"DO THEY ALL DIE?" SHE ASKED

"We've had so few cases so far," Amelia hedged. "We have two on life support who seem to be holding their own, and another who's shown some signs of improvement without any special treatment. He's had the vaccine, of course."

"Teddy Marsh?" Sharon said. "I visit him every day. Yesterday he just looked at me and didn't even talk."

Amelia nodded.

"Such a cute kid," Sharon said, looking out the hospital window at the flowers below. I *will* get out of this, she told herself. And maybe I will have kids someday, a boy just like Teddy Marsh, and—

A noise at the door made her turn; and there, of all people, was Teddy himself. She laughed. "We were just—"

The expression on Teddy's face cut her off. His eyes went wide, he bared his teeth, and from somewhere deep in his throat came a noise like a growl.

THE LYSSA SYNDROME

CHRISTOPHER FAHY

ZEBRA BOOKS
KENSINGTON PUBLISHING CORP.

ZEBRA BOOKS

are published by

Kensington Publishing Corp.
475 Park Avenue South
New York, NY 10016

First printing: April, 1990

Printed in the United States of America

To Mike and Judie, Lani and Bob

ONE

Above the stand of spruce and pine, the moon went under a cloud and the low brick building across the lawn turned black. "Jesus, Gary," Miranda said, "I'm scared."

Gary Simmons kept digging. Another five minutes and they would be under the fence. "Hey, babe," he said, "there aren't any sensors. There aren't any guards with tommy guns. All we got to fear is Skinny Watts, and on weekends he's comatose. You could come through here with the Blue Harbor marching band and he wouldn't blink."

The moon came back brighter than ever, lighting Miranda's freckled face and turning her red hair blue. Far down the rocky slope, the ocean crashed. "What if they have guard dogs?" she said.

Gary jabbed at the earth with the short-handled shovel; his muscular forearms bulged. "We'd know it by now if they did," he said. "You think they'd be locked away somewhere, like the monkeys and beagles and mice?"

Miranda looked out at the bay. A path of moonlight stretched to Granite Island, twelve miles off. Gary lay on his side and chopped at the dirt. The shovel's handle

7

hit the fence, making its links vibrate.

"Be *careful*," Miranda said.

Gary grunted and said, "So who's gonna hear us? The closest cottage is Mrs. Watson's, a quarter-mile from here. People break into nuclear *warhead* plants, and you're worried about a stupid *animal* lab."

"If I get caught . . ."

He laughed. "Hey, babe, it was your idea." He lifted another spadeful of soil, emptied it, dug in again, and struck a rock. Miranda winced.

Gary said, "What a great pair of criminals. Nerves of steel."

"*They're* the criminals," Miranda said. "Not us."

"Keep thinking that," he said. He took a last shot at the ditch he had made, set the shovel aside, and said, "That's got it with room to spare." He rolled onto his back, sliding his head and shoulders into the ditch, grabbed the fence, gave a push with his feet, and was in. "Piece of cake," he said.

Miranda handed the gym bag through the hole, along with the shovel, then lay down as Gary had done. He caught her under the armpits and pulled her clear.

They stood up and brushed off their shirts and jeans. Gary pushed back his curly brown hair and said, "We'll do it the same way going out. I'll go first."

"Okay," Miranda said. She smiled and said, "Oh Gary, this is *exciting,* we're really *doing* it."

"We really are, babe."

They started across the lawn. To their left, on the crest of the bluff that fronted the bay, sat the mansion, which now housed a visitors' center, a library, and administrative offices. Straight ahead stood Building 8, its windows now silver with moonlight. That's where the monkeys were. There was no use setting them free, they would never survive in Maine, but the beagles would do just fine.

8

The beagles were in the gardener's cottage, down the steep hill behind the mansion. Miranda had seen them on visitors' day. The gardener's cottage hadn't been part of the tour, but Miranda had slipped away from the group and gone to the cottage and peeked in the cellar windows . . . and there were the beagles, three of them: two of them brown and white and one honey tan, caged, with tubes up their noses and under their skins. She had almost cried. Those innocent animals, pumped full of chemicals, tortured, maimed . . .

The Jillson Lab had done wonderful things: it had given animals lung cancer, cancer of the colon, liver and spleen, had given them herpes, had given them diabetes. The problem was, it hadn't yet learned how to take back these gifts. Not that it hadn't tried—and tried, and tried. The animals were mutilated, chopped to pieces, operated on until they were totally hopeless, and then were destroyed—in the crematorium on the complex's eastern edge. Miranda wouldn't have been surprised if some of the poor things were still alive when they went to the ovens.

Your tax dollars at work, she thought as she and Gary crept up to the cottage. All to save a bunch of people too lazy to care for themselves, too lazy to eat the right foods and give up the booze and cigarettes and fats that had caused their disease.

"Okay," Gary said. "Up we go."

Gary was well acquainted with the Jillson Lab. Two years ago, the summer between his freshman and sophomore years at Maine Maritime, he'd worked for J&R Small and painted the buildings. Had painted the gardener's cottage. Its skylight. Its fire escape.

The fire escape—a state requirement—had been installed when Jillson took over the complex, the former Rowland estate, in 1949, two years after the Great Blue Harbor Fire had wiped out half the island.

9

Its stairs went up to the second floor. From there, a steel ladder led up to the roof.

Gary and Miranda climbed. Miranda's sneakers squeaked on the ladder's rungs. When she reached the roof she squatted, her hands on the asphalt, and looked at the bay, and the buildings and the trees. The complex lay in silence under the moon.

Gary knelt down, opened the gym bag, took out a roll of contac paper, peeled off the backing, and spread the paper over the skylight's glass. He put on a pair of leather gloves and tapped the glass with his hammer, lifted the paper, pried the cracked glass away from the metal frame, and said, "Just like the movies, right?"

Miranda's heart was hard in her throat. She whispered, "Gary?"

"What?" he said, not looking up.

"I love you."

He smiled at her. "After this, you better, babe." He lowered himself through the skylight; let go.

As his feet hit the floor, a dog started barking, and Miranda froze.

"Come on!" he said.

She handed the gym bag through the hole; he took it and helped her down. "No turning back now, babe."

"No," she said.

She followed him down the moonlit stairs, and the barking grew fierce.

"They'll catch us," she said.

"Too late to think about that," he said. "Let's just *do* it."

They went down the hallway and stopped at the basement door. Gary set down the gym bag and took out a flashlight, clicked it on, shined its beam on the lock. "A nightlatch. Piece of cake," he said.

Miranda said, "Gary, look."

A sign on the door: three interlocking rings and the warning: Biohazard.

"Hell, they probably put that on all the doors."

"But maybe—"

"Bullshit," Gary said. He took his hammer out of the gym bag, along with a chisel, and quickly attacked the lock. Four blows and it sprang. He put the tools back in the bag, picked it up, shined his light on the steps. He went down and Miranda followed.

The beagles were right in front of them. Two of them lay there listlessly, their tongues hanging out, but the third one was frantic. It was he who was making the racket.

"My god, the poor *things,*" Miranda said.

"Christ, but beagles can bark," Gary said. "We better get going before Skinny Watts *does* wake up."

He took a pair of bolt cutters out of the bag and went at the padlocks. Hard clinking sounds, and they fell to the floor. Miranda opened the closest cage and the beagle, one of the brown and white ones, crawled shakily into her arms.

"He's sick. They've made him *sick.* Oh, Gary."

"He'll feel all right when he gets some fresh air," Gary said. "He'll feel all right when he's *free.*" He opened the second cage, lifting the honey tan beagle out. "There you go, boy—girl, I mean." He set the dog down. It wandered clumsily over the concrete, sniffing and bumping into the legs of the table.

Miranda frowned. "She acts like she's drunk."

"Maybe Skinny's been down here with some of his weekend special," Gary said.

He touched the third beagle's cage, and the barking became a low growl. "Hey, they turned this one into a Doberman. I knew they did great things here, but this is too much." The dog showed its teeth. "Come on, pup, cool it, we're your liberators." He turned to Miranda.

11

"You sure you want to let this one go, babe?"

She nodded, almost in tears, petting the head of the dog in her arms. "Let him go. And let's get *out* of here."

Gary opened the cage. The beagle sprang out with a snarl and ran up the steps into darkness. "Wow!" Gary said. He put the tools back in the gym bag, scooped up the female beagle, and said, "Let's go!"

At the top of the stairs, they saw the third beagle down at the end of the hall in the slash of bright moonlight that came through the pane in the door. For a moment its legs gave way. It got up and ran into the wall.

They ran past it. As Gary's hip hit the door's release bar, he felt sudden pain in his foot. "Shit!" He gritted his teeth and kicked. The third beagle fell away with a yelp, rolled over, and shot out the door.

It was gone into the night. Miranda and Gary ran through moonlight and reached the chain link fence. Gary shoved his sick dog through the hole, Miranda followed suit, and both animals limped and staggered into the trees.

Gary lay on his back in the ditch, pulled himself through the hole, and helped Miranda through. They ran into the spruces, firs, and pines and flopped down on the ground, their sides heaving. No sign of the dogs.

A blade of pain stabbed Miranda's ribs. "Whew," she said.

Gary smiled, his breath coming hard, and said, "He bit me."

"No. Is it bad?"

"Just a scratch. I had my tetanus shot three years ago, so no sweat. But I'm worried about that sucker, he's mean. What if he bites some kid?"

"He won't," Miranda said. "He was scared, that's all. Being caged up like that and tortured like that, it's no

12

wonder he's mean. Once he's out for a while, he'll be fine."

"I sure hope you're right."

A soft breeze whistled high in the trees. Ten feet away, moonlight broke through a gap in the canopy, dappling the ground.

Miranda whispered, "You were wonderful, Gary."

"You weren't too bad yourself."

She came close, put her arms around him, kissed him below his ear. "Wounded in action," she said.

"Do I get a medal?"

"You get more than a medal . . . make love to me."

He laughed. "What? Here?"

"Right here. Right now. I want you to."

"But babe, we're all sweaty."

"We'll get all sweaty anyway."

"Well, what if Skinny decides to walk off his buzz and comes cruising through here?"

"That's his good luck." She stood; her hands went to her waist; a button popped; she slid out of her jeans. Her hips and legs were solid black against the pale light of the moon.

He kissed her knee. It was salty and hot on his lips. He said, "You talked me into it, Miss Shore."

She knelt on the spongy carpet of spruce needles, cradled his face in her hands, and kissed his mouth. Her tongue went deep. He sank to the earth, his hands in her thick red hair.

In the dream, there was a prison break. Skinny watched from outside somewhere as men swarmed through the corridors, lights flashed, bells rang. Then swiftly, inexplicably, he was with them, among them, a part of the frantic whirl. There were dogs, there were shouts, he was racing across the packed clay of the

13

yard, he was scaling the high stone wall. The spotlight caught him in its glare, the shots rang out, it was bright on his bleeding hands, as bright as the sun . . .

He woke up. The guys on the TV were laughing. He groaned. His lids were gummy and his tongue was thick. His foot crashed into the bottles and sent them rolling. He cursed.

And heard the alarm.

Jesus Christ, the alarm! A red light blinked on the console above the desk. He shoved himself up, dazed, and went to the board.

The gardener's cottage. His brain tried to focus. Farrow and Kessler. The dogs in the cellar.

He turned the alarm off, strapped his shoulder holster on, and went outside.

The tops of the fir trees swayed in the breeze, and he sighed with relief. So that's all it was. The alarm had been adjusted twice this year because of the way it went off in the wind, and now, by God, the damn thing had done it again. But hell, he thought, I've gone this far, I might as well check things out, and he stepped off the concrete path and into the shadows.

At five-foot-six and a hundred and twenty pounds, Skinny himself was not much more than a shadow. He crossed the lawn, staying close to the line of trees, and went down the hill.

The gardener's cottage was dark, which was finest kind. No lights were ever left on in there, as they were in the other buildings. He came up to the dark north wall and a tension closed in on his heart.

He tripped on a rock and lurched forward, his hand on his holster, Skinny stood straight again—or as straight as he ever got—and searched the trees and shadows with his eyes.

No movement. No sound but the wind. He slid into the moonlight, crept up to the door, and sneaked a

14

peek through the metal-meshed glass. Put his hand on the latch, slowly lowered his thumb. Locked. Finest kind.

He went back into darkness, circled the building, examined the door on the west. Also locked. Okay. There was one other entrance, the door at the top of the fire escape. He stood back and looked up, convincing himself that the glass was unbroken, then set about checking the windows.

The grilles were intact and no glass was shattered, but something . . . something seemed wrong. What? Damned if he could put his finger on it. He stood there frowning for a minute, then went back up the hill again to the mansion, his breath coming hard. I'm too damn old for this, he thought. Too goddamn old. He stopped for a minute, his heart thumping rapidly. "Shit," he muttered out loud.

In front of the TV set again, his lids closed down. He still had a nagging uneasy feeling, but couldn't say why. He belched, and a fat sour bubble of Bud dissolved on his upper plate. He shut his mouth again and settled back. He'd report the false alarm first thing tomorrow, they'd have to fix that goddamn system, it would drive him nuts.

He was drifting into a dream, a dream about the Masons' secret symbol—what it *really* meant—when it came to him.

No barking. That was wrong. Very wrong. Every time he had checked that cottage before, those beagles had barked their fool heads off. Should've shined my light in the windows, he thought. Should've gone inside. I ought to go back, he thought.

But the cottage was so far away, and his lids weighed tons, and a voice in his head said the dogs were just sleeping, that's all. You don't have to go back, forget it, they're just asleep.

15

"You're right," Skinny muttered aloud. "You are goddamn-A right," and soon he himself was asleep.

They came out to the lane. At its end, where it met the paved road, they would find Gary's van.

They held hands, with the moon now incredibly bright, and Miranda said, "I feel so good, don't you?"

"You bet," Gary grinned.

With her free hand she punched his arm and said, "I don't mean *that,* I mean about what we *did.* So many people *talk* about making a contribution, but so few act. We *acted.*"

"We sure did, babe. Now let's hope we don't get caught. Maine Maritime doesn't look too kindly on students who break and enter."

"I'm sure Bennington doesn't either."

"And your mother?"

"She'd die," Miranda said. "She'd simply die. She's been in the Jillson Ladies' Club since before I was born. It's okay with her if *these* dogs are cut up, but just let somebody try it on Buffy or Fritz—" She stopped, her eyes fixed on the side of the lane. She let go of his hand and said, "Oh Gary, look."

The female beagle, the tan one, was lying stretched out on the ground. They went to it. Gary, the gym bag in his hand, knelt down and touched its side.

"She's dead," he said.

Miranda pressed her lips together and said, "We got there too late. Damn!"

"At least she had a taste of freedom."

Miranda shook her head. "It just makes me so mad. I want to go back and let *all* of the animals loose."

"Yeah, I know how you feel. But we've made our statement, babe."

She looked at him. "Can we bury her?"

16

"If you want to, sure."

He stepped into the trees, took the shovel, and fashioned a shallow grave; then went back to the roadside and lifted the dog, set it into the hole, and covered it up with earth. "Rest in peace," he said.

As they walked to the van, Miranda said, "Killers. Murderers and terrorists, that's what they are."

Gary sat in the driver's seat. When he pressed on the clutch a hot pain hit his ankle. He winced.

Miranda didn't notice. "I wonder what they gave those poor creatures that made them act so confused," she said. "And so mean."

The van's engine started and Gary pulled out, the flesh at his ankle throbbing. "I guess we'll never know," he said.

"I guess not," Miranda said.

TWO

For Paul Kessler, the weekend had been sublime. The weather had been close to eighty, cloudless, with a gentle breeze; he'd gone out on his comet, *Concentric* (named by his eighteen-year-old, Jeff, who joked that his dad ran around in circles most of the time); and on Saturday, when he'd sailed to Great Northern Island, Angela had joined him. She had seemed like her old self again, not preoccupied as she was so often these days, and yesterday at the clambake down on the shore they had really had fun. He'd played Frisbee with Jeff, who was back from Vermont for a week, and with Mindy, his fourteen-year-old, now off to summer camp, and before they ate he had gone for an ocean swim, his first of the season. It had felt terrific.

His spirits were high as he strode down the walk to the gardener's cottage. Another fantastic day: blue sky, high clouds, sun kissing the tops of the trees. It was going to be that kind of summer, he knew it was. And it looked as if Angela might be about to emerge from her shell or cocoon or whatever the hell she'd been in these past few months. He sure hoped so.

It was seven thirteen, and as usual, Kessler was the

18

first of the staff of a hundred and eight to arrive on Jillson's grounds. He'd been a morning person all his life. Nothing wrong with that, unless your partner had the opposite metabolism, the kind that—like Martin Farrow's—didn't rev up until noon. When Farrow began to shift into high around four, Kessler was ripe for a shower, martini, and dinner. He was often asleep in his lounge chair by ten, while Farrow would grudgingly call it a day at 1:00 or 2:00 A.M.

Kessler was forty-five, with a fringe of light reddish brown hair, short, a bit overweight, a bit sloppy, and liked good jokes, though he often appeared not to get them. Farrow, two years his senior, was tall, slender, neat, with a trim salt-and-pepper beard. He hated jokes, and anyone who told him one would be met with an icy glare. An odd couple, Farrow and Kessler, but a highly effective one.

Their field was animal virology, and they had been working together for the last eight years. Kessler had grown up in Hartford, had taken a Ph.D. in microbiology at Wisconsin, and had come to the Jillson Lab as a postdoctoral fellow. While there, he'd met Angela James, only eighteen years old at the time, at a dance in a Route 1 hangout called The Purple Drake. They had fallen in love, married, and no matter where his work had taken him, they'd managed to spend a part of each summer in Maine. For the past five years, thanks to his work with Farrow, they'd *lived* in Maine. And would always live in Maine, if their luck held out.

Usually, Kessler went straight to his office in Building 6 on Mondays, but this morning he wanted to check on those three series IVs. They'd been perfect for nearly a month, and then all of a sudden, last week— the same damn thing, all over again. Which was truly upsetting.

19

He reached the door of the gardener's cottage, set his briefcase down on the concrete walk, and selected the proper key from the mess on the ring. He inserted it into the lock, turned, pulled, kept the keys in his hand as he picked up his briefcase again, and went inside.

As always on Monday mornings, he felt a slight twinge of misgiving. His research at Jillson was fascinating, challenging, yet its purpose was not always clear to him. Farrow insisted the work was crucial, but Kessler felt it might create more problems than it solved. He'd often wished for opinions other than Farrow's, but his wish was futile: the work was classified. He and Farrow had sworn to speak of it only in general terms to their Jillson colleagues. Of course, with the setup they had (their own lab), the positions they held (senior staff scientists), and their reputations (National Academy of Science Commended Scholars), they were virtually on their own. Each year so far, they'd come up with a paper of more than ordinary merit, and that was sufficient to keep the board of directors happy.

But the doubts always rose to the surface again on Mondays. The decreasing incubation time was the major worry. Yet, what if the incubation time was also decreasing outside the lab, somewhere in those Pennsylvania woods? How would he feel, if he'd had the chance to intervene in the process, and hadn't seized it? Good question. And every Monday, Kessler found himself posing it once again.

He unlocked the office, stepped inside, set his briefcase beside the desk. He went to the cabinet behind the desk and took out the metal-mesh gloves, then went back to the hallway.

Sun streamed through the doors behind and in front of him, giving the stuccoed walls a mellow glow. Sun

20

from the skylight flowed down the stairs and into the vestibule. Yes, he said to himself, it's going to be one of those summers. He thought of Saturday, with Angela, the sail to Great Northern Island. He stopped at the cellar door, a smile on his face—and saw that the lock was gone.

His breath stuck in his throat. The lock was *gone*. It had been punched out, was lying there on the floor. He opened the door, his mind racing, and went down the steps.

No barking, no noise at all. The dogs were either very sick, or dead, or—

At the foot of the steps he stared at the open cages, the ruined padlocks there on the concrete floor. Numbness spread through his chest and along his arms and he thought: No. No! He gritted his teeth, made his hands into fists. The center of his chest seized up and he suddenly gasped for breath. He pressed his fist to his sternum and stared at the cages and whispered a trembling No to the empty room. Then he hurried upstairs and called Farrow.

Martin Farrow was ripped. He'd forgotten to unplug the phone, and here it was chirping away at the ungodly hour of what? Seven thirty? This had better be good, he thought as he reached across the mattress. *Damn* good.

"Hello," he said flatly, his voice cracked and thick.

"Hello, Martin? It's Paul. Martin, listen, the fours are gone."

Farrow thought for a second he'd heard it wrong. "What?"

"They're out, they're gone, someone broke in and let them go."

"Jesus Christ!"

21

A long pause, then: "Why? I don't understand it. Who in the world would *do* such a crazy thing?"

"God knows," Farrow said. "Look, don't tell anybody, don't go anywhere, just stay there until I arrive, okay?"

Another pause. "The fools," Kessler said. "The goddamn *fools.*"

"Just stay there, Paul."

As Farrow dressed he thought back seven years: to Kromer's disconcerting eyes, his tight thin smile. "The chickens are coming home to roost, you prick," he said to the empty room. "The bitch of it is, though, they're not going to roost on *you.*"

Farrow had been dissecting a monkey brain at the Wistar Institute when the call came from Graduate Hospital. He had hesitated a second, frowning at the scalpel in his hand, then said he would be right over. And his life had changed forever.

What he saw, when he got to the morgue, was the naked body of a swarthy, powerful-looking man in his thirties, his face twisted into an ugly, menacing snarl. One side of his mouth was raised, exposing his broad, tobacco-stained teeth. The top of his head had been cleanly sawed off, and his brain was gone. The man was Guiseppe "Little Joe" Flowers of South Philadelphia, and the story on him was this:

Flowers and some of his pals had been on a summer outing near Upper Black Eddy, Pa., at a property owned by Mickey "The Hatchet" Russo, who had gone to New York for the day on company business. There was plenty of chicken cacciatore and garlic bread and plenty of everything else, including female companionship. It was hot, the drinking was steady, and Little

Joe, needing to lose a pint or two of the St. Pauli Girl he'd consumed, and not wishing to take the long walk up to the gray stone manor at the crest of the spacious lawn, strolled casually into the trees.

He was halfway through his business—the smoke of his panatella floating up through the sunlight that streamed through the beeches and oaks, his water streaming out of him—thinking how lucky he was to have such a successful career and such fine friends; when a rustle and a flash the color of rust made him jerk to the right—and spray his white filigreed shoe.

Which wasn't of any concern at the moment, as the rust-colored flash was a fox. Little Joe had never seen a fox outside a zoo, and no zoo fox had ever looked like this. This fox looked mean. It looked more than mean, it looked crazy. Its fur was mangy, running in cross directions, and its eyes were hard and glazed. It lowered its head, fixed Joe in its glare, and as it did, it growled. Its lips curled back, revealing a row of vicious-looking teeth. Slobber dripped from its jowls.

The panatella fell out of Joe's mouth. He tucked himself in, damn near catching a chunk in his zipper. He backed off slowly, his blood thick and loud in his ears, and the crazy fox sprang.

A hot jolt tore into Joe's ankle. He yelled, "You bastard! You goddamn prick!" He kicked, teeth clenched, and caught the fox square in the ribs. It yelped and tumbled backward, and Little Joe ran.

He was met in the clearing by Al Palucci and Danny Walls and screamed, "A fox! The fucker bit my foot!" He was gasping for breath, his burly chest heaving. "I'll blast that bastard from here to Atlantic City, I swear I will!"

The fox hunt that followed was not as elegant as most that take place in southeastern Pennsylvania, but what it lacked in style was more than made up for in thoroughness. When they found the fox lying dazed near a log not far from where Joe had dropped his cigar, they did such a number with their .38 Magnums, the aftermath looked like eighteen-wheeler road kill.

Three weeks later, Joe was making his rounds on South Philly's Catherine Street, when a wave of dizziness made him drop to his knees. That night he got a headache that Excedrin Plus wouldn't touch, and his throat turned sore. Three days later he hurt all over. His girlfriend said he should see a doctor, and he yelled she should shut the fuck up. He turned hot. He began to feel weak and his thirst was huge. When he tried to drink, he clutched his throat, made a horrible face, and dropped the glass on the floor.

He ran outside and into the Three Coins Bar on Christian Street. Without warning or provocation he attacked the cop in there, Pete Pignatano, beating him with his fists and tearing his flesh with his teeth. Cop-biting was not unusual, but the frenzy of Little Joe's fury was such that the Three Coins cleared out in a flash. Joe's teeth were still in Pignatano's neck when he shivered into a slobbering fit and passed out. He was taken to Graduate Hospital in a coma.

Two days later he died, much to the consternation of his physicians. They suspected a form of influenza, but flu almost never caused convulsions, unless its fever climbed much higher than Flowers' one hundred and two point four. And for influenza to kill a healthy adult in his thirties was rare indeed—unless the afflicted suffered from immune system breakdown, which was certainly not the case with Little Joe Flowers.

It was an intern, a fuzzy-faced kid named Washburn—certainly not the most perceptive of the budding doctors roaming the hospital's halls—who had ventured a timid, "Could it maybe be rabies?" at the Tuesday staff conference. The question had struck a chord with Glickstein, the resident assigned to the Flowers case, who recalled the incompletely healed lacerations on the dead man's ankle. He called Joe's girlfriend, Nina Field, and was fascinated to learn that a fox had bitten Joe at a picnic four weekends ago. Glickstein rapidly wrote down all the details in a typical doctor's hand, one that he alone could decipher: Upper Black Eddy; the Russo estate; the fox had been destroyed. The folder said that Joe's next of kin was his mother. Was that correct? Miss Field said as far as she knew, it was.

Rosella Florello, seventy-two, who had come to the States from Palermo as a five-year-old, was a stubborn woman. No matter how much the doctors coaxed and explained, she would not be moved. Allow her youngest son to be cut up? What were they asking? It wasn't enough that the poor boy had died in such pain? Her baby, her Little Joe, who was always so good to her, who never hurt a flea—unless, of course, it hurt him first? When she left, Glickstein looked at Hall, the physician in charge, who merely shrugged—and scheduled Joe Flowers for autopsy.

Horst, the staff pathologist, took off the top of Flowers's head and removed the brain. Examination confirmed Washburn's hunch: it was rabies. The Philadelphia and Pennsylvania Departments of Health and the Centers for Disease Control in Atlanta were notified; the policeman, Pignatano, was told to report for further treatment; and Martin Farrow, Wistar's international authority on rabies, received word of a case that warranted his attention.

Horst considered it damned good fortune to have a man of Farrow's stature in the area, because the virus

25

he'd noticed in Flowers was different from what he'd expected. His expectations, of course, were based on animal studies: he'd never encountered human rabies before, and he'd studied the animal tissues in medical school, not as part of his job. In the city of Philadelphia, animal rabies was only slightly more common than bubonic plague.

Farrow checked Horst's slides with the electron microscope. Negri bodies, the bullet shape . . . the age-old terror, rabies, *Lyssa* to the ancient Greeks, there was no doubt about it, Horst was right: this rabies was different—those spiked projections—and Farrow cursed under his breath. A variant strain could mean he and Kessler would have to begin again, start a whole new project from scratch.

For decades the only rabies treatment had been a series of abdominal injections—twenty-three in all—that were very painful, did not always work, and sometimes had serious side effects—the worst of which was to actually *cause* the disease. After long years of work at Wistar and other centers, a new vaccine had evolved, one cultured in human diploid cells. Its latest version consisted of four injections in the deltoid muscle, given a week apart, and the side effects were minimal. Farrow and his colleague, Paul Kessler, were on the verge of breaking through to a two-shot treatment with virtually no side effects, and now, goddamn it all, *this*.

Stroking his pointed, graying beard, Farrow went over and looked at Joe Flowers again. That was one mean face. Well, rabies was one mean disease. There weren't many uglier ways to die: hallucinations, fever, paralysis, joint pain—and throat pain made so severe by attempts to drink, that victims feared the very sight of water. Thank God there were very few victims. In his

26

thirteen years of research, this was only the second case of human rabies that Farrow had come across.

He turned to Horst. "When was he bitten?"

"Four weeks ago."

"What?"

"That's what they say."

"Impossible. The bites are on the ankle. To reach the brain that fast from there, the virus would have to travel at ten times the speed of the virus we know."

"Exactly," Horst said.

Farrow made a quick sucking sound. "Jesus Christ," he said.

"And the cop he bit is still out there somewhere." Horst nodded to the door.

"He bit somebody?" Farrow said.

"Yeah, didn't they tell you that? Did they ask you to bring vaccine?"

"Yes, but I thought—" He looked at the corpse.

"No, Flowers was already dead. It's for the cop. The guy really got chewed, they put three dozen stitches in his neck. But of course the wound's the least of it, poor bastard. We had him scheduled to come in this morning, but he didn't show."

Farrow's mouth went dry as he said, "So what's the follow-up?"

"We called police headquarters. He didn't report for work, so they're searching for him."

"Christ."

Horst frowned and said, "You think—?"

"I don't know what to think," Farrow said. "All I know is this virus is different—*real* different. We've got to find that cop and find him fast."

When Farrow learned that Flowers had bitten somebody, an alarm had gone off in his head. Rabies was self-limiting in humans: they were "dead-end

27

hosts"—that is, they didn't pass the virus on as foxes and bats and similar mammals did. They suffered horribly, but for some unknown reason did not go into the frenzy of other animals, the frenzy that caused the biting that spread the disease.

Of course, Joe Flowers's biting might well have been simply an aspect of rage and not of rabies. Farrow fervently hoped this was so. If it wasn't, the implications were huge, but no use engaging in speculation on that at this juncture, he told himself. A bite was a bite, infectious no matter what its cause, and this missing cop was in trouble. Big trouble. At the speed with which this rabies worked, a bite in the neck could mean that the virus would hit his brain in less than a week and a half.

"When the cop shows up, I want to see him," he said. "And let's just hope to God he shows up soon."

He showed up three days later, face down in an alley five blocks from his home.

Millie, his wife, was in shock. He'd been desperately ill, she said, but refused to return to the hospital. He'd perspired profusely for three days straight and said crazy things. Light hurt his eyes, and he covered the windows with towels. He pulled out the phones and hid them away, wouldn't let her leave the apartment, and alternated snatches of sleep with fits of pacing and shouting. When she ran some water in the kitchen sink, he became a wild man, throwing dishes and trying to scream, but no sound would come out. He chased her outside and she ran to a neighbor's house. Late that night they discovered his body.

Farrow was there when they found the virus in Pignatano's brain. Nine days had elapsed from the time

28

of initial lesion to the time of death. It was terrifying. He spoke to CDC in Atlanta. They'd never heard of rabies acting that fast. They called the state and city health departments, and southeastern Pennsylvania was put on a rabies alert.

Farrow was totally unprepared for the next development: Three weeks later, Nina Field, Joe Flowers' girlfriend, was admitted to Graduate Hospital, suffering from fever, hallucinations, weakness, and unbearable thirst. Vaccine was administered right away, but the rabies had already passed the point where immunization would work. The woman's rages were so explosive, she had to be put in restraints.

The first time Farrow went to see her, she was raving and incoherent. The second time, she lay weakly against the pillow, her skin slimy yellow, her red-rimmed eyes half-closed.

"Did Joe hurt you? Did he scratch you or bite you?"

She nodded no, once, slowly, her black hair damp on the pillow. Her mouth was open, her tongue was purple, her lips were chalky-looking, cracked.

"Did you have any cuts or open sores at the time Joe was sick?"

She simply stared. Then her features contorted with pain, and she made a small whispery rasping sound somewhere deep in her throat.

Farrow went to the foot of her bed, read the chart that was hanging there. No lesions at time of admission—he thought that's what Glickstein's scrawl said—but hell, a scratch was all it took to let the virus enter.

"Miss Field, I'd like to do another exam. Just a short one, to see if you've had any recent cuts, cold sores—"

The sunken eyes flashed and the cracked lips curled. The rasping sound became a growl; there was no other way to describe it. Frowning, Farrow left the room.

He examined her the following day, shortly after she died—and found nothing at all: no scratches or cuts less than six weeks old. Then how had she caught the disease?

There were cases on record of airborne rabies transmission. A Kentucky spelunker had once been infected by breathing the air in a cave filled with mounds of bat guano. But there had been tons of droppings in that cave, the area was enclosed . . . Airborne transmission seemed out of the question in Nina Field's case. If the rabies was potent enough for her to have caught it like that, he and Horst and most of the hospital staff and patients would no doubt already be sick.

Another possibility occurred to Farrow, and he cursed himself for not having thought of it sooner. He called in Millie Pignatano, and told her about Nina Field. After listening gravely and silently, she consented to an exam. Farrow found no lesions on her body, and once she was dressed again, he asked: "Did you and your husband have sexual relations after his neck was bitten?"

She flushed bright red. "My god, of course not, he was in such pain—"

"I'm sorry, forgive me for asking." He fingered his beard and said, "You seem fine. Even so, you should have the vaccine."

A frown crossed the woman's face, and she said, "I don't want the vaccine, I'm scared of it. Can't I just have a test or something?"

"There isn't any," Farrow said. "Well, there is, but it's not very accurate. We can't really tell if people have rabies until they develop symptoms, and by then it's too late to help. To be on the safe side, you've got to

30

have shots."

She consented . . . and never got sick. But why? Had the vaccine worked? Or had she never been infected in the first place? The only way to know for sure if the standard vaccine would stop this variant strain was through lab experimentation.

Three weeks after he filed his final report with the Centers for Disease Control, Farrow found himself in the Pentagon, sitting across the desk from Major General William Kromer, a trim and powerful-looking man with a silver brushcut and disturbing eyes.

Ever since the reports from CDC had started to cross his desk, Kromer had been intrigued, and his fascination had deepened as time went by. He leaned back in his leather swivel chair, crossed his legs, and said, "This theory of sexual transmission, Dr. Farrow. You actually think it's viable?"

One of his eyes was clear, brown, sharp. The other had a milky cast, and Farrow thought: corneal leukoma. Alkali burns. No transplant would work. He said, "I can't see how else Nina Field would have caught the disease."

The strange eyes blinked. "But if I remember my medicine right—and I may not remember it right, it's been a long time—rabies is always spread through infected saliva."

"Almost always," Farrow said. "There have been a few cases of airborne transmission. Or so the researchers think. There's even been at least one case of transmission through corneal transplant."

Kromer looked doubtful. "But *sexual* transmission?"

"We're dealing with something new," Farrow said.

31

"AIDS was new once, too, and we couldn't believe that, either."

"In a way, we still can't," Kromer said. "And we still don't know why it appeared." He leaned forward again, picked up a pencil, creased its eraser with his thumbnail, and said, "Where do you think this rabies has come from?"

"God," Farrow said.

"From whom all blessings flow," Kromer said. "Most likely so. But maybe not."

Oh? Farrow thought. He said, "A fox in southeastern Pennsylvania carried a mutant form of rabies. That fox was killed by the man it attacked. Its remains were found and cremated."

"End of case," Kromer said. Then he smiled, just slightly, and said, "Or maybe not. Maybe scavengers sampled the carrion before it was burned."

"Maybe so," Farrow said. "Or maybe that fox infected another animal. That's why the rabies alert."

"Yes," Kromer said. He dropped the pencil, ran his fingertips over his chin, and said, "What are the odds against a mutant virus cropping up like this?"

Farrow shrugged. "I don't know."

"Maybe millions to one?"

"Maybe so. But viruses *do* mutate."

"Yes, they certainly do," Kromer said. He swiveled slightly in his chair, glanced out the window, turned to Farrow again. "In our Fort Detrick labs, we have four strains of smallpox, four strains the world has never encountered before. Do you know where they came from?"

"Let me guess," Farrow said.

"I'm sure you can."

"And you think—?"

Kromer shrugged. "Why not?"

32

"They'd release one infected fox in rural southeastern Pennsylvania?"

Kromer grinned. "Not likely. They'd probably decide to spread a disease of this type through migratory birds, who'd die, be eaten, and infect dogs, cats, skunks, foxes . . ."

"There have been no reports of other infected animals, or of any unusual behavior in birds."

"Not yet," Kromer said, his gray eyebrows rising. "The point is, however, that it *could* be a man-made mutation. But let's say it's not. Let's say it came about naturally. It still could serve as a highly potent biological weapon, agreed?"

The back of Farrow's neck was starting to hurt. "I don't know," he said. "I don't think along those lines."

"Of course not," Kromer said. He leaned back in his chair again and said, "The problem with smallpox or influenza or any other airborne or casual contact virus as a weapon is one of control. Once the genie is out of the bottle, it doesn't know where to stop. It may want to wipe you out, as well as your enemies. Something like AIDS or rabies, however, something that depends on more than casual contact, is so much more predictable—and so much more useful."

He smiled again; light gleamed in his silvery hair. He said, "We have two new types of bubonic plague at Detrick that would decimate the Soviets . . . and would spread to Eastern Europe, Western Europe, China, Alaska. I'd take nuclear winter any day over what that stuff would do. The problem with plague is the problem we have with the bomb: We've created a weapon we can't ever use without destroying ourselves in the process." Leaning forward again, he picked up the pencil and tapped his fingertips with it. "Rabies," he said, "is a different story, however."

33

Farrow frowned and said, "What are you driving at?"

"A fast-acting, deep contact transmissible, violence-inducing disease that can be surreptitiously introduced. Something like that has *potential.*"

"Interesting way of putting it," Farrow said.

"All in a day's work," Kromer said. His milky eye shifted. He said, "The problem with contact diseases is: How do we guarantee contact? The rabies virus has found an ingenious solution: Give your host an overwhelming urge to bite other living creatures. Add *sexual* transmission to this . . ." He was thoughtful a moment, then said: "The social disruption caused by the 1918 flu epidemic was *nothing* compared to what this disease would do. Imagine, an illness that can't be detected by any test, that turns everyone's neighbor into a threat. The implications are staggering."

"And revolting," Farrow said.

Kromer nodded. "Agreed." Then he smiled his hard smile and said, "I assume you want to publish your findings concerning this Flowers episode."

"Of course."

"Maybe have them appear in *Science* or *Scientific American?*"

"If I'm lucky, yes."

Kromer kept smiling. "You won't be lucky. Your findings will not be published."

Farrow stiffened and said, "What the hell do you mean?"

Kromer turned to the window again and said, "Fort Detrick generates hundreds of papers each year. Care to guess what percentage of all that work reaches people like you?"

Farrow's face felt hot. "I'm not in the mood for games," he said.

34

Facing the room again, Kromer said, "Fifteen percent. That's all, fifteen percent. There's a very good reason for that."

"I'm sure there is," Farrow said. "But I don't work for Fort Detrick."

"Not yet."

"Not ever."

Kromer dented the pencil's eraser again and said, "Never say never." He paused for a second, ostensibly reading the print on the pencil's side, then said, "Look, the ball's in our hands. I don't know how it got there, but it's there, and we can't afford to drop it."

"Meaning?"

"Meaning we've got some pretty bright people at Detrick, but the fact is, you're way ahead of them. You know more about rabies than anyone else in the world—or so we've been told."

"I suppose it's possible," Farrow said.

"And you're gearing up to do some research on this mutant form, am I right? You're not going to simply forget about it, pretend that it never existed."

Farrow sniffed. "That isn't how science works, and you know it. Chances are slim that more animals have the disease, but if they do, we have to be ready."

"Exactly," Kromer said. "That's precisely my point."

Farrow's neck was killing him as he said, "I prefer to keep working for Wistar."

"I can understand that," Kromer said. "But Wistar may not have the funds to support your research. Their grant money might dry up."

Farrow stared at the flat impassive face. "Of course," he said.

Kromer lifted his eyebrows; his bad eye turned out. "On the other hand, there's a place in Blue Harbor, Maine, that can give you open-ended funding, your own private lab, more than Wistar could ever *dream* of providing. You and Kessler have wanted to switch to Jillson for years, am I right? Well, now you can do it."

Farrow thought of the satellites that could read a license plate from thirty thousand miles out in space. He felt suddenly transparent, totally vulnerable. In short, he felt like a patient. It was a feeling that doctors loathed.

His head was pounding. He felt like murdering Kromer. He slowly caressed his beard and said, "All right, then, when do I start?"

Christian Charity. That was the label that Kromer had given the project, after the name of the street where the tavern stood that Little Joe Flowers had run to in his rabid daze. Farrow's mission was threefold: (1) To see if the new strain of rabies could be transmitted through sexual contact as well as through saliva; (2) to see if it caused biting behavior in mammals not prone to such behavior; and (3) to develop a vaccine. The new disease—foreign invention or natural mutation—had to be neutralized. There was no telling where and when it would turn up again, and in what potency. A disease of such strength, if it got out of hand, could bring a nation down in a matter of months.

The work on sexual transmission went quickly: Farrow and Kessler used mice. It took less than three months to learn that the Flowers serotype was carried in semen as well as saliva, and spread by osmosis: absorption through the mucous membranes lining body cavities. The research on biting was done with cows—which, like human beings, didn't turn violent with conventional rabies—and was inconclusive. Four cows became quite irritable, but none of

36

the three dozen used in the tests became vicious. (Would *anything* make a cow vicious? Farrow wondered.)

Progress on a vaccine came slowly, just as it had with the known rabies strains. Mice responded well to the earliest version, but cats and dogs did not. Cats did well on Series II, but eighty percent of the dogs developed serious side effects. Series III seemed promising, but Farrow discarded it suddenly—capriciously, Kessler thought—though he had to admit that the new direction in which Farrow steered the project was looking quite good. The incubation time, though. God, the incubation time!

Kessler had noticed the change early on, in the work with mice. Each successive batch of animals developed symptoms faster, which appeared to indicate that the more the virus was transmitted, the more it gained in strength.

"The configuration doesn't change, but the damn thing's acting quicker," he said in Farrow's office one day, his high forehead shiny with sweat. "It scares me, Martin. Maybe we ought to just drop this project."

He knew nothing about William Kromer, of course. He believed that his sponsor was NIH, and the move from Wistar to Maine had been sheer good luck.

"To beat a virus, you have to grow it," Farrow replied, looking up at his wall, at a painting that hung there, a seascape. Something about the whitecaps was not quite right.

"Yes, yes," Kessler said, "in order to make an omelet . . . The question is, is this omelet worth making?"

They're just not alive, Farrow thought as he looked at the waves, there's no movement in them. Frowning

37

and turning to Kessler, he said, "It's worth making, believe me, Paul."

Farrow stared at the empty cages. In spite of his many misgivings about Christian Charity, he'd consoled himself with the thought that, after all was said and done, he was striving to cure the disease. The research on sexual transmission, biting, that terrible business with Luce—all fed into this goal. This rationalization was shattered now. He said, "How the hell did they get in?"

"Through the skylight," said Kessler. Adjusting his horn-rimmed glasses and raising his eyebrows, he said, "We have to tell CDC."

"No," Farrow said. "We tell the Blue Harbor police and the county sheriff that dogs have escaped from the lab. We tell them the dogs have herpes, a form that human beings can catch, and tell them to shoot them on sight. If we're lucky enough, they'll kill them all before the infection spreads."

Little droplets of sweat covered Kessler's bald scalp. "And if one of the dogs has already bitten somebody?"

"Let's not think about that," Farrow said. "The bitch of it is, we're probably not going to know till the victim comes down with symptoms."

"Unless we notify the *Herald* and spread the word that anyone bitten has got to report for treatment."

"Treatment," Farrow said sarcastically.

"All right, confinement, then. We tell them they have to report for confinement, so we can make sure their horrible manner of death isn't duplicated."

Farrow sniffed. "Good idea." He looked at the ceiling a second, then said, "We don't tell the *Herald*. We do, and the town will panic. We tell the police and ask them to keep it quiet till the dogs are found. As far as anyone already being bitten goes, we'll just have to take our chances."

"I don't like those chances," Kessler said.

"Well, you think I like them? That goddamn Watts, how the hell did he let this happen?"

Kessler shrugged his soft shoulders and said, "For God's sake, Martin, we know he drinks, we've known it for over a year. And now somebody here, in Blue Harbor, Maine, has let rabid dogs escape. Jesus, you might expect it in Philadelphia . . ." He wiped his sweaty forehead with trembling fingers and said, "Okay, okay, look, maybe they'll get the dogs right off, maybe no one was bitten. Even if they were, there's still no proof the disease will make them act violent. Chances are they'll die without infecting anyone else. Right?"

"Right," Farrow said, thinking: Luce. He looked at the empty cages and said, "We better get down to the station."

Randall "Cowboy" Luce had first run afoul of the law at the age of nine, for stealing a thirty ought six from a hardware store in the town of Wayne in his native North Carolina. After a series of offenses ranging from vandalism to car theft to assault with a deadly weapon, he was sent to the Boys Correctional Center at Guilford at the age of sixteen. While there, he was accused of beating a fellow inmate nearly to death, but was cleared. Upon his release he got into dealing drugs and was apprehended three times. He was twenty when he killed the owners of a Florida inn and their four-year-old son with an axe, in the course of stealing two hundred thirty-four dollars and a Sony stereo.

39

The American wheels of justice moved at their average rate in Luce's case; by the time his appeals were exhausted, the electric chair had gone through two revisions, the most recent of which was rather cheerful: a modern, quasi-Scandinavian design in international orange.

Luce's date with that chair was less than a month away when he met Martin Farrow. As Farrow prepared the syringe, Luce squinted and said, "If I don't get sick, I'm outta here, right?"

"I don't know," Farrow said. "All I know is, you won't be executed."

"They told me I'm outta here."

"Then I guess you are," Farrow said.

God only knew what Luce had been told. Certainly not that his chances of not coming down with a fatal case of rabies were slim indeed. Series III had worked in eighty percent of dogs, but dogs weren't people. Luce could be lucky, of course, and if he was, Farrow would count *himself* lucky. If would mean he and Kessler were close . . . damn close.

He gave three shots of pre-exposure vaccine spread four days apart, and five days after the last of these he visited Luce again—with something different.

"Okay," he said, "put your leg up here."

Luce set his foot on the stool and said, "Weird place to stick a needle, ain't it?"

Farrow didn't reply. He thought: If it isn't this, it's the electric chair, I just might be saving his life. Right, he thought, and inserted the needle. He felt Luce jerk. This tough guy, who'd split three people apart with an axe and maimed countless others, had flinched during every injection. Farrow applied even pressure as Luce watched with narrowed gray eyes, and the deed was done.

40

Farrow stood. "I'll see you tomorrow again," he said. "Good luck." The guard led him out of the cell.

He started the postexposure series the following morning. At the end of a week, as he gave him the second dose, Luce said with a crooked grin, "Well, doc, I ain't sick yet."

"Good for you," Farrow said. "Keep it up."

He'd injected the virus in the ankle, the spot where the fox had bitten Joe Flowers eight years after Luce had murdered the Florida family. Without any vaccine, it had taken Flowers three weeks to develop rabies. In spite of the Series III vaccine, it only took Cowboy Luce two. Shortly after his third postexposure injection, his temperature rose, he complained of soreness and pain in his joints, and said that the light hurt his eyes. He started to shake, became incoherent, and turned so vicious he had to be felled by a tranquilizer dart before he could be restrained. Strapped to his infirmary cot, he tried to bite those who approached him. He screamed in terror when offered water, foamed at the mouth, lost the use of his arms and legs. Four days later, paralyzed, he died. The official announcement said he'd succumbed to pneumonia. Farrow sectioned his brain.

Examination revealed no difference between this virus and the virus in Little Joe Flowers. Farrow hadn't expected any. Mutant strains of a virus usually differed so slightly in purines and pyrimidines that they couldn't be detected by analysis: the only observable changes were in how they acted. Luce's symptoms had been the same as those reported in Flowers and those observed in his girlfriend, Nina Field, but the virus had only taken fifteen days to reach Luce's brain, as opposed to twenty in Flowers. Differences in physical resistance could account for the different incubation

41

times, but combined with Kessler's observations, the results were highly suggestive. They could only be verified by running tests on large numbers of human beings, something Kromer hadn't suggested yet, though Farrow wasn't about to put it past him.

Kessler had never been told about Cowboy Luce. Farrow's report—which he'd typed himself—had been sent by army courier directly to Kromer. As far as Kessler knew, Farrow had been visiting the Merieux Institute in Miami, whose studies complemented Jillson's.

"They advised us to switch to DM-1609-3M."

"But what about the reactions, Martin? That strain caused rabies in twenty percent of the cats."

"They feel it's our best bet."

"Really? God."

Farrow fingered his beard. "They have confirmed that the Flowers strain causes humans to bite."

"Any other good news?"

"You were right about incubation time. It's getting shorter."

"Jesus."

"A *highly* contagious form of herpes," Kessler was telling Captain Leeds, and Farrow remembered the snarl on Luce's face, the violent feral snapping of his jaws. Leeds asked if they had any pictures of the dogs, and Farrow said no, Jillson didn't routinely photograph its animals. All three of the dogs were beagles, two females and one male, and he described their markings and coloration. Leeds wrote it all down impassively, but Farrow sensed a certain disapproval in his manner; a certain dismay that dogs—or perhaps

42

more specifically beagles—had been used in their research.

On the way back to Jillson, Kessler said, "It's going to get out, the cops will leak it."

"You don't know that," Farrow said.

"The hell I don't, this is Blue Harbor. You can't keep a secret here."

Maybe *you* can't, Farrow thought.

THREE

A breeze rippled the bay, which was almost black in the failing rose-colored light. The granite boulder Miranda sat on was cold. She hugged herself and stood up, looking at Great Northern Island, lonely and dark in the twilight, then turned toward the house.

On the crest of the sloping lawn, in front of the sprawling turreted "cottage" of twenty-four rooms, guests in tuxes and gowns stood in clusters, drinking. On the flagstone terrace, Japanese lanterns swayed on cords as older couples danced. A late arrival, a forest green BMW, pulled into the lot near the tennis courts. Miranda wished she had brought her car so that she could go home, but now she was stuck till her parents decided to leave.

She wished Gary were here, but even if he had been feeling okay, he would never have come to a party at Juniper Heights. "Those Wadsworths make me feel like dirt," he had said to her once. "*All* those fancy summer people make me feel like dirt. You have to come from around here to understand that, I guess."

She had said, "Do I make you feel like dirt?" and he'd laughed, "No, babe, you make me feel good. Anyway,

44

you're not fancy. Rich, yes—but not fancy."

Gary was in his last year at Maine Maritime down in Castine. "I know what they think, the Wadsworths and people like that," he'd said. "Typical native. No ambition. Goes to college to learn how to be a sailor."

"My parents don't feel that way," Miranda had said.

"I wonder," he'd said.

Two ten-year-olds, a girl in a yellow chiffon dress and a boy in shorts and a striped boat shirt, tumbled into the pines. Miranda smiled. Ten years ago she had been like those kids; in another ten years she'd be thirty. Too fast, too fast! The breeze kicked up, she shivered again, and kept walking.

"Miranda!"

Catherine Wadsworth's granddaughter, Jennie. She floated over, holding a half-drained gin and tonic, a too-wide smile on her oval face. "Miranda, I haven't seen you in *ages.*"

"Since last summer, as a matter of fact."

"Since last summer."

Her fair-skinned face was flushed. She stumbled slightly and Miranda smiled. "You sure you can handle that stuff?"

Tossing her long brown hair, Jennie laughed. "Where's yours? Don't they drink at Bennington?"

"No."

"They don't at Middlebury, either."

"So I've heard," said Miranda, thinking, Was I this silly two years ago? "So how was your freshman year?"

"Oh, great. Super, really, I only flunked math."

"Terrific. I hope it's not your major."

"I don't have one yet, do you? Oh, of course you do, you're a senior."

"Mine's history."

"American?"

45

"Ancient. The ancient Egyptians fascinate me. They worshipped animals."

"And the sun, right?"

"Right."

"I worship the sun, too," Jennie said. Her tan gave ample evidence of this. "A history major, what will you do with that?"

"Find out where I stand in the scheme of things, I hope."

"There's a scheme?"

"I'm not sure yet. Listen, Jennie, have you seen my parents?"

"No, but you might ask Grandmother where they are, she's over there." The slender pale arm with the drink lurched backward.

Miranda saw her up by the gazebo, with her husband, Marvin, standing at her side. She was holding forth to a half-dozen guests, her coon cat, Precious, cradled in her arms. Her eyebrows were characteristically arched and her thin wrinkled mouth was puckered. Catherine the Great, remarkably intact for a woman past eighty. She had not, of course, led a highly demanding life.

Miranda said, "Nice seeing you, Jennie."

"You're not leaving, are you? The party's just started."

"I'm kind of tired."

"Oh," Jennie said, and she looked unaccountably grieved. Her glass, now empty of all but a sad wedge of lime, was practically horizontal. "Well, get some rest, and I'll see you soon. You'll be at the fireworks on the Fourth?"

She meant the private display at the Marlton estate, of course. "I suppose so," Miranda said.

"Well, I'll see you then."

46

High thin blue light was dying on Dutchman's Bay. The dance band looked like ghosts in the lanterns' glow. As Miranda approached the gazebo, Catherine said, "It's the same old story all over again—inferiority. And to overcome that, you have to conquer ignorance." She stroked Precious, who absorbed the affection with squinting, complacent eyes. "Now take this Jillson incident. Pure ignorance. You just *know* it was natives who did it. They resent the lab and always have. Of course, they won't exert the effort it takes to understand what's going on down there, they'd rather go *clamming* or something. Until that attitude's overcome, they'll never advance."

"That isn't fair," Miranda said, and everyone turned her way.

Catherine Wadsworth, eyebrows raised imperiously, said, "Ah-hah, an alternative viewpoint." The coon cat shuddered and flicked its whiskers, and Marvin Wadsworth, who looked for all the world like an overgrown frog with his baggy dark eyes and olive skin and flabby purple mouth, sucked his pipe with a little smile.

"Well, it *isn't* fair," Miranda said. "Plenty of natives have gotten an education, plenty have been successful in business and the professions. And some of those people who clam for a living are the nicest people on earth. Take Artie Hall."

"Well, Artie's a *dear,* of course," Catherine said. "But for every Artie, I could give you ten . . . well, I could give you ten."

She grinned, and Miranda's face went hot. "And I don't think letting the Jillson dogs escape was a stupid act," she said. "I think it's about time someone protested the work they're doing. A hundred and fifty animals are sacrificed to the gods of research each

47

minute in this country. Each *minute.*"

Nobody spoke. Miranda looked at the faces around her: Howard Barnes, a Washington lawyer, and his wife, Sandra, a legislative consultant, both in their thirties; Wilson Pickett, a slender, short, sixtyish artist with frizzy white hair; Engard Caswell, a psychiatrist from Boston; and Marcella Dumont, a professor of history at Cornell. Heavy hitters, and Miranda felt overwhelmed.

"I agree that it sounds atrocious," Sandra Barnes said gently, "but not very long ago, Miranda, children got measles, German measles, mumps, and every summer polio terrified people. Those diseases are practically gone today. And smallpox *is* gone—gone from the entire *world.* Without research on animals, it wouldn't have been possible."

"But they use them in *pain* experiments," Miranda said. "They torture them—like the Nazis used to torture prisoners in concentration camps—and most of it leads to nothing."

Howard Barnes raised his bushy pale eyebrows and said, "They don't do pain experiments at Jillson, Miranda, they do disease research."

"But they cut the animals *up.*"

Howard shrugged. "Better them than us."

"Agreed," said Marcella Dumont, a heavy-set woman with flabby pale arms.

Howard said, "I can't sympathize in the least with vandalism, and as Jillson's attorney, I'll prosecute the perpetrators to the fullest extent of the law."

Miranda looked at Howard's wide face, his sandy, curly hair. She had always liked him, but right at this moment she felt like wringing his neck. "Some laws are higher than the laws of man," she said.

"The anarchist manifesto," Wilson Pickett said.

Miranda had hoped that the artist would take her side, and she was furious. "Civil disobedience," she said. "Thoreau."

Marcella Dumont said, "Thoreau may not be the best one to quote in this case. He spent his later years growing plants for laboratories."

"Plants aren't animals," Miranda said. "Plants don't have eyes and ears and feet and tongues and brains. You know what they do to cats at Jillson? Test cosmetics on them. Shove oven cleaner down their throats, put nail polish in their eyes." Looking at Catherine Wadsworth, she said, "You wouldn't want someone to torture Precious, would you?"

"Torture, child?" Catherine said. Light glittered on the diamonds at her throat. "That term's a bit . . . excessive, don't you think?" She stroked the cat and said, "We wouldn't permit anybody to harm you, would we, sweetie? Of course, if it came to a choice between you and one of these children here, I wouldn't hesitate."

The dance band struck up a faster tempo, forties swing. Miranda tried to find her mother in the crowd. She saw Amelia Rose, Frank Hamilton . . . The dancing made her dizzy, and she looked away.

"It's a matter of ethics *and* pragmatics," Marvin Wadsworth said, looking more like a frog than ever. "Consider how Sandra here handled the Pyramid Chemical threat. Following your line of thought, Miranda, she should have gone over to Pelham and bombed the place. Destroying property, maiming innocent people—and dooming her cause in the process. There are *channels,* Miranda. Sandra twisted a couple of arms in Augusta, a couple more in Washington, and hazardous waste is not being burned on the shores of Dutchman's Bay. If someone has a

49

complaint about Jillson, it should go through *channels.*" He tilted his head back and puffed on his pipe, as if he'd said something profound.

"And in the meantime, animals die," Miranda said. "You talk about innocent people, well what about innocent cats and dogs? The Jillson animals might not have papers, but they *do* have feelings."

Catherine Wadsworth, looking pained, said, "We'll defend the natives' homespun dignity next, I suppose."

Miranda's mother, Dorothy, appeared near the terrace's steps with Amelia Rose, and Miranda thought, Thank God. She was feeling very tired now, and very cross. She opened her mouth to excuse herself from the group when a child's soft distant crying split the air.

Heads turned toward the source of the sound, the shore, where the water was nothing but darkness now. The swath of field between the trees was dotted with fireflies, and Miranda saw somebody climbing the slope, someone carrying something. It was Rachel Stemmer, holding her daughter, Tricia. She approached, breathing hard, and set Tricia down on the grass.

The child—three years old, Miranda guessed—rubbed a fist in her eye and whined.

"Why, sweetheart, what's wrong?" Catherine said in her gravelly voice. Precious jumped from her arms, and Tricia flinched.

"A dog just bit her," Rachel said, kneeling down, still fighting for breath.

Catherine said, "Good heavens. *What* dog?"

"I didn't see it—but look."

There were three sharp punctures above the ankle, and two purple lines.

"Are you certain that it was a dog?" Marvin

50

Wadsworth asked, his pipe in the cup of his hand.

"Not absolutely, no," Rachel said. "Tricia told me it was."

"Mmm," Marvin said.

Tricia started to sob again.

"It's okay, Trish," Rachel said as she hugged her. "He's gone now, it's all right now."

"Let's go inside and clean that up," Catherine said. "Imagine. Where in the world would a dog come from?"

Howard Barnes turned his wide pale eyes on Miranda. She looked away.

Marvin Wadsworth said, "She's had her DPT's, of course."

"Of course," Rachel said.

"But it ought to be looked at anyway. Nasty thing."

"I'll take her into town as soon as we've washed it," Rachel said. "Have you seen Fred?"

"Not recently," Marvin said.

Miranda felt suddenly weak. She said, "He's on the terrace. With Mother."

Sandra Barnes stared at the dark slope of lawn and said, "Howard, find Lucy and Matty. I don't want them out of my sight."

"God no," Howard said.

"Now what other children are there?" Catherine said. "The Telfords' boy."

"And Mary Walker," Marvin said.

"They were playing together, down by the pines. We'll need them back here right away."

Miranda walked toward the house with Rachel, who was carrying Tricia again. The child wiped her eye and whimpered, "Bad doggie."

"He certainly was," Rachel said. "He certainly was."

"Trish, what did he look like?" Miranda asked.

"I don't know," Tricia said in a petulant voice.

"Was he big or little? What color was he?"

"I don't *know*."

The dog that had bitten Gary was brown and white, with a white spot between its eyes. Miranda remembered its nasty snarl, the way it had leapt from its cage. Near the terrace, her mother was talking to Mr. Stemmer, Fred, a broker with Paine Webber, and Wendell Renshaw, editor and owner of the *Blue Harbor Herald*. Heads turned as Rachel mounted the flagstone steps. "Sally?" she said to an angular woman in a strapless gown, "you better call Mary up to the house, there's a dog on the loose down there, and not a very pleasant one."

In the background Miranda heard Howard Barnes call, "Lucy! Matty!" in singsong tones. As she went up the steps, she shivered.

The Great Fire of 1947 had started on Blue Harbor's northwest rim and swept the whole island in twenty-four hours, destroying its link to the mainland, the Taggart bridge, consuming two-thirds of its buildings and most of its trees, and driving a third of its population into the numbing sea. Most of the summer people were back in their permanent homes by the time it broke out in early fall, and kept abreast of the tragedy by telephone or radio or through accounts in the *Boston Globe* or *New York Times* or *Philadelphia Bulletin*. Many did not see the ruins until the next spring.

Juniper Heights, tucked into the island's southwest corner, had been spared in the conflagration, along with twenty-six other Sunday Point mansions. Sunday Point was the wealthiest section of town, and Juniper

Heights was its pride. Constructed in 1892 from a Stanford White design, its original owners were Catherine Wadsworth's paternal grandparents, Herbert and Eleanor Holmes, owners of the Folger Ball Bearing Company of Providence, Rhode Island.

From the very beginning, the house had contained three bathrooms. Such opulence was rare in any turn of the century dwelling, and its presence in a Maine vacation cottage had once set tongues to wagging. The third-floor bathroom, the smallest of the three, only twelve feet long by ten feet wide, was nevertheless the most striking. Its walls were tiled in black, its tub was black, and the twin sink vanity top was made of Ethiopian onyx, black with white bands.

A huge mirror ran the length of this vanity. Reflected in it at this moment were Angela Kessler, Paul Kessler's wife, and her lover, Jim Morgan, chief loan officer at the Blue Harbor National Bank.

In his hand Morgan held a small cardboard square. On this square was the face of Jeff Sanderson, a third baseman for the New York Mets, and on this face were two short rows of white powder. Laughing, Angela took a new ten-dollar bill, rolled it into a tube, placed one end of it into her right nostril and the other end on the baseball card. She sniffed, and a row of the powder disappeared.

Jim took the bill and snorted the other line. He breathed, a smile on his face, and said, "That's nice."

Leaning against the onyx sinktop, Angela echoed, "Nice." The row of bulbs above the mirror sparkled in her dark blond hair. "Now let's get out of here."

Jim held up a hand. "Whoa," he said. "We have further business."

A laugh. "Oh, really? Not *serious* business, I hope."

"Quite serious," Jim said.

Angela tossed her hair and said, "Jim, don't be crazy. We shouldn't have gone this far."

"Come on, no one's going to use the third-floor john."

"They will if the downstairs johns are filled."

"That's a hell of a lot of simultaneous pissing, isn't it?" Jim said.

Another laugh, and Angela's cheeks were flushed. Jim held her shoulders, kissed her ear, pressed into her, and said, "Come on, Paul's not going to show."

She sniffed. "Just when I thought he might finally relax, he's a madman again. Ever since those goddamn dogs got loose."

"Married to his microbes, and so much the better for us." He ran his hand along her thigh and a wave of heat rushed through her.

"Jim . . ."

He kissed her again, on the mouth, pressed against her again. This time there was more to press with. Quite a bit more.

"Jim," Angela said again, hotly this time, and this time her eyes were closed, and he raised her flimsy skirt above her hips. "So the doctor's wife runs around without any panties," he said.

Her breathing was loud. "Too confining in summer weather," she said.

"I agree," Jim said. He lifted her up on the vanity top, her skirt around her waist. She leaned against the mirror, the white of her thighs reflected in gleaming black onyx. He ran his hand along her pale silk stocking, over the snap of the blue garter belt, and cupped his palm on her crotch.

"Jim, they'll catch us. Please." Her voice was quick, high, thin.

"That only makes it more fun," he said, and worked

54

his zipper.

"Jim, oh my god . . ."

She was moist and hot, and said, "Do it fast." Her eyes were closed again, she was biting her lip, her fingers dug into his back. She thrust her hips hard and said, "I hear somebody!"

"Yes," he said. "Yes!" and spasmed and shook. She cried out, "Oh!" and her head went back.

He withdrew. "Damn," he said. "I'll go down first, you wait ten minutes."

She was limp against the mirror, still gasping, her cheeks bright crimson, her eyes half-closed. Her dress was still high on her waist as Jim fixed his pants. "All right," she said.

Jim checked himself in the mirror, ran his hand through his thick black hair, set his bowtie straight, and walked out into the hall.

They were all in the kitchen. Rachel Stemmer was at the sink, washing Tricia's leg. Her husband, Fred, was kneeling, holding his child's hand as Amelia Rose, a nurse at Blue Harbor hospital, showed her a picture book. Dorothy Shore and her daughter Miranda looked on.

Jim Morgan walked in casually and said, "What's all the commotion?"

From behind him Catherine Wadsworth said, "The poor girl was bitten by a dog, a stray, down by the dock. So much for Blue Harbor's leash law. I don't know one of my friends who disobeys it, but as for *others* . . . That Frenchy Goselin lets his animals roam all over the place, and that bunch at the end of the Flatiron Road, whatever their name is—"

"Sparrow," Fred Stemmer said. Tricia pouted

and winced.

"Yes, whatever. They have a Doberman—a *Doberman,* mind you—that's up and down that road ten times a day. Absolutely outrageous. But talk to animal control about it, hah! They're *cousins* of those people! Outrageous. I'll see what Howard can do, this can't be allowed to continue."

Fred, still holding his daughter's hand, said: "It might have been one of the Jillson dogs."

"They're supposed to be docile," Jim Morgan said. "Right, Wendell?"

Wendell Renshaw, the newspaper editor, stood near the stove. He puffed on his pipe and said, "That's what Dick Leeds told me. That's what the people at Jillson told *him.*"

Miranda thought of the beagle again; saw its teeth. She thought about Gary last night, making love to her, sweating, complaining about his sore throat.

Her mother, Dorothy, said in her calm way, "The odds are pretty great against it being a Jillson dog, I suppose."

"I suppose," Fred said. "But the last I heard, there were two of them still on the loose."

"They caught one?" Dorothy asked.

"They found it dead. Someone buried it out on the lane near Jillson."

"But what did it die of? I thought they had herpes."

Fred Stemmer just shrugged.

"I'll call the police and find out what it died of," Catherine Wadsworth said. "And see if they caught the other dogs—and give them a piece of my mind while I'm at it, too." She swept out of the kitchen and into the hall.

Jennie Wadsworth came in. Miranda went over to her and said, "Did they find the other kids?"

56

Jennie's eyes looked a little bit crooked. "Yes," she said.

"Thank God," Miranda said.

Jennie shrugged. "Well, what's the big deal? It isn't the end of the world. It isn't like it's a werewolf or something."

"No," Miranda said. She felt small and weak and scared and said, "Can I see you alone for a minute?"

They went into the dining room. In the hallway, Catherine Wadsworth's voice was making stern demands. Miranda said, "You got any dope?"

Jennie smiled and said, "Follow me."

The breeze had died, and the Japanese lanterns hung still. Mary Walker, Lucy, and Matty Barnes, still with plenty of zip, were playing hide and seek in the boxwood hedge that surrounded the formal gardens. Angela Kessler, sitting on the low stone wall that surrounded the terrace, had been cornered by Wilson Pickett, who said in his squeaky voice, "The problem with superrealism, as I see it, is one of *dimension.*" Angela's eyes were fixed on the darkness—or maybe on nothing at all.

Miranda sank into a canvas chair that sat near a towering pine and listened to the band's soft swing. Down near the water, an owl made a lonely cold sound.

The dope had mellowed Miranda out for a while, but now all her sadness and fear were back. She stared down the slope to the heavy black trees and thought of Tricia again. Gary wasn't feeling well, and he had been bitten . . .

She hadn't prayed since the age of twelve, but now she stared up at the stars and prayed that the dog that had bitten Tricia had not been a Jillson dog. She prayed that Tricia and Gary would not get herpes. She prayed that she herself would not get herpes.

The sky looked down on her, empty and endless. She buried her face in her hands and thought, *Please, please.* Then, tired and scared and confused, she began to cry.

FOUR

In Kessler's dream, the Doberman had him trapped. He'd returned to the lab after dinner, and was sectioning some rabbit tissue, when he suddenly heard the growl. He turned on his stool, looked up—and there was the dog, in the doorway, fangs bared, a string of white drool hanging down from its lower jaw.

Numbness spread through his chest as he thought: Impossible. The cages were locked, the dog couldn't have gotten out . . . unless somebody let it out, but who . . . ?

Again, low in its throat, the dog growled. Kessler swallowed hard, gripping his scalpel, and didn't move. Sweat bloomed on his skin. Go away, he thought. Go away, go away.

The dog had a wild cast in its eye, an almost human look, as it started forward. "Go away!" Kessler cried.

And awoke saying "What?" his voice muffled and dead in the living room, his eyes fighting to focus. His hands gripped the arms of the easy chair. "Is that you?" he said, his heart racing, and yes, it was Angela, there at the door, in the shadows.

"Paul," she said.

"I dozed off."

She came into the room, to the circle of lamplight, a worried frown on her face. "A dog bit a child," she said.

Kessler's mind sharpened instantly. "What? Jesus! Where?"

"At the Wadsworth cottage."

He let out a breath. "Did they see it? Do they know whose it was?"

Angela put her clutch bag down on the table beside the easy chair. "No. The child was down in the woods, chasing fireflies. No adults were there."

"Damn." He stared at the floor. "Who was it?"

"Fred and Rachel Stemmer's girl."

"Damn."

"And you know what they're thinking, of course."

"Of course. They took her to the hospital, I hope."

"Amelia Rose was there—the nurse? She drove."

"They cleaned the wound right away?"

"Yes."

Kessler sat there a moment, eyes closed; then he opened his eyes again, and picked up the phone on the table. Punched the buttons and waited.

Six rings, then, "Hello?" Martin Farrow's flat voice.

"Martin. Paul. Martin, listen, a child's been bitten—"

"I know. The doctor at the emergency room called Leeds, and Leeds called me."

"And you didn't call *me?*"

"I just found out."

Kessler let out a breath. "So what did they say?"

"They used benzalkonium on the wound and started a PM-1403-4M."

"Completely worthless."

"We don't know that. It could be it wasn't our dog. It could be it wasn't a dog at all. In the morning the cops will start combing the woods to see what they can find."

Kessler frowned at the table beside the chair; at the rug.

"There's nothing we can do right now," Farrow said, "except hope for the best."

"Yeah."

"Okay?"

"Okay."

"We'll talk tomorrow."

"Okay," Kessler said, and hung up.

Angela had fixed a drink. She stood in the dining room doorway with it. "Want one?" she said.

"No thanks," Kessler said. He closed his eyes again and said, "I'm calling Jeff tomorrow. I'm going to tell him to stay in Vermont."

"What?" Angela said, walking into the room. "He wants to compete in that race next weekend."

"No," Kessler said, looking up. "I don't want him to come here."

"Well, isn't this just a bit of an overreaction? I mean what are we talking about here? Herpes, or the plague?"

"I don't want him to come to Blue Harbor, that's all."

Angela shook her head, then sipped her drink. "You're totally absurd sometimes, do you know that, Paul? If it hadn't been for me, you wouldn't have let Jeff learn how to drive a car."

"Don't start, okay?"

"You're the one who 'started,' Paul." She drank, walked past him, and went up the stairs.

He sat in the chair, a dull pounding behind his eyes. He remembered the dog in his dream. If the Stemmer child's bite had come from a Jillson beagle . . .

There was no way to save her.

Christ, he thought, and the weight of his work these

61

last few years pressed down again. We have to end it, he thought. Destroy the rest of the animals, destroy the virus. We should have done it long ago. But Martin, goddamn him . . .

We'll talk about it tomorrow, he thought. And this time, he'll listen. This time, he'll have to listen.

FIVE

Teddy Marsh, age eight, held the megabomb in both hands.

The Russians had shot down the missiles, but his bomber—totally silent and radar invisible—had slipped through all their defenses. Moscow was on his screen, and in less than a minute now, it would disappear.

The megabomb would evaporate it: each girder and brick, each man, woman, and child. Each animal, too, and Teddy felt bad about that—the dogs and cats and gerbils and hamsters didn't deserve to die. Then again, if they lived with Russkies . . .

He stopped for a minute to wipe his nose on the sleeve of his torn T-shirt and looked at Moscow, there in his old sandbox. It had taken him hours to build it of sticks, and in no time at all, boom—destroyed. But that's why he'd built it. To bomb it. During all those minutes of patiently placing stick upon stick upon stick, he'd been thinking about this moment, the moment of doom.

He scanned the city carefully. No citizens were to be seen. They'd been hiding for hours, most of them down in the subways, but that wouldn't help them today. The megabomb would pulverize them, blasting the subways to dust. Good. The Russians were bad. They were all like Billy Webber, who'd stolen his penknife and lied about it. Closer and closer death came . . .

He stopped again. In the trees at the edge of the lawn—he'd heard something.

He stood there, not moving, the rock in his hands. Moscow's fate hung suspended. A thin breeze failed; a mosquito came zeroing in on his ear. He rubbed it away on his T-shirt, annoyed, and looked at the woods.

The brush at the edge of the trees shivered slightly. Something was in there.

The world was suddenly real again: too real. Teddy started to sweat. He would use the rock. No, he'd run. Just drop the rock and run.

The brush moved again, and an animal tumbled out. A dog; a beagle. It wobbled and fell; stood shakily, panting; collapsed again.

Teddy's eyes went wide. He dropped the rock and said, "Marley! Marley, you're back!"

He ran up to the dog. It lay wearily on its side, looking up through glazed eyes. A thin white froth covered its lips. "Marley, what's wrong, boy?"

The dog tried to rise, but flopped over again, its tail limp.

"Wait here," Teddy said. "Stay right here."

He ran over the patchy lawn, up the steps of the back porch, and into the house. "Dad, Dad!"

Walt Marsh, settled deep in his La-Z-Boy, set his can of beer on the floor. The Red Sox had runners on first and third with one out, and what now?

Teddy stood in the living room doorway, his forehead smudged, his spikey hair sticking up this way and that. "Marley's back!" he cried.

Walt Marsh grunted and thought: Oh, no. He watched the batter ground into a double play, took a swig of his beer, set the can down again, and stood up. Jesus. Marley. He'd thought this might happen. "Where is he?" he said.

"Out back. He came out of the woods."

The two of them went outside. The dog hadn't moved. It lay there, sides heaving, its eyes half-closed.

"Is he sick?" Teddy asked.

Walt squatted. He lifted the beagle's ear, let it fall. "He sure looks it," he said.

"You're not gonna send him away again, are you, Dad?"

"Ted, I told you before, we can't keep him."

"Why *not?*"

"You know very well why not."

"I'll keep him inside, he won't bark anymore."

"We tried that, Ted."

"But—"

"We'll keep him tonight, and tomorrow we'll take him to see Dr. Borden."

"Why not today?"

"He's not open today. It's Sunday."

"And then what? You'll send him back?"

"We'll see what Dr. Borden says. But Ted, we've been through it and through it. We can't keep him here."

"But what kind of a home did you send him to where they let him get sick?"

"Dogs just get sick sometimes," Walt said. "It's not the owners' fault." He petted the beagle, who just lay there, panting. "What's wrong, Marley? What's wrong, old boy?" He slipped his hands under the dog and lifted him gently. Drool clung to the animal's lips.

Slowly Walt walked to the house, thinking: Animals, Christ, they're amazing. He'd shipped Marley off to the Brewster shelter, fifty-five miles northwest of Blue Harbor, thinking that if he was placed with a family up

65

there, so far away, he would never come home again, but mother of God, here he was. Even sick like this he had found his way back.

"Please can we keep him, Dad?"

"You heard me, Ted."

"For a week?"

"Ted . . ."

SIX

"I think we should stop the work on the Flowers strain."

Farrow, seated behind his desk, leaned back in his chair, and said, "Paul, we've already been through this."

"Yes. And if you had listened to me before, a little girl—"

"We don't know about that little girl yet, Paul."

Kessler took out a handkerchief—a bandana, really—and patted his shiny scalp. "It's too dangerous, Martin. I worry myself to death about our staff. All it takes is one scratch . . ."

Farrow picked up a paper clip. He bent it, tossed it down among the papers, folders and books on his desktop, and said, "We don't force them to work here, Paul. It's not slave labor. They know what they're dealing with, and you'll have to agree, we take every precaution."

"That doesn't mean an accident won't happen," Kessler said. "Christ, it's *already* happened."

"That wasn't an accident, it was sabotage."

Kessler dabbed at his forehead. "Well, call it whatever you want, the dogs got loose. That's scary as

67

hell, I mean it. Two dogs are running around out there that—" He let out a breath and said, "Christ."

Farrow picked up the paper clip; straightened it out. "So you want us to stop the research. When maybe somewhere else in this country, other animals are running around with this stuff."

Kessler licked his full lips. "It's been years since that fox bit Flowers. *Years,* Martin. If anything else was going to happen, it would have happened by now. In the meantime, we're *growing* this stuff. There's more danger in that than there is in taking the chance it will show up again somewhere."

Farrow tugged at his beard, his gray eyes on Kessler; said nothing.

"Look," Kessler said, "if it shows up again somewhere, we resume our research."

Farrow looked out the window: the long line of maples across the lawn, the clouds piled up in the powder blue sky. He glanced at the painting, the seascape—that surf, not right—then looked back at his desk. "So you'd let these criminals, these terrorists— because that's what they are—negate five years of work? We're getting so close, Paul, so close. In another year—maybe less—we'll beat this thing."

Kessler looked at his handkerchief, shaking his head. "I'd love to believe that," he said, "but I can't. I think we're still five years away, and I don't think it's worth it. Three known victims of this stuff, all dead. It just isn't *worth* it."

Four known cases, Farrow thought, and pictured Cowboy Luce's agonized face.

"I have to live with myself," Kessler said. "This thing with the Stemmer girl had me up all night. And I told my son not to visit next weekend."

"You don't even know it was one of our dogs," Farrow said.

68

"But what if it was?" The hand with the handkerchief quivered.

"For Christ's sake, calm down," Farrow said.

Kessler took a deep breath; wiped his cheeks. "I know those people, they're Angela's friends, if anything happens to that girl—"

The telephone rang. Farrow answered it, eyes still on Kessler's flushed face. "Hello?" He listened, nodding, and then said, "Good. Where was it?" He listened. "I certainly do," he said. "I'll be right there."

He hung up. "Leeds. His men shot a beagle this morning, down near the Wadsworth estate. He wants me to see if it's ours."

Kessler's eyebrows went up.

Farrow stood. "Yeah, I better get moving. Someone's likely to get some bright ideas about doing some lab work on it."

Kessler clutched his handkerchief, his eyes still wide. "If it's one of ours, and was down near the Wadsworth estate—"

"Paul, for God's sake, relax," Farrow said, and was out the door.

One more, Kessler thought as he looked out the window at nothing. If this one's ours, there's just one more dog left. In a few days, a week at the most, its disease will kill it. Most likely it's already dead. But if something eats the cadaver . . .

Don't think about that, he told himself, breaking into a sweat again. Don't think about that, it won't happen.

He thought again of Tricia Stemmer. Sick, he went back to his office.

SEVEN

The monster was moving across the lake with terrifying speed, its eight legs churning hard. Unless a miracle occurred, the entire town was doomed. Buildings would be reduced to rubble, people would be crushed and devoured alive.

But a miracle *would* occur, and he, Teddy Marsh, was its agent. His plane would guide the megabomb to its goal.

He was over the lake now; the monster was right below. Easy, easy, he told himself, sighting with one eye shut. You get one chance. If you blow it . . .

He held his breath, blinked once, said a prayer, and let go.

Blam! The rock landed right on target, smack in the center of the metal plate that served as Marley's water bowl, and the beetle went flying.

It landed three feet away on its back, its spindly legs scratching the air. Teddy snuffed out its life with his shoe.

There, he said to himself. No wonder Marley wouldn't drink with a thing like that in his dish. Though, to tell the truth, he wasn't too fussy, he used to drink out of the toilet, which, at least in Teddy's view of things, was much, much worse.

Teddy looked at the dog. It had stayed outside on its chain all night and hadn't made a sound. All morning it had lain in the dust, hardly moving, its tongue hanging out, a ring of foam coating its lips. When Teddy's father had brought out the water, the dog had stared and shown its teeth and hadn't drunk a drop. All day, in this heat, and no water. Teddy himself had drunk glass after glass, because they were out of juice; they would go to the store on the way back home from the vet.

Teddy picked up the metal dish and went back to the house. If Marley would only drink, he might feel better, and if he felt better, maybe Dad would let him stay. Teddy went to the outside faucet and turned it on, then went to the end of the hose and sprayed Marley's dish. Cleaned it good. Then filled it with fresh cold water and turned off the faucet again.

Walking with utmost care, he took the dish back to the dog, hardly spilling a drop. Placing it gingerly on the dirt, he said, "Come on, Mar, take a drink. It's so hot, you gotta drink. Please? If you can get better, we'll keep you. Okay? Come on."

He pushed the dish close to the beagle, right under its nose. "Just a little bit, Mar."

The dog's eyes came open; its lip curled back. It showed no inclination to sample the water.

Teddy dipped his right hand in the dish. He held it over the beagle's head and shook it gently, twice. A couple of drops fell onto the animal's purple black ugly gums. "Come on, Mar—"

"Ow! *Ow!*" Teddy clutched his right hand and fell backward.

The whole thing had happened so fast Teddy couldn't believe it: the dog's eyes and mouth snapping open, the teeth clamping down . . . and a bright red streak stained Teddy's palm.

"Marley," he said, shocked, frightened, betrayed, scrambling onto his feet. "What's *wrong* with you?"

He held his hand next to his chest, and tears came to his eyes. "Mar . . ." he said in a feeble voice, and quickly ran into the house to wash his wound.

As Gary Simmons wiped his hot forehead, his hand shook violently, his arm weighed tons.

He looked at the showroom, where Hachett, the manager, sat leaning over his desk, hunched forward, writing up another sale. It was five-fifteen, he had to get out of this goddamn place, and the bastard was making him finish this goddamn job.

When he looked at the top of the car he was cleaning, its glare stunned his eyes. Pain contracted inside his hot skull. He looked out at the street, at the cars whizzing past on Route 1, and felt giddy and faint.

"Screw this," he hissed softly, and tossed his rag into the car. He rolled up the windows and locked the doors and walked to the showroom. His legs felt weak, and his goddamn ankle . . .

He stood in the showroom doorway. Hachett kept writing, ignoring him. Clearing his aching throat, Gary said, "Excuse me."

The manager looked at him coldly.

"I have an appointment," Gary said. "I've got to go."

Hachett said, "Did you finish that job?"

"Almost," Gary said. "I'll have it done before nine in the morning."

The manager scowled. "The customer's likely to show before that. I want that car ready when he arrives."

"I'll come in early," Gary said. "I'll have it done by eight."

"I'd prefer that you finish it now," Hachett said, and he turned away and looked at the customer signing the forms on his desk, a woman with purple slacks and glasses like orange mirrors. "And this one is for the title," he said. "Is it going to be in your name or your husband's, too?"

"I'm leaving," Gary said.

Hachett looked at him hard again. When he did, a terrible urge welled up in Gary, an urge to strangle the man. He'd never felt quite this way before in his life, and it scared him. He opened his mouth to speak, thought better of it, and turned on his heels and walked quickly outside again.

He went to his car and got inside and started the engine and thought: Screw you. You don't like it, go get some other slave to do your dirty work. His right ankle tingled and burned and itched, and his forehead was soaked with sweat. He backed up sharply, spun the steering wheel hard, and peeled violently onto Route 1.

"Gary, make an appointment with Dr. Welch. Please."

Miranda sat next to him on the porch, on the flowered settee. He wiped his brow with his hand again and said, "I'll be okay."

"You don't look okay."

A surge of that anger he'd felt at work welled up and he forced it down. "Thanks," he said.

"I just mean—I'm just trying to help." She looked at the gray painted boards of the floor. "I want you to be all better, that's all I mean."

Taking her hand, he said, "I'll be fine. It's the flu, it's been going around."

His fingers were hot and damp on her flesh. "I guess so," she said.

73

"You're feeling okay?"

"I'm fine," she said, but it wasn't true. She'd been tired these past two days, and she had the strangest sensation between her legs: a tingling itchy heat that was driving her crazy.

He squeezed her hand, then let it go. He looked out at the lawn, at the water, the islands out there, and the brightness hurt his eyes. He squinted; pain throbbed at the base of his skull.

She looked at him with worried eyes. "Gary?"

A wave of quick dizziness hit him; he licked his lips and brushed back his curly brown hair. "Yeah?"

"What if they lied to us? What if the dogs didn't really have herpes? What if they had something worse than that—and you've caught it?"

Again, that anger rising. "I didn't catch anything from the dogs," he said. "I have the goddamn flu!"

She looked at him sadly, then sighed, and looked out at the sea. "Please go to the doctor," she said. "For me, okay?" She turned to him with blue, blue eyes, a shaft of sun on the part in her rust red hair.

"Okay," he said, and swallowed, his throat really sore.

"Tomorrow. Don't go to work."

"I have to go to work, I'm in the middle of a job."

"Oh Gary, forget the job. This is more important."

He spat out the words, surprising himself. "Oh, is it? I'm not independently wealthy, Miranda! I need this money to go back to school! I guess people like you wouldn't understand that."

The hurt on her face made him sorry for what he'd just said. "I just want you to be all better, that's all."

He nodded, a giddiness rushing through him, along with a flash of shame. "I know, babe. I'll go to the doctor."

That pain at the back of his head. And his ankle

again, that burning raw tingling.

"I'm tired," she said. "I'm going in."

"Take care of yourself."

"I will."

She stood, and to Gary it happened too slowly. Her pale blue dress and sandals looked spotty, as if he'd been smoking dope.

"You'll call me tomorrow," she said in a slow voice, "as soon as you're through at the doctor's."

"Yeah. If I can get an appointment."

"You make him give you one."

"Right," he said.

He held her then, and their bodies burned, and he kissed her pale forehead with pale clammy lips. The pain in his ankle flared into his knee and he thought: I have to learn more about Jillson. Who *knows* what they do down there? He knew a guy who had worked on the grounds there, he'd ask—

Against him, Miranda's tight chest was heaving. As she fought the tears, he said, "No, babe. No, babe, it's just the flu."

EIGHT

"Ow!"

Dr. Butler withdrew the needle and Teddy watched as the nurse put the Band-Aid on. He wouldn't cry. He was much too big to cry.

"Now you're sure your dog was up to date on his rabies shots," Butler said.

"Absolutely," Walt Marsh replied. "I took him last year, and they're good for two years, right?"

Stripping off his plastic gloves and tossing them into the trash, Butler said, "That's right." He squinted at Walt through glasses with pale plastic frames and said, "Did you know that only forty percent of the dogs in this country are immunized against rabies?"

"You're kidding," Walt said. He was wearing his work clothes, dark blue, with "Walt's Burner Service" in white above his left pocket.

"It's true," Butler said. "Most of the people who don't get licenses for their dogs don't bother with rabies shots either. And only four percent of cats are immunized."

"Cats? I didn't know cats were dangerous."

The nurse left the room, closing the door, and Butler squinted at Teddy. "They're dangerous, all right," he

76

said, then turned to Walt. "You were ready to take the dog to the vet."

"Yeah."

"Who's your vet?"

"Dr. Borden."

"I'll call him and ask him to come to your house. I don't want you touching the dog."

"I don't want to touch him," Walt said.

Butler tilted his head back; light caught in his glasses. "A dog bit a child a few nights ago and they brought her here to ER. We were worried it might have been one of those dogs that got out of the Jillson lab. Could be it was your dog instead."

"Christ, I hope not," Walt said.

Teddy, scowling, was clutching his arm. Butler patted his shoulder. "You're all done, pal. Say hi to Dr. Hayes for me, when you see him again, okay?"

Teddy slid off the table quickly, relieved to be finished, glad that he only needed one shot.

"Take this slip to the front desk," Butler said, and handed a paper to Walt, whose hand was clammy as he took it.

"Tetanus? It's something you get from bites and rusty nails and stuff," Walt said as he pulled the car into the dooryard.

"Well, what does it do to you?" Teddy asked. He had finally let go of his arm.

"You can't open your mouth."

"You can't eat?"

In front of the garage, Walt stopped, put the lever in park, and turned off the engine. "You're not gonna get it, Teddy, that's why he gave you the shot."

"I know," Teddy said.

They got out of the car. Marley was lying stretched

out on his rope on the other side of the lawn. Teddy looked at him sadly. "Can Dr. Borden make him better? Give him some shots?"

"We'll see, Ted. But even if he gets better, you know we can't keep him."

"But Dad . . ."

The door to the porch came open and June Marsh stood there, looking worried. "So what did he do?" she asked.

"The usual," Walt said. "Tetanus booster."

June Marsh pushed her hand through her graying hair. "Dr. Borden just called," she said. "He'll be here in half an hour or so."

"Can he make Marley better?" Teddy asked.

"We'll see," his mother said.

Dr. Borden, squatting with Marley's paw in his plastic-gloved hand, looked up at Walt Marsh. "He's dead," he said.

Teddy's eyes went shut. Tears rolled down his cheeks and he covered his face with his hands. His mother put her arm around him and held him.

"It's sad, but it's better this way," Walt said. "He was very sick, Ted."

Teddy nodded, his fists at his eyes.

Standing up, Borden said, "I'm going to take him to be examined. We have to find out what he had."

June Marsh frowned sharply. "What do you mean? What do you *think* he had?"

"Just to be on the safe side," Borden said.

"But what *could* it be?" June said.

"Any number of things—most of which human beings can't catch." He went to his car, a pale blue Volvo, came back with a green plastic bag, and asked Walt to hold it.

Walt did. Borden carefully lifted Marley, put him in the trash bag, then took the bag from Walt.

"Are you just going to throw him *away?*" Teddy said, his face shiny with tears.

"Oh no, no, no, don't you worry about that," Borden said. "We'll take good care of him."

Teddy turned away, crying again. Borden said, "Walt, I'd like the name of the people you gave him to, so we can check to see if they have any other animals."

"Oh, yeah," Walt said. "I have it in the house somewhere. It'll take me a while to find it. I'll give you a call."

June's arm was across Teddy's shoulder again. "Let's go inside," she said.

The two of them walked toward the house, and Walt went to the Volvo with Borden, who carried the bag. "I gave it to the Brewster pound," Walt said in a quiet voice. "I don't know who they gave it to, you'll have to check with them."

Borden nodded. He opened his trunk, set the bag inside, then closed the lid again. As he got behind the wheel he said, "I'm sure there's nothing to worry about."

"Thanks for coming," Walt said.

Borden nodded and pulled away.

Walt walked across the lawn to the metal dish, the bare patch of lawn and the rope that had held the dog. He untied the rope from the tree, then took it to the oil drum where he burned his trash and dropped it on top of the ashes.

He stared at it there in the drum's rusty darkness and thought: He bit Teddy. He had something that killed him, some kind of disease.

He went back to the bare spot where Marley had died and picked up the metal dish.

The police had found one of the Jillson dogs dead

and had shot another dog, but the third one was still on the loose. Could Marley have come into contact . . . ?

Nah, Walt said to himself. Christ, you think of the damnedest things.

When he looked at the metal dish in his hands, he discovered he'd bent it in half.

NINE

As Sharon Jensen frowned up at the screen, sweat broke out on her high pale forehead. She took a deep breath through her mask and looked away and checked the sketch she had made; looked back at the screen again.

Impossible, she thought.

Impossible on two counts: One, the dog had had its rabies shots; and two, this rabies was different, she was sure it was.

Or almost sure. In almost twelve years in the Maine State Department of Health's pathology lab, she'd only seen four rabies cases: one bat, two skunks, one cat— all precisely the same as what she'd studied in school. But this one, those odd projections, those spikes . . .

Breathing deeply again, she looked back at her sketch. That could explain it, of course. If this *was* a new form of rabies, a *really* new form, the standard vaccine wouldn't work.

She was frightened, but also thrilled. A new form of rabies, and she, Sharon Jensen, had found it. The Jensen rabies. A matter of chance, of course—right place, right time—but then again, what wasn't? God knew she deserved some good luck, things hadn't gone well at all since she broke up with John, but to think that she, a pathologist in a state health lab, not some tenured professor at Stanford or Duke, had actually found—

She laughed to herself and said aloud, "You're getting a little carried away, aren't you, Sharon?"

She got up from her stool, went to the door, opened it, and lowered her sterile mask; walked down the dingy mint green corridor twenty feet and stopped at Steve Burlingame's office. "Knock-knock," she said.

He looked up from his desk with that flat obtuse expression she truly despised.

"Got a minute?" she said.

He studied the screen for a long time, his chin in his hand, then turned to her slowly, and said, "It's rabies. Absolutely."

Beside him, she said, "But those spikey projections."

Steve Burlingame shook his large head. "It's different, all right. Whether that difference is significant is something else again, and something we'll have to find out. I'll call Atlanta. And I guess you better call that vet. There's a kid out there that needs some rabies shots."

"Positive," Borden said into the phone. "July of last year. Rabies, distemper, and heartworm." He stared at the folder that sat on his desk. "I can't understand this. I can't understand it at all."

On the other end of the line, Sharon Jensen said, "We can't either, unless . . ."

"Unless what?"

"The virus is different. It has these projections."

"You mean it's a new strain of rabies?"

82

"We don't know yet."

"My God."

"We don't know how else to explain it. How can a dog that's been immunized get rabies? Unless it's a brand new strain?"

"Yes," Borden said. He was quiet a moment, then said, "Maybe he didn't just 'get' it."

"What?" Sharon said.

"Maybe he didn't just get it," Borden repeated. "Maybe . . . he was given it."

"By whom? How?" Sharon said.

"I think you better get in touch with Jillson," Borden said.

The receiver was hard and hot in Walt Marsh's hand. He looked out the window, sick, and said again, "I just don't believe this. They have to be wrong."

Borden's voice, on the other end of the line, said, "They're quite sure it's rabies, Walt."

"But you gave him his shot, I know you did, I had the papers. The pound asked me for them."

"The dog's shots were up to date. I can't understand it either, all I know is, it's true."

"Jesus Christ," Walt said.

June appeared in the kitchen doorway, frowning. "What's wrong, Walt?"

His tongue wasn't working right. "The dog," he said. "Oh Christ, it had rabies."

June covered her mouth with her hand.

Borden's voice on the phone was sharp and thin. "Eastern Maine Medical, that's where they have the vaccine. You get right over there, time is crucial." A pause. "Remember now, the new vaccines are excellent."

"Okay," Walt said, his heart loud in his ears. "Okay,

83

and . . . thanks."

June was sobbing, her face in her hands.

"He'll be okay," Walt said. "We just have to get him there right away, they can stop this stuff, he said—"

"Mom?"

Teddy was there in the doorway, his face confused. June knelt and threw her arms around him; held him, tightly, tightly.

"Mom?" he said, his voice very weak and small.

Walt said, "Get your shoes on, Ted, we have to go back to the doctor."

"What?"

"You heard me."

"I need more shots?"

"Just a little one, Ted."

TEN

Kessler stared at the table, sweating hard, pushing his glasses up on his slippery nose. It was one of the missing dogs, there was no doubt about it. He swallowed behind his sterile mask, his throat tight.

When the call from the state pathology lab had come through, he had tried to reach Farrow, but today was Wednesday, Farrow's day off, and as always on Farrow's day off, no one answered his phone. The caller, a woman, had stressed the great urgency of the matter, and Kessler, without hesitation, had driven the sixty miles to Augusta.

And now he stood next to the caller, Sharon Jensen, and her colleague, Steven Burlingame, and stared with them at the dog on the slab of steel. The top of the beagle's head had been sawed away and its brain had been sectioned.

"I can't really tell," Kessler said, his mouth dry and his heart high and quick. "There are certain similarities, but this dog was a pet?"

"That's right," Sharon said. "It was given to the Brewster shelter."

"Then I don't see how it *can* be ours," Kessler said. "Maine law won't allow shelter dogs to be used in research."

85

"I'm aware of that," Sharon said. "But what if the shelter found it a home—"

"And the people gave it to us?" Kessler said. "We don't accept offers like that. Our dogs are kennel-raised."

Steve Burlingame grunted. "So, this isn't yours?"

"I would have to say no," Kessler said. He looked at the sawed-off skull again and said, "May I ask what you found?"

Above her mask, Sharon's brown eyes blinked twice. "I'm afraid we found rabies," she said.

Kessler's forehead was slimy with sweat and his palms were damp. "God," he said. "And a child's been bitten? Has he started his shots?"

"He's started them," Sharon said. "But I want you to look at something."

She went up to the screen on the far wall and Kessler followed. "What do you make of these?" she said. "These here?"

Kessler looked at the screen through his heavy glasses, the sweat coming heavily now.

"Have you ever seen spikes like that before?"

"No," Kessler said.

"We think it's a radically different form," Steve Burlingame said. "If so . . ."

"The current vaccine might not touch it," said Kessler. "We can't be certain of that, of course, but— My God, this is awful, just awful. And how do you plan to proceed?"

"We've issued a rabies alert," Sharon said. "And we've sent a tissue sample to CDC."

Kessler's head was swimming. "That's good," he said. "Good."

"If this *was* a Jillson dog," Steve Burlingame said with a frown, "we'd suspect that the rabies had come from you, that you people were working on rabies

86

out there."

"No, we're working on herpes," Kessler said quickly.

"You did work on rabies at Wistar, though."

The bottoms of Kessler's lenses were steamy. "Where did you hear that?" he said.

"I remember reading about it once, when you first came to Jillson. You and another researcher, right?"

"Right," Kessler said, "but we've concentrated on herpes at Jillson." He frowned at the screen. "Well, I've got to get back."

"We appreciate your coming out," Sharon said.

Kessler looked at the stainless steel table again. "Don't mention it," he said. "I suppose you'll cremate the dog?"

"Eventually," Sharon said.

Kessler nodded. "Good meeting you both," he said, and went outside.

He sat behind the wheel of his car, rolled down the windows, and stared at the lone linden tree near the door to the yellow state building. No way they can prove that it's one of our dogs, he told himself, but once that tissue sample hits CDC . . . Damn. At least all the dogs are accounted for, he thought as he wiped his forehead with his fingertips. The threat is over at least, and thank God for that.

The linden's dark green leaves shuddered quickly in a passing breeze. But the boy, he thought. He shook his head and thought, Maybe he won't contract rabies, some people don't. The lesion was cleaned right away, so he stands a good chance, and the Stemmer girl's still okay. And if, God forbid, the children get sick, they'll die and that will be that, the disease will die with them. Unless, of course, before biting the children, the dogs had bitten—

"No," he said as he gripped the wheel. "No, that didn't happen, damn it." He thought of the tissue

87

sample again, on its way to CDC, then turned the key and started the engine and headed for Gilman cove.

In 1841, at the age of nineteen, Louis Pasteur stopped painting forever to give himself wholly to science. By all accounts he had been a quite gifted artist, but at last found the lure of research too strong to resist. Pasteurization, inoculation, the first rabies vaccine—worth any number of landscapes and still lifes and portraits, certainly, and history applauded his choice.

And as Martin Farrow dabbed at his easel, he wondered again: If he had quit painting, would he have become a Pasteur? Not likely. At any rate, unlike his boyhood idol, he had never been able to quit. And, unlike Pasteur, who felt he could not serve two masters, Farrow felt that his painting helped make him a better scientist—if not a better person.

At least once a week for the past twenty years, he had worked on his art. An outlet? Therapy? Others might see it that way, but Farrow did not. He was not a dilettante—at anything. His approach to painting was serious, as serious as his approach to his work at the lab. Time, that was the problem, not dedication. Well, he thought, standing back from his canvas, a number two brush in his hand, some day . . .

It was coming along, he thought as he squinted. Damn right, it was coming along, he might have something here. What incredible luck to hit weather like this today.

He looked out at the emerald green water. Already a change there, a shift in the light. He stepped up to the easel again.

Although Farrow was salaried, not in a private practice like most other area doctors, he took

Wednesdays off in the summer. If they could do it, hell, he could, too. He deserved it as much as they did; deserved it more. For while most of the other MDs were out golfing and sailing, wasting their time, he was working at this, his art. Creating.

Three weeks ago he had gotten back into acrylic with adequate, if not outstanding, results. But today's work had gone very well, extremely well. Yes, he had something here, the real thing, he might even be able to fix that seascape now. He dipped his brush quickly in permanent blue—

"Martin!"

Cursing, he turned and looked up at the field. Not today, he thought. Not now. Goddamn you, Paul!

His partner came out of the field and onto the stony beach, walking in that tentative way Farrow hated. He looks like a goddamn duck, Farrow thought. A myopic, overweight duck.

"Martin." Kessler was out of breath, and his eyes were wide. "Bad news. They've got one of our dogs at the state pathology lab. He bit some boy."

"What?" The brush in Farrow's hand turned hot.

"But they don't know it's ours," Kessler said, "it belonged to the boy. They sent it away and it came back sick and bit him."

"Then how can it be our dog?" Farrow said.

"I don't know, but it is. It's one of the three that escaped."

Farrow looked past Kessler to the top of the hill and his house. "And?" he said.

"Well, they've put out a rabies alert, of course. And they've sent a tissue sample to CDC."

"Goddamn it," Farrow said.

"A pathologist there, Sharon Jensen, she's pretty sharp. She saw those projections and jumped right on it."

89

"When did they send the sample?"

"This morning."

Farrow looked at the tip of his brush, at the blue, at the dregs of his ruined day.

Kessler licked his full lips. "They'll know where it came from. They'll realize we let it out."

"We didn't let it out," Farrow said. "Some idiot let it out."

"So we aren't to blame for what's happened?" said Kessler, a strident note in his voice. "We shouldn't feel bad that two innocent kids have been bitten and maybe will die?"

"Of course we should," Farrow snapped. He looked down at his brush again and said, "I'll be in later on."

Kessler looked at the stones at his feet and said, "I can't go on with it, Martin. I'll move from Maine, I'll live in Africa, anywhere, I don't care. This work on the Flowers strain's crazy. It's always been crazy."

"We'll talk about it later," Farrow said.

Kromer's voice on the phone was razor sharp. "How the hell did a pet get involved in your lab experiments?"

"We haven't found out yet," Farrow said. He looked across the room at the largest painting, the cliff with the jagged lone tree growing out of its crown.

"I'll take care of Atlanta," Kromer said. "People from CDC will arrive at your state lab tomorrow and talk to those people and tell them this strain isn't new. They'll say a case turned up some years ago, that it never spread, there's no reason to panic, etcetera, etcetera. They'll make sure the boy is hospitalized. There's always the danger he might become vicious and bite someone else. As for the girl . . ."

"We're not sure about her," Farrow said.

"We'll see that she's put in the hospital, too. We can't

90

take chances."

"Right," Farrow said.

Kromer missed or ignored his sarcastic tone. "Has she had rabies shots?"

"Not to my knowledge."

"We'll give them to her as soon as she's hospitalized. And tell the parents she'll be fine."

"Yes," Farrow said.

"And remember, it wasn't your dog. This dog was a pet, not a Jillson dog. The disease had nothing to do with Jillson. The CDC will back you up on this."

"Okay." Farrow said. He looked at the painting, the cliff, the tree. Something not quite right with that tree. He had always known it.

"A goddamn pet," Kromer said. "And who knows what it contacted while it was loose. Well, let's hope we're lucky."

"Let's hope," Farrow said. He thought of the children again and said, "We continue with Christian Charity, I suppose."

A silence on the line, and then: "After this, do we have a choice?"

ELEVEN

The newspaper covered Miranda's knees like a shroud. She stared at it, faint and dizzy and sick, and a small weak whimper escaped from her burning throat. She fell back on the pillow.

Rabies, the article said. A new kind of rabies that might not respond to vaccine. The boy's dog had it, the boy might get it, and Tricia Stemmer? And Gary? And she herself, is that why she felt so bad?

Every day she felt weaker. Her throat was sore, and that heat in her stomach, that fire between her legs . . . Today she'd decided to rest in bed and beat this thing, and she'd slept all morning and woken up hot with a low-grade fever, and now—

Now this.

She broke into a sweat. She couldn't have rabies, she told herself, she hadn't been bitten, the dogs hadn't touched her. But maybe this new kind . . . And Gary was feeling so awful.

The paper across her knees was blindingly white. Without warning her stomach rebelled and she threw off the covers; the newspaper scattered, hurting her ears. She ran to the bathroom, reaching the toilet just as she started to retch. She stared at the bowl, confused and frightened, then clung to the sink and pulled herself up and rinsed out her mouth, splashed her face with cold water. Dried off with a towel.

Her face in the mirror was pasty and drawn. She'd lost five pounds in four days and she looked it. Summer flu, Dr. Welch had said. That's all, just the flu. . . .

She left the bathroom and went to the bedroom again, and the soles of her feet felt numb. She sat on the bed and picked up the phone. The noise when she punched the buttons was piercing, sharp. She felt giddy behind her eyes.

The ring of the phone echoed darkly, three long times, then a man's voice said, "Scudder Motors."

"Gary Simmons, please," Miranda said, and her voice sounded soft and thin in her head.

A pause, then: "Gary's not here right now."

"He's not? Do you know where he is? Is he home?"

"I'm not sure," the voice said. "Hold on."

Some discussion took place, then another voice said, "Hello?"

Feeling suddenly drained, Miranda said, "Hello? Is Gary Simmons there?"

"He's sick," the new voice said.

"He went home?"

"No, we sent him down the emergency room."

"The emergency room?" Miranda said. "He's hurt?"

"No, just sick," the voice said. "That's all I know, okay?"

Miranda breathed thickly. "Okay," she said, and hung up.

She stared down at the rug and the pattern blurred as hot tears welled up in her eyes.

Behind his desk, his knees still shaking, Mike Hachett stared down at his palm. A bright spot of

93

blood had appeared on the gauze and he thought, Why *this* hand, damn it, when I have all these orders to write? What a son of a bitch.

He still couldn't sort out what had happened. He'd seen Simmons standing out there in the lot with the hose, staring off into space, the water rushing out to beat the band; seen the customer pull up and park; seen Simmons, looking drugged, slowly turn as she left her car and splash both her nyloned legs.

Hachett had left his desk like a shot and rushed outside. This was it, this boy was through! Then Simmons's head had snapped back and the fiery look in his eyes had stopped Hachett dead in his tracks. And before the idea of retreat had fully formed in Hachett's shocked brain, Gary Simmons had thrown down the hose and was on him, screaming wildly, pounding him with his fists.

Help came instantly, in the form of the assistant service manager and six mechanics, and Simmons was laid out cold by Butch Dodd, a former amateur boxer who weighed over two hundred pounds. But before this, he'd managed to clamp his teeth into Hachett's right palm, and Hachett had run to the bathroom, clutching his wound, washing it long and hard with soap and hot water and getting Sue Bellows, the office manager, to wrap it up tightly in gauze.

That had happened three hours ago, and the sucker still stung. The human bite is the dirtiest bite of all, he remembered reading that once. Probably ought to see a doctor about it, get a tetanus shot. Wasn't he up to date on those? He tried to remember when he'd had one last. Before moving to Maine? That was eight years ago, and it might be getting a little bit thin by now.

Through floor-to-ceiling tinted glass he saw a Mercedes pull into the lot; a two-year-old silver Mercedes with sunroof. It stopped, and a silver-haired

94

man with tinted glasses opened its door and got out and surveyed the scene, his cleft chin tilted skyward.

A thrill went through Hachett's chest. This, he said to himself, is a *customer.*

He forgot his hand for the moment and hustled outside.

The receptionist, peering over the tops of her glasses, repeated, "Simmons?"

"Gary Simmons," Miranda said.

The receptionist swiveled around in her chair and said to a woman behind her, "Isn't he the one . . . ?"

"He's in isolation," the other woman said crisply. She had hair like spun sugar, sparkling and golden.

Bracing herself against the counter, Miranda said, "I have to see him." Her groin was burning again, and her calves and knees felt weak.

"That won't be possible," the receptionist said.

"But—" Miranda swallowed; it hurt. "Is Amelia Rose here?"

"She's off today," said the spun sugar woman.

Miranda steadied herself on the counter. "I'm Gary's sister," she said. "I'll just be a minute. Please?"

The receptionist sighed and leaned toward a microphone. "Joan, to reception. Joan, to reception," came out of ceiling speakers along the hall.

Several minutes went by before a dark-haired, attractive, middle-aged woman appeared. The badge on her uniform said, "Joan Mildrum, R.N." Miranda, tired and flushed and very hot now, gave her request.

"I'm afraid he's quite ill," Nurse Mildrum said. "I can let you say hi, but that's all."

"That's fine," Miranda said.

They went down the hallway. The door at its end was crooked and far too bright, and its light sent splinters

95

of pain at Miranda's eyes. "Has Mother visited yet?" she asked.

"No, you're the first," Nurse Mildrum said. "We haven't been able to reach his mother—your mother— he only came in two hours ago." She looked at Miranda. "How did you know he was here?"

"I called him at work. I needed some information from him."

"Oh," Nurse Mildrum said. "Then you know."

Know? Miranda said to herself, and the thought was a dark echo deep in her brain. "Yes," she said.

They turned down another corridor, passed through a pair of swinging doors, and then, at the second door on the left, they stopped. Miranda looked through the doorway. Gary lay on his back, eyes shut, with a sheet drawn up to his neck.

As they entered the room, Nurse Mildrum said, "He's heavily sedated. He attacked the orderlies, too."

Too? said Miranda's echo, and her stomach tightened. "Did he hurt them?" she asked.

"Not badly. One had his hand bitten, one got his arm scratched up. Your brother's quite a fighter."

Miranda approached the bed. In the dim light, Gary's closed eyes looked bruised and his skin was a mottled yellow. "Gary?" she said in a soft voice. "Gary?"

He gave no reply, just lay there, mouth open. "His arm," she said. "Why is it strapped to the bed like that?"

"He was wild," Nurse Mildrum said, "and we had to restrain him. He knocked an orderly flat on his back and elbowed a nurse in the stomach."

"A nurse?" Miranda said. "He hit a *nurse?*" Throat suddenly swollen, she said, "What's wrong with him?"

"It's some sort of brain inflammation, we don't know what kind. He's negative for meningitis."

"It's rabies," Miranda said, staring at Gary's white

face, her voice breaking.

Nurse Mildrum, eyebrows raised, said, "What?"

"It's rabies," Miranda repeated. "A dog—" Her hands went to her face and she started to cry. Gary started to moan.

"I'm sorry, I'm sorry," Miranda said, sobbing. "You wouldn't have done it except for me. I'm sorry. Oh God."

The nurse stood there, watching her weep. Miranda pressed her hand to her breastbone and said, "He was bitten. His ankle, didn't you see it?"

Nurse Mildrum, frowning, went to the foot of the bed. She folded the sheet back. "We didn't undress him, we wanted to let him calm down."

"His left ankle," Miranda said.

The nurse pulled Gary's left sock down, revealing a huge wad of gauze. She pulled at the tape and the gauze came away. "My God," she said. The bruise was four inches wide and almost black.

"We're the ones," said Miranda, crying again. "We freed the dogs and one of them bit him. It isn't herpes, it's rabies, I read about it, a little boy— Oh—"

She wept uncontrollably now.

Nurse Mildrum put her hand on her shoulder and led her into the chair by the window. "I'm sorry, I'm sorry," Miranda sobbed, rocking forward and back in the chair. "Oh, Gary, I'm sorry."

She kept rocking, as if in pain. When she stopped, Nurse Mildrum said gently, "The dog that bit that boy was his pet. It wasn't the dog that bit your brother."

Miranda looked up, her face shiny with tears. "He's not my brother," she said, "he's my boyfriend." She wiped her eyes and swallowed, stood and went up to the bed again. "Gary, say something, please," and she reached out and shook his shoulder.

"Miss, don't, let him rest," Nurse Mildrum said.

Miranda's eyes flashed. "Let him rest!" she said. "He doesn't need rest, he needs rabies shots! I told you what's wrong with him, don't you believe me?"

Nurse Mildrum looked startled.

"You don't," Miranda said. "You don't believe me. You're going to let us both die. Don't you understand? I've got it, too! I didn't even get bitten, and I've got it, too!"

"Miss—"

Miranda made her hands into fists, then turned and ran out of the room.

TWELVE

The conference room was musty and airless and hot, and to make things worse, a CDC guy was smoking.

Sharon Jensen, practically gagging, just wanted to get this over with. Her disappointment huge, she said, "That happened seven years ago."

The man with the cigarette, Peyton his name was, said, "Seven years ago. And we haven't found one single case of it since."

David Woodruff, from Maine Disease Control, looked down at the pen in his hand. "The thing that's got me worried," he said, "is that rabies vaccine didn't work."

The other CDC man, Lauer, said, "But that was a very different vaccine. We've come a long way since then."

Peyton glanced at his colleague, then said, "Jim's right. Of course, we're not saying the new kind will work on this either, that hasn't been proven yet."

"I guess we'll find out pretty soon," Sharon said.

Dr. Lauer, a slim balding man with wire glasses, said, "We can only hope for the best. The boy's under constant surveillance. So far, so good."

"If the lesion was on the hand," Sharon said, "the

virus should act fairly quickly, right?"

"That's the thing about this one, Peyton said, blowing smoke. "It acts *very* quickly. Much faster than other strains."

To Sharon's relief, he extinguished his cigarette. A doctor smoking. Behavior like that was beyond her.

"There's really nothing more to do, but to keep us completely informed," Peyton said. "You'll keep the boy in isolation, cremate the dog . . ." He turned to Herbert Tibbetts, the other person from Maine Disease Control, "And you'll get those releases out. We want to make sure that everyone's fully aware of this thing."

Tibbetts, blond, in his thirties, and thick at the waist, said, "When will the new research get going?"

"Instantly," Peyton said. "We've put it in the hands of Martin Farrow at Jillson, he's one of the best. He helped develop the five-shot series at Wistar, years ago. Don't expect results overnight, though, rabies is tricky stuff."

Remembering Kessler's sweaty face, Sharon Jensen said, "Farrow's been working on herpes, right?"

"Right," Peyton said.

"Why didn't he work on this instead, if you knew about it seven years ago?"

"His interests changed."

"Then why didn't somebody else work on it?"

Smiling a little, Peyton shrugged. "If we'd found more than one case, I guess they would have. Looking back on it, maybe they should have. Well, it's easy to look back, isn't it?" He glanced at Tibbetts and then at Woodruff. "More questions?"

"I guess we've pretty well covered it," Woodruff said. He ran his hand through his thick white hair. "What a hell of a thing."

"Indeed," Peyton said. "Let's just hope this is it—

and the boy stays well."

They stood, shook hands, and Peyton and Lauer left. Woodruff and Tibbetts stayed on for a while, reviewing the situation with Sharon, then they left, too.

Sharon went to her office and stood by the open window. Her office was down the hall from the lab, in the basement, the window was over her head, and no matter how deeply she breathed, she just couldn't get enough air. That damn Peyton. How anyone the least concerned with health could smoke cigarettes . . .

Let's hope the boy stays well, he'd said. And what were the chances of that? The standard vaccine didn't work seven years ago, why should it work today? Five shots, four shots—what was the difference? The standard vaccine wasn't made for this stuff. That poor kid, his poor parents . . .

And, to a much, much lesser extent, poor Sharon Jensen. For the rabies was not something new after all, and would not become known as the Jensen strain. No fame for Sharon, not this time around.

She picked at her tender cuticle and, laughing softly, said, "Not this time, but maybe next week. Or the week after that."

Damn, she thought as she looked at her finger. That cuticle had bothered her all through the meeting. It was red and sore, she ought to put something on it.

A noise at the doorway. She turned to see a woman there, a pretty young woman with dark red hair and a flushed red freckled face and intense blue eyes.

"Dr. Jensen?" the woman said in a hesitant voice.

"Yes?" Sharon said.

"My name's Miranda—Miranda Shore. They told me to wait, but I couldn't, I had to see you."

Sweat clung to her forehead; her hands were shaking; in spite of—or maybe because of—her ruddy complexion, she looked quite ill.

"Come in," Sharon said. "Have a seat."

Miranda sank into the chair beside Sharon's desk. "I wanted to look at the dog," she said. "The one with the rabies."

"Oh?" Sharon said, frowning. "Why?"

"I think maybe it came from the Jillson lab."

A shock went through Sharon's chest. "And why would you think that?" she asked.

Miranda looked down at the floor, her hands clasped together. "Because—" Her voice suddenly rose as she looked up again, "I'm the person who freed the dogs. They were sick, really sick, I mean one of them died right away, that night, and one bit Gary . . ." She covered her face with her hands and broke into tears.

A flash of fear struck Sharon's heart. "Who's Gary?" she said.

"My boyfriend," Miranda said, sobbing. "He's in the hospital now, he's so sick, he didn't even recognize me . . ." She shook her head back and forth, her hands still on her face.

Sharon's heart speeded up. She was suddenly very alert. For a second her mind went blank, then slowly she said, "Good God."

Miranda kept crying. Sharon stood up. "We've got to get moving," she said. "Fast."

Miranda took her hands down. "What?" Her face was wet with tears.

Sharon helped her to rise, and she braced herself on the desk.

"Okay?" Sharon said.

"Not really," Miranda said.

"Do you think you can walk for about ten minutes?"

"I guess so." She didn't let go of the desk.

"No, you stay here," Sharon said. "Would you like a drink? I'll have somebody bring you one."

102

"Okay," Miranda said, slumping into the chair again.

Sharon asked Steve Burlingame to look after Miranda, then hurried down the hall.

The crematorium wasn't far—out back, across the quad—but the dog had been sent there an hour ago. At least an hour ago. Goddamn, Sharon thought as she ran down the concrete steps, slammed the bar on the metal door, and rushed into the sun.

She ran down the walk, her eyes on the column of smoke rising up from the quad's far end. Diseased organs and body parts, dead animals—that's where that smoke came from. She rounded a corner and saw the brick building, Miranda's image bright in the back of her mind. Two women stared as she ran past them, ran to the door, flung it open.

In the vestibule's silence, her breathing was loud. Another door said No Admittance. She went to it, yanked on its handle.

Across the room, a man in a mask and gloves and green work clothing whirled. On the floor beside him were dozens of white plastic bags.

Fighting for breath, Sharon said, "I sent . . . a dog over here . . . an hour ago." The pain in her side made her wince.

The man looked around at the stuff on the floor. He poked at a bag with his foot. "Must be this one," he said. "The rest of them come from the fridge." Frowning, he added, "You shouldn't be in here without no mask."

"I know," Sharon said, taking hold of the bag. She opened it quickly and looked inside. Thank God, she thought. Thank *God*.

"We need another tissue sample," she said. "Then I'll

103

bring it right back." And before the man could protest, she was out of the room.

Miranda stared at the severed head, at the open skull, the brain. She was sitting in the lab now, masked. Her hot eyes filled with tears again as she said, "Yes, that's one of the Jillson dogs."

"You're positive," Sharon said.

Miranda's tongue was sluggish, stuck. With great effort, she forced it to move. "I'm positive. That spot between the eyes."

The skull was missing above the spot, and the sight made Miranda feel sick. She turned away.

Sharon looked at Steve Burlingame. "What do you think?"

"I don't *know* what to think."

Miranda said tearfully, "That little boy owned this dog, it was somebody's *pet*. It had shots and it still got rabies, the shots didn't work."

Looking at Burlingame's frowning, masked face Sharon said, "Her boyfriend was bitten. He's pretty sick."

"And I am, too," Miranda said. "Oh God . . ." She was soaking with sweat and shaking all over.

"But you told me you weren't bitten," Sharon said.

"I never was." She wept softly, head down.

"Maybe some her boyfriend's saliva got into a cut," said Burlingame.

"Maybe so," Sharon said. Closing the bag on the dog and twisting it shut, she said, "He lied to us."

"If you were Kessler, what would you do?" said Burlingame.

She sighed and said, "Well, maybe he couldn't be sure. After all, the dog was a pet, and how would a pet end up at the Jillson lab?" To Miranda she said,

"You're sure this is one of the dogs, now."

Miranda nodded. "Yes. It's the crazy one, the one that bit Gary."

"Could Gary identify him?"

Miranda's voice broke again. "He's too sick," she wailed. "Unless maybe, by now . . ." She looked up at Sharon, face wet and pathetic. "By now—do you think?" she said. Then her eyes rolled back up in her head and she slid to the floor.

THIRTEEN

"'The elephant said, "Hello down there! Would you like a ride on my back?"'"

Tricia Stemmer looked up from the bed with a petulant frown. "Can we go home now? Please, Mommy?"

"Not yet, Muffin," Rachel said. "Pretty soon. Let's finish the story, and then you can go to the playroom."

"I already *went* to the playroom."

"I know, sweetheart. We'll go again. We'll find something new. Now let's finish the story." She tilted the book towards her daughter. "Now, look at the mouse. He's going to sit on the elephant's trunk, and the elephant's going to lift him right onto his back!"

Tricia sighed. "I'm thirsty, Mommy."

Rachel looked at her watch. They had been in the hospital less than two hours. It already seemed like two days, and God only knew how long they would have to stay. Dr. Thurman had called before noon, saying Tricia would have to go into the hospital right away and stay there till further notice. He'd had a long talk with Maine Disease Control, and just to be on the safe side, they wanted to watch Tricia closely for several weeks.

Several weeks! Rachel's heart had contracted as Thurman explained that while chances were very slim, the dog that bit Tricia could be—just *could* be, mind you—the dog that bit Teddy Marsh. Had she heard about Teddy Marsh?

She had. She'd read the article that morning in the *Blue Harbor Herald.* Fred had finished the last of his coffee, frowning deeply and looking off into space, then had shown her the column. "But Tricia's fine," she'd said, feeling sudden deep fright. "So's the boy," Fred had said, "but it takes a while for rabies to incubate." "Well what should we do?" "I guess we should call Dr. Thurman," Fred said; and had kissed her and said not to worry and left for work. She'd called Dr. Thurman right away, but his line had been busy all morning. Before she was able to reach him, he called her.

She had packed Tricia's clothes in a daze, feeling distant and light, almost the same way she'd felt when she'd given birth. Of course nothing's wrong, she'd told herself, or Tricia would be sick by now. How long had it been since the bite? A week? No, more than that. Ten days? This dialogue failed to convince, for she had no idea how long it took for rabies to manifest.

"I'm *thirsty,* Mommy."

Rachel looked at her daughter. Blue eyes, pale hands, pink ruffled pajamas. She'd grown so much these last few months, her hair had turned darker . . . "I'll get you some juice, sweetheart, you wait right here. Don't go anywhere now, okay?"

"Okay."

Handing Tricia the book, she stood up. At the door she faked a smile, waved, then hurried down the hall.

They would start the shots soon. The thought of it made Rachel sick to her stomach. Tricia hated shots so. Well, what child didn't? Tricia had survived other

107

shots, and she'd survive these. The series was necessary, that's all there was to it, and no use feeling upset about it. At least Dr. Thurman had *said* it was necessary, She'd hate to put Tricia through all this for nothing. Well, better than putting her through it for *something*, she thought.

She was heading for the vending machine that stood near the waiting room. If it didn't have juice, she would settle for Coke. Tricia loved Coke, of course, but they tried to restrict it to special occasions. This isn't a special occasion? she said to herself.

She went past the X-ray department, the laser lab, turned left. At the end of the hall, past the business office, the vending machine was a beacon of light in the gloom of the seats filled with sad-looking anxious people. No juice, unfortunately.

"Rachel?"

Amelia Rose, in her uniform, crisp and efficient-looking.

"Amelia."

"What brings you here?"

A feeling of vast relief flowed through Rachel's chest. It was so good to see a friend here, a friend on the other side of the fence. "I brought Tricia in for some tests. You know, this rabies thing."

"She's not sick?" said Amelia, sounding concerned.

"No, she's fine. It's just a precaution. They want to observe her—and give her some rabies shots."

"What fun."

"Oh yes, delightful. They want her to stay three weeks. Can you imagine?"

A sudden commotion broke out at the nurses' station. Two of the nurses stood up, and one of them— dark-haired, attractive—came out from behind the counter. She looked outside through the sliding glass doors and muttered, "Not *you* again."

Amelia walked the few steps to the end of the hallway, and Rachel followed. They looked through the sliding doors at the ambulance parked out there. An attendant was crouched near a stretcher that lay on the ground. He shouted something, then ran behind the ambulance.

"What's happening?" Amelia said to Joan Mildrum, the dark-haired nurse.

"They were bringing that nut in, and all of a sudden she jumped off the stretcher and started to hit them. Scratched one of them pretty good. You have that sedative ready?"

A nurse at the counter replied, "All set."

"She came in a couple of hours ago," Nurse Mildrum said. "A real looney tune, we may have to call the cops."

"And they'll be here in half an hour," the nurse at the counter said.

At the rear of the ambulance, then, the woman appeared. Her eyes were wild, her hands were claws, and she screamed and screamed and screamed. The sound was barely audible thought the glass.

An attendant appeared and she lunged at him, slashing out viciously. Shielding himself with his arms, he retreated again.

Rachel Stemmer looked stunned. "Amelia, it's— God."

"It's Miranda," Amelia Rose said.

FOURTEEN

"The girl claims it's one of your dogs," Woodruff said, leaning forward and resting his arms on the conference table. He shrugged, his white eyebrows raised.

Farrow looked at him coolly. "She's wrong," he said. "That dog was a pet. We don't use pets at Jillson. The girl's confused."

Woodruff glanced at his partner, Tibbetts, then looked at the table: blond oak, and the chairs were chrome, with padded tweed navy blue seats. Quite a contrast to Maine Disease Control. Half an hour in Woodruff's chairs could put you in traction. He ran his right hand through his wavy white hair and wondered what Farrow and Kessler got paid.

"How long do you plan to keep the dog in storage?" Kessler asked.

"We don't know yet," Woodruff replied.

Farrow glared. "I'd suggest you destroy it right now," he said, "as directed by CDC. They have samples of virus and so do we, and that's plenty to have around."

Blond-haired Tibbetts looked down at his hand. "So the dogs that were freed just had herpes," he said. "You never studied the variant rabies here."

"No, never," Paul Kessler said. "We're studying it now, of course, at CDC's request."

Tibbetts frowned at his finger. "It just seems strange," he said, "that you found this virus in Pennsylvania, move to Maine, don't work on the virus, and suddenly, there it is again." He looked up.

Farrow sniffed and said, "We must be carriers." He turned sharply to Woodruff. "These orderlies, how were they treated?"

"Thorough cleansing of the wound, benzalkonium chloride, and immunization."

"Excellent," Farrow said. "How's the Simmons boy doing?"

"Not well. He appears to be in the final stages. Can't talk, severe pain. He's heavily drugged."

Farrow grunted. "And the girl's confused, quite obviously."

"She's very sick. High fever, sweats, still violent. They have her in restraints, of course."

Farrow looked at the window. "The fools," he said. "If they'd gotten the shots right away . . ."

Tibbetts coughed at his hand. "You still feel the standard vaccine will work?"

"Time will tell," Farrow said. "We can only hope. I assume that the children are still okay?"

"They're still okay," Woodruff said. "Thank God."

"Thank God," Kessler said. "The important thing is that we work together on this."

"Of course," Woodruff said.

"I expect to visit the hospital every day," Farrow said.

"So do I," Woodruff said. "What about your research?"

"You'll receive weekly updates. If there's any big

111

news, a breakthrough of any kind, you'll know right away."

"Fine," Woodruff said.

An uncomfortable silence descended. Herbert Tibbetts pursed his lips and said, "Weird. Two known instances of this stuff, and you were there both times."

"Yes, isn't life strange," Farrow said.

FIFTEEN

*The barge she sat in, like a burnished throne, burned
on the water,* and the river was red, was her hair, was on
fire, was her, on fire, was blood, she burned—
"Miranda?"
Yes, that was her name. The river turned white, so
bright, so bright—

Farrow, dressed in his white lab coat, leaned over the
hospital bed. "Can you hear me, Miranda? Miranda?"
Her right eyelid twitched. The ruddiness had left her
skin, and her face was now waxy and pale, her eye
sockets sunken and brown. Her slightly parted lips
were white and cracked, and her breathing was ragged
and thick. Tubes of clear plastic ran out of her nose and
into an oxygen tank. Her wrists were secured to the
rails of the bed with heavy fabric straps.
Her lips drew back as if registering pain and her
plaintive voice said, "Hatasu. Daddy, please."
A chill traveled through Farrow's spine. "Miranda,"
he said, "I'm Dr. Farrow."
She bared her teeth further. "There's too much wind
on this boat. Stop it. Please, please, stop it."

Farrow looked at the drapes, which were tightly closed, since light caused Miranda pain. It was evening now and perfectly calm. "The windows are closed," he said. "It's all right now."

"No, no," she said, twisting her torso. For a second her eyes came open and looked at his, unfocused, then closed again. She turned her head away.

Farrow took a deep breath. He had been to see both of the children, and both were still well. On his own, he had started the Marsh boy on Series IV. It might very well react with the standard vaccine, but without it, he'd surely die.

As for the little Stemmer girl, he could only hope that the dog that bit her was not an infected dog. Her wound was ugly, highly suggestive, but since she'd been given the standard vaccine, he didn't want to subject her to Series IV unless he was sure she needed it.

He looked at Miranda's pale agonized face. Her boyfriend Gary was bad, very bad. He was comatose now and unable to swallow, salivating heavily. He'd been like that since last night, and the end was near. It would soon be near for Miranda Shore, too.

Miranda began to weep without sound, her features contorted, her shoulders writhing. "He's dead," she whimpered. "He's dead, he's dead."

Farrow looked at her, thinking: Miranda, you are to blame for this. There are hundreds of deadly viruses locked away in labs all over this country, every one of which could start an epidemic. We're so careful, so careful, and then a young fool like you, who knows nothing—Christ! Do you think we *like* to make animals sick? We're doing it to save human lives, to save people like you. If you hadn't done this stupid thing, you'd have your whole life ahead of you. Damn you!

Someone entered the room; two people, a man and a

114

woman. The man was stocky, with dark red hair and heavily freckled skin, and the woman—the woman made Farrow's breath catch in his throat.

She was fair-skinned, of medium height, with light brown hair and green eyes. Those eyes, those cheekbones—she could have been Janice's sister.

The couple approached the bed. The man looked down at Miranda and said, "Honey?"

No reply.

"Honey?"

Nothing. He looked up at Farrow. "She's worse," he said, and the woman who looked like Janice had tears in her eyes.

"Her temperature's higher," Farrow said. "She's a bit confused."

The man nodded. "How high?"

"A hundred and four the last time we checked."

The man grunted and took a quick breath. He held out his hand and said, "I'm Richard Shore, her father."

The hand in Farrow's hand was hot and firm. "Martin Farrow. And you're Mrs. Shore."

"Dorothy Shore," said the woman quietly; and even her voice was a lot like Janice's voice. "Have there been any signs of improvement?"

"I'm afraid I'm not really the person to ask," Farrow said. "Dr. Finch has been caring for her."

"Where is he?"

"He's eating. He'll be back soon."

"And you—?"

"I work at the Jillson lab," Farrow said. "We're doing research on this new rabies strain."

With a sudden dark scowl, Richard Shore said, "Research! It's your research that made my daughter sick!"

"Oh?" Farrow said, raising his eyebrows.

"Don't act so goddamn innocent," Richard Shore

said. "You gave those dogs this new rabies. If it hadn't been for you and your goddamn research, my daughter would still be well!"

"No," Farrow said. "Your daughter—"

"That Marsh dog was one of your dogs. Miranda identified it."

"No, it was not our dog, it was a family pet."

"Family pet or not, it was one of your dogs."

"I can see I'm not going to convince you," Farrow said.

"Damn right you're not."

"You work with Paul Kessler, don't you?" Dorothy Shore said.

"That's right."

"I know his wife. I've met him, too, but I can't say I know him. He seems to be out at Jillson most of the time."

"He's very dedicated."

Richard Shore snorted. "Dedicated? To what? Creating suffering? Creating death?"

In her sickness, Miranda stirred. Her mother said, "Sweetheart?"

"Hatasu? Necho?" Miranda said, then moaned and fell silent again. Dorothy Shore closed her eyes.

"Where the hell is the goddamn doctor?" Richard Shore fumed. "The *real* doctor." To Farrow he said: "You'll pay for this, I swear to God you will."

Without answering, Farrow left.

He had planned to go back to the lab, but instead he drove home. At the dining room cabinet he took out the bottle of scotch, poured a glass half-full, and thought: I've paid enough, Mr. Shore. I'm through paying, I've paid enough.

As he drank, he looked out at the cove, watched the

116

blue in the trees turn to gray. That light, the day's last light, to get that down on canvas . . .

He sat at the dining room table and poured more scotch and thought: those cheekbones, those eyes . . .

He'd been seeing Janice for almost a year when the illness struck. One little mosquito bite at the end of the summer. Encephalitis: high fever, delirium, death. Not so different from rabies, really. Not as violent or painful, but not really so different.

He'd been in his third year of general practice when Janice had died. He had gone back to school and had been in research ever since. Research could help thousands of people, millions of people, while direct care could reach so few, he had told himself. But the truth of it was, he could no longer bear to see people in pain, because all of them, somehow, were Janice. The lab was a buffer against the past; a demanding, enchanting mistress. And after long years without Janice or anyone else, Farrow's work turned as abstract as mathematics. Divorced from all human concerns, it was only a series of puzzles to solve, a game.

Now the game was up. After all the years of slides and cells and stains and microscopes, he was next to people's beds again, responsible for their pain. And this time, the pain was his fault.

Farrow swallowed more scotch and looked through the sliding glass doors. The light on the cove had faded now; the trees on its rim were black. Janice had only been twenty-two, so incredibly young, and this poor girl, Miranda, was not even that.

He sighed and looked back at his glass. The researchers from CDC and NIH had arrived today, and with their help, he and Kessler might beat this thing. But when? In a year? Two years? Five years? The standard rabies vaccine had evolved so slowly.

117

He finished the last of the scotch and thought: No matter how fast we progress, Gary Simmons is dead. And Miranda Shore, and maybe Teddy Marsh and the Stemmer girl, too.

He gripped his glass tightly and gritted his teeth, and again he saw Dorothy Shore's face; saw Janice's face. "Goddamn you, Miranda!" he said out loud, and surprising tears came to his eyes.

He flung the glass hard at the hearth, where it shattered to bits.

SIXTEEN

"The doctor could not have committed the crime," Inspector Roberts said, "for the following reasons: One—"

Wendell Renshaw leaned back in his chair, frowning hard at the words on the screen. The cursor blinked at him, urging him on. One, he thought as he tapped his pipe on the ashtray. He could not have committed the crime because . . .

Had the doctor committed the crime? Renshaw swiveled to face the window, the *Blue Harbor Herald* in large black letters backward on the glass. Yesterday he'd been certain the doctor had done it, but now— Damn, he said to himself, and turned back to the screen with a scowl.

Renshaw worked on a novel every day—or almost every day, at any rate. Not the same novel, though, and that was the problem. The longest he'd ever stuck with the same one was slightly less than two weeks. And then he'd deleted the mess and gone on with his new idea—which after a week had turned into another mess. He was seventy-three, and said to himself: Time's running out in the novel department, old boy. The cursor blinked.

At the end of the hallway, the bell that hung over the door jangled twice, and Renshaw peered over his glasses. The man coming at him looked somewhat familiar, but Renshaw couldn't quite place him. He muttered, hit "save" on his word processor, exited the file.

The man stood at his doorway. He was middle-aged, of medium height, and had dark red hair. Renshaw picked up his pipe. "May I help you?" he said.

"My name's Richard Shore," the man said. "Can we talk for a minute?"

Tempted to say, "Why, shore," Renshaw said instead, "Of course. Have a seat."

Shore sat in the molded plastic chair beside Renshaw's ancient oak desk and said, "I have a story for you."

"Well, that's what I'm here for," Renshaw said.

Shore looked at the floor for a second, clasping his freckled hands, then looked up at Renshaw again. "You wrote the piece about the boy who was bitten by the rabid dog—that it might be a new kind of rabies?"

"Yes?" Renshaw said. He had been with the *Blue Harbor Herald* for forty-six years; there were damn few names in town he didn't recognize, except for some of the newer summer people, of course. He set his pipe down in the ashtray again. "We met at the Wadsworths', right?" he said. "About three summers ago?"

"That's right," Shore said.

"I thought you looked kind of familiar. Your wife was at the Wadsworths' again this year, and your daughter, too, right?"

"Right."

"And you came here to tell me something about Teddy Marsh?"

"No," Shore said. "I came here to tell you something about my daughter. She's ill, very ill—with rabies."

120

This news sent a shock of alarm into Renshaw's heart. "My God," he said. "The Marsh dog bit her, too?" He thought of that night at the Wadsworths' a few weeks ago: Tricia Stemmer.

"The Marsh dog bit her boyfriend," Shore said. Sighing, he added, "The truth of it is, she and her boyfriend broke into the Jillson lab. It's crazy, but they're the ones. Her boyfriend is Gary Simmons, you know him?"

"I know him, his dad works at Coastal Marine. He goes to Maine Maritime."

"Yes. Well, Gary was bitten by one of the dogs the night they broke into the lab, and now he's got rabies. He's terribly sick, in a coma, and now—Miranda's sick too."

"The same dog bit her?"

Shore shook his head. "No, that's just it, it didn't. She was never bitten at all."

"Then how did she get it?"

"Exactly what I'd like to know," Shore said. "The story you wrote said this rabies was new, a new kind."

"The department of health thinks it is."

"I *know* it is," Shore said. "It's a new kind developed by Jillson, a kind for which there's no vaccine. A kind you can get without being bitten—which is now on the loose in Blue Harbor."

Renshaw lifted his shaggy eyebrows. "Whoa," he said.

"The Marsh dog was one of the Jillson dogs," Shore said. "And the dog that bit Gary Simmons, Miranda identified it. Ask Sharon Jensen at the state pathology lab, she'll give you all the details."

"Sharon Jensen," said Renshaw. "I've spoken to her before. She's the one who discovered the new form of rabies."

Shore snorted. "She *thought* she did. Then she found

121

out the Centers for Disease Control had known all about it for years. They swore that Jillson wasn't growing it, but that's not true. The Jillson people infected those dogs, and one of those dogs bit Gary and Teddy Marsh."

"But not your daughter."

"No. Which means the disease is transmitted in some other way. Through a sneeze? A kiss? I don't know. All I know is, we've got something serious here."

Renshaw picked up his pipe again; studied its bowl. "There are two sick people, possibly three. All the dogs are dead . . ." He stopped, instantly sorry for what he'd just said. "What I mean is—" He looked up to see that Shore's eyes were wet.

"You mean the disease is contained. But we don't know that. We can't explain how Miranda caught it. If she caught it, others can, too. Maybe I've caught it, maybe the Marsh boy's parents have caught it." He swallowed and looked at the ashtray on Renshaw's desk. It was glass, with *Blue Harbor Herald* along its rim. "The community should be warned of the danger," he said. "I assume you'll run my story. Or, at the very least, you'll call Sharon Jensen."

"I'll call Sharon Jensen," Renshaw said, "and then I'll get back to you. Where can I reach you?"

"Blue Harbor Hospital," Richard Shore said. "I'll be there the rest of the day."

SEVENTEEN

Walt Marsh sat at his kitchen table and stared at the *Blue Harbor Herald*'s front page. She's wrong, he thought. She's gotta be, and that's all there is to it.

Miranda Shore, over on Carver's Cove. Never heard of the girl. He didn't have friends among summer people, but he'd fixed a lot of their furnaces, knew who a lot of them were. The Shores, though? Never heard of the Shores.

He looked back at the paper, frowning. Uh-uh, no way, Marley couldn't have been a Jillson dog, he told himself. Like the story said, she'd seen the animal briefly, once, in the dark, and now she was sick, so there was a very good chance she was way off base.

Walt looked at the kitchen sink, the dishrag limp on its hook, the lamp on its nail on the wall between the two windows. Without Teddy around it was so damn *quiet*. They'd visit him this afternoon, and that would be boring as hell. There was nothing to do with him. Bring him some baseball cards, and after two minutes, that was the end of that. Then watch TV as he kept on asking, "When can I go home?"

Which, after all, was a very good question, Walt thought. If the kid wasn't sick, why did he have to stay hospitalized? He'd had all his rabies shots, so what more did they have to do? Observe him, they said. It was almost like being in jail. A nice jail, but jail all the same. A beautiful Saturday morning like this, they ought to be swimming together, fishing. Maine summers were short enough as it was without losing whole pieces of them to crap like this.

He looked at the paper spread out on the table, grunted and thought: Pure bullshit. Not Marley, she's wrong, he *couldn't* end up at Jillson.

He swallowed the last of his coffee, looked into the cup at the thin band of grounds, then turned in his chair and reached into the drawer of the table that held the phone. He took out the Brewster directory, thumbed through the pages. Stared at the listing. Bullshit, he told himself. But the doubts wouldn't go away.

With his callused and grease-stained index finger, he punched out the number.

Three rings, then, "Brewster Rescue League." A woman's voice.

"Hi, my name's Walter Marsh. A couple of months ago, it was back in April, I left a dog with you, a beagle named Marley. You said you'd try to find it a home. I wondered if you ever did."

"Hang on for a minute."

Walt waited. He looked through the window above the sink to the trees on the edge of the yard; the trees that Marley had wandered out of. He looked at the clock that sat over the door, the large black second hand.

"Hello?"

"Yeah."

"Our records show that we put him down."

Walt frowned. "What?"

"We get so many animals here, Mr. Marsh. We try to

124

find homes for them all, but it just isn't possible. Even with purebred beagles."

"You couldn't have put him down," Walt said.

"I'm sorry. But as we explained when you signed the release—"

"I don't mean that," Walt said.

"What?"

"You're sure that you got the right dog?"

"Absolutely. You live at 39 Linden Street in Blue Harbor, right?"

"Right," Walt said.

"Well . . ."

"Jesus," Walt said.

"I'm sorry."

"It's okay," Walt said, and hung up.

He turned to the table again and stared at the paper and said to himself: What the hell's going on? What the *hell* is going on?

He heard June's feet on the living room stairs and then she was in the doorway. "Were you just on the phone?" she said. "Is something wrong?"

Walt looked at her worried, lined face. "It was just a customer," he said. "You ready to go?" He folded the newspaper carefully, turning its front page face down.

"I'm ready," June said. "Did you get any baseball cards?"

"I'll have to stop for some," Walt said.

A nurse was sitting beside Teddy's bed, and Teddy was lying down. His face was flushed and he looked worn out.

June hurried up to him. "Teddy?"

The nurse said, "He's got a sore throat and a little fever. We gave him some Tylenol."

125

June put her hand on Teddy's head. Warm, but not burning. "A cold, right?" she said to the nurse. "That flu that's been going around?"

"Probably so," the nurse said.

"Hi, Mom," Teddy said.

June's voice was thin as she said, "Hi, Ted."

"My throat is sore."

"I know. It'll get better soon."

"Yeah."

Walt joined them. He fished in his pocket. "Hey, Ted, I brought something for you."

Teddy looked at the packs of baseball cards with slow eyes, then looked up at his father.

"You want me to open them for you?"

A sluggish nod.

As Walt opened the first of the packs, he felt weak in his chest. "Here we go. Hey, a Red Sox guy," and he held it up.

Teddy looked at it listlessly.

"He's tired," the nurse said. "Maybe you better let him rest for a while."

"Yeah," Walt said.

June took her son's hand. It was clammy and hot. "Mom?"

"Yes?"

Teddy looked up, but said no more. June gently squeezed his hand and said to Walt, "I'm going to stay here with him."

"Okay," Walt said, his chest heavy and sad now. "I've got a few things to do. What time do you want me back?"

In a faltering voice, June said, "Around five?"

"Okay."

In the hallway, Walt quietly said to the nurse, "You think he's got it?"

126

"The tests show signs of a viral invasion," she said, "but we're not sure yet."

"But if he does have it?"

Her face was grim. "It would be very bad," she said.

"How bad?"

"You better talk to Dr. Finch about it."

"Yeah," Walt said, his throat suddenly tight. He nodded, said, "Thanks," and left.

The Bluebird Tavern was down on the Hook, the "working" part of the waterfront—which didn't work much anymore these days, since most of it was owned by developers biding their time, apparently waiting to act in concert. Soon—no one knew precisely when—the clock would strike the proper hour, and down would go the lobster shacks and up would rise the condos. People had seen it coming for ages. The rusted railroad tracks had carried their last load more than a dozen years ago, and the grass between the ties was a foot high now.

The Bluebird's days were clearly numbered; the pressure of money would soon be too much to resist. And where would the fishermen go for their beers after that? To the Silver Oyster on Danbury Street? The Harrison Publick House? Would Blue Harbor's native sons have no place in town to wet their whistles and tell their tales and raise their brand of hell?

Walt Marsh parked next to the railroad tracks. The gravel glittered with broken glass in the sun. The bay shone bright; its light hurt his eyes. He looked across to the Bluebird Tavern, squinting against the glare.

With a sagging weather-worn porch on three sides and a second-floor false-front facade, it looked like a transplant direct from Dodge City, a hunk of the Wild

West in old New England. For the first time, Walt wondered who'd built this place.

He got out of the car and crossed the street and went up the steps of the porch. The smell of beer and cigarettes was thick in the summer air. He stood at the doorway a second, then stepped inside.

Noise, darkness, and smoke. The bottles behind the bar glowed faintly in front of the dingy mirror. The only other source of light was the jukebox, a wavy red yellow and green machine that loudly wailed rhythm and blues. At least that's what Walt thought it was; he never listened to music.

He glanced at the tables, and then at the booths that lined the wall on the right. Mickey Davis and Pee Wee Dodd, but he hadn't come here for them.

Then he saw who he wanted, down in the last booth, next to the hallway that led to the mensroom, sitting with somebody, someone that Walt didn't know.

He went up to the booth and said, "Hey, Skinny."

The man craned his leathery neck. He was smoking, and squinted suspiciously. "Yeah?"

"Walt Marsh. Can I see you a minute?"

Skinny kept squinting. "Walt Marsh. Jesus Christ, I ain't seen you in years." He took a long drag on his cigarette. "What's new?"

"I have somethin' to ask you about. It might mean some money for you."

Skinny stubbed out his cigarette in the metal ashtray, blew out a stream of smoke, and said to the guy he was with, "Guard my beer. You drink it, I'll bust your head."

He braced himself on the table in order to stand, revealing slack workpants cinched tight with a thick leather belt. "So where you wanna talk?" he said.

"Outside," Walt said.

They went into the sunlight and stood on the porch.

"You still work at the Jillson Lab?" Walt asked.

Again Skinny squinted. "That's right," he said.

"I want to know somethin'."

"Yeah?"

"Where do they get their animals from?"

Skinny held up a wrinkled hand. "I can't talk about that kinda stuff," he said. "They don't like us to talk about that."

Walt reached into his right rear pocket and brought out his wallet. He took out a twenty and shoved it at Skinny's hand. Skinny looked at it, took it, then folded it slowly, and tucked it away in his shirt. "Well," he said, "it depends. They raise all the mice right there, they're famous for 'em. I guess you know that."

"Yeah," Walt said. "But what about other things?"

"Well, the rabbits they get from a couple a places, one in Wiscasset, one in Rockland." He wrinkled his forehead. "You thinkin' of goin' into the business?"

"I might be," Walt said. "Let's go over and sit in my car a minute, I might have a deal for you."

The two of them went down the rickety steps, crossed the street and the shimmering gravel, and got in the car. In the driver's seat, his hands on the wheel, Walt said, "So where do they get their dogs?"

Skinny scrunched up his face. "Oh, a couple a different kennels," he said. "One in Ellsworth, one in Brooks."

"And the Brewster Rescue League?"

Skinny looked as if someone had punched him. "No, never, no sir," he said, "we don't get our dogs from no pounds."

"But you do," Walt said. "I took my dog to the Brewster pound, and it turned up at Jillson."

"No way, Ho-Zay," Skinny said. "Uh-uh, no sir."

It was sweltering in the car. Walt wiped at his brow with his grease-stained palm, then rubbed the sweat off

129

on his workpants. "I think somebody's got a deal going," he said. "They're trading kennel dogs for dogs from the pound. They sell the dogs that Jillson's supposed to be getting and substitute pound dogs for them."

"Bullshit," Skinny said with a snort. He groped for the handle of the door.

Walt reached under his seat and Skinny froze, a .38 caliber snub-nosed revolver aimed squarely between his eyes.

"Jesus! What the hell—?"

"Someone's trading those dogs," Walt said. "Who is it?"

"I don't know!" Skinny screeched. "Honest! Honest to God!"

The barrel was now at his temple. "Don't move one goddamn inch," Walt said, "and you listen to me. My boy was bitten by our dog, a dog that got loose from the Jillson Lab. A dog that I sent to the Brewster pound, a dog the pound says they put down. That dog had rabies, a new kind of rabies, and now my boy's sick." He touched Skinny's skull with the gun. "Now who's trading the dogs?"

Skinny's face was the color of chalk. "I can't tell you," he said. "Nobody! Jesus!"

"I'll give you five seconds," Walt said, and he started to count: "One . . ."

Sweat trickled along Skinny's cheeks. He swallowed, his sharp Adam's apple bobbing.

"Two . . ."

"Okay, okay, for Christ's sake, *I* done it, I got a friend up there! He lets me know if he's got a beagle, an' then when I go on a kennel run, I pull a swap an' sell the kennel dog an' we split whatever we get. They're one-year-old purebreds, real easy to sell, an' the pound dogs get put down anyways half the time, so . . . Four times

130

in the last five years, that's all, an' how in the hell did I know that some asshole would let them go?"

Shoving the pistol back under the seat, Walt started the car and pulled out.

"Hey?" Skinny yelled. "Where you goin'?"

"Blue Harbor Herald," Walt said through clenched teeth. "You've got a story to tell."

EIGHTEEN

"You categorically deny, then, that you use pound dogs in your work?"

Heads craned to regard the questioner: Ruth Hickey of the *Portland Press Herald*.

At the table that stood at the front of the room, Norman Sargent, Jillson's chief administrator, said, "It's against Maine law. We abide by Maine law. The use of the Marsh dog and other pound dogs was due to the action of one individual, one employee who has been dismissed. We understand that his partner at the Brewster Rescue League has also been dismissed."

The Blue Harbor Trust's conference room was stifling in spite of the wide open windows. Wendell Renshaw, who stood near the open door, looked over the heads of the crowd, through the windows, and out at the distant ocean. In front of the water he saw the flat roof of his office, a black square of tar.

"Do I understand," said a matronly woman with wisps of gray hair poking out from beneath a white hat, "that you people from CDC kept the lid on all this?"

Jim Peyton, who sat at one end of the table, glanced at his partner, Irving Lauer, then looked at the woman and said, "We didn't 'keep the lid' on anything. We

132

didn't see any reason to start any wild rumors going, that's all. We still don't. If this story hadn't appeared in the local paper, we wouldn't be here today—and the town would be better off."

Indeed, Wendell Renshaw thought.

The matronly woman, Nancy Keaton from the *Boston Globe,* persisted: "But you told Dr. Farrow and Dr. Kessler to say the disease was herpes."

A man with a camcorder over his shoulder moved close to the table; a bright white light went on. Peyton, looking dazzled, cleared his throat. "That's right," he said. "We wanted the town to know of the missing animals, but not have it panic."

"But weren't you playing with people's lives by lying to them like that?"

Slim bespectacled Lauer said, "We didn't see it that way. Sometimes you play with lives when you tell the truth, if that truth can be readily distorted."

A murmur went through the crowd, and another reporter took over: Wesley Rudd, from the *Bangor Daily News.* "Tell us about the Shore girl," he said. "She has the disease, but she claims that she's never been bitten."

Peyton deferred to Martin Farrow, who said, "She's a very unusual case. Apparently some infected saliva got into an open cut."

"You can catch it like that?"

"It's possible. But ninety-nine percent of cases result from a bite, let me emphasize that."

"But the Shore girl got it from a cut?"

"It appears that way."

A man that Renshaw didn't like, a man with long shaggy white hair and a beard but a young-looking face, asked, "Dr. Peyton, there's no vaccine?" He was Oliver Emmet, AP, Boston. Renshaw had met him at one of the few conventions he'd gone to there, and

133

remembered him saying, "So we get things wrong every once in a while, so what? Journalism is not an exact science." Wonderful, Renshaw had thought.

In response to the question Emmet had posed, Peyton nodded to Farrow, who turned to Paul Kessler. "That's right," Kessler said, his eyes owlish behind his thick glasses. "There's no vaccine, not yet, but we're getting close. Now that we have the NIH and CDC working with us, we're quite optimistic."

"By close"—it was Nancy Keaton again—"just what do you mean? Six weeks? Six months? Six years?"

"I can't give you a time frame," Kessler replied, drenched with sweat.

"So you could still be years away."

"I'm afraid so, yes," Kessler said.

The murmur that went through the crowd was louder this time. Farrow said, "Or we could crack it any day now, we just don't know." He saw Tibbetts look at him, Tibbetts from Maine Disease Control, to whom he had lied about working on the Flowers strain. His look said: You're lying again.

"You're talking about preventive vaccine, right?" Wesley Rudd said. "Not a cure."

"That's right," Kessler said. "We still don't have a cure for rabies—any form of rabies. Once the symptoms appear . . ." He shrugged.

The crowd came alive with talk again, and another white light went on. Renshaw looked at the roof of his office and thought: If I were to make a novel out of this . . .

"Tell us about the law suit," a trim man with wavy black hair said, standing. Michael Frame from AP in Augusta.

Howard Barnes, Jillson's lawyer, who sat at one end of the table, had so far been silent, but now he spoke up. "I'm afraid we can't."

"The Shores aren't going to drop it?"

"No comment," Barnes said.

Wendell Renshaw spoke out from his post near the door. "What's the danger of this new disease getting out of control?"

Heads turned to the back of the room. At the table, Farrow stroked his beard, as Lauer said, "Very slight."

Renshaw reached in his pocket and fingered his pipe. "An untreatable form of rabies is loose in this town, and you say, 'Very slight'?"

More noise. When it quieted, Peyton said, "No one's saying it's loose. The infected dogs are dead, and the people who have the disease, or *might* have the disease, are confined. And the hospital personnel are protected, of course. Well protected."

"Okay," Renshaw said. "But what if those dogs infected other animals, animals still at large?"

Peyton shrugged. "Please, remember, this isn't a new thing to CDC, we've known about it for years. It didn't spread in Pennsylvania, and chances are it's not going to spread in Maine."

More questions, more taping, and Renshaw looked out at the ocean again. The last crisis of any proportion this town had faced had occurred years ago: the Great Fire. Everyone talked of the danger that summer, yet nobody really believed . . . Well, maybe these people are right, Renshaw thought, and the danger is slight. In my novel, however . . .

NINETEEN

Deep in her chintz-covered living room chair Mabel Dodge thought: Mabel, you're getting old.

She had just finished cleaning the whole downstairs, including the kitchen floor, but should that wear a body out? At her age? Her mother had put in a good day's work till she broke her hip at ninety-two, and even after the accident, it was hard to keep her down. Well, maybe it's more than just age, Mabel thought, slumping back with her arms on the arms of the chair. Maybe I ought to see Dr. Lewis. It's been ten years.

She didn't much care for the idea, though, undressing in front of a man so young, only sixty-three, and she said to herself, Well, it could be the heat. Eighty-four, the same as her age, pretty hot for the coast of Maine, and although it was mid-July, her blood was still thick from the winter. It seemed to take longer to thin out each year, and then every fall it was slower to thicken again. Old age, well, you couldn't do much about it. She guessed she was lucky to still be around, to be able to clean her own place, make her meals, when a lot of her friends were in nursing homes or in heaven.

She sighed heavily, wiping some sweat from her

neck. Soon she'd have to start making those pies for the supper tonight. If she didn't get after them soon, they wouldn't cool, and then they'd be runny at serving time. And how would that look? Mabel Dodge serving runny pies! They'd really think she was on the skids, if she let that come to pass.

Two more minutes, she told herself, just two more minutes' rest.

She looked up at the wall, at the pictures of Nellie and Bobby and all their kids, fine kids every one, even Rick, who was kind of slow; at the picture of Elston, dead twelve years now, framed on the polished tabletop. He'd only been eighty years old when he'd died. So young. If they hadn't put that fool pacemaker in, he would still be alive, she was sure. Fool thing made him sweat like a pig, even in winter. These doctors nowadays.

Her eyes stopped at the window, the yellow drapes. Land alive, a big leaf on the drapes. Now how in the world had she ever missed that? She'd been to Dr. Willard about her eyes two years ago, were they already getting worse? Or maybe it wasn't two years ago, it might've been longer than that. It was right after Bobby flew in last time. Let's see . . .

God help her, she couldn't remember. Bobby lived in San Diego, three thousand miles away. His kids were just about all grown up, and she hardly knew them now. Cindy, the oldest, had a child of her own. Her great-grandchild, and she'd only seen pictures of her.

Well, that's how it is these days, she thought as she sighed again and heaved herself out of the chair. Robert, her middle one, Bobby's father, still lived nearby, but Grace and Leonard were miles away. That's how it was, and no use thinking about it.

Time to get at those pies, that was enough to think about. Strawberry rhubarb, her last batch of those, for

137

blueberry season was just about here. She loved blueberry pie. And oh, didn't Nellie? While Bobby loved apple so much.

Oh . . . that leaf, she remembered, and went to the drapes. Just look at that, would you? she thought, and adjusted her glasses. An old brown leaf that size and she'd missed it. Well, maybe her mind was going, not just her eyes. It had happened to Elston a bit, but that was because of that fool machine they'd planted in his chest. Messed the blood up somehow. She tilted her head back and reached for the leaf—

And it suddenly came alive. A needle-sharp pain struck her palm, and the leaf was flapping and swirling around her head—

A bat! Not a leaf, a bat! It swooped close to her ear with a soft thudding sound, and she ducked and flailed her arms and cried out.

When she looked up again, it was gone. Where? She looked at her hand, at the blood flowing over her palm, and her heart was suddenly thick and loud in her ears.

There—on top of the TV set. Keeping her eyes on it, Mabel Dodge went to the airtight stove, reached into the bucket beside it, and hefted a stick of white birch.

She advanced on the TV set, feet quiet, heart loud. The bat sat there perfectly still. Mabel raised the log high in the air, her breath stuck in her throat, then brought it swiftly down.

The TV exploded; glass flew at her knees. The bat, squashed, fell onto the floor.

Mabel stood there as if in a trance, her chest heaving, her breath coming hard. The pain in her hand brought her back to her senses. She put the log back in its bucket and went to the kitchen and pulled paper towels off the roll. Her blood stained their printed blue flowers. She went to the living room, draped the towels

138

over the bat, and gingerly lifted its corpse. She could feel its soft heat in her fingers. Quickly she took it out back and gave it a heave. Up it sailed, then plunged into the weeds at the edge of the yard.

Had that been the right thing to do? she wondered. She should maybe have kept it? The very idea made her shudder.

She went back inside and disposed of the towels and washed her hands with plenty of soap and hot water. The bite wasn't really that bad and the bleeding had stopped, but when had she had her last tetanus shot? She couldn't remember. That time she'd stabbed her foot with the pitchfork? Twenty years ago?

She looked at the sink, at the boxes of strawberries there. Now how was she going to cook all those pies and take care of this, too? And that mess in the living room. Good heavens, she'd ruined her TV set! The whole thing had happened so fast.

Shaking her head, she told herself maybe it wouldn't take too long to get her tetanus shot. If things were slow at the hospital, she might still have time for her baking. But not enough time for the pies to set.

"Oh let them be runny, then," she said to the empty house. "They'll still taste better'n what Elvira Higgins makes, and that's the truth."

With that, she took her pocketbook from its perch on the hook near the door, and went out to her car.

Amelia Rose looked at her watch as she held Tricia Stemmer's limp wrist: pulse one hundred and twenty-two, and her temperature was now one hundred and three.

"I'm hot," Tricia said, looking up at Amelia with half-closed eyes, face flushed.

"I know it, darling," Amelia said. "Here, drink some more juice."

Tricia took the cup slowly and sucked at the straw half-heartedly. Wincing, she said, "My throat hurts," and gave the cup back.

"Just a little bit more?"

Tricia shook her head no.

Amelia gently placed the cup on the stainless steel stand by the bed, and said, "Try to sleep now, darling."

Tricia looked at her dully.

"I'll be back in a moment," Amelia said. "Just rest."

She left the room, a knot in the pit of her stomach, and went to the nurses' station. Dora Trask, a blond plump nurse in her early forties, was sitting behind the counter. "Tricia Stemmer is running a fever," Amelia said. "We'd better page Dr. Finch."

Dora Trask leaned into the microphone. Her voice called Dr. Finch through the ceiling speakers. "He's here," she said to Amelia. "I saw him a little while ago."

Amelia nodded.

"How high is her fever?"

"A hundred and three point two," Amelia said.

"Oh my," Dora said.

Two voices came from around the corner. One belonged to an older woman, who said, "It makes no sense at all."

The other voice, also a woman's, said, "I'm sorry, but it's doctor's orders."

"Well, what does that mean? That I'm under arrest? Is this a free country or not?"

The antagonists came into view: Joan Mildrum, head nurse, and a sturdy-looking woman with curly white hair. "All I came for was a tetanus shot," said the white-haired woman. "I have pies to bake and a supper to go to tonight."

"Mrs. Dodge—"

140

"I promised to bake six pies, and it's already almost too late," Mabel Dodge said testily. Scowling at her watch, she said, "I believe it *is* too late. Such foolishness. You don't get rabies overnight, do you? Can't I go to my supper and come back later if I'm sick?"

Hearing this, Amelia Rose said, "Oh my God," and started up the hall.

"You'll need shots, as the doctor explained," said Nurse Mildrum, guiding her antagonist into a room. "And you'll need to be kept under observation."

"For how long?" Mabel Dodge protested. "I've never spent one day in the hospital, not one minute. My husband went in and it killed him, and that's the truth."

Joan Mildrum sighed. At the doorway, Amelia said, "She was bitten?"

"By a bat," Joan said.

"Oh," said Amelia, suddenly weak. "My young patient has a fever now."

Joan Mildrum frowned.

"Who's that?" Mabel said. "Did a bat bite him, too?"

"Her," Joan said. "No, a dog."

"Well, I been bitten by dogs, too, years ago, before they all had rabies shots, and nobody made such a fuss. These days they all have shots, so how can you get it?"

"They don't all have shots," Amelia said.

"And it wasn't a dog that bit you," Joan Mildrum said.

"I never," Mabel said with a shake of her head. "I never in all my life— When's that doctor coming back?"

"Soon," Jane said.

Mabel plopped herself down in the chair in the corner. "Soon. Well it better be soon, I have pies to bake. It's my right to leave, he can't keep me here, I didn't commit any crime."

141

"You'll have to talk to him about it, Mrs. Dodge."

"Oh, I will," Mabel said. "I will indeed." Scowling and gripping the arms of the chair, she looked out the window. Pure blue sky, a few low clouds, and behind them the sun high but on its way down. She thought of those strawberries, there on her sink, and sighed.

TWENTY

The child peered over the edge of the drop. An explosion of white spray shot into the sky, framing his sturdy form. Sandra Barnes caught her breath.

"Matthew!" Howard Barnes shouted.

His son gave another look into the gorge, then turned and came running back.

"I told you not to go close to the edge," Sandra scolded.

"I wasn't close," three-year-old Matty insisted, cheeks flushed, his brown eyes wide.

"You were. You were very close. You wait for us before you go running ahead."

"But I wanted to see the water come up."

"You'll see it come up with us," his father said.

His sister, Lucy, five and a half, said, "What makes it go so high?"

"What do you think, Lulu?" Howard said.

She looked thoughtful. "The wind?"

"That's right. And the tide. They push it right up through that hole and —kaboom!"

"Kaboom!" echoed Matty, pure joy on his face. His mother had taken his hand and he strained against it.

"Matty!"

143

"I want to *see!*"

Laughing, Sandra shook her head. The four of them walked over thin mossy soil covered with lichen and bunchberry plants, and onto the bare granite ledge. Once again, spray flew into the air. As the tiny cold droplets hit Matty's tanned forearms, he shrieked.

"You keep holding my hand, young man," Sandra said. "Don't you dare let go."

They stood six feet away from the edge. Before them lay miles of dark blue sea punctuated with islands bristling with trees. Behind the islands, the sun formed a halo of gold.

Forty feet down, a deep stream of water rushed angrily up through a channel of jagged rock. When it crashed at the base of the cliff this time, the roar was deafening; spray flew at least twenty feet over their heads. "Wow!" Matty said, and Howard, laughing, said, "Now we're cookin', kids."

Roaring Spout was a favorite of Matty's, and Howard and Lucy liked it, too, but Sandra felt nervous here. The water came in from the open sea through a natural bridge in the rocks, and even when the tide was out and the air was calm, its force was astounding, terrifying. When she was here with the kids, she couldn't help thinking—

"Did anyone ever fall in?" Lucy asked.

My daughter the psychic, Sandra thought. "I don't know," she said. Which was true.

"If they did fall in, would they die?"

"I guess."

"But you wouldn't, would you, Mom?" Lucy said, looking up with a quizzical frown. "You're a real good swimmer, right?"

"Not quite that good, I'm afraid. At seventeen I might have been, but not at thirty-four."

"How far is it through the tunnel?"

"I don't know. Fifteen feet?"

"More like twenty," Howard said.

Lucy flinched as the surf hit again with a terrible bang, and Matty laughed.

"Do you want to go back by the trees?" Sandra asked.

Lucy nodded.

"Okay, go ahead, we'll be back in a minute."

"Hey Matty! Let's go find old man's beard!"

"Yeah!" Matty said, his interest in the water suddenly gone.

"Don't you pick any," Sandra said. "Just look."

"Okay," Lucy said.

"And stay in sight."

"Aw."

"You heard me."

The children ran into the darkening woods, and Sandra laughed. The water below her tore up through the granite, smashed into the cliff. She jumped back.

"Gotcha," Howard said.

Wiping the wet off her cheek, she laughed again.

Howard put his arm across her broad, tanned back. Together they stared at the sunset, its purple and lemon and crimson bands. "Incredible," Sandra said.

"Absolutely," her husband said.

She slapped at a bug on her neck and said, "Can't you stay?"

"Not this weekend, love."

"Can't Smith or Wilkinson pick up some more of the load?"

"They're loaded already. This damn Jillson thing."

She frowned at him. "Sometimes I think that we ought to come with you."

"Because of the rabies?"

"Because of the rabies."

"Hey, love, if I thought there was any danger, you

145

think I'd be here in the woods?"

"I guess not." She shrugged.

"Love, believe me. The dogs are dead. The people who have the disease are confined."

"I know. Tricia Stemmer is still okay?"

"She was okay this morning."

"That poor little boy. And Miranda and Gary."

"It's horrible," Howard said. "But Miranda and Gary—what can I say? They let the damn dogs loose."

The sea hit the rocks with a harsh grinding sound. Sandra looked at the islands. The sun was behind them in layers of deep tangerine. "It's so beautiful here, the most beautiful place in the world. I hope to God—"

A mosquito attacked her ear. She swatted it, then frowned and said, "Where are the kids?"

They made their way back over granite to spongy earth. The woods were quite dark now. As Sandra stared into them, tension arose in her chest.

"Lucy?" Howard said sharply. His voice hit the trees and died.

Behind them, the Spout exploded. A vacuum of silence, a crisp rustling noise—

—And Lucy and Matty ran out of the bushes, laughing. "We fooled you, we fooled you," Lucy said, and Matty echoed, "Fooled you."

Sandra let out a breath. "You sure did," she said. "Okay, don't run ahead on the way back now, it's too dark."

"I can see perfectly," Lucy said.

"I'm sure," Howard said. "But you do as your mother says."

They started down the path through the trees, the children leading the way. The air had turned cool, and Sandra had a sudden feeling that something was following her. She looked behind her: nothing. A shiver went down her spine. As she took Howard's hand she thought of Tricia Stemmer and Teddy Marsh. "Matty! Slow down!" she called, and a firefly winked, and the smaller of the moving shadows ahead of her in the dark called back, "Oh, Mom."

Paul Kessler looked up at the slide on the screen. "This makes me sick," he said. "I mean literally sick."

Farrow, sitting across from him, snapped: "Look, it isn't the end of the world."

It was nine twenty-five and his nerves were frayed and he needed something. Something more than a drink. It had been a long day. The press conference this morning, and now, goddamn it, this.

"Not the end of the world?" Kessler said. "It damn well might be, Martin. The stuff is *out* there, damn it, and we're to blame."

"Like hell we are."

"Well, who is, then?" Kessler said. "Those two kids?" He took his handkerchief out of his left rear pocket and wiped his forehead. "A bat. A goddamn bat. This is very bad, Martin."

"We're lucky they found it," Farrow said. "The old woman tossed it outside in the weeds."

"And a cop probably caught the disease when he picked it up."

"He wore gloves," Farrow said.

"Gloves aren't foolproof, Martin."

"Damn near."

Kessler let out a breath. "So what's with the woman?"

"They used ultrasound, benzalkonium . . . The bite's on her palm, not terribly deep. She hasn't allowed me to use the vaccine."

Kessler wiped at his forehead again. "If you had been bitten, would you allow it?"

"I know a bit more than she does about side effects."
Kessler shook his bald head. "I'm just sick."

"So you've said."

"I told you before, we should never have started on this. Was I right? Huh? Was I?"

He glanced at Farrow, and Farrow said tersely: "We're not the ones who created this, Paul. Iranians, Libyans, Syrians—God only knows who created it—but it wasn't us. But we do have to fight it. What would you have us do, just roll over dead? Have our whole country roll over dead?"

Kessler's look said: You're crazy, you're out of your mind. "You think someone *created* this thing?" he said.

"Of course," Farrow said. "Where do *you* think it came from? Let's not be naive, Paul. Look at the stuff at Detrick, at Harley, at Dugway. If our fellow Americans knew what people like us have cooked up in those places, they'd never sleep at night."

"Oh, they'd sleep," Kessler said. "They'd sleep fine. They'd believe that the stuff would stay under control, that accidents couldn't happen. They'd never dream that a place like Jillson would hire a Skinny Watts, who'd go around swapping dogs with a pound, or get so drunk that a couple of college kids could sneak right past him in the night."

"Maybe so," Farrow said. "Maybe so. And maybe they'll also believe that we've got the Flowers rabies under control."

"Fat chance," Kessler said. "When they find out a bat bit a person, Jesus." He dabbed at his forehead again. "People—children—are going to die because we brought this rabies here. Does that mean anything to you? No?" He sniffed. "I swear to God you aren't human, Martin. You have no heart."

Farrow fingered his beard and stayed silent.

"And when do we let people know about sexual

148

transmission?" Kessler said.

"We don't."

"It's bound to come out."

"Why? Who's going to spread it sexually? A couple of little kids? An old lady? Two comatose college students?"

"No heart," Kessler said again. "All brain and no heart, I ought to, I ought to just—"

"Quit?" Farrow said. "If you're thinking of that, Paul, forget it, we need you to beat this thing."

Kessler looked at the table and sighed. "Martin, how—"

The phone rang. Farrow went to the desk and answered it. "Yes?"

A silence, then Farrow said, "All right. Thanks. Good-bye," and hung up.

Kessler looked at him. "Well?"

Farrow frowned at the door to the room—solid white, metal, closed—unable to meet Kessler's eyes. "It was Sargent," he said in a quiet voice. "The hospital called him just now. Gary Simmons is dead."

TWENTY-ONE

HEALTH OFFICIALS DENY EPIDEMIC OF RARE FORM OF RABIES

by Oliver Emmet

BLUE HARBOR (AP)—Residents of this coastal resort town fear an epidemic of a fast-acting new kind of rabies, in spite of assurances from public health officials.

These assurances were made at a press conference yesterday morning, before a Blue Harbor woman was bitten by a bat while cleaning her house. Examination of the bat last night showed that it carried the new disease.

Earlier in the day, Maine State Health officials downplayed the threat of an epidemic. "There is absolutely no basis to the assertion that this disease represents a significant threat to the general public," said Dr. David Woodruff, an official with Maine Disease Control. But three hours later, Mabel Dodge, 84, of the Highlands section of Blue Harbor, admitted herself to Blue Harbor

Hospital, claiming that a bat had bitten her on her hand, and that she had killed it by hitting it with a log. A search was made of her property by police, who recovered the bat in the grass behind her house, but no more bats were found in the house itself.

Concern has been high in this coastal resort, ever since it was learned that a mutant form of rabies escaped from the Jillson Laboratory, which has been doing research on various diseases here since its founding in 1949. But scientists from the lab, backed up by officials from both Maine Disease Control and the Centers for Disease Control in Atlanta, insisted that the situation was well in hand.

"All the infected animals have been accounted for," said Dr. Martin Farrow, senior staff scientist at Jillson, "and all of the people exposed to these animals are currently receiving treatment." An attempt was made to get Farrow to update his statement in light of the recent developments, but he could not be reached. Yesterday, when asked whether treatment would be effective against this new disease, Farrow said it was still too early to tell.

The mutant form of rabies was first identified in Pennsylvania seven years ago, according to the CDC officials. Since only three cases were reported at that time, and since no new cases have been seen since then, research on prevention and cure has not been a top priority.

When asked if any existing vaccine would prevent the disease in animals, Dr. Farrow said that while Jillson has made great strides in this direction, there is as yet no one hundred percent effective prevention measure. The rabies vaccine

151

in current use, he said, is worthless against this new form. This led to intense questioning by the media, which at times became rather heated. At one point, when Farrow was accused of unleashing a potential epidemic on the community, he replied, "If vandals had not broken into the Jillson Lab, there would be no disease in Blue Harbor."

The "vandals" to whom he referred were both infected by the rabies, and one of them, Gary Simmons, 22, of Blue Harbor, died last night. The other, Miranda Shore, 20, of Blue Harbor and Summit, New Jersey, is in critical condition. Ms. Shore has confessed that she and Simmons released three infected dogs from Jillson on the night of June 18th. Teddy Marsh, 8, of Blue Harbor, was bitten by one of the dogs and is also in critical condition. Another child also bitten by a dog has begun to develop flulike symptoms, but doctors are not yet certain whether she has the new rabies.

State police emphasize that people should avoid all strange-acting animals—wild animals that appear overly friendly or docile, pets that seem confused or aggressive or sick. Any suspicious animals should be reported immediately to state or local police. They urge the public to remember that rabies is extremely rare in human beings and the chance of infection is slight, and that appropriate measures are now being taken to minimize the danger to the population at large.

When Wendell Renshaw finished the story, he read Gary Simmons's death notice once again. He had known the boy; had known who he was, at least, as he'd made the high school soccer all-star team. His father still worked down to Coastal Marine. He thought of that other kid's father, Richard Shore, saw him sitting across from him here at this desk. What a pity, he thought. What a shame. So smart. So young.

His own story had been quite low-key, but he'd filed it shortly after the press conference, yesterday afternoon, before he'd found out about Mabel Dodge. Mabel Dodge made everything different. Very different.

He looked at the AP article again. Not bad for Oliver Emmet, really. Emmet loved to sensationalize, and for him this story was uncharacteristically mild. This "epidemic" nonsense, though, was all Emmet's doing, as was the "heated questioning." Anything to sell papers, that was his motto. Well, you had to expect it from somebody raised in Boston.

He looked at the cursor blinking away on his monitor. No novel today, no novel today, it said. Or yesterday, either. He picked up his pipe, frowned, sucked at its stem, then laid it back down again. With his index fingers he typed: A TIME FOR CALM.

He stared at the green words, the cursor urging him on. "Don't be so impatient," he said out loud to the screen. "This has to be done just right. We aren't talking about the school board here, or a hike in the property tax."

He looked at Emmet's article again. Appropriate measures will be taken to minimize the danger. And what might these measures be? he asked himself.

He picked up the phone and punched out a number he knew as well as his own, the number of the state police.

TWENTY-TWO

Brad Hawkins stood in the bedroom doorway and said, "This is totally nuts, you know."

His wife, Nancy, wiry and thin, her brown hair pulled back in a knot, picked up another shirt and folded it expertly, placing it in the suitcase that sat on the bed. She reached into her bureau drawer again; pulled out a sweater. "You can stay if you want to," she said, "but the kids and I are getting out of here."

"But we just *got* here," Brad said. "We just unpacked all this stuff. I look forward all year to this, and you tell me we're going home?"

The sweater was packed. Nancy folded another shirt. "Would you rather be alive in Baltimore or dead in Blue Harbor?" she said.

Brad rolled his eyes. "The paper said don't panic. So what do you do? At the very first chance you get?"

She glared at him. "I don't care what the paper said, I want the children out of here. I know how much Maine means to you, but I just can't stay. I won't be able to sleep at night. My heart's been racing ever since I read about this stuff."

At this, Max Hawkins, five, ran into the room. "We're going home?" he said.

154

"That's right," Nancy said.

"But I wanted to catch some fish."

"I know that, honey, but we can't this time. We'll catch some at home. Where's your sister?"

"Outside."

"What?" Nancy said, looking startled. "Didn't I tell you—?"

She dropped a bra on the bed and went through the doorway, rushed through the cottage's living room and out through the screen door, which slapped like a pistol shot. On the deck she instantly spotted Lisa, playing in the sandpile with a car.

"Lisa!"

The three-year-old looked up, eyes wide.

"Come in here. Right this minute."

Still in a squat, Lisa said, "But—"

"Right now!"

Lisa dropped the car in the sand, her fingers splayed. She gave it a lingering look, then walked up to the deck.

Nancy held the screen door open; her daughter took an age to maneuver the steps and cross the pressure-treated planks. "Come on, come on," Nancy said, and when Lisa was in and the door was closed, she said, "You can't play out in the yard today, I told you that."

"Max pinched my arm," Lisa said.

"If he does it again, you tell me," Nancy said. "But you can't go outside. Now wash your hands."

Lisa looked at her sandy palms. "I saw a funny cat," she said.

"What?" Nancy said.

"He was in the trees."

"A cat? Like Bimbo?" Nancy said.

"No, a *funny* cat," Lisa said. "He had a real big tail, this long," and she held her arms apart as far as they'd go.

Nancy shuddered. "You stay in the house now, understand? Now go wash your hands."

Lisa frowned.

Brad came into the room. "So I have to get Willis to close the place? He just opened it up.'

"Like I said, Brad, stay if you want, but I'm leaving, and so are the kids."

"You are just impossible sometimes," Brad said.

"Likewise," Nancy said.

Route 6, Island Road, was the only way into or out of Blue Harbor, and now, for the first time in eight years of coming to Maine, Brad Hawkins was caught in a traffic jam.

"What the hell's going on?" he said testily, squeezing the steering wheel.

"An exodus," Nancy said.

In the back seat, Lisa pummeled Max, who stuck out his tongue and laughed.

"Stop it! Both of you!" Nancy said. It had taken all morning to pack, and now it was after three.

"Bimbo's hot," Max said.

"We're all hot," Nancy said.

"Drive faster, Daddy," Lisa said.

"Don't you see all the cars?" Max said. "Can he drive through the cars, dumbhead?"

"Just stop!" Nancy said.

It took seventeen minutes to reach the roadblock. The trooper leaned over and looked in the window and said, "Looks like you folks are going away for a while."

"You got it," Brad said. There was stuff piled under the kids' feet, stuff under Nancy's feet, and two bikes on the roof of the car.

Looking into the back seat, the trooper said, "That a cat in that box?"

"That's Bimbo," Max said proudly.

156

"A cat."

"Yes," Nancy said.

The trooper shook his head. "I'm afraid you can't leave with a cat."

"What?" Brad said.

"No animals can leave Blue Harbor."

A moment of silence; the heat weighed down. Then Brad said, "Well, what can we do?"

"You can either stay, or turn the cat over to us. We'll keep it safe till the rabies alert is over."

With a sigh, Brad said, "Can you reach it, Nance?"

Nancy reached back and grabbed the box, and Bimbo yowled. Brad passed the box out the window.

"We have to give him Bimbo?" Max said frowning, and Lisa began to cry.

"We'll get her back," Brad said. "Don't worry, they're just going to keep her awhile."

The trooper had set the box on the ground. "May I see your license, sir?"

Brad reached into his pocket and Lisa kept crying.

"We have to make sure the disease doesn't spread," the trooper said, taking the license. He straightened up. They saw only his stomach and belt.

"I want . . . my Bimbo," Lisa said, choking, tears staining her cheeks.

"Bimbo's going to be fine," Nancy said. "She's just going to stay with this nice policeman awhile and have a vacation."

"Which is more than we'll have," Brad said.

The trooper attached a tag to Bimbo's box, then gave Brad his license and looked in the car again. "None of you folks have been bitten by animals, have you?"

"No," Brad said.

"Not even by your cat?"

"Our cat doesn't bite," Brad said.

"That's good," said the trooper with a little smile.

157

"Okay, you can go. And we'll send you a notice about your cat."

"Thanks," Brad said.

As he drove off he said, "So we have to come all the way back here for Bimbo? From Baltimore?"

"Will they give her the right kind of food?" Max asked. His sister, still sniffling, was standing up and looking out the rear window.

"They'll give her the right kind of food," Nancy said. "Lisa, Daddy can't see. Sit down."

Lisa's face crumpled up and the crying began again.

"Good god," Brad said.

"Look at all the cars, there's *millions* of them," Max said.

"Lisa, here, wipe your nose," Nancy said.

Milt Hancock turned the .38 snubnose around in his hands and said, "Boy, this *is* an antique. Where'd you get 'er?" Boxes of ammo filled the shelves behind his bullet-shaped head.

"It belonged to my grandfather," Walt Marsh said.

"You ever fire 'er?"

"No," Walt replied, remembering Skinny Watts, the terrified look on his face as he'd stared at the empty gun. "Never had any bullets. Never needed any."

"Uh-huh," Milt Hancock said. "Lotta people who never shot guns before been in here these last few days. Those newspapers got everybody stirred up, it's unbelievable." He looked at the pistol again. "She's a beauty, an' clean as a whistle, you musta done some piece a work on this thing."

"Yeah," Walt said.

He had cleaned the gun over and over. It made him feel better to clean the gun. Yesterday, when he got back home, after seeing Teddy so limp and so flushed,

158

he had taken the gun out and cleaned it still one more time. Now the girl was sick, the Stemmer girl, and the doctors were pretty sure she had rabies, too.

"You have the right bullets for it?" he asked.

"Oh, sure, sure," Hancock said. "She just takes regular thirty-eights, that's all." He turned to the shelves and took down a box. "One?"

"I guess that'll do," Walt said.

"That's six ninety-five," Hancock said as he set the box down on the counter. Beside it he placed the gun.

Walt reached into his workpants' pocket and brought out a wad of bills. He peeled off a ten and gave it to Hancock, who rang up the sale, tore the slip from the register, gave Walt his change, put the bullets and slip in a bag. "So who's gonna teach you to shoot this thing?" he said.

"I guess I'll teach myself," Walt said.

"Uh-huh," Milt Hancock said. "What you might wanta do, though, is head for the Blue River Range, they'll teach you all you need to know about this job. If you have any problems with 'er, they'll fix 'em right quick."

Walt Marsh slid the gun off the counter and looked at its chamber, then picked up the bag with the bullets. "Thanks," he said. "Maybe I'll do that."

"Ask for Dick," Milt Hancock said. "He's the owner. Tell him I sent you. He knows his guns."

Walt was getting the feeling again, that feeling he'd had these last few days of being closed in, constrained. The gun shop seemed suddenly tight, confining. "Okay," he said, and turned and left the store.

Milt Hancock watched him get into his station wagon. Another greenhorn packing a gun. It was downright scary. Blue Harbor, like most American towns, was already armed to the teeth, and now, because of this rabies thing, it seemed like anyone who

159

didn't already own a gun was in the market for one.

Milt shrugged as he saw Walt close his door and thought: What the hell, it's their right to buy and my business to sell. He had certain misgivings, but what could he do? Except caution the buyers to learn how to handle their purchases, tell them about the Blue River Range, where they could get expert help. The thought of these people out in a field or woods somewhere, taking potshots at bottles or cans, made him shudder. More people were going to die of gunshot wounds than of rabies, if this kind of nonsense kept up.

As he watched Walt pull away, he thought, That man looks sick, and a sick man shouldn't be fooling around with a gun. Then again, it's his constitutional right, and I sure as hell don't want those gun control wimps to take away our means of protecting ourselves. You can't count on the cops to protect you, and what with these bats an' shit on the loose . . . Must be harder'n shit to shoot a bat, those suckers can *move*.

A pickup came barreling into Milt's lot, an old junker with battered fenders and sagging doors. It screeched to a stop, dust flew into the air, and a long-haired young man in a T-shirt slunk out of its cab. His arms and shoulders were dark with tattoos, and he flicked the butt of his cigarette at the bushes that bordered the path.

Oh my, Milt Hancock said to himself.

The door came open. The young man approached. "I need shells for a thirty-thirty," he said, his words whistling through crooked black teeth.

"Uh-huh," Milt said, and he turned to the shelves.

Almost out of the thirty-thirties. This was better'n huntin' season. Much better, since the big chain stores didn't stock this stuff in summer. He picked up a box, turned, and set it in front of the man. "These are twenty-two fifty," he said.

"I need a dozen," the young man said.

"A dozen!" Milt said. "I can't sell you that much, I'm low."

"It's for Dick," said the young man, tossing his head and pulling a rumpled paper out of his jeans. "For the Blue River Range. He took me on as a teacher there, he's got so much business now. You're his cousin, right? You own it with him, right?"

Milt looked at the paper the young man had flung on the counter—from Dick. "Right," he said with a little nod, and turned back to the shelves.

TWENTY-THREE

Angela Kessler, naked, leaned back on the pillow and reached for her cigarettes; shook one out of the pack and lit it. Smoke streamed from her nose, then rose to the ceiling, flattening out in gray bands. "What's the matter?" she said.

Jim Morgan, naked beside her, said, "The matter?"

"You seemed so distracted tonight."

"I'm not feeling that great."

"That damn bank. It's about time you took a vacation."

"It isn't the bank."

"What is it, then?"

Running his hand through his curly black hair, he said, "I don't know, sore throat, kind of tired." The lamp on the table beside the bed made his wide white shoulders gleam.

"Flu," Angela said decisively, blowing out smoke. "And now I'll catch it. Thanks a lot."

They were quiet a minute. Then Angela, looking at him, said, "What's that?"

"What's what?"

"That scratch on your arm."

162

"That isn't a scratch, it's a bite. That goddamn Mickey . . ."

Angela shifted position, frowning. "A cat did that?"

"I chased him off the couch and he turned on me. I took the damn thing in out of the cold and fed it for five years, and this is the thanks I get."

Angela's frown deepened. "When did this happen?"

"I don't know. A week ago. Maybe longer than that. Why?"

"Is Mickey still acting strange?"

"I booted him out that night and he never came back."

Angela sat up; her hair in the light was bright gold. "Have you seen a doctor about this?" she said.

"It's better now."

"That's not what I mean."

"Well, what *do* you mean? Like cat scratch fever or something? You think that's why I don't feel well?"

She looked at the tip of her cigarette, at the smoke rising up in a line. Her heart had begun to quicken. "You know what I mean," she said.

"Come on," he said.

"I'm serious," she said. "Your cat did that and you didn't report it?"

"It happened a week ago," he said, "ten days ago. Nobody knew about rabies back then."

"But now you know, and you still haven't told anyone? That cat could be infected, and it's out there somewhere . . . and you . . . Jim, you have to go see somebody."

He sighed. "Angela, I just have a little sore throat, okay?"

"But you don't know that."

"I do know that."

Angela snuffed out her cigarette in the ashtray next

163

to her thigh. The air from the lake, through the open window, felt cold, and she pulled up the sheet. "I want you to see somebody," she said.

He laughed. "Are you my lover or my mother?"

A shiver went down her back. "It's nothing to joke about," she said.

"They don't have a cure for the damn stuff anyway," he said. "If I've got it, I've got it, I guess." He was looking down at his leg, which was bent at the knee. "Or has Paul made a breakthrough?"

"Paul," she said. "He'll live in that damn lab now. Not that he didn't anyway."

"So much the better."

"Yeah," Angela said.

"You want a drink?"

She shook her head no.

"I'm going to have one. This goddamn throat . . ." She turned to him. "Jim."

"What?"

"Promise you'll see somebody. Tomorrow."

"Angela . . ."

"Promise me. Please."

"Okay," he said, laughing again. "Okay."

She looked at the scar on his arm. It ran from the base of his palm on an angle across his wrist. Ugly-looking. Mean-looking. "You do it," she said.

Skinny Watts was right wicked pissed off; and indignant and tired and drunk as a coot. It was dark as a pocket, with just a slim sliver of moon, but that was no problem for Skinny. He knew this dirt road like the back of his friggin' hand.

It was right off this road, as a matter of fact, that he'd started the fire that, years ago, had destroyed two-thirds of this island. He wasn't aware that he'd started it, though. It was way back in '47. He'd walked off his job at Bayside Lumber, and had come down here to drink some vodka and make some plans concerning lifetime goals. He had drunk half a pint and smoked half a pack before moseying on, planless, leaving a smoldering Lucky Strike butt on the tinder-dry forest floor. When he'd learned of the fire, he'd thought: started up near Harper's fields! Good Christ, I was lucky to get outta there when I did, if I'd fell asleep . . .

Sleep, good God, he was sleepy right now. And under the double moon his worn-out shoe hooked a root and he tripped, caught his balance and kept from falling, his vodka sloshing. He looked at the spray of weak stars and those moons, then lifted the bottle and drank. When the liquid hit bottom he said, "Ah," belched loudly, and started to walk again.

Twenty years. Twenty years he had worked for that goddamn place and this was the thanks he got. Driving all over God's earth to get animals, taking dead animals down to the furnace, keeping an eye on the place every weekend . . . and, last but not least, taking care of the shit.

Animals shit like mad, they shit plenty, and Jillson had animals up the wazoo. And had shit up the wazoo, too, shit that he, Skinny Watts, had disposed of for twenty years. He snorted and drank from the bottle again. Well, now they could get someone else to take care of their shit. Maybe Farrow would like to do it, or Kessler. Or maybe that bastard Sargent, who'd let him go. Yeah, let *him* clean the cages out and see how he liked the job.

Skinny thought of the look on the bastard's face as he sat in his nice shitless office and gave him the news. Lucky they didn't take legal action. Yeah, lucky, you bet, lucky, that was his middle name. His last piece of luck was not getting fried up in the fire of '47. Since

165

then it had all been downhill: Ten years at Paradise Cement, a dozen more at friggin' Star Rope, and twenty years cleaning up shit. Now out of a job at sixty-one, that was pretty damn lucky, all right.

He stopped, took a drink, and looked up at the stars again, at the pointed tops of the spruces and pines dead black in the velvet sky.

At the end of this road was his home. Just a couple of tiny rooms and a backhouse, but that was enough—and his garden, a half an acre. The potatoes and turnips were doing real good this year. He had lived on potatoes and turnips before, and he'd do it again. It wasn't a whole lot of fun, but it kept you going, especially when you used the peelings for mash. His social security would cut in next spring, and maybe his cousin Al would take him on at the treatment plant. More shit. Christ, he'd never escape it. He drank.

A shadow came out of the woods maybe ten feet away, and he froze. It moved slowly across the road and into the bushes, its tail arched high.

A skunk. A goddamn skunk. Now that's all he needed, to get tangled up with a skunk. Shit was one thing, but skunks, well, skunks was another. He stood there, his eyes straining hard at the dark. Was it gone? Yeah, it was. Seeing nothing, hearing nothing, he started to walk again.

Skunks were sort of a joke to most people, but not to him. Skunks were nothing to mess with. The smell was awful, of course, but it wouldn't kill you. But skunks got rabies. They got it a lot.

Skinny muttered out loud, "An' they're tryin' to blame me for *that*. They invented the goddamn stuff, been growin' it down there for years an' years, an' now it's escaped, sure, they try to blame *me*. Hell, did I let them animals go? Did I grow the shit? As far as the dogs go, they pay me enough, I wouldn't *have* to deal in no goddamn dogs. Damn right."

He passed the spot where the skunk had been; caught a whiff of it, not too strong. Clutching the neck of his bottle, he raised it high, took a swallow, and wiped the wet off his mouth with the back of his grimy sleeve.

His bladder was aching badly now, and he set the bottle down with care in the weeds by the side of the road. Reminding himself not to piss on the bottle, he moved through the weeds to the edge of the trees, then unzipped his fly and brought his limp organ into the cool night air.

A sound. He froze. That goddamn skunk? A different goddamn skunk? He stood there, holding himself.

And he heard it again—a scratching, almost. Not on the ground, he realized now, but somewhere up in the trees. An owl? A squirrel? A sudden chill struck him. He stood there. For Christ's sake, he said to himself, are you pissin' or not?

He listened intently. His breath was the only sound. He flatulated, relaxing some, and the urine began to stream out.

Then a rustle in front of him, over his head, and a ball of black flew at his face. A strangled cry left his throat and he stumbled back as the animal struck, its claws in his scalp and its vicious hot hiss in his ear. A bobcat for Christ's sake! his frantic mind screamed as he tore at the beast, at its bristling thick fur, and he fell, landing flat on his back on his bottle. It broke. A rank feral smell and a slash of bright pain on his cheek. His bladder let go all the way, and the beast was gone.

He sat up, panting, dazed, afraid, his hand on his wounded cheek. Not big enough for a bobcat, he said to himself, just a regular cat. Jesus Christ, do you think—?

No, he said to himself as he pushed himself up,

breathing hard with a pain in his ribs. No, it can't be. Not that.

His hand was hot and sticky now. Goddamn, goddamn, he said to himself. Got to wash that cut, put some alcohol on it. Jesus. I have some rum.

Dizzy, he stumbled along the road, his heart pounding frantically now. At his cabin at last, he threw open the door, grabbed his flashlight, and went to the kerosene lamp. With quivering fingers, he struck a match.

And saw blood on his hands; saw his penis, still out, and the stain on the crotch of his pants. "Goddamn it," he said, feeling not at all drunk as the lantern's glow brightened the room.

Tucking himself away, he went for the rum.

TWENTY-FOUR

Sharon Jensen sat on the lab stool, her feet on its rungs, her hot hands clasped between her thighs. Her eyes were fixed on the gray tile floor. Across from her, on another stool, John Henderson sat with his hands on his knees. He started to speak, then stopped; exhaled and began again. "There's a chance," he said, then stopped again, shaking his head.

Sharon's eyes remained downcast. "There's always a chance," she said, so tired, her throat so sore, and her voice sounded wrong in her ears, flat, dead. "But John . . . oh, John."

He was quiet a minute, then said, "Sharon, please, don't jump to conclusions."

She nodded and looked at her thumb again; it was swollen and red and stung with a tingling heat. That stupid nervous habit of chewing her cuticle—had killed her? "I'm so careful," she said. "I'm always so careful, John."

"Of course you are," he said softly, "but gloves aren't fail safe. You know it, we all do. Sometimes you get a bad one."

"I know," she said.

Time seemed to be standing still. Sharon stared at

the floor and her thoughts were scattered, drowned out by the huge swell of sadness and fear that grew and grew in her chest. "Oh John," she said.

He got up from the stool and held her. She started to cry. A long time ago, when she'd first come to work for the state, she and John had been lovers. For years now they'd just been friends.

"Sharon, no," he said. "There's a good chance it's not what you think, and if it is, they're working like mad at Jillson. They've got some of the best in the country down there, and they're going to beat this stuff."

"But when?" Sharon said. "Two years from now? I have two weeks, a month . . ."

"You don't know that," he said, his arm still around her.

She did know that. She didn't believe it, couldn't believe it, but knew it. She sat there, feeling his warmth on her shoulders, and stared at the floor through wet eyes.

She was thirty-three. She had hardly lived. Her entire life seemed like a matter of days. There was so much she wanted to do, had planned to do. She had thought there was time. There just *had* to be time, it couldn't all end so soon. Thoughts flickered and flashed in a dizzy dance, and she couldn't sort anything out.

"John," she said.

He squeezed her, then took his arm down. "You're going to Blue Harbor Hospital," he said.

She looked at him. "Blue Harbor? But why?"

"It's the best place," he said. "The Jillson people are close by."

"But I don't want to go down there, it's too far from home."

"I'm afraid you don't have any choice," he said.

She frowned at him. "What?"

170

"Anybody suspected of having rabies goes to Blue Harbor Hospital. You can understand that."

"Yes," she said, nodding. "Yes." The fear welled up in her chest again. "I washed that lesion," she said. "I kept it clean. What more was I supposed to do, cut off my goddamn thumb?" Closing her eyes and shaking her head, she covered her face with her hands.

Her entire past was a huge ball of pain, with strobelight images flashing; that day in elementary school, when she'd fallen down on the playground and split her lip; that time she had gotten sick during finals as a freshman; the day she had broken up with John eight years ago. Her life had gone by so fast, too fast, and she wanted to do so much more. She *deserved* to do so much more, this couldn't be it.

But it was, and she wanted to hold every moment; savor it slowly, totally; remember every nuance of sight, sound, taste, touch, smell. And why? she thought. What good will it do to store up memories, when memory itself will soon dissolve?

"I'll help you any way I can," John said. "I'll help you pack, I'll drive you down to Blue Harbor . . ."

"Thanks," Sharon said. She wiped her eyes, thinking: Good I didn't get married, after all. Good I didn't have children. If this had happened and I had children . . .

Tears came again, stinging. She'd always been sure she'd have children. Sure she would marry someday and have children, and so many wonderful things would happen. someday.

"Well, we better get going," John said.

TWENTY-FIVE

The bee at Eddie Mason's head just wouldn't go away. He swatted at it again, ducked, ran a few yards toward the pond, crouched down, and there it was, right back in his ears again. "Get outta here! Geez!" he yelled and batted the air with both hands.

He couldn't get a good look at the bee, but it was a big sucker, huge, as big as a sparrow. No, he thought with a scowl, it can't be that big, what kind of a bee is that? And the buzzing, it's so . . .

His dream popped apart in a bright white puff, but the buzzing continued, right next to his ear.

The phone. He reached out blindly and sent the receiver crashing down onto the floor. He scrambled for it, trying to focus, retrieved it, half out of the bed. "Hello?" His mouth tasted like dust.

"Hello, Mason?"

"Yeah?"

"This is Bob Waters."

Eddie's brain was enmeshed in cobwebs. Bob Waters. Waters? The squad leader? "Yeah?"

"We're being called up. Report to the Brewster armory at thirteen hundred hours."

Eddie frowned at the window, the shade bright with

sunlight. He pushed himself up and rolled back on the bed. "We are?"

"Do you hear me, Mason?"

"I thought it was next month. In August."

"I'm not talking about maneuvers, Mason. We're being called *up.*"

"Oh."

"Be there, in fatigues. Thirteen hundred hours. That's one o'clock, right?"

"Right." His mind hummed blankly. "What happened?" he said. "I mean where are we going?"

"You'll find out later. I'll see you there."

A click. Eddie hung up the phone. He blinked at the window; the light hurt his eyes. He looked at the clock; ten fifteen. This was awful, criminal, somebody waking him up at this hour on Saturday morning.

"Crap," Eddie said as he swung his legs over the side of the bed and ran his hand through his tangled brown hair. Well, he thought, his mind starting to clear, it's something to do, at least. He'd had two crummy jobs pumping gas since he got out of high school last year, had quit them both, and ever since then the Guard had been the closest he'd come to work. His mom was kinda ticked about it, but didn't kick him out. She was pretty lonely now that his dad was gone. Heart attack mowing the grass last summer. He'd only been forty-five years old, and Eddie had been shattered, especially since it was his job to mow, not his dad's, and if he hadn't hurt his hand playing touch football—Well, you couldn't think about things like that, it would drive you nuts.

Eddie went to the trailer's bathroom, showered, then dressed in his Guard fatigues. He liked the khaki underwear, thought it was cool. He liked the whole uniform. It made him feel like he fit in somewhere, belonged to something. So far he had drilled once a month, and he liked that okay, but he'd really looked

173

forward to summer maneuvers. But this would be better, whatever it was, the real thing. A strike somewhere, at one of the paper mills? Or maybe an earthquake had struck while he'd slept?

He went to the kitchen. His mom wasn't there, she worked Saturdays now. She worked too much, in Eddie's opinion, but his mom said she liked to work a lot, it kept her mind off things. Mr. T, his terrier, nuzzled his leg, and he reached down and ruffled his fur. "Hey T," he said. "What's up? You want to know what's up, you read the news."

The *Journal* sat on the kitchen table, next to his mom's coffee cup. He took the cup to the white steel sink and poured the remains down the drain; put the coffee maker on heat—there was plenty left, she always made some for him—then sat at the gold formica table and looked at the *Journal's* headlines.

No earthquake, no strike, nothing big like that. Some guy robbed a bank in Portland, but they caught him two blocks away. Big deal.

Now here was something, though. Two women had died of rabies down to Blue Harbor, and so had a little girl, and a bunch of people were sick with it. Geez, that was awful. A man had died of it, too, a few days back. A new kinda rabies, the article said, a real bad kind. The girl was only five years old and one of the women was only as old as he was. Well, a year older, twenty. Geez.

The coffee was hot and he got up and poured a steaming cup, brought it back to the table. Put three spoons of sugar in it, then went to the fridge for the milk, stirred a shitload of that in, too.

As he drank the coffee, he looked at the paper again. The Red Sox had lost four games in a row and were five games in back of the Yankees. No pitching. As usual. Last year he'd been playing third base for his high

174

school team. It seemed so long ago. He wondered if he could even hit anymore.

He checked the clock above the door. Still plenty of time, and he went to the fridge again and took out the eggs. Mr. T watched his movements with interest, head cocked to the side. As he cracked the eggs into the frying pan, he looked at the clock again and a twinge of excitement stirred in his stomach. Or maybe a twinge of hunger, he couldn't tell.

As they fell out, Bulkhead Morrison said with a grin, "This is gonna be just like deer season, only better."

They went to the wall and joined the line. Voices rang off the armory's ceiling.

Pete Richert, a muscular, good-looking guy about five eleven, said, "Deer season shit. You wouldn't want to eat this meat. You don't even want to *touch* this meat."

"You can get it that easy?" Eddie said. "If all you do is touch it?"

"You heard what the captain said."

"I didn't think he meant if you only *touched* it."

Richert scowled. "It gets into a cut on your hand or somethin', you're dead."

"Well, they want us to cart the animals off? Or just kill 'em?"

"Some of us got to cart 'em off, there's nobody else gonna do it."

"Geez," Eddie said.

The armory was filled with men in fatigues, more men than had ever shown up at the drills. "M-15s," Eddie said. "That's what they used in Nam, right?"

"Right," Richert said. "Some of these babies probably blasted some gooks."

175

Bulkhead Morrison laughed, revealing his chipped front tooth. He was six foot six and weighed two hundred and forty-five pounds, and his face was a perfect circle. His hair was an eighth of an inch of bristle, and his ears stuck out. "You hit some skunk or a cat with a M-15, an—" He laughed again.

Eddie had never killed anything. Not deer, squirrels, rabbits, or anything else, but now he was going to have to. "Well, who's gonna set out the poison?" he asked.

Richert slapped Eddie's shoulder. "You are, my man. We'll see you get poison detail."

"But that's gonna kill all the animals, right? I mean not just the sick ones."

"It's gotta be done."

"Well, it don't seem right."

Bulkhead moved up a couple of steps in the line. "I never been to Blue Harbor," he said. "What's it like down there?"

"Nice," Richert said. "Yachts, tennis courts, the whole nine yards."

"Hey, maybe I'll meet a rich widow or somethin'."

"An' maybe I'll win the lottery," Richert said.

TWENTY-SIX

As a child, Farrow had played with fire. He didn't remember exactly when, but he must have been only seven or eight years old. He passed a field on his way to school every day, and every day for two weeks, he threw a match into that field and watched as the fire caught in the curled brown grass, then quickly spread in a circle and started to crackle. He would stare at the flames, in love with them; they were magical, thrilling, hypnotic. Each day he would wait a bit longer before he would stamp them out excitedly, his heart beating fast and high in his skinny chest. When the fire was dead and the acrid smell of burnt grass was thick in the sweet spring air, he would laugh. He'd stopped it. Stopped *that*. He had won again.

Then one day he didn't win. He had let the circle of flame grow wider than ever, supremely confident, had jumped in quickly and started to stomp it out, when a sudden brisk wind arose. The fire leapt happily under its urging, escaping his feet—and was out of control. He kept trying: frantically running first here, then there, and stamping as fast and as hard as he could, but nothing would stop its spread. A wall of flame flickered above his head. He gasped at its power and ran.

He ran six blocks to the firehouse. "There's a field on fire!" he yelled. The firemen were playing cards and reading magazines. One of them, next to the huge open door, tilted back in a wooden chair with a toothpick lolling in the corner of his mouth, said, "So? Let it burn."

"There are houses down there!" Farrow said. "*My* house is down there!"

Which was true. The field was several acres deep, with a thin line of trees on its southern edge, and his house lay beyond those trees. He had threatened his home and all that his parents had worked for, threatened their very existence, with his deadly game. The firemen jumped up suddenly, dropping their cards, and in seconds the engine was roaring its rich throaty growl and its siren was filling the air, and he stood there watching it rush away, feeling weak in the chest and knees.

Farrow thought of all this as he sat at the desk in the gardener's cottage and fixed the syringe. He had never set fires again after that, but he'd never lost the urge. Now, as he watched the fluid rise in the tube, he thought, No firehouse to run to this time around.

He had not been present at Miranda Shore's death; her parents had not let him into the room. The nurse, Amelia Rose, assured him her end had been peaceful. She'd been heavily tranquilized, of course, and filled with morphine.

The Stemmer girl, also heavily drugged, had gone quietly, too. Not so the old woman, Mabel Dodge. In her, the disease had run its course with frightening rapidity. She'd refused all injections, and once symptoms began, they peaked in less than three days. Seemingly comatose, she had not been restrained or tranquilized, and suddenly she'd come alive and torn her room apart and maimed two nurses with her teeth and nails before she could be subdued.

Four deaths, six active cases, and how many others waiting in the wings? These nurses, Sharon Jensen . . .

Sharon Jensen, that was a tough one. That was really a tough one. By rights, he and Kessler should have caught the disease by now, not her. They'd been fooling around with this stuff for years, and she'd handled one lousy dog. She'd had no pre-exposure prophylaxis, but could that account for the difference? The pre-exposure series they'd given themselves didn't work on the Flowers strain—at least not by itself. He thought of that childhood field and the circle of flame growing wider, wider, until it was leaping and laughing and making him sick to his heart.

He pushed the needle into his arm, his head bent low. And was Kessler right? They should never have started the work on the Flowers virus? Hell, if people like Kessler ran the world, we'd be back in the Stone Age, he thought. No skyscrapers, airplanes, open heart surgery; no cures for smallpox and polio. Freud, Halstead, and even Pasteur had been willing to play with fire, and had changed the world.

To Farrow, the substance in this syringe was not fire. It certainly could be, but he was so careful, had always been careful. This substance had turned on its chief proponent, Sigmund Freud, and William Steward Halstead, John Hopkins' first professor of surgery, had gotten quite badly burned. In 1885, the year that the aged, partially paralyzed Pasteur successfully treated his first rabies case, the brilliant young Halstead injected this substance—cocaine—directly into human nerves and discovered regional anesthesia.

Self-experimentation had paved the way to this triumph—and had led to Halstead's addiction. Freud was still extolling the drug when Halstead was hospitalized for a lengthy and difficult treatment. When Freud killed a patient with an overdose, his enthusiasm waned, and in 1887 he at last renounced cocaine. Oh, it could be fire, all right.

But never for me, Farrow thought as he eased the syringe out from under his skin. For his was a well-controlled habit of very long standing. After Janice had died, when he thought he'd go mad, he had tried a number of different drugs, and found this one suited him best. Deprived of marrying lovely Janice, he'd married Freud's "magical drug," the leaf of the coca plant.

He had been a faithful husband, using less than a gram a week—often quite a bit less—since that time. Supply was no problem; it came through the lab for his ongoing pain experiments, the pain in this instance being his own. The quality of his anodyne, government issue, was superb.

This was another reason he'd quit direct care. If someone got hurt because of an error in judgment caused by his habit, he'd never forgive himself. Research was so much safer, allowed so much room to maneuver—or so he had always thought.

He dropped the syringe in the waste can, along with the metal tray that had held the cocaine. His mind was as brilliant as crystal now, and confidence rose in his veins. They were going to beat this rabies, he knew it, he knew it down deep in his blood. He and Kessler had made such great strides on their own. And now with all the help they had . . .

Just look at these Series V, Protocol 4's. Two minor reactions, out of a dozen dogs. And the four they'd infected were still all right—after almost three weeks! He thought of Miranda Shore again, and her mother, so much like Janice. The Stemmer girl.

180

The air in Farrow's nostrils was silver and cold; he got up and went to the door, turned the overhead lights on. The blue flourescents blinked and held. He went back to the desk, turned the desk lamp out, and went to the door again. Turned the overhead lights out and locked the door.

The air was soft and deliciously clean, and the sky was alive with stars as he walked down to Building 6. An owl called out from a distance, a lonely sound, but Farrow felt confident, buoyant. The bushes and trees held no fear for him and would hold no fear for anyone soon. He was sure of it.

The spotlight over the door shone down on his hands in a beautiful way as he pushed the buttons, and the lock clicked open.

A thin yellow shaft of light sliced the dark at the end of the hall and he started toward it, his soft-soled shoes making almost no sound on the vinyl. The door was open a crack and he looked inside at Paul Kessler asleep on a stool at the lab table, his head in the crook of his arm.

At another time, he might have seemed rather pathetic, but not tonight, not now. The cocaine in Farrow's brain declared all was well. They were all working hard and well, Kessler more than the rest, but Kessler liked to punish himself, worked best that way. Farrow looked at him there. In his dreams, was he still running tests? Awake, could he really not know that his wife was cheating, when so many others knew?

Farrow left him there and went on. Soon he passed through another door and was in with the dogs.

Their smell came to him sharp and clean. The sound of their barking was crisp in his ears, and the overhead light when he threw the switch was as bright as the light of the sun.

He went to the Series V, Protocol 4's. They were

making a racket, and only two slept. With the length of dowel that leaned on the wall, he poked one of the sleepers. "Come on, up, up," he said, and kept poking until it stood.

It looked good, damn good. He poked the other sleeper awake, and it looked just fine.

He and Kessler had come so far. From attempts to inactivate the Flowers serotype with beta-propiolactone and the year of frustrating failure with mice—when the vaccine had killed them all—to the trials with DM-1507-2N, the Kenya strain—also a failure—to the shift to DM-1609-3M, from Zaire, which had worked well on mice but caused the disease in twenty percent of cats. The success with the rabbits and dogs with Protocol 2 of DM-1609-2M (Series III), which he'd given to Cowboy Luce. The elation and then dismay over Series IV, which had failed in the dogs that Miranda and Gary had freed. And now Series V, which was highly unstable in Protocol 3, but in Protocol 4 looked so good.

He had given the Protocol 3 to Teddy Marsh and the orderlies, Bill Marcotte and Evan Cole, and it hadn't worked: they were all gravely ill. But these dogs, look at them! he thought, mind bright. Two months!

Of course, they could still get sick, but with each passing day, things looked better and better. Whether the new formulation would work on humans, though, was another question—that would have to be answered soon. Very soon. They didn't have months and years to play with now, this was life and death now, not an abstract game.

Confidence surged through Farrow's brain. He walked back through the cages, quickly, lightly, setting the dowel against the wall, and went through the door to the hall. The streak of light still came from the lab, and Kessler still slept at the table.

182

Farrow went to him. Looking down at his balding head, he thought: You never played with fire, did you, Paul? Too smart for that. Too dull for that. Straight-arrow Paul. He placed his hand on the soft pudgy shoulder and Kessler jerked, raised his head, and said "What?" in a startled, thick voice. He groped for his glasses, which lay near his arm.

"Paul, you better go home."

Kessler blinked as he put on his glasses. "Oh. Martin," he said. "What time is it, anyway?"

"One fifteen."

"God. You been here, too? All this time?"

"Yes."

Wiping his lips with his hand, Kessler said, "Yes. I better get home."

"The Protocol 4's look good," Farrow said.

"Yes."

"We have to start human trials."

"But we only finished the series two months ago."

"Two months is a long time these days."

Kessler groggily nodded. "You leaving now?"

"I'm going to stay a few minutes. I'll lock the place up."

"Okay," Kessler said. He ran his hand through his fringe of hair, looked back at the lab table, frowning, then left the room.

When Farrow heard the outside door click shut, he went to the wall, to the refrigerator there, and unlocked its stainless steel door. The vials sat on the rack in rows. He picked one up and took it to the desk across the room.

From the desk's lower drawer, he took a syringe and inserted its needle into the top of the vial. Slowly he drew up the amber fluid, his breath cold and clean in his throat. He held the needle up to the light, then inserted it into his arm, in the deltoid this time.

183

As the fluid sank into his flesh, he thought of Miranda Shore. And Mabel Dodge and Tricia Stemmer and Randall "Cowboy" Luce. And Freud and Halstead and all the others who had used themselves as subjects. He thought of Pasteur.

He pulled out the needle, exhilarated, pocketed the syringe and vial, then went to the refrigerator, opened it again, and took out three more vials. As he slipped them into his lab coat, he laughed to himself.

Still playing with fire, he thought. After all these years.

TWENTY-SEVEN

TROOPS OCCUPY BLUE HARBOR

By Oliver Emmet

BLUE HARBOR (AP)—A National Guard unit set up camp on the outskirts of this small coastal town last night as part of a government effort to contain a spreading rabies epidemic.

The unit, under the command of Lieutenant Colonel Michael Tower and comprised of nearly five hundred men, took over the area known as Harper's fields late yesterday afternoon. Harper's fields is a stretch of forty-three acres which spans the northern border of the island. Large khaki tents can be seen on both sides of Route 6, Island Road, the only access into or out of Blue Harbor.

According to Lieutenant Colonel Tower, the Guard was called up by Governor Cinton Laycock as a precautionary measure in the wake of three recent rabies-related deaths. Up to ten other victims of the disease are said to be in critical condition, and new cases are being reported daily. Tower refused to comment on the Guard's speci-

185

fic duties in the area, but sources at the Maine State Department of Health say that guardsmen will be setting out poison for wild animals in the Blue Harbor region in an effort to control the disease, which has area residents close to hysteria.

Guardsmen will also be sent on forays into the woods that border the town, with orders to shoot all animals on sight. Residents are urged to confine all pets to their properties during this period, and to stay out of wooded areas. While elimination of the wild animal population may seem like overkill to many, Dr. Marilyn Blount, head of Maine's Department of Health, says that the state has never before been faced with such a grave public health threat. "It is tragic to have to take the lives of these animals," she said. "But it would be much more tragic if people's lives were lost because we failed to take this step." When asked how bats could be controlled, Dr. Blount admitted that this was a difficult problem, but one which could be surmounted.

Wendell Renshaw threw the paper down on the floor of his office in utter disgust. *Troops occupy. Close to hysteria.* The Guard ought to shoot that goddamn Emmet, forget about the animals! Anything to sell papers. The people of this town had handled this threat damn well, *damn* well, nobody was in hysterics as far as he knew, and this creep with a hit man's ethics . . .

With a frown, he took his pipe out of his ashtray and filled it from the pouch in his desk's top drawer; lit a match and sucked at the pipe's black stem; leaned back in his oak swivel chair and exhaled.

Slowly he rocked back and forth, smoking, biting the stem of his pipe, and thought of the Second World War, the Great Fire. The town had responded so valiantly, and its character hadn't changed since then: once again it would rise to the challenge. Nothing to fear but fear itself. Damn right.

He smoked. How long ago all that seemed. FDR, the Fire. It *was* long ago. "Damn it, Wendell, you're getting up there," he said out loud. "It's about time you realized that."

He rocked; he smoked. Ten patients critical? Could that be right? The Marsh boy, two orderlies, the girl from the state health lab, a guy from Tully's Cove . . . He leaned forward and reached for the phone, but before he could touch it, it rang.

Oh God, he thought as the voice came screeching across the line. Catherine Wadsworth was bad enough sober, but once she was in the bag . . .

"Outrageous!," she sputtered into his ear. "Absolutely outrageous! Poisoning our wildlife! Shooting our pets! The next thing you know, they'll be taking a bead on *us!*"

Wendell sucked on his pipe. "I doubt that, Catherine."

"Get them to call off this madness, Wendell. Stop them! You must!"

God save me, Renshaw thought, and said, "I'm afraid your idea of my power's distorted, Catherine." The clock on the wall read ten thirteen, and the old girl was totally blotto.

"You stopped them from burning hazardous waste here, and you can stop this," Catherine said.

"I didn't stop them," Renshaw said. "I wrote some editorials, that's all. It was you and Howard and Sandra Barnes who stopped them."

"You had a big hand in it, Wendell."

His pipe was out. He laid it down. "So what do you want me to do?"

"Write editorials, naturally, that goes without

187

saying. And get on the backs of Winslow and Steele."

Bill Winslow was U.S. Senator, and David Steele was a congressman. "I would have thought you'd already taken care of that," Renshaw said.

"I can't get through to them, damn it," Catherine said. "Those damn silly girls won't let me. They're supposed to call me. Fat chance." She paused a few seconds, then added, "My Precious is out there somewhere."

"Excuse me?"

"My Precious! My coon cat!"

Of course, Renshaw thought. I should have known.

"They're liable to poison the darling! Or shoot her! She's been missing for weeks, ever since—" She stopped to loudly clear her throat, then said, "She ran off the night of our party. I've been worried sick ever since, and now, with this . . ." A few seconds of silence, and then: "The girls simply won't let me through. There's no access these days. Bill Winslow's mother was in the DAR with me, and now . . . For God's sake, *do* something, Wendell! They let the criminals do what they will in the cities, they don't call the army in on *them,* but as soon as a quiet, law-abiding town like this has a little trouble? Occupation! Invasion!"

"I'll write the editorial," Renshaw said. He had planned to do that anyway; had been mulling it over when Catherine called.

"I should hope so," Catherine said. "And I hope that's not all you'll do."

"You'll try to reach Winslow and Steele again?"

"Of course!" Catherine said. "And you will, too, I hope."

"Yes," Renshaw said. "Well, I have to get off now, Catherine. Been a pleasure to talk with you."

When he hung up he thought, A real pleasure indeed. As usual. He punched the phone's buttons and fingered his pipe as he waited for someone to answer. The phone rang fifteen times before a voice said, "Blue Harbor Hospital. Hold, please."

Renshaw toyed with his pipe as what passed for music these days assaulted his ear.

Frowning at the dead receiver, Catherine Wadsworth thought: newspaper people, always in such a rush, so scattered, no wonder they always get everything wrong. She had yet to read an article about herself or about a situation she was familiar with which didn't contain at least one glaring error. Those people called their writing "stories" for a very good reason.

She looked at the number on the yellow pad that sat beside the phone and slowly, finger shaking, dialed again.

Busy. Not even the stupid girls this time. Why didn't he have more lines put in and hire more staff? He certainly got paid enough. If his mother were still alive . . . Well, no use thinking of that.

The other number gave her a helpless feeling. She didn't even *know* this David Steele. Came from up north, from the County somewhere. Raised on potatoes, no doubt. She decided to wait till later to give him a try, as her glass was now empty.

She hung up the phone and left the study, crossed the parlor with its Empire divans, walked through the dining room and into the spacious kitchen. As she poured herself another drink from the pitcher that sat on the black slate counter, she thought about Tricia Stemmer.

She had spoken to Rachel once since her child's death. Rachel had been so brave. As one would expect from a Wilkinson, they had such good breeding. But brave or not, she would never be right again. Catherine

189

was fully aware of that from her own loss, her Davis, who'd died in Korea, that foolish "conflict" brought on by that madman Truman. A miracle this country still survived with those reckless Democrats tearing away at its roots.

She thought of her Davis every day; she would never get over his loss. The telegram had killed something deep inside that had never come back. And that was how it would be for Rachel, too.

Miranda, you foolish child, she thought as she sipped a Bloody Mary and looked outside at the acres of lawn, at the bay. To think that only a few short weeks ago, you stood right here and spouted that radical nonsense. Animal rights indeed. Of course, at the time, I had no idea it was you. That lowlife, that Simmons boy, a mistake from the very start. Obvious to your mother, I'm sure, as obvious as it was to me, but control these days is simply not possible, not with television. We've all lost our children, one way or another.

Thoughts muddled, she drank. She was tiring of Bloody Marys now and couldn't wait till noon, when she'd switch to Manhattans. She had very strict rules about drinking. Manhattans permitted from noon until Marvin came home from the club at four, when martinis began. Wine with dinner, and afterwards scotch. She placed great stock in regularity. It was the key to a healthy, long life.

Miranda, Miranda, the trouble you've caused, she thought. Your poor mother grieving, and Rachel grieving, and now the entire town subjected to this, this nonsense with the National Guard. My lord, it was a virtual siege! Hard to believe a Republican governor would overreact this way. And the summer colony, some of her best friends, running around like a bunch of scared sheep, going home. Frowning into the pulpy

190

red dregs of her glass, she thought, You won't catch *me* going home, I *deserve* this holiday. Ninety-five in Boston the past three days, and air-conditioning or not . . . All blown out of proportion. Sensationalism, the modern world with a vengeance. Those newspaper people.

She drank, thinking, Time to try that Winslow boy again, then said to herself: *Boy.* He must be forty-five if he's a day. You're starting to sound like the locals, Catherine. She shivered, and drank again.

And heard something then, heard a sound she could scarcely believe. From outside. She stood perfectly still, head cocked. Could it actually be?

Oh absolutely, yes.

Setting her glass on the counter, she went to the door and opened it quickly; stepped onto the patio, shielding her eyes with her hand. The sound again. And there she was. Oh there she *was!*

She was curled up under the bench near the wall, and did not look good. Her fur was matted, greasy-looking, and her eyes were narrowed and dull.

"Precious," Catherine cried, hurrying towards her. "My darling, you had me so worried, you naughty girl! They're setting out *poison,* of all things. You naughty, naughty girl, to worry me so," and she bent down and scooped the cat up in her ample arms.

Precious lay in them, practically lifeless. And then, with a furious hiss, she leaped at Catherine Wadsworth's face and sank her teeth into her throat.

Catherine lurched backwards. Precious hung from the sagging flesh of her neck, then fell with a yowl and ran to the end of the patio. She turned and looked at Catherine, baring her fangs, then ran off.

Catherine clutched at her neck with both hands. She had felt the pain of the bite, but now felt nothing; nothing but hot sticky blood on the skin of her palm.

191

"Precious," she gasped. Her mind swimming, she made her way back through the door. The kitchen was dark, too dark, and the blood as she stared at her palm looked almost black.

My God, she thought, Oh God, and she quickly went to the sink and ran hot water. She splashed the water on the wound and cleaned it thoroughly with soap, then pressed a wad of paper towels to her neck.

Dr. Nelson, she thought. He'll know what to do, he'll be able to help. If they don't have the right vaccine around here, they *must* have it somewhere. I'll go there, wherever it is.

She paged through the book for the number. In order to dial, she had to let go of her neck, and she felt the blood starting to flow again. Two-three-four-six, *there*. She pressed the towels to the wound again as the phone line clicked.

And the busy signal began.

TWENTY-EIGHT

Amelia Rose removed the thermometer, read it, looked up and said, "It's normal."

Sharon Jensen exhaled. "I don't understand it," she said. "I mean how could it drop? I could just have a regular virus?"

"It's possible," Amelia said.

And what more could she say? That Gary Simmons, as sick as he was, had suddenly woken up one morning demanding that he be sent home? His fever was gone, he was perfectly lucid, and all of his strength had returned. He'd fumed at her and the rest of the staff and chewed his doctor out, but they'd made him stay. And late that night he could hardly breathe, and two days later he was dead.

Sharon sat by the window that filled the east wall of the room. Outside was a lawn with a circular bed of petunias and marigolds; past that stood a thick stand of spruce. She felt fine today. A bit tired, perhaps, but her sore throat was gone. "How long will I have to be symptom-free before they'll let me go?" she said.

Amelia Rose shrugged her thin shoulders. "You'll have to ask Dr. Finch," she said. "A week, perhaps."

"Oh," Sharon said, and thought: If I get out of this, it

will all be different, I'll live an entirely different life. She had saved up enough to get by for a couple of years without working, and that's what she'd do. She would go back to school or travel or just hang around, who knew, but she wouldn't continue to spin her wheels at the state health lab. She'd eat better, put on some weight, frost her hair, and use makeup again. Study Buddhism, maybe. Or hypnotism. She'd always been interested in that. *If* she got out of this—a very big if.

"Do they all die?" she asked.

"The ones who develop symptoms?"

"Yes."

"We've had so few cases so far," Amelia hedged. "We have two on life support who seem to be holding their own, and another who's shown some signs of improvement without any special treatment. He's had the vaccine, of course."

"Teddy Marsh," Sharon said.

"I can't give out names, it's against the rules."

"I know, but that's who it is. I visit him every day. Yesterday he just looked at me and didn't even talk."

Amelia nodded.

"Such a cute kid," Sharon said, looking out at the flowers again. I *will* get out of this, she told herself. And maybe I will have kids someday, a boy just like Teddy Marsh, and—

A noise at the door made her turn; and there, of all people, was Teddy himself. She laughed. "We were just—"

The expression on Teddy's face cut her off. His eyes went wide, he bared his teeth, and from somewhere deep in his throat came a noise like a growl.

"Teddy?"

Looking suddenly frightened, Amelia Rose stood, saying, "Teddy, you're not allowed in the hall, you'll have to go back—"

194

Teddy turned and took off.

Amelia Rose ran to the doorway, followed by Sharon. An aide rounded the corner, pushing a cart, and Teddy plowed into her, roaring. The cart went down, and so did the aide, an older woman with gray hair in tight tiny curls. She screamed in terror as Teddy attacked her, biting her fiercely and tearing away at her clothes.

Amelia screamed, "Teddy!" and ran down the hall, Sharon right on her heels. "Sharon, no, please, don't, this isn't your concern," Amelia said, but Sharon did not go back. A nurse at the station around the corner came out from the counter, then hurried behind it again when she saw Teddy coming. He ran on by, eyes glazed, his lips retracted and covered with thick white foam. "Seconal," Amelia said as she passed the station. "Page Dr. Finch and security."

Teddy ran through a set of doors and into another wing. In a flash he ducked into a room, and a woman's loud screams filled the air. He was biting her shoulder viciously when Amelia and Sharon arrived. The woman flailed wildly, screaming her lungs out. Her sheet flew across the room.

"Teddy! Stop!" Sharon cried.

But he seemed not to hear. He had fastened himself to the woman now with both arms and was biting her neck.

"Teddy!"

"No!" cried Amelia, "keep back!" She pushed past Sharon and rushed to the tray that sat by the woman's bed; grabbed the pitcher of water that sat on the tray and poured it on Teddy's back.

Teddy screamed as if he were burning. He rolled off the woman and onto the floor, both his hands digging into his neck. His eyes bulged out, froth flew from his lips, and a series of hoarse hacking sounds issued forth

195

from his throat. His trunk spasmed and twitched as the woman ran out of the room in hysterics, sobbing and choking. He rolled to the window, gagging and jerking, and suddenly Dr. Finch was there with two security guards, and they had Teddy's arms and legs and gave him the shot.

His teeth chattered; his skull made a cracking noise on the tile floor; he went limp. Dr. Finch looked up at Amelia. "How the hell did this happen?" he said. "Who let him out?"

"I don't know," she said.

"Who undid his restraints?"

"I don't think he was in restraints."

"What?"

"He was passive, he never showed any signs—"

"They should all be restrained," Finch said, his teeth on edge. "Or heavily tranquilized, do you understand that?"

"Yes," Amelia Rose said.

"Even me?" Sharon said.

Dr. Finch looked at Sharon. "My God, what are you doing here?"

"I was trying to help. Should I be restrained, too? Or tranquilized?"

Finch sighed. "Please go back to your room," he said.

In his sleep, Teddy twitched. His mouth, covered with slobber, jerked to the side. Two orderlies entered the room with a stretcher.

They set it down on the floor beside Teddy and Dr. Finch said, "Stay away from his head."

"Let's go," Amelia said to Sharon; and Sharon was staring at Teddy and shaking her head as she backed away toward the door. She frowned at Amelia and said, "But I don't understand."

In the hallway, the patient that Teddy had bitten was

196

crouched on the floor, her arms over her face, and three nurses were trying to budge her. "Mrs. Dorn, it's okay now," one said. "Mrs. Dorn," said another, "please, we have to clean your arm."

Sharon started to shake. "I don't get it," she said as she walked down the hall, her voice thin in her head, "this disease makes *people* violent? The way regular rabies makes animals violent? You mean," and she looked at Amelia, "you mean *people* spread the disease? By *biting*?"

Amelia Rose didn't reply as she walked; just continued to stare straight ahead.

"Amelia? Is that how it works?"

"I don't know," said Amelia. "I really don't know how it works."

"But the others, were they violent, too?"

"I can't tell you," Amelia said softly, biting her lip. "You'll have to ask Dr. Finch."

TWENTY-NINE

Dear Mom,

You can't even get a phone line their always busy, so I thought I'd write and tell you how it is here. Well its okay here, its not like being in my own room of coarse, but I have my walkman and tapes, but, I sure do miss you're cooking. The food here is barf, like macaroni that all sticks together, we did get blueberrie pie once but it was not like you'res! You're crust is so good, this must of been made with motor oil! Hows Mr. T? Its good we don't live here in Blue Harbor, he'd be in the pound. Its awful. I go there sometimes and look at all the poor cats and dogs a lot of them all ready died. Theres this big hole they put them in. I don't like it here and hope this is over soon but I don't know. Maybe I should of went to collage, like you wanted me to, I don't know, but I probaly won't be here to long, and then I can think about stuff like that, like maybe I should take forestary at Orono, I've always liked trees, but i'm not so sure about that anymore, either.

Anyway, say hi to Mr. Terreir for me and don't work to hard.

love, xxx

you're son

Eddie Mason

"What the hell's that?"

Under his army blanket, Eddie stiffened. He was one of forty men in the tent, in one of the twenty cots that lined each wall. "I don't hear anything,' he said.

Pete Richert whispered hoarsely, "Sack out, will you, Morrison? There's nothin' there."

Bulkhead, in the cot between the two, croaked softly, "The hell there ain't. Listen up."

Dead quiet, except for a couple of crickets out in the field.

Then Eddie *did* hear something: a tiny scratching sound. His shoulders tensed.

"You hear it now?" Bulkhead whispered.

"Yeah," Eddie said.

Scritch-scritch, somewhere down near the floor. "You hear it, Richert?"

Now Pete Richert was stiff in his cot. "I hear it," he said, and he whapped the side of the tent with the back of his hand. A guy down the line said, "Knock it off, asshole!"

"Yeah, yeah," Richert said.

They were silent again; the sound was gone.

"You musta scared it off, whatever it was," Bulkhead said.

"Yeah," Richert said. He made both his hands into fists, then let them go limp.

199

"What was it, you think?" Bulkhead said. "A bat?"

"Geez, Bulkhead, will you shut up?" Eddie said.

"No, I mean it. A lady got bit by a bat and got rabies, you know. That couldn't a been the only one. And we gotta sleep in these goddamn tents in a goddamn field like this, all kindsa things could come through here. Skunks, foxes . . ."

"No fox is gonna come anywhere close to here," Richert said.

"You never know," Bulkhead said. "Once they get rabies, they ain't the same, it takes away all their fear. All they want is to bite things, kill things, and they don't give a shit what it is, they ain't scared."

"Okay, okay," Richert said. "Will you go to sleep now?" He rolled over, clutching his blanket.

Eddie lay on his back, wide-awake now, and stared at the roof of the tent, its black canvas expanse. A guy across the way was snoring like mad. Eddie wished he was home in his mother's trailer, back in his own bed again. He wished he had never signed up for the Guard, but who the hell knew this would happen? All he could get was dumb-ass jobs pumping gas, the Guard was something steady at least, and he'd thought it might break the monotony, too: there were summer maneuvers, and maybe they'd get called up to put out a forest fire or break up a strike somewhere. But geez, this rabies stuff . . . There were animals all the hell over the place: bats, cats, dogs, foxes, skunks . . . They said squirrels and rats and mice didn't get the disease, but who knew for sure? They always said stuff like that so you wouldn't get scared.

He wriggled his shoulders and closed his eyes and told himself to relax.

And geez, there it was again!

He rose up on his elbows, eyes wide. "Hey, Bulk-head!" he whispered.

"Yeah?"

"I can hear it again."

The crickets outside; and again, the scratching.

"Yeah," Bulkhead said. "Me, too."

Pete Richert sat up. "God *damn* it," he said. And again he whapped the tent.

"Hey!" somebody yelled. "Knock it off!"

"There's a goddamn bat or somethin' in here," Richert said.

"Go the fuck to sleep."

They were quiet again. Eddie's heart thumped hard in his ears. Sweat poured over his temples and down his jaw and trickled onto his neck.

Then Bulkhead began to giggle, softly. And then he was sniffling and shaking his cot.

"What the hell's the big joke?" Richert said.

Bulkhead rolled in his cot. "You wimps," he said. "You friggin' wimps. Were you ready to piss yourselves or not? Tell the truth. Huh?"

"You lousy creep," Richert said. "You scumbag. They oughta call you Dickhead, not Bulkhead."

"One more time and you guys'd be screamin'," Bulkhead said. He scratched the wall of the tent again and said, "A bat! Roll out the howitzers, men."

"Some joke," Eddie said. His heart was still racing; then suddenly slowed, and his face felt suddenly cool.

"Dickhead," Richert muttered, yanking his blanket up, smacking his fist in his pillow and lying down.

It was silent again, except for the crickets and Bulkhead's occasional giggle.

"Shut up!" Richert whispered.

Bulkhead quieted down. Then an owl started up in the woods past the field. Eddie lay on his back with his blanket pulled up to his chin. It had been a good summer for weather so far; warm days, cool nights, and not much rain or fog. The rain and fog were bound to

201

come, Eddie thought, probably now, while he lived in this tent. He hoped they'd get this job over with soon so he could go home. Would there still be summer maneuvers after this? He didn't know.

"Hey, listen," Bulkhead suddenly whispered.

"I'll friggin' kill you," Richert said.

"No, I mean it this time."

"You asshole."

"No, *listen.*"

The sound was different this time: both softer and sharper.

"I hear it," Richert said. "What do you want me to do, shoot your friggin' hand off?"

"It ain't me doin' it, Richert, swear to God."

"You asshole."

A silence. Then the sound started up again.

"Bulkhead, I will—"

"Aagh! Aagh!" Bulkhead suddenly shouted and shot up out of his cot. A yowl, a flailing of arms in the dark and a dark streak of fur jumping onto the dirt. Something scooted across the floor.

"Jesus Christ!" Bulkhead cried. "Jesus Christ!"

"Shut up!" someone shouted. In cots down the line, people stirred.

"What was it?" Eddie said, sitting up, his arms stiff and his heart banging hard.

"A cat," Bulkhead said. "A friggin' cat."

"Did it bite you?"

A pause. Eddie's breathing was loud.

Bulkhead's hands clutched his chest, then his neck, then he let himself go. "No," he said.

"An' you call *us* wimps," Richert said.

"Oh yeah?" Bulkhead said. "Somethin' jumps on your throat in the dark? It could have the goddamn rabies, how do you know? You don't. Friggin' animals all around us, sick, Jesus Christ."

Four cots away, Jimmy Hibbert said, "What's goin' on?"

"Aah, Dickhead got scared by a cat," Richert said.

"A cat?" Hibbert said. "Who let a cat in here?"

"It let itself in," Bulkhead said. *"Anything* can get in here, Jesus Christ."

"So what do you want to do?" Richert said. "Go home to your mommy?"

"Aah shut your mouth," Bulkhead said.

"Yeah, shut your mouth," someone said down the line.

They lay down again. Eddie stared at the roof of the tent. The owl started up in the trees again. Bats, foxes, who knew what was waiting out there?

Eddie wished he was home in the trailer again: with its red wooden tulips stuck into the lawn, its wishing well, and on top of T's doghouse, Sylvester and Tweety with legs that spun fast in the wind. He wished he was back there with Mr. T. With his Mommy, safe in his very own bed. He really did.

THIRTY

Mike Hachett was really ripped. Cindy had asked him not to go in for three days in a row now. Goddamn it, he wasn't that sick! Always trying to boss him around like that. It made him so mad he had wanted to choke her this morning. The feeling had welled up all through him, his hands had been shaking, he'd broken out into a thick drenching sweat and felt dizzy, and when she said, "Mike? Mike? What's wrong with you?" it had sounded far off, like her voice was in cotton somewhere, in another room, and her face didn't look just right as she stared at him hard with a frown and frightened eyes. Then the feeling had drained away and he'd felt all limp, and the ache at the base of his neck had come on, and the sharp tight pains in his chest, and he'd turned from her, gasping for breath, and had gone to the den and stayed there, resting, till the worst of the feeling passed. "I'm calling the doctor," Cindy had said, and he'd shouted, "Like hell you are!" and had shot straight up from the couch with his hands in fists. And she'd left the den in a hurry and gone upstairs.

And now as he sat at his desk by the showroom window, the sun beating down through the high glass wall with the gray plastic film doing nothing to stem the heat, he couldn't remember driving here. He had done it, he had to have done it, but couldn't remember. The time between Cindy leaving the den and his walking through the showroom door was a blank, simply didn't exist. And the customer across from him, the pudgy man with the fringe of red hair (What the hell was his name? he had known it a moment ago, the guy had just said it), was smeary and bloated, as if he were under water, and Mike Hatchett hated his guts.

"That's the price with the sunroof, right?" the man said as he arched his thick brows.

It was? Mike just couldn't remember. He didn't think so, and said, "That's the price without it."

"You said *with* the sunroof," the pudgy man said.

Sweat poured over Mike's forehead. The base of his skull pounded hard and knives stabbed at his ears, which were humming a high silver tune.

"Sunroof and radio, that's what you told me."

Mike didn't remember. He just knew he hated this man: his fuzzy hair, his shiny scalp, the ring of fat at his neck. A tightness seized his chest and spread into his throat. "All right," he said in a strangled voice. "It's a deal."

The man sucked at his teeth. "And you said air-conditioning, too."

Mike narrowed his eyes; at their edges he saw yellow rings. He had not said that. He knew he had not said that. "No," he said.

The fat man's eyes widened. "Oh?" he said. "Then I think Curtis Ford beats your deal."

The rings in Mike Hachett's eyes grew darker; coppery, then brown. The fat man sat at the end of a tunnel, a hot brown tunnel lined with blood. The humming grew loud in Mike's ears, seemed about to explode. The fat man was talking, but Mike couldn't hear him; he could just about see the thick lips moving slowly, like snails.

In a flash, he was up from his seat and around the table and choking the fat man's neck. The man staggered backwards, knocking his chair down. "You bastard!" Mike said. "You son of a bitch, I give you a good goddamn deal and you have the nerve—!"

The man, still in Mike's grasp, was against the window. His head banged the plate glass hard as Mike shook him and choked him. His face turned purple. Then somebody had an elbow around Mike's neck and Mike bit him. Whoever it was fell back screaming. The fat man's head hit the window again, again, again, again, till the glass gave way with a frightening crack, then somebody had Mike's legs and they brought him down. And they had him then as he thrashed and raved in the hot brown rage in his brain.

"I'm covering this for the AP, okay? Associated Press?"

The guardsman, officious with helmet and rifle, did not respond.

"You want to see my card, I guess," said Oliver Emmet, smacking his gum, letting go of the steering wheel. He reached in his pocket and brought out his wallet, flipped it open, held it out. "Okay?"

The guardsman, tall, with serious eyes, barely glanced at the plastic card. "I have orders," he said. "No one comes through."

Shrugging and putting his wallet away, Emmet said, "Hey, you have your job, I have mine. My job is to write this story. I was here two days ago and talked to Colonel Tower, the guy at the lab, the hospital guys. And now I'm not allowed in town?"

"No sir," the guardsman said. "Unless you get clearance from headquarters, sir. And sir, if you do get

206

in, you won't get out again."

"What?"

"That's right, sir. Once people come in, they stay in."

"What is this, Hitler's Germany?"

"I'm sorry, sir. You better call headquarters, sir."

There were guardsmen all over the place. On the side of the road leading out of Blue Harbor, a dozen cars, most of them loaded with stuff on roof racks, were stopped behind the barricade. In his rearview mirror, Emmet saw two cars behind him on the causeway.

"The order went out half an hour ago," the guardsman said. "It will be on the TV and radio soon, then people will know not to try. And we'll put up the signs."

"I don't believe this," Emmet said. "They won't get away with this."

"If you'll pull right up to the barricade, sir, you can turn around."

In his room at the Starbuck Motel, Emmet called Colonel Tower. The line was busy. He smoked a cigarette and tried again, and then again. No luck.

Sealing the town off. Why? Was the stuff that contagious? Rabies? An animal had to bite you, so why keep *people* from leaving the town? Restrict their pets, okay, but the people themselves?

Outrageous, he thought as he smoked—and precisely what people wanted to read. A juicy dose of outrage, terror, shock, along with a cigarette and coffee—what better way to start off the day, to get the old bloodstream flowing? This was fabulous, great, and he had to get the story first, before that turkey Renshaw or some other clown.

He tried Tower again, still without any luck, then dialed another number. It took five attempts, but the

207

phone finally rang.

"Department of Health."

"This is Oliver Emmet, Associated Press. I'd like to speak to Dr. Gilbert, please."

"One moment, please."

Another ring, then: "This is Frank Gilbert."

"Hi, Oliver Emmet, Associated Press. We've spoken before, about the Blue Harbor rabies outbreak."

A pause, "Oh, yes."

"Apparently the town's been quarantined. Do you know why?"

Another pause. "I have no idea why. I just found out about it myself. My secretary heard it on the radio."

"Well, where did the order come from, then?"

"From whoever's in charge of the National Guard."

"The governor?"

"I guess so, yes."

"Well, why would he do that?"

"I really don't know."

"Can people spread the disease? Is it that contagious?"

"People *can* spread it," Gilbert said, "but they usually don't, because they don't bite other people. Rabies doesn't enrage them. If their saliva should get into somebody else's cut or open sore, however, that person would be at risk. One of our workers caught rabies this way—we think—and she was wearing gloves. She caught it from an animal, not a person, but my point is, this stuff is potent. Still, I don't see why they'd quarantine the town, unless . . ."

"Unless what?"

"Nothing," Gilbert said. "I just had a crazy thought, that's all."

Emmet flipped to the back of his notebook. "Your worker who caught it, that would be Sharon Jensen, right?"

208

"I'm afraid I can't give out names."

"Okay," Emmet said, "but whoever it was, they got it from touching saliva."

"More likely blood, in this case. From dissecting a rabid dog."

"This person is hospitalized, right?"

"Right."

"How's she doing?"

"Quite well, the last I heard."

"That's good, real good," Emmet said. "Well, thanks for your help."

He hung up and called the hospital. It took half an hour, but he finally got through. He introduced himself, then said: "Blue Harbor was recently quarantined. They won't let anyone in or out. Do you have any idea why?"

"I certainly do," Sharon Jensen said.

By the time he hung up, Emmet's notebook was nearly full.

THIRTY-ONE

It took Sandra Barnes two hours to get through to Washington. By the time Howard got on the line, she was frantic.

"There has to be *some* way to get us out of here. Ed Lynch?"

"I'll try him, Sandra. Dick Miller, too. I think he knows Laycock."

"I'm just about out of my mind," Sandra said. "The whole town is." Eyes shut, jaw clenched, she said, "Why didn't we all leave together, damn it. I knew we should have, that day down at Roaring Spout . . ."

"You couldn't have known they'd do this."

"No, but somehow I knew things were going to get really bad, I just did. And they're worse than I ever guessed, or else why are they keeping us here?"

"I don't know," Howard said, "but I'll damn well find out, you can count on that. This is absolute madness."

"I still can't believe it," Sandra said. "This isn't Russia or China for God's sake."

"First, let me find out where the order came from. We'll file an injunction."

"Howard, God—"

"Are the kids okay?"

"Not really, I guess."

"Put them on."

She called them both in from the living room. Lucy took the phone first. "Hi, Daddy."

"Hi, Lulu, how are you?"

"Okay. Are you coming back soon?"

"Just as soon as I can, honey."

"Daddy?"

"Yes?"

"Tricia died."

Sandra's throat seized up and a burning sensation spread through the back of her nose.

"I know, honey," Howard said. "And I know you're sad."

"I am," Lucy said.

"Have you done any swimming?"

"A little."

"That's good, keep it up. I love you, Lu. Let me talk to your brother now."

Lucy handed the phone to Matty, whose conversation was brief, consisting, at his end, of three "Uh-huhs." Sandra took the receiver again, and Matty ran out of the room with Lucy pursuing.

"Is she very upset?" Howard asked.

"It's been a hard time."

"Nightmares?"

"You bet."

"You think they need to see someone? A therapist?"

"I don't know yet."

"How's Rachel?"

"She was awful the last time I saw her. They have her on Ativan, a pretty large dose."

"And Fred?"

"He's held up pretty well—on the surface, at least."

"What a horrible thing."

211

A shout from the living room: Matty. "Calm down in there," Sandra hollered, then said, "I don't think you ever get over a thing like that, not really. Poor Dorothy Shore . . . Miranda was twenty, and oh my God . . ."

"That goddamn kid, if she hadn't—Well, damn it, she did, and what's done is done. Look, I'll find out about this quarantine and get back to you."

"Soon. Please."

"As soon as I can. And listen."

"Yes?"

"That pistol that's in my bureau?"

"Yes?"

"You know how to load it, right?"

"I still remember."

"The bullets are in the box on top of the bookcase. You see any strange-acting animals, shoot."

"I don't know if I can."

"You can. You must."

"All right."

"You take care of yourself."

"I love you, Howard."

"I love you, too. Just try to stay calm now."

"I will."

When she hung up she sat at the dining room table, her head in her hands.

The days since Tricia's death had been dreadful. The Stemmers had had a funeral, and she had gone, leaving the kids with a neighbor, Jane Carter. Unable to eat that evening, she made the kids hot dogs and beans, and Lucy had taken one spoonful of beans and then asked: "Is it nice in heaven? Are there toys up there?" "It's lovely there, sweetheart. Sure there are toys," Sandra said, and Lucy ate half of her hot dog. They got into bed together, the king-size bed, Sandra read them *Miss Rumphius,* and they both fell asleep at her side. Then at three in the morning Lucy had woken up screaming, "He's trying to get me! I'm scared!" and Matty woke up and the both of them cried and cried, and Sandra said, "No, no, nobody's coming, we're all just fine," and at last they settled down again as Sandra, her heart like a stone in her chest, caressed them and spoke to them softly of flowers and birds.

In the living room Matty was shouting and Lucy was answering back. They'd been hyper for days, and she just didn't have the strength to be after them all the time. Maybe they needed to shout and be hyper at this point, who knew. She'd gone to the beach with them yesterday, to help them let off steam, but the whole time there she'd felt shaky, uneasy, and kept looking back at the bushes and trees, as if death were lurking there in those shadows, just waiting, waiting.

She closed her eyes and saw Tricia Stemmer lying in white in her casket. No, she thought. Inconceivable. No.

She took a deep breath; let it out. Please call, she thought. Please call me, Howard. Soon.

THIRTY-TWO

HUMAN BITE SPREADS RABIES, CDC ADMITS MAINE TOWN IS QUARANTINED

by Oliver Emmet

BLUE HARBOR, MAINE (AP)—The Maine resort town of Blue Harbor was placed under strict quarantine by Governor Clinton Laycock yesterday once it was learned that the rabies strain which has already claimed a half dozen lives here is spread by human contact.

James Peyton, an official at the Centers for Disease Control in Atlanta, Georgia, admitted yesterday that the new form of rabies is transmitted by the bite of human beings. "While this had been suspected," he said, "it was only recently confirmed. Rabies enrages certain animals, making them bite and thus assuring its perpetuation. We have never before seen it have this effect on humans. This is a first—and, I may add, an extremely disturbing first."

The quarantine was placed in effect shortly after Michael Hachett, a local auto dealer who contracted rabies from a former employee who subsequently died, allegedly attacked a customer, biting him and two coworkers before he could be subdued. Those attacked were given emergency treatment consisting of ultrasonic cleansing and disinfecting of the bites and were confined to the rabies wing of Blue Harbor Hospital, which now contains twenty-eight patients. "If bites are given immediate attention," Peyton said, "there is an excellent chance the disease will never develop."

Oliver Emmet looked up from the paper that lay on his naked thighs, exhaled a stream of smoke, and said, "We'll see about that one, Jimmy."

The woman beside him in the bed, her voice groggy and sluggish, said, "What?"

"Just talking to myself," Emmet answered, running his hand through his long white hair and taking another drag. It was almost eleven o'clock, and his stomach growled. He looked at it, frowning. In spite of his running, he still had a gut. Shit, you can't outrun time, he thought.

He smoked again and thought about Sharon Jensen, who'd cleaned and disinfected her thumb but got sick anyway. She was two years younger than he was, thirty-three, and yesterday, when he talked to her, she hadn't sounded good. She denied that anything was wrong and said she was just under observation, but later admitted she felt just a little bit tired. Sore throat? he had asked. No. Fever? No. But Emmet, his shit-detector sharpened by sixteen years of dealing with politicians, hadn't believed her.

"She's got it," he said.

215

"What?"

"She has got the friggin' disease," he said, and smoked, and thought: What the hell is this woman's name? Candy? Cookie? He couldn't remember. Taffy? Something to eat, he was sure.

He had picked her up in a bar in Rockhurst last night after filing the story. "You actually interviewed Elvis?" she'd said, her eyes shining. "You bet," he'd said, "and John Lennon, too." "Oh my God," she'd said, and had come on super strong after that, as they nearly all did when he gave them that line.

She'd been waiting on tables in Spats in Blue Harbor, and now what the hell was she going to do? she complained, they wouldn't let her in town anymore, she'd be lucky to make half those tips here in Rockhurst, the people were so damn cheap. The Blue Harbor people, the summer pukes, you wouldn't believe how rich they were with their yachts and all, and some of the year-rounders, rich as shit too, if they liked you, they'd pile it on. She always made sure they got extra dessert, those chocolate-covered ice cream bonbons? They fell for it every time, and now what? she said draining her glass. And they went to his room, and she hadn't been bad at all.

He looked at her now with her hair sticking up and her makeup gone and thought: Kitty? Nah, you can't eat a kitty. At least I can't. She rolled over, away from him, groaning. He smoked, then read his own words again:

In an effort to contain the virus, Blue Harbor has been sealed off. No one is allowed to enter or leave. Armed National Guardsmen man a roadblock on Route 6, the town's only access road, and other guardsmen patrol an electrified barbed

216

wire fence that stretches across the island's north shore. All boating and fishing, including commercial fishing and lobstering, has been suspended, and the Coast Guard is patrolling Blue Harbor's waters to assure that no one tries to leave the town by boat.

All foxes, skunks, coyotes, and other susceptible animals are being exterminated by the National Guard, and all cats and dogs are being impounded till the crisis subsides. When questioned about this policy, Lieutenant Colonel Michael Tower, Guard commander, said: "The problem is, standard rabies vaccines don't work on this new variety. That means all pets are vulnerable, cats especially so, as they come and go as they please and can easily contact an animal that's infected. We ask all owners of dogs and cats to bring their pets to the pound at National Guard headquarters at Harper's fields on the north end of town. Those who do not comply will have their pets forcibly removed.

"These measures may seem drastic, but we are faced with a dangerous situation which must not get out of hand," Tower added. "The disease is currently well contained, and these measures will assure that it remains so, and will give us the best chance to eradicate it before it can spread any further."

Emmet laughed to himself. Yeah, tell me another one, Mike. Well contained. And who says it hasn't already spread out of the town? Who says that people who worked in the town and now aren't allowed back in don't already have it? Who says that bats haven't left Blue Harbor chock-full of the goddamn stuff and are

217

flying from here to Miami?

He thought about Sharon Jensen again. He would call her again today and see how she was. If she wasn't so great, it might be time for the story on how standard treatments don't work. How *nothing* works. Wouldn't that send a nice bolt of fear through old mother and dad in the breakfast nook? Give them heartburn till noon, and newspaper sales would soar.

The woman beside him stirred again. Not much in the brains department, but so? The receptacle of desire was basically the same, regardless of the contents of the skull.

She turned and looked at him, smiling, and uttered a soft "Mmm," and started to rub his leg. His stomach rumbled again, but it could wait.

Cherry, he thought as he stubbed out his cigarette in the ashtray and fondled her rump. That's her name, Cherry White.

Tough job, this reporting, he thought with a laugh as she threw her thigh over his hip, but somebody's gotta do it.

Others might have been surprised, but Merrill Lodge was not. He'd seen it coming years ago, and he was prepared.

Merrill had sold his dairy farm precisely because of this—because of them. They'd changed the rules so honest men just couldn't make a living anymore. You'd work your fingers to the bone eight days a week and still couldn't make ends meet, you had to depend on subsidies from *them*.

The Jews.

Oh, that's who it was, all right. He had read about it for years. They controlled the banks all over the world;

they controlled the Federal Reserve. And whenever they wanted, they'd put on the heat, and make the white men sweat. Make the God-fearing Christian white men sweat to death.

And their doctors would kill you, too. Like with Hilda. She'd never of died if it wasn't for them. They talked her into going to their hospital, then killed her. And then when his headaches started, they tried to get him to go there, too, in order to mess up his mind with X-rays and turn him into a slave.

But he was too smart for that. He'd read the books. About what they controlled and how they controlled it, all over the world. About how they infested each part of the country, no matter how white and pure it was, and spread their evil ways.

He'd tried to tell people. They just wouldn't listen. He never dealt with Midcoast Furniture, owned by the Weinbergs, but plenty of others did, other people who should've known better: God-fearing Christian people who strengthened the anti-Christ. They thought that Merrill's ideas were peculiar, and now they were paying the price.

Years ago, when he was a boy, they wouldn't have thought him peculiar. Years ago, they didn't let Jews in this town. The big hotels had signs in their windows: No Jews. Just like that. And God help the kikes who tried to pretend they were white.

Merrill spit out the hayloft's window. The gob hit the dirt by the open barn doors below him and sent up a short puff of dust. He looked at the rifle's blue steel barrel, then back at his house over there, at the peeling white paint on the eaves. You fixed it up, repainted, and they'd raise your assessment. It was part of the plot. They took and took, till the Christians were slaves and the devil ruled over all.

219

It was hot in the hayloft, damn hot. He wiped his forehead again with his red bandana, adjusted his wire-rimmed glasses. The back of his head hurt wicked now. The headaches had left him alone for a while, but now they were worse than ever. It was hard to think straight when your head hurt like that. The Jews had got into his well again, in the night, he was sure of it; had loaded it up again. No sense having it tested, for who did the tests?

They had been in the Jillson Lab from the very start. They had come from all over, New York, Philadelphia, the cities they'd had in their grip for years and years, and the Jillson Lab was their foothold in Maine. One of the people behind all this was Kessler, a Jew for sure. So quietly they had come to this town, so smoothly. He'd written the paper about it a few years back, but they hadn't printed his letter. No wonder. That Renshaw was almost a kike himself, he'd gone to NYU.

Well now all the nonbelievers were paying the price, the whole town was paying the price. Like it said in the books, the worst had happened: they ran the army now.

But he still had his gun. They'd tried for years to take them away, but so far the NRA had been able to stop them. And those who still had their guns would go down fighting. At least he would.

He leaned against the bales of hay and wiped his forehead again. The smell of the hay was strong in the heat, and it made him sad. He missed his cows; he really did. He was sixty-eight and probably would've had to quit soon anyway, but that wasn't the point. A hard-working man like him should not be forced out of his work. They couldn't be allowed to have their way again and again and again. To destroy this country and all

220

that it stood for.

The pain in the back of his neck jabbed his eyes. Yes, this was the time for his stand. They had taken his cows and his wife, but would not take Chief. The others could scream and fuss, but that wasn't his way. His way was to fight. He'd done plenty of it on Guadalcanal, back when he was no more than a kid, and he still knew how. Chief would never go into that pound. If he did, he would suffer and die, just like Hilda had died in the hospital. He was twelve years old, and you didn't do things like that to a dog his age.

Last night, Roscoe Farnum had called up and told him they'd taken his Katy. They got all the names of the dogs from the town. It was harder to track down the cats since they weren't licensed, but the Jews, with their army, had threatened the animal doctors and got them to give up their records. Roscoe was crying, since Katy was all he had. Both his boys had been killed in Vietnam, and his wife had died nine years ago, and he'd got Katy right after that and she'd kept him alive.

Roscoe had tried to talk to the National Guard, but they wouldn't listen. The Jews didn't care. All they wanted was money and power. That and the end of the Aryan race, of course.

He looked at the gleam on the rifle's barrel. This rifle had killed a deer every fall for thirty-six years, till he'd stopped hunting four years ago because of his eyes. Mike Porter had killed Dick Boles, swore to God he looked just like a buck, and he hadn't even been drinking, his eyes were just gone. And Merrill knew enough to take the hint.

But from here he could see clear enough. It wasn't very far to his kitchen door from here, probably less than a hundred feet, and today, with the sun as high and bright as it was, he could see real good. He cradled the gun in his arms. Good gun. He'd always kept it clean. And no one would ever take it away from him, ever.

He sat there, leaning against the bales and thinking about his cows, flies buzzing around the window frame, the heat pouring down on the hay, and he drifted off.

It was voices that woke him. He sat up quickly, adjusting his glasses, and sure enough, there they were.

The one was short and wiry and dark, and was almost surely a kike. The other one was tall and blond. Well, that didn't mean a damn. They both had rifles over their shoulders, short little things, looked like toys. They had battle fatigues but no helmets. They stood by the doors of the van they had come in, then strode up the walk to his house.

They knocked on the weatherworn kitchen door, and behind it Chief started to bark. Merrill's hands raised the rifle, the pain in the back of his head so intense now he trembled all over. His target, the kike, weaved into, then out of the sight. He steadied the gun on the window frame. His breath was hot on his thumb as he fingered the trigger.

Chief barked. Poor Chief, he thought, and what would the end of this be? If he got these two, they'd send more. If he got those, more would come, and at last he'd lose. The time to have stopped all this was years ago, but nobody wanted to listen. Now the town was a concentration camp, that's what it had come to. But if he could take a stand, right here and now, he could wake people up. He was not afraid. Superpatriots had no fear. Nathan Hale, Thomas Paine . . .

The blond one banged on the door again, and Chief barked like mad. Merrill gritted his teeth but he couldn't stop shaking. Salty sweat burned the corners of his mouth. If he let these two go, they would only come back. Or maybe they'd break his door down, was that what they planned to do?

The little dark short one, the kike, was heading around back now. Merrill followed him with the gun. When he got to the edge of the house, his image dissolved, and when Merrill looked up from the barrel, the guy was gone.

Damn these eyes, Merrill said to himself. Damn these hands, damn all of it, he was no damn good anymore. He set down the rifle and took off his glasses and wiped them against his shirt; put them on again. Took the gun up again and aimed at the blond guy, who banged at the door again.

Chief barked, and it hurt Merrill's ears; was electrical jolts of pain. They can't do this, they can't, Merrill said in his mind, and the dark guy came around the side of the house again, and Merrill saw him good this time and fired.

The bullet hit the Jewboy's arm and he spun around with a scream. He fell to the ground, his mouth open wide, and the blond guy yelled, "Corelli!" and Merrill fired again and the bullet missed and shattered the kitchen door. The blond guy ran for the barn, straight towards Merrill, who fired again, but the guy was too quick, he was inside the barn, and Merrill turned, his back to the window, his heart pounding hard in his throat. He glanced over his shoulder and out the window at the sunny dirt of the dooryard.

The Jewboy was gone. He had gotten away somehow. In the house, behind the splintered door, Chief barked and barked and barked.

223

"All right, get down outta there," the blond guy yelled from below. Merrill gripped his gun tightly, sweat thick on his upper lip.

"Did you hear me? Get down outta there."

Dead silence. Then Merrill could hear the guy running again. He looked out the window, but couldn't see him; then did, he was already in the van, behind the wheel, he was already starting his engine. Before Merrill could get him into his sights, he was pulling away.

They were gone. Both gone. Merrill stared out the window.

Ten minutes later he left the loft and crossed the dooryard, hay sticking to his coveralls, the rifle still in his hands. He looked around back. Yes, the Jewboy was gone. They had both escaped. He had failed. And now the blond one would send a whole slew of them in.

He went into the house through the broken door. Chief greeted him, whimpering, tail between his legs. "I failed, Chief," Merrill said. "I'm just too old to take a stand. I thought I had the one and he got away. Maybe I scared 'em off for a bit, but soon they'll be back in force."

Sun streamed through the holes in the broken door and shone on the worn linoleum. The dog licked Merrill's hand and Merrill said, "They'll never take us, Chief. Not us, they won't. We're goin' where they can't get us."

The pain in his head was blinding now and his heart was a roar in his ears. He pointed the gun at his dog, at his eyes, and said, "I love you, Chief," and fired.

And once that was done and the dog lay still, Merrill sat at the table and reached in his pocket and took out another round. It felt heavy and cool in his hand. He was not afraid. He put the round in the chamber, and

224

said a short prayer. "We're goin' to heaven, Chief," he said. "Where the Jews can't get us. Ever."

The barrel was bitter and cold in his mouth. The last thing he saw was the needlepoint cushion that Hilda had done the first year they'd been married, its blood red rose on the seat of the ladderback chair.

THIRTY-THREE

Shooting the skunks and coyotes and foxes and all of the other stuff had been fun, but this, Bulkhead Morrison thought, this setting out poison bait wasn't fun at all. Especially today, in this goddamn fog, when you couldn't see more than a few feet in front of your goddamn face. It was scary the way people came up like ghosts out of nowhere all white like that, and his hand kept going to his gun, he was just so jumpy. Orders were not to shoot in this stuff unless something attacked you, a fox or something, but everybody was jumpy as hell, he'd be lucky not to get wasted. What looked like a fox one minute turned into a guardsman the next, it was goddamn spooky.

The air was clammy and cold, and Bulkhead shivered. Tossing a cake of the bait near the base of a scraggly spruce he said, "I can't wait to get outta these goddamn woods. That Richert's so goddamn lucky."

"You think so," Eddie Mason said. "All the people ticked off at those labs?"

Spitting a noisy bullet of mucus, Bulkhead reached into his sack for another cake. "Better'n this," he said. "Better'n tryin' to take people's dogs. Christ, they shot at another guy yesterday, just missed his head. We

226

oughta just teargas the bastards. They don't wanta give up their goddamn dogs, we teargas 'em."

"Teargas old ladies?" Eddie said.

Bulkhead flung down the bait. "I don't mean old ladies, asshole. Did I say old ladies?"

"Old ladies have dogs," Eddie said.

"Well, that's not what I mean. I mean nuts like that psycho who picked off Corelli." He reached for another cake and said, "Corelli's lucky, too."

"He is?" Eddie said. "You think getting your arm blown apart is lucky?"

"Jesus, you're dumb," Bulkhead said, "sometimes I wonder. He's lucky because they sent him home." He tossed the cake of poisoned bait. "You get hurt like that, you go to the field hospital, then you go home, they don't put you in with the biters." He spit again. "Anyway, the real hospital's full."

"Get out," Eddie said.

"You don't believe it," Bulkhead said, "you ask Captain Taylor. This shit is bad, man, it's spreadin' like crazy, we're gonna be shootin' people soon, you wait and see."

Eddie reached in his sack; it was almost empty. "When we finish with these ones we gotta get more, right?" he said.

"Did you hear Sergeant Bledsoe?"

"Yeah."

Eddie hated this job. All these perfectly healthy animals dying, not only the wild animals, but the cats who liked to roam. He thought about Mr. T, about somebody poisoning Mr. T or trying to take him away.

"I wonder if there's bears in these woods," Bulkhead said.

"Bears," Eddie said, trying to laugh. He looked over his shoulder, at spruce trees fading into gray, gray hanging above his head. They were doing this job in a cloud.

"It's possible," Bulkhead said. "These are pretty big woods."

"This is freakin' Blue Harbor," Eddie said. "The bears left here before World War One, I bet."

"Don't be so sure," Bulkhead said. "I seen a bear at Reid State Park once."

"Come on."

"I did," Bulkhead said. "And there's moose here, for sure."

"A moose won't hurt you."

"Like hell it won't. Them suckers get mad, watch out."

"I'm empty," Eddie said. "What about you?"

"I got a few more."

Bulkhead tossed down the rest of his bait and said, "Let's head back."

"Which way?" Eddie said.

"This way. No, wait a second . . ."

"Oh geez," Eddie said.

Bulkhead snickered. "You think we're lost? All the guys who are out here doin' this, and we're lost?" He shouted, "Hey!"

From far off to their right came an answering, "Hey."

"There you go," Bulkhead said. "Just as easy as that."

They started off, sacks over their shoulders, their feet sinking into the spongy, needle-thick earth. "What I don't want to meet is a bobcat," Bulkhead said. "Them suckers are *mean.*"

"Cut it out," Eddie said.

"I'm just sayin' you never know what you'll run into, that's all," Bulkhead said with a laugh.

They trudged along in the damp and gloom, avoiding the sharp black branches of spruce and pine, not talking, and suddenly Eddie said, "Geez, look at that."

They stopped. Off to their left, just a few feet away, lay a fawn.

"God," Eddie said.

They approached the dead body. Its side had been eaten away.

"Them things don't eat this poison," Bulkhead said.

"They're not supposed to."

"Somebody shot it? Who the hell would do that?"

"It looks like coyotes got it, or maybe foxes."

"Shit."

"Maybe somebody thought it was somethin' else, something dangerous," Eddie said. "A coyote or somethin'."

"Yeah," Bulkhead said. "Hope nobody thinks I'm somethin' dangerous, like one a them crazy vigilantes. They're crazy, them guys. This goddamn fog. We better keep talkin.'"

"What about?"

"About baseball, anything, Jesus, how do I know?"

They moved on again—in silence—and came to a one-lane dirt road. "Here we are," Bulkhead said. He looked up and down both ways into thick gray gloom. "Down here," he said jerking his head.

"You sure?"

Bulkhead hollered again, "Hey!"

No answer this time. "Yeah, I'm sure," he said. "If we're wrong, we'll turn around. At least we're on the friggin' road again."

They walked down the rutted lane through the tunnel of fog, their empty sacks over their shoulders, their boots crunching hollowly on the stones.

"Red Sox pitchin' is lousy this year," Eddie said.

"Huh?" Bulkhead said.

"Red Sox pitchin' is lousy this year."

"Oh, yeah?" Bulkhead said. "I wouldn't know, I don't follow baseball."

"I thought you said we should talk about baseball."

Bulkhead spit. "That was just an example," he said. "Baseball, Jesus."

They walked. Eddie wondered what he was doing here. This assignment had seemed like an easy job at first, but what with the stuff that had happened the last few days, he was really nervous. That head case shooting Corelli, another whole bunch of people sick (The whole hospital full? So soon? Bulkhead couldn't be right about that), all the people pissed off because they were forced to stay here—and worst of all, the vigilantes out here in the woods taking potshots at everything. That was scary, real scary. That poor little fawn.

Eddie's breath made gray puffs in the raw wet air. Setting out bait was boring, but not as boring as unloading food and stuff. A lot of the guys had got stuck doing that, since no trucks were allowed into the town anymore: unloading everything at the causeway, loading it back into army trucks, delivering it to the stores. Real boring, and hard work, too. He was lucky to get this detail.

But this fog made him jumpy. He wondered how guys had been able to stand Vietnam. Those booby traps, where every step you took could mean your death, it must've been awful. This was nothing, a piece of cake. But right now he wished he was out of here and back in the trailer with Mr. T. He hadn't realized how good things had been at home. If only he could have found a job. Well, now he was stuck with the Guard for seven more years, job or not. Seven years was a long time, geez, he'd be old by the time he was through, twenty-six. That was really old.

"I think we're goin' the wrong way," he said.

Bulkhead spit. "Nah, this is right."

"We should of found the cart by now."

"We walked farther into them woods than we thought, that's all."

Eddie stopped. "Hey!" he yelled. His voice disappeared in the mist.

No answer. The two of them stood there, breathing white plumes.

"They probably went back and left us here," Eddie said.

"Nah," Bulkhead said, "they wouldn't do that. Go back without us?" His eyebrows curved into a scowl. "Shit, where is that goddamn cart?"

They looked down the lane at the fog. "Shit," Bulkhead said.

A sound off to their right, like the snap of a twig.

"You hear that?" Eddie said.

They froze; breathed fog.

And the man came crashing out of the brush straight at Eddie, arms raised.

"Hey! Hey!" Eddie cried, falling back, and the man was on him.

Terrified, Eddie kicked out. The man screeched like an animal, clawing the air. He was old, with a thin wild tuft of white hair and thin arms, and as Eddie kicked, he retracted his lips and made a hissing sound.

Bulkhead stood motionless, dark eyes wide. "Help! Help me!" Eddie yelled, and Bulkhead, sucking in breath, drew his gun. Thoughts collided inside his head as he held out his arm and said, "Back off, you son of a bitch! Back off!"

But the man paid no attention, and Bulkhead fired.

The man screamed in pain and jumped backwards, clutching his wrist. Eddie fell to the ground. Then the man charged at Bulkhead, his good hand curved into a claw. "No!" Bulkhead said. "No, don't!" The man's

231

crazed eyes came closer, closer, and Bulkhead fired again.

This time the bullet struck him squarely, flinging him onto the road. He lay doubled up, his thin legs twitching, his head jerking back, then was still.

"Is he dead?" Eddie asked. "You killed him?"

"I—Christ," Bulkhead said, out of breath.

Not taking his eyes off the man, Eddie got to his feet. "Holy God," he said.

"Did he get you?" Bulkhead said. "Did he bite you?"

"No," Eddie said. "I'm okay."

Bulkhead started to shake, and then, to Eddie's great surprise, he made a groaning sound.

Eddie stared at the fallen Skinny Watts, whose blue tongue protruded, its tip smeared with blood, eyes were glassy and blank.

"I didn't mean it," Bulkhead said. "Honest to God, Eddie, honest to God."

"You had to do it," Eddie said.

"Honest to God," Bulkhead said once again, and then doubled up quickly and puked. Vomit splashed on the road's mud and stones. Gasping and moaning, he wiped his wide mouth. His other hand, still holding the pistol, hung limp and pale at his side.

"You couldn't have helped it," Eddie said. "It wasn't your fault."

"Yeah," Bulkhead said, nodding, his words tight and thin. "Yeah, you're right. You'll tell 'em that?"

"Yeah," Eddie said, sick to his heart and touched his neck, where the bite was now starting to sting.

THIRTY-FOUR

In vain have I scourged my flesh with the other penitents, for my wife has perished, my five children have perished, and I have labored to bury them all with my own two hands, as no one remains to do such tasks. The serfs are dying, and fields lie untended. Mothers abandon their feverish children, husbands abandon their wives, no man is a neighbor to any other, no loyalty holds. The streets reek with the stench of death, the river is thick with corpses, the charnel pits overflow. Even the holiest of men fall ill and are dead within days. Lord, why have you forsaken us, your faithful servants?

Alfonzo Passini

Diary of the Plague

Florence, 1347

It took Eddie Mason two weeks to begin to get sick. Not a long space of time, but enough to transform

Blue Harbor.

Except for the guardsmen, the streets were deserted now. For who knew who might have the disease and turn suddenly violent? Who knew when a stray cat or dog, infected, would suddenly turn a corner, eyes wild, fangs dripping with slime, its crazed mind driven to bite and bite again? Who knew when a neighbor might go off the deep end like Merrill Lodge, or, worse, Clay Ferris, an ex-marine survivalist who went on a rampage one night with an AK47, killing six innocent people, two of them children?

In the post office, mail piled up on the floor; there was only one person to sort it and no one to deliver it— except the courier who took it to the Jillson Lab, the hospital, the police. The exclusive shops on Harbor Lane off the center of Main Street were closed, as were most of the other businesses: the clothing stores, the sandwich shops, the Pizza Hut, the Dairy Queen, insurance agencies and beauty shops, the hardware stores. On Main Street, aside from the post office, only Schofield's Drugs, with its window of flasks of pastel water, and the *Blue Harbor Herald* were open. The North End Market, not far from the causeway, did almost all of the grocery business, as it could be easily stocked and protected by the National Guard. It was in this market's parking lot that the Guard gave away the powdered milk and rice and cheese that kept so many alive.

But many would not venture out to the North End Market, and tried to make do with what food was on hand and whatever they grew in their gardens. Some even feared venturing into their gardens, remembering Sadie Copperthwaite, whose next door neighbor, Sara French, had attacked her when she leaned down to get her paper on the last day of paper deliveries; remembering Harry Buchanan, the retired investment

234

banker, who stepped outside to pick some lettuce and found himself face to face with a snarling chow.

All pets had not yet been confiscated, and many now hid in the fields and woods, locked out of their homes by their owners. For who knew where they'd roamed, and what they had come into contact with in those roamings? No vaccine could prevent this dreaded disease, and who could say for sure that Champ, the family's beloved labrador, who had run off last week for an hour or two, might not wake in the night with the hot lust for flesh in his bones? The Guard roamed Blue Harbor around the clock, and all animals on the loose, both domestic and wild, were shot on sight.

A number of people had tried to flee, but all had been quickly caught. The electrified barbed wire fence that spanned the north shore was manned by a permanent Guard detail. At its western terminus it curved into water too broad for all but the best long distance swimmers to attempt; on the east it ended at the cliffs near the Roaring Spout, which fronted another daunting stretch of bay. The three escape attempts by boat had all been easily foiled; lobster boats and pleasure craft were no match for the Coast Guard cutters patrolling the island's waters night and day.

The town had just barely begun to cope with its grief and confusion. The first few dozen dead had been given funerals with eulogies in churches and viewings in the town's lone funeral home, run by Timothy Blair. But that stage had quickly passed, for Timothy Blair would not handle the dead anymore; could not handle the dead, for he wasn't well. That job was left to a National Guard detail in surgical masks and gloves. The burials and occasional hasty memorial services—which were sparsely attended if attended at all—took place in Seaview Cemetery only if the victims already owned plots there. If, like most of the summer visitors, they owned no plots, they were buried in Harper's fields, a half mile west of the Guard encampment. Ezra Ward, a carpenter, and his two sons, Rick and Steve, worked sixteen hours a day making caskets of native pine. Their new-found prosperity, though, was short lived, as Harold Dunn, who ran the only lumber mill, had to cease production. He wasn't feeling just right, and took to his bed.

The Wadsworth mansion, which had sparkled with music and laughter and light at the start of the summer, spent its nights in darkness now. Also dark were the cottages owned by the Hollinses of Fairfax, Virginia, the Groats of Austin, Texas, the Feathergills of Saddle River, New Jersey, and the Larsons of Philadelphia, all of whom were descended from the summer colony's founders and all of whom had contributed mightily to Blue Harbor's welfare, providing initial funds for the library, the art museum, and the hospital in which they now lay burning, aching and delirious.

Blue Harbor Hospital, for rabies victims exclusively now, was staffed by army physicians. Every available bed, including the cots in the hallways, was occupied with patients in various states of distress, many of whom, despite being sedated, were subject to outbursts of rage. All were placed in restraints at the time of admission, adults and children both, for the virus was unpredictable: some victims would be struck with rage just days after being infected, while others would not take the turn until weeks had passed. Some never turned violent at all, but went out passively, writhing in pain as the virus tore at their throats and muscles, making them spasm and shiver and froth at the mouth.

Accident victims or people with illnesses other than rabies were treated at the Blue Harbor elementary school, which was now filled with cots. Its staff was comprised of the town's five doctors, who'd suspended their private practices, and a small group of volunteers, most of them older retired people who'd been through difficult times before and would not be cowed by the current turn of events. As Gloria Samson, a nurse in England in World War II, said crisply to Wendell Renshaw, "If I lived through Hitler's London blitz, I can damn well live through this!" And she and a dozen other kindred souls drew blood, assisted in minor surgery, dispensed medications, and prepared and delivered meals.

Thanks largely to Oliver Emmet's article: FLOWERS RABIES—THE NEW BLACK DEATH? which appeared in *Sunday Magazine*, the Blue Harbor story had gone worldwide and had generated intense debate regarding the cause of the crisis and what should be done about it. Blue Harbor's residents, prisoners in rented cottages or year-round homes, saw the surgeon general, in a nationwide TV address, say the rabies must be stopped at all costs. Extreme measures, while painful to all, were absolutely essential if a tragedy of epic proportions was to be avoided. The quarantine would continue as long as necessary. He was sure that the people affected would understand.

Sandra Barnes punched the knob on the TV set and the surgeon general died. I understand, all right, she said to herself. I understand you're safe in your Dupont Circle townhouse, you don't have to hustle the kids in the car and drive to the store for your ration of food with the doors locked and windows rolled up. You don't have to worry about what to do if the kids break a bone or get chicken pox. Where the hell do you take them? Out to the elementary school? Where some sicko can come bursting in and bite everybody?

Sandra had not been able to sleep through the night

237

since Tricia Stemmer died. She kept a light on in her room so whenever she woke with her hand at her throat and her heart pounding hard, she would see the picture of Howard on top of the dresser and know where she was. She woke up every night and lay there, tormented, and didn't dare take a sleeping pill, for what if Lucy or Matty should need her and, caught in the depths of the drug, she ignored their cries? She was chronically tired, a total wreck. Stuck in this house all the time with the children, with Howard gone, with the constant threat of disease outside, cut off from her friends except for the phone, which was damn near impossible now . . .

Her daily swim was the only thing keeping her sane: that familiar rhythm, linking her to the glorious days of her teenage triumphs. But she'd gone for her swim before noon today, and its soothing effects had worn off.

She went to the table beside the couch and dialed again. In her mind she could see Howard's office; its chrome and wool couches, its plate glass window, Pennsylvania Avenue out there. She pictured her townhouse, where Howard still lived, alone. What wouldn't she give to be there?

After ten rings, she slammed the receiver down. The government claimed they had put in more lines, but they claimed lots of things: that the rabies would soon be brought under control, that calm reigned in Blue Harbor, that people were managing well. You bet, she said to herself. You bet. If I don't get through to him soon, I swear—

The telephone rang and she picked it up quickly. "Hello?"

"I've been trying to call you for over an hour."

"Oh, Howard, thank God, I've been trying to call you, too."

"I'll come if you want, I can get the clearance. I just won't be able to leave again."

If I want? she thought. The only thing I want more is to have this nightmare end. She sucked in breath and said, "Don't come, there's no use your being here, too. If something should happen to both of us, what would the children do? It's safer this way."

The line crackled and hummed. "I miss you, Sandra. I miss you so much. I worry about you constantly."

She felt weak in her throat as she said, "I wish with all my heart that you were here, but it wouldn't be right, it wouldn't be smart. And you have to stay in Washington to try to get us out of here. To get *all* of us out of here."

More static, and Howard said, "It doesn't look good."

"But Howard, Jesus, they can't . . . I mean how can they do this to us?"

"They can do it," he said. "In national emergencies, they can do what they damn well please."

"Goddamn it," she said.

"That's just how it is. How it has to be. How are the kids?"

"All right. Better than I am, really. They're bananas with cabin fever, of course, but other than that, they're not bad. Back here in the cove we don't see all the stuff that the people in town have to see."

"Lulu's sleeping okay again?"

"Better than I am, let's put it that way."

"Kids are tough. And have short memories."

"I hope so."

"They'll both be fine. All they'll remember of this is that they weren't allowed to go out anywhere. Matt won't even remember that much."

"Lucy won't forget Tricia. Not ever."

"You don't know that."

239

I *do* know that, she thought, but said instead, "Can there be any truth to this stuff that Libya's saying?"

"The biological warfare crap? Of course not."

"I hope not."

"They'll jump on us every chance they get."

"Yeah," Sandra said, feeling time pressing in. You were only supposed to talk for five minutes, no more, but she hated to let Howard go. "Can't you hijack a helicopter and rescue us?"

"I wish I could. But if I come to Blue Harbor, I stay in Blue Harbor."

"I'll be okay," she said.

"Of course you will, Sandra, you've always been strong. Are the kids available?"

"They must be upstairs, I don't hear them."

"Well, next time then. Give them both a big kiss for me."

"I love you, Howard."

"I love you, too. With all my heart."

When she hung up, the emptiness hit her, hard and huge. She pressed her lips together and told herself to get busy with something, to clean the goddamn bathrooms again or do *something*.

She went to the kitchen and poured some more coffee. Just what the old nerves need, she thought, and drank the bitter stuff in the quiet. The quiet. *Too* quiet. With sudden alarm, she thought, Where *are* the kids, anyway?

She set her mug down on the countertop and went to the foot of the stairs and called, "Lulu?"

No answer. "Lulu!" she said tensely, louder.

Behind her, beyond the kitchen, from out in the rear entryway, came: "Mommy!"

She hurried back into the kitchen, and there were the children, both of them. Lucy was crying and saying something that Sandra could not understand. She

240

knelt; put her hands on her daughter's shoulders. "Lucy, calm down, what—?"

And then on the back of her daughter's neck, she saw the blood.

"Lu—"

"The kitty cat bit us," Lucy wailed. And Matty was frowning hard at his palm, at three angry red lines.

"What?" Sandra said, her heart in her throat, her mind blazing.

"We didn't hurt him, all we did was pet him, and he—"

Sandra jumped up and went out through the entry; scanned the deck quickly; saw no cat. Saw no cat on the lawn or in the trees. She came back to the kitchen, sick and faint. "A cat?" she said.

"He bited," Matty said with worried eyes.

"But I told you not to go outside!" Sandra said. "I told you! Didn't I tell you?"

Both children were crying now, and Sandra's mind was saying, No, no, no, and she lifted Lucy up to the sink and ran hot water and scrubbed her scratches with soap, then did the same for Matty. No, her frozen mind kept saying, no. Her mouth felt numb and her heart was sick as she shook her head and said in a whisper, "No," then louder: "We have to go for a ride now."

"Where?" Lucy asked with fear in her voice, and Sandra didn't reply.

THIRTY-FIVE

Farrow's chest felt tight as he looked at the woman lying before him, her limp brown hair brushed back, her dark eyes staring up at his. "Has anyone survived it yet?" she asked.

Farrow shifted his gaze to the window: saw flowers outside in the hospital garden, neglected, a wild tangle. "Not yet," he said, looking back at the bed but avoiding those eyes. "Let me qualify that. There are several people doing well, but they aren't yet out of the woods. We're quite optimistic about their chances, though."

"Yeah," Sharon Jensen said.

"We have state-of-the-art support now. The best in the world."

Sharon swallowed and turned to the window, to the rank and failing garden; a tear left a trail of silver on her cheek. In the hallway, on one of the cots, someone moaned.

Farrow took a deep breath. "Your symptoms disappeared before," he said, "and it's possible they'll do so again. You're under constant surveillance, and if

242

things get worse, we'll start supportive treatment."

"Wonderful," Sharon said.

Farrow started to turn away when she said, "You created this, didn't you?"

"I beg your pardon?"

"You created this rabies at Jillson."

"No," Farrow said, "we did not. We were given a grant to study it."

She bit her lip; said nothing. The patient in the hallway moaned again.

"That's the truth."

"Okay," Sharon said.

"I'll see you tomorrow," Farrow said, and quickly left the room.

Outside the door Nurse Mildrum stopped him and said, "Mrs. Wadsworth died."

"Damn," Farrow said.

Catherine Wadsworth was one of the first to receive the new state-of-the art support. Until two days ago, she seemed to be doing well.

"She went downhill in less than two hours," Nurse Mildrum said.

"She was fairly old."

"Eighty-two."

Farrow nodded. "I want you to keep close tabs on Sharon. If she gets any worse, I want to know—right away."

"All right."

"What's the latest?"

"Five new ones and several maybes, including a couple of kids."

"Christ," Farrow said, and looked down at the tile floor. He fingered his beard, looked up again, and said, "Keep me posted."

"I always do."

"Of course," he said.

He walked down the hallway briskly, turned right, and went down another hall to the emergency room. Only people suspected of having rabies came here now, and as Farrow looked through the glass in the swinging door he first saw a guardsman, standing at ease, a pistol at his hip, then a frightened-looking old man slumping down in a chair near the window. A dumpy, sallow-faced woman sat two chairs away, and then Farrow saw the children, a boy and a girl, with their mother.

His breath stuck in his throat. He knew that woman. He'd been to some function, some party that she had attended. The boy stood on her right and the girl on her left, looking down at the book in her lap. She was reading aloud to them, slowly, her face devoid of expression.

"Christ," Farrow muttered, turned away, and walked down the hall to the exit.

There were dozens of false alarms every day in ER: people who'd scratched themselves on nails, people who had a slight touch of the flu, people who were merely scared. He hoped with all his heart that these kids were a false alarm.

But you couldn't tell. There was no way to tell. So damn it, it's worth the risk, he thought as he gave a curt nod to the guard at the door and walked across the parking lot to his car.

He had given himself the preexposure series of Protocol 4 and two of the postexposure shots, and so far was perfectly fine. All the dogs were still fine and it just might be time to try it on somebody else. He could save those kids' lives—or could kill them. But wasn't it worth the risk?

He started the car and pulled away. As he stopped

244

at the checkpoint on the lane, he wished he had tried it on Sharon. At lease she'd have had a chance, but now . . .

Paul Kessler, seated at his desk, stared out at the shaggy lawn. He turned with a frown as Farrow came into the room.

"I was just at the hospital."

Kessler waited:

"Sharon Jensen's not feeling well. And someone came in with a couple of kids, a woman you know."

"Who?" Kessler said.

"Her name escapes me, but she was the one who did all that work to keep Pyramid Chemical—"

"Sandra Barnes? Do you mean Sandra Barnes?"

"That's the one. Ironic, isn't it? She keeps that chemical plant from filling our air with poison, and now this happens."

"Ironic," said Kessler. "Is that how you see it, Martin? Ironic? Not tragic?"

"Of course, it's tragic, I didn't imply that it wasn't."

"Damn," Kessler said, shaking his head. "She's one of Angela's friends. And the children? Lucy and Matty? Not them, Martin, damn it." He gritted his teeth and banged his hand on his desk.

Rarely had Farrow seen Kessler display such emotion. "It's awful," he said.

Kessler looked at him hard. "We've created a modern day plague, and all you can say is, 'It's awful'?"

Jerking his head back, Farrow said, "Plague. You've been reading those newspaper fools? We didn't create any plague, Paul, we've worked on a prophylaxis for a

245

vicious disease, and for all we know, we've found it. *That's* what we've created, if my hunch is correct." He looked down at the desk, at the stacks of papers near Kessler's clenched hand, and said, "It's time we found out. It's time to start human trials with Protocol 4."

Kessler stared at his fist on the desk. "I'm afraid not, Martin."

"Oh?" Farrow said. There was no need to ask why not; he already knew. "A dog is sick."

Kessler nodded.

"One we infected?"

"No."

The word echoed in Farrow's head, going down into darkness. "All right," he said. "But that still doesn't mean the vaccine doesn't work. We have to expect some reactions. The other dogs are okay?"

"They're okay, yes, including the ones we infected. But now this happens."

"All right," Farrow said, "it's a setback, but it isn't the end. We've still got fifteen dogs that might beat this thing. I mean, Jesus, their lesions are in the neck—"

"They were only infected two weeks ago."

"All the same—"

"It's too early to start human trials."

Farrow's jaw tightened up. "Too early?" he said. "Paul, what have we got to lose?"

Looking up at him slowly, Kessler said, "What if the people we try it on aren't infected, and the vaccine kills them? How would you feel if that happened?"

"We can't tell who's infected, Paul."

"You're avoiding the issue."

"I'm willing to take the risk. I think it's time."

"Well, I don't," Kessler said. "You'd give those Barnes children Protocol 4?"

"Yes."

246

"I wouldn't. I won't."

Farrow looked outside at the overgrown lawn, which hadn't been cut in weeks. Tonight was the night of his final injection. "I'm going to call the committee together," he said. "I have data that might be of interest to them."

THIRTY-SIX

In 1918, when the Great Flu Epidemic struck Boston, Emily Mitchell had been twelve years old. All these many years later, that tragic time was still perfectly clear in her mind. Her mother and her sister Lillian, two years older than she, had died of that dreadful disease, and she had become the woman of the house, cooking and cleaning for heartbroken Papa, up to the day he departed this earth at the age of eighty-six. Once he was buried and all his affairs were in order, she sold the house on Beacon Hill and moved to the summer place in Blue Harbor to spend the rest of her spinster days by the sea.

It seemed to her now that the world had come full circle. The new epidemic was carrying off her neighbors just as the old one had. This time it was different, though. Back then, in Boston, when people got sick they stayed in their homes and the doctor would visit, and home was where you either lived or died. Hospitals weren't the thing they were now, and medicine wasn't either, and you did just as well to stay in your bed as to go off to somewhere strange. And they let you stay in your bed. But not today.

Today, if you got this rabies, you had no choice, you

had to be hospitalized. If you couldn't or wouldn't go on your own, the army would come and take you. And that was the way it had to be, because unlike the Spanish flu, this disease made you ugly, mean, turned you into a beast. Before you went into a swoon, you were fighting mad at anyone—your own family, best friends—as if they were somehow to blame for the plight you were in.

At the height of the 1918 flu, Mr. Harmes, the undertaker, came daily to Beacon Street. He and his men would arrive in the horse-drawn carriage, enter a house, bring out the dead in a box, and cart them away. He had come for her sister and then for her mother, for Mrs. Folsom across the street and the Bingham boys down the block. Then Emily had fallen ill and had not seen the cart when it came for the Higginses, Walshes, and old Mr. Cobb, the banker. But she heard the clop of the horse's shod hooves through her third-floor bedroom window, and thought through her fever, For me? This time has he come for me?

But no, the horse never came for her, and the heat in her flesh went away, her mind stopped turning, and after a few months she felt like herself; but older, a different, sober Emily, the child burned out of her now. And Mama and Lillian both were gone, and her life with Papa began.

She thought of this now as she watched through the window, the curtain a thin film of white in front of her glasses; saw the olive drab jeep pull up and the three men, the soldiers, climb out; saw one of them go to the door of the house over there while the other two lagged behind on the concrete walk. All three of them wore those strange padded jackets, helmets, masks, and gloves. So uncomfortable in this heat, she said to herself.

The soldier who'd gone to the door rang the bell. He waited, but nobody came. Emily's breath was loud in her ears as she watched from behind the curtain. The soldier rang the bell again and knocked on the paneled door with a white-gloved fist. Still no response, and all three soldiers went around back.

Emily watched from behind the lace curtain. She knew what was going to happen, she'd seen it before, with Mrs. Potts down the street. The grandfather clock in the dining room ticked off the seconds; she shifted position and straightened the antimacassars.

Then the door of the house over there flew open and out they came with Mr. King. Mr. King was a big man, over six feet, with large shoulders and arms and an ample stomach. His face was contorted with rage as the soldiers held him and pushed him along the walk. Mr. King had been handcuffed. He shouted and kicked, and Emily, behind her curtain, winced. He had always been such a pleasant man, a good family man, this was all such a shame. His wife stood in the doorway, helplessly, clasping her hands. For a moment her eyes looked up, and Emily drew back slightly. Well of course Mrs. King couldn't see through the curtain. Of course not.

Soon the jeep and the soldiers were gone. Mrs. King closed the door. One of these days, no doubt, the soldiers would come back and take her off, too, because people who lived with infected people got rabies, nobody knew how. At first they had thought that you had to get bitten or scratched, but that wasn't the case, some people who'd never been bitten or scratched had caught it. By breathing infected air? The same way you could catch the flu?

It was awful to see them accost Mr. King like that. But once you got sick and you tried to hide it, that happened. If you were sick with anything, you had to

250

go to the grammar school, and if they suspected rabies, you went to the hospital. You had no choice in the matter.

And that's how it had to be. For this rabies was so much worse than the Spanish flu. Five hundred thousand had died of the flu in 1918. Five hundred thousand, when the country was so much smaller. If this rabies got out of Blue Harbor, how many would die? In 1918, people got sick and went quietly, peacefully, not with this terrible fuss. Her mama and sister had lain in their beds breathing thickly, their faces flushed, eyes closed, and after a spell they were gone. People back then could infect other people, of course, but not like this, not by scratching or biting. They didn't scream and foam at the mouth and fight with the strength of ten men. The world had mourned, but it hadn't turned ugly like this. These days, when somebody died, half the time you were glad they were gone, you had been so frightened of them.

She'd been frightened of Mr. King. Not of what he was now, but of what he might soon become. For she'd known he was sick. A man like that, so regular, who went to work at the same time every day and then suddenly never appeared, you knew something was wrong. A lot of people stayed home when they felt a bit under the weather, but not Mr. King. He'd never missed one day of work till a week ago, and he'd already had his vacation in May, so his disappearance wasn't because of that. And the way he looked when she saw him outside that time: so sallow, so tired, so *sick*.

She'd had to report him; really, she'd had no choice. It was for his own good and the general good, for he wouldn't get better at home. No one ever got better at home. Quite possibly, no one got better no matter where they went, but they had a better chance in the hospital, surely. She'd had her gall bladder out down there and they'd done a marvelous job. Mr. King would be better off down there, and she would sleep better at night.

Slowly she rose from her chair and went into the kitchen. So dreadful, this rabies, she thought with a shiver. People spreading it, animals spreading it—not only dogs, but rats and mice, like the plague. How could a sickness like that ever be contained? Could all of the Blue Harbor rats and mice be accounted for? Wouldn't some of them manage to cross that causeway and multiply on the mainland? Especially now that most of the cats were gone?

She opened her refrigerator door, the image of poor Mr. King in her mind again. So sad. But she'd had to report him. And Mr. and Mrs. Powell had a cat, she knew they did, she'd seen it last night on their windowsill, and she'd have to report them, too.

She poured some milk into her glass and sat down at the kitchen table. She'd turned in her cat, Isabel, at the very start; it was still at the army pound—or so she'd been told. She missed that cat so. It was terribly lonely without her.

In the dining room, the grandfather clock ticked on. She was so aware of time these days. There seemed so much of it.

She drank some milk; and heard, below the ticking of the clock, another sound. A scratching: sharp, insistent, in the wall, not far from the outside door.

A mouse? A rat? Her heartbeat quickened. She rose from the table and went to the closet and took out her dusting mop. Went quietly to the door, then banged the mop hard on the wall.

The scratching stopped. She stood there, listening, breathing loudly, her heartbeat thick in her throat.

She was lonely and scared and she wished she had

252

Isabel back. She put the mop back in the closet, then sat at the table again. Her appetite for milk was gone. She said a prayer.

As Wendell Renshaw stared at the bay, at the brilliant slash of sun on the blue morning water, he thought: It's as lovely as ever. So lovely you could almost forget the truth.

Almost, but not quite. For in normal times these boats that now clung to their moorings would be far out to sea, and these empty docks would be humming with locals and tourists. How distant those times seemed now.

Renshaw turned in his swivel chair and looked at his desk, which was littered with newspapers, letters, and notes. He looked at his word processor's screen, at his editorial. Same old stuff, he thought. What more could he say that he hadn't already said?

The *Blue Harbor Herald* was four pages long these days. There was nothing much to report on except *the story* and its ramifications—including, of course, the list of the sick and the dead. The paper was almost a throwback to what it had been at the turn of the century ("Word has come to us that Sarah Hepplewhite of the Washington Road is gravely ill with softening of the brain"), but skimpier and much more grave. There was no town business to write about, no summer softball, no lectures or art shows or concerts, nobody trying to violate zoning laws, nobody filling in wetlands. There was still the occasional auto accident, the occasional fire, but most of the news was body count, or what the authorities had in the works (facts only, none of the rumors that people like Oliver Emmet fed on), or who had tried and failed to escape by boat. Man's cruelty to man in these difficult times got little

253

ink. People were scared enough without that, Wendell figured. Why add to their woes?

The paper's advertising base had evaporated. Three quarters of its staff either couldn't or wouldn't work, and Renshaw and a handful of others struggled to keep things going. What they faithfully turned out each week was a broadside, something of which Thomas Paine might approve, with its rousing editorials calling for courage and calm. Renshaw was keeping the paper afloat on subscription money and savings, and gave it away outside the office, at the grammar school clinic, at the North End Market food drop. With mail delivery suspended and carriers out of the question, if you wanted a paper, you had to go out and get it.

Renshaw gave it away, because, with their businesses dead, a lot of the locals were broke. They didn't have the money for clothes, let alone for the news. The government was providing phone and electrical service now along with food and medical care, and to charge for a paper in times like these would have made Renshaw feel like a crook.

As he looked at the blinking cursor, he thought, I guess Oliver Emmet, star reporter, has already filed his piece for the day. He's dug up another sensational item—*made* up another sensational item—and sent it off to an eager, gullible world. What a hell of a guy. He'd sell his grandmother's teeth to get ahead.

Renshaw stared at the screen. Why the hell did he bother with this? Did the town really need it? Or did only *he* need it?—to keep himself sane. No, damn it, it wasn't that, you had to preserve the word, the word was life.

He sighed. Well, life or not and free or not, most people could do without it. They'd pick it up if they had to go out, but most got their news via TV and phone. Locked in their houses, living on government food, they existed like moles. A bunch of suspicious, mean moles for the most part, too. But he'd vowed not to write about that.

He looked at the water again and thought: What a shame. What a shame that Blue Harbor should come to this. One of the world's most beautiful towns, and one of its nicest towns, too. No crime to speak of, friendly, church-going people who always treated the summer folk well in spite of their big city ways. Blue Harbor did not deserve this fate. Newark, maybe, maybe Detroit, Philadelphia . . .

When you got right down to it, though, was anything disconnected? Was one part of the country immune to the ills of another? Blue Harbor had certainly acted as if this were so. It knew how to live, and if New York or Boston or Washington didn't, that was their problem, not Blue Harbor's.

There were questions when Jillson came to the island; some folks were suspicious. But nobody pressed those suspicions, and once the scientists settled down and started to spend good money in town and started to hire locals, the questions died. The Jillson people were doing good work, life-saving work, cancer research and all kinds of wonderful stuff. One hell of a lot of animals died down there, but most of them, after all, were only mice.

The sun flashed on the water. So beautiful. And so still, so deathly still: like before man had come to these shores.

Renshaw turned to his desk again, running his hand through his shaggy hair, which hadn't been cut in weeks. The barber was still in business and so were the dentists, up at the grammar school, but the wait was endless.

He took his pipe out of the ashtray, cleaned it, filled it, and sucked it to life. Tobacco was at a premium now, and he'd sharply curtailed his smoking. Just as well, he thought, and the thought was amusing, as comical as those wire service items that kept on coming in spite of the holocaust. About baking a great chocolate cake or growing begonias. Where was one they could use? How to Build a Good Coffin, or Gourmet Cooking with Powdered Milk.

He took a long comforting drag on the pipe and told himself, This too shall pass. Of course it shall. But when? And where? The plague had passed, and so had the Spanish flu, after millions had died. Could the government actually keep this disease from spreading? It seemed like a pipe dream, but had to be tried. If people were allowed to leave Blue Harbor, all hope was lost. Not even the National Guardsmen could leave now, as thirteen were already ill.

The Pentagon big shots had come and gone, but others who came had to stay. Howard Barnes, for example, who'd come yesterday to help his wife care for their children. Such wonderful people, who'd done so much for this town, stopping the Pyramid Chemical threat, raising funds for the library's children's room. Those beautiful children of theirs, it just didn't seem right. But who could say what was right in God's great plan? Every now and again the world needed a good cleaning out? Was that how it worked?

He stared at his monitor, smoked his pipe, frowning, and looked at the stuff on his desk. Since the post office was only two doors away, he still got his mail. The letters to the editor were interesting these days.

He picked up some envelopes, tossed them all down except one. This should be *very* interesting, he thought. G. Rutherford Weems, The Ledges. The former U.S. Senator, retired for the last twelve years.

A good one to start with indeed. If anyone knew about God's great plan, it was surely G. Rutherford

256

Weems. He opened the envelope, puffed on his pipe, and read:

Dear Mr. Renshaw:

Three weeks ago, I shot my wonderful collie dog, Bruce. In spite of the fact that I kept him chained, he somehow came down with rabies, and attacked my wife, Louise.

An hour ago, I shot Louise. As I write this, she lies in the bedroom, covered with blankets. She'd been sick for three days. We both knew what it was, and we knew that there was no cure. Louise begged me not to send her away to the hospital; she didn't want to spend her last days among strangers. I did what I thought was right. If Louise felt any pain, it was very short-lived.

By the time you receive this letter, I will also be dead. As soon as I return from posting it, I will turn the gun on myself.

How many marvelous summers I spent in this town as a child, a youth, a man! And these years of retirement—splendid. The beauty of this town, the goodness of its citizens, are surely unsurpassed. I thank God for granting me so many hours here.

And now as I see this terrible tragedy deepen, I ask myself if I could have done something, anything, to prevent it. If only I had bothered to learn about Jillson's work. If only I had protested against the work in Maryland and Utah that I knew about only too well—and which continues, even as I write. I achieved some good things in the senate. But all my achievements are dust in my mouth in the light of today's events.

Thank you for your uplifting editorials. As Faulkner said, Man will prevail. But not this particular man, who is broken and sick to his heart.

Keep up the good fight.

Best wishes,

G. Rutherford Weems

Renshaw's hand was shaking. He set his pipe back in the ashtray, breathed deeply, then dialed the police. More grist for Emmet's sensation mill, he said to himself. Poor Senator Weems and his wife! Poor Blue Harbor!

And oh, how the world will love it and thirst for more.

THIRTY-SEVEN

Oliver Emmet's official "informed source" was an attache assigned to Lt. Colonel Tower, and every day on the dot of three in the afternoon, he'd call the guy, whose name was Hook, and get the new list of the dead. Hook was a pretty closed-mouth character, and unless someone really prominent had bit the dust, the stuff Emmet got wasn't much to hang a column on.

He got his best stuff from his unofficial sources, and the best of these was Cherry White, the woman who most often shared his motel room. Cherry worked at the Great Day Cafe in Ellington, a bustling Route One truck stop, founded by born-again Christians and now owned by Polish Catholics, the Walinskis, the same folks who owned the Starbuck Motel, where Emmet now made his home. The truckers who shipped supplies to Blue Harbor all ate at the Great Day Cafe, and Cherry knew every one of them by name. She'd worked in Blue Harbor for years as a waitress, knew plenty of people there, too, and what she didn't learn while dishing out coffee and muffins and blueberry pie wouldn't fit on the head of a pin.

But Cherry hadn't been at the diner these past few days, and Emmet hadn't been able to reach her at home, and his column had felt the loss. Yesterday the thing with the senator blowing away his wife had bailed him out, but today he had nothing but standard body count, so after he hung up on Hooks, he walked down to the diner.

Ellington was a beautiful town, with its white-spired churches, its tidy Main Street, its village green, Masonic Hall, and all the rest, and Emmet was sick to death of the goddamn place. It had gotten real old real fast, in less than a week, as a matter of fact. The rabies story was old now, too, but it had been very good to him, and he'd stick it out in Ellington to the end— which looked like it wasn't going to come for quite some time, and how he would keep from going nuts in this burg was beyond him.

He entered the diner, the coffee and bacon smell sharp in his nose, and went to the counter, where Abigail, one of the owners, was shoving a yellow sponge across the formica.

"Hi, Abby. No Cherry again?"

A guy with a solid fat stomach, his arm protecting his coffee cup, glanced at him, sucking his teeth, and Abby said brusquely, "They took her away to Blue Harbor."

Her words seemed to hang in the steamy air. "Blue Harbor?" Emmet said.

"She thought she just had a sore throat," Abby said, bearing savagely down on the sponge. "But then she started to feel like shit and went to Doc Peters, he said that she had to go down there. The National Guard took her down."

"It's a goddamn police state," the man with the coffee cup said in a heavy voice. "You get a goddamn cold and they haul you away."

Feeling light-headed, Emmet sat down on a stool. The quilted aluminum boxes behind Abby's head had a sick dull glow. A clink of cup on saucer hurt his ears.

"Police state is right," Abby said. "They try to haul *me* off when I get the sniffles, they'll have a fight on their hands." She tossed the sponge at the sink and said, "So, what'll it be?"

Emmet's throat was sore. He'd woken up with it feeling scratchy and thought it would pass, but it hadn't—which hadn't concerned him till now. "Black coffee," he said.

He drank half a cup in silence, acutely aware of his throat, then left and walked back to his motel room and dialed Blue Harbor Hospital. It took him nearly an hour to reach his party.

"Hey, Cherry, it's Oliver. What's going on?"

Her voice sounded fearful and broken. "They think I've got it."

"Hold on, how can you? You mean something bit you?"

"No."

"Well then, how in the hell can you have it?"

"That's what I want to know. They have to be wrong, right?"

"Right. If nothing bit you—"

"They have to be wrong. You can only get it through bites, or touching dead animals, stuff like that." She was silent a moment. "I feel like shit."

"It's the flu," Emmet said. "That's all, it's been going around. These doctors are goddamn paranoid. Every time somebody gets the flu, they're going to lock them up? I'll write about it, Cherry, they won't get away with this shit. I'll get you out of there."

"They won't let me out," Cherry said. "Out of the hospital maybe, not out of Blue Harbor, though. Once you're here, it's for good."

"Yeah? We'll see about that."

A moment of silence, then Cherry said, "It's horrible here. All these sick people crying and screaming and

261

moaning, you can't even sleep. The hallways are full of them now."

"Christ," Emmet said, taking notes.

"Last night I saw Jimmy Hurd. He's so sick. They have him strapped down and doped up, he already looks dead. But he screams so loud, it's horrible, even with all the dope."

"So who's Jimmy Hurd?" Emmet said.

"This guy I used to go with. We broke off a month ago. He worked at the Mobil station."

"Where? In Blue Harbor?"

"Yeah."

"He didn't"—it sounded foolish—"he didn't bite you?"

"Jimmy? Jesus no, why would Jimmy do that?"

"Yeah. Well look, hang in there, kid. I'll see what I can do."

"You're a doll, Ollie."

"Catch you later, kid."

He hung up, hands shaking, a thin sweat coating his skin. He stared at nothing, at the beige heating/air-conditioning unit below the window, the closed orange drapes, and thought, Could it possibly be? She went with a guy who was sick and now *she* was sick, so maybe you didn't have to be bitten, maybe you could get it—

Jesus Christ, that *couldn't* be!

A sudden flush swept over him. He swallowed and his throat felt worse. Just a cold, he told himself. Just a cold or a touch of flu.

"A goddamn cold," he said out loud, and reached for his cigarettes. When he tried to light up, his hands were shaking so hard the match went out.

THIRTY-EIGHT

Walt Marsh had quit school in the eighth grade, the year his father dropped dead of a heart attack. He had gone to work in a lumberyard, loading and unloading trucks, and two years later had gotten a job as a driver for Seavey Fuels, delivering tanks of propane. When one of the old hands retired with emphysema, Walt had been taught to install heating ducts and clean out furnaces. He'd liked the work and had done so well that Seavey had trained him in all the various aspects of furnace installation and repair. After six years with Seavey, he'd started his own operation, and for twenty years now he had worked twelve hours a day, six days a week, installing and servicing domestic and commercial heating systems.

It had been a hard life, but a good one. He had a nice house, two late model cars, and a pretty good chunk of dough in the Blue Harbor Bank and Trust. He took off for a couple of weeks in the summer to fish at his camp on Lake Lincoln. His business was well established by the time his only child arrived, and Teddy lacked for nothing; clothes, sporting equipment, toys. Yet he was a worker, not spoiled, a really good kid. And smart.

Walt Marsh had a plan for his son. That money he'd sacked away had a definite purpose: Teddy was going to college. If once he had finished, he chose to fix oil burners, fine, but he'd have an education. An education was important to Walt; he felt his own lack of one dearly. There was so much he wanted to understand, but couldn't quite grasp, and his son would go to college and learn all that stuff.

Walt's plan was supported by Teddy a hundred percent. He had dozens of pennants on his wall and followed college athletic teams with a passion. His sights were set on Bowdoin and Bates and possibly Stanford, and what with his brains and the way he worked, he could probably take his pick. Walt hadn't been sure if he wanted kids, but June had talked him into it, and once they had Teddy, he was just so proud, and the world was a better place than he'd ever dreamed.

And now that Teddy was dead and buried and June was locked away with a breakdown, unable to walk or talk, the world was a hell and would be so forever. Walt moved through time detached, oblivious, as if he were watching himself from afar, and deep in the empty sleepless night without June and Teddy, he prayed for his heart to explode.

But his prayers went unanswered. Slow numb anger infused his flesh, informed his bruised soul, and loaded the .38 snub-nosed revolver, his grandfather's gun, and sent him on stunned electric feet to the source of all his pain.

Pete Richert felt lucky. Night after night he sat at the desk in the hallway of Building 6, whiling away the boring hours with Cokes and old magazines. The lab emptied out by eleven, except for Kessler and Farrow and maybe a couple of others, and once they left at one or so, the place was totally dead.

Late at night it was creepy there in that hallway with all the rooms locked, just the whine or bark of a dog now and then and scarcely another sound. Sometimes he'd go to the door at the end of the hall and call out to the guard at the gate, Dick Foster, and have a chat in the late night stillness, surrounded by acres of spruce, balsam, and pine; just a few crickets stirring. He'd let the door click shut again and go back in and wander around, use the bathroom, then sit at the desk again. Read magazines. At six in the morning Skip Dawes would relieve him, and Pete and Foster would drive the jeep back to base, chow down and sleep. Johnson would go relieve Dawes at two, and Pete, in turn, would take over for Johnson at ten, and so it went, day after day.

It was boring as hell. Richert liked it that way. The guys who patrolled the causeway and beach had to be on the ball, especially at night, for—believe it or not—an occasional moron still tried to escape, and some of those morons had guns. Blue Harbor was loaded with guns and tempers were short, and walking along that causeway you never relaxed, for the fear of a sniper was always, but *always* there. And the guys who'd drawn hospital duty, my god, to try to stay sane in that chaos, that sickness and pain, that screaming and groaning, with people like wild animals . . . Seeing your friends, like Eddie Mason, get worse and worse, go crazy, die . . .

Yes, magazines and Cokes and quiet suited him just fine.

Tonight they had all gone home except Kessler and Farrow, and soon, in an hour or so, they would call it quits, too. And six hours from now, while he was asleep, those two would be back here again, or over at

Blue Harbor Hospital or one of the other treatment centers, the houses they now occupied. Incredible, the way they worked, the energy they had, and Richert wondered, Were they doing drugs? There must be every drug in the world around here.

He looked up from his magazine, *Popular Science*, and yawned. At the end of the hallway, the reinforced panel of glass in the door reflected the outdoor spotlight. Time for a bathroom break, then a chat with Dick.

The MAC 10's holster under his arm, he went down the hallway and into the men's room. When he zipped up and turned to the sink, the holster hit the urinal. As always. It never failed.

As he dried his hands on the paper towel, he heard some popping sounds. From where? Where they kept the dogs? The lab? He frowned and dropped the towel in the trash and went to the hallway again.

As the men's room door swished shut behind him, he looked at the door at the end of the hall, and an arm was protruding through the glass, which hung in shreds on its reinforcement wires. The arm pushed the locking bar down, the door came open, and Richert yelled, "Hey!" and a man was there, a big man with a pistol, and Richert's mind went suddenly white and he dived for the desk near the wall. As he hit the floor, three shots rang out, one entered the metal desk with a loud whanging sound, and Richert, the MAC 10 now in his hands, yelled, "Hey!" again, but the man kept shooting. Richert lifted the gun high and, not even looking, fired.

The rounds poured out at the rate of nine hundred per minute, jarring his bones and teeth, and he heard a strangled cry and risked a quick glance, and the man was squirming on the floor, his pistol ten feet away. The bullets had taken the top of his head off and blood was everywhere. He suddenly jerked and went limp and a hot dead silence filled the hall. Richert, his ears whining loudly, stood up, eyes wide, and said, "For Christ's sake, for Christ's sake," then ran past the body and down the hall and opened the hallway door.

Dick Foster lay slumped on the walk near the gate. Richert ran to him quickly, crying, "Dick!" but Foster's chest was dark with blood and it wasn't moving at all. "Dick," and this time it came out a whimper and Richert knew Foster was dead, and he sucked in a hard deep audible breath and turned away and ran back to the building again.

In the light of the hallway, Kessler and Farrow were standing above the body. The puddle of blood was monstrous now, a yard wide, dark maroon. "I know this man," Kessler was saying, his face pasty white. "He put my furnace in."

"Walter Marsh," Farrow said. "His son was one of the first to die."

"My god," Kessler said.

"Call the base," Farrow said to Richert, who just kept staring.

"Call the base, I said!"

"Yes sir," Richert said, and went into the lab, his knees weak, his skin clammy and pale. He reached for the phone on the wall and its outline faded, disappeared, and the tables and vials and instruments faded, too, and his head hit the floor with a crack.

At his kitchen table, Paul Kessler stared down at his hands. Even now, three hours after the incident, his fingers still trembled, and his chest felt hard and splintered at its core.

Blood and exposed brains were part of his job, but to see Walter Marsh like that . . . the man who'd installed

267

his furnace, a good man, good neighbor. He could not rid his mind of the image for even a second, and lifted the glass of bourbon again, drank again, and told himself, I'm just not strong enough. I'm not like Farrow, a block of ice, I just can't take this stuff.

But he had to. What else could he do? The town depended on Farrow and him and the others, and what could he do, walk away? Walk away, right, he thought with a sour sniff. As if that were an option. No, he was a prisoner here till the end of this thing, whenever, whatever that was. And not only the town but the country depended on him, maybe even the world.

The thought was too huge to bear. He reminded himself that others had picked up the ball now, too: Sweden, Russia, Germany, and maybe one of them, free of the terrible pressure he labored under, would see through fresh eyes, find the key.

A letter from Jeff, his son in Vermont, lay in front of him on the table. How he ached to see him and his daughter, Mindy, who was still at camp. But the way things were going, who knew when they'd meet again?

He sipped at the bourbon; it burned all the way to his stomach. He thought of what Martin had said about Protocol 4, that they ought to start human trials. Perhaps he was right. Only one dog had had a reaction so far, and even that dog, while very sick, was still alive. On support, but alive.

His eyes were burning, his ears were ringing, he needed to get some sleep. *Had* to get some sleep, had to put in a full day tomorrow—and everyday. He looked forward to tomorrow's work: it would speed up time and help mute the horror he'd seen. He sighed and held his head again, and his elbow hit the glass of bourbon, sending it to the floor, where it shattered loudly.

"Oh Jesus," he said, and went to the kitchen closet for the dustpan and brush. He was sweeping the pieces

268

into the pan when Angela entered the room.

She was wearing a thin blue robe, and her eyes were dark and her golden hair looked dull. "Paul, it's after three thirty, what are you doing?"

The trashcan was under the sink. He went to it with the dustpan, disposed of the broken glass, then set the pan down on the floor again and pulled a bunch of paper towels off the roll near the cabinets. He knelt and wiped at the wet on the floor and said, "Something horrible happened. Remember that man who put in our furnace?"

"Not really, no."

"Walter Marsh? He came last summer. Kind of heavy, black hair?"

"I sort of remember him, why?"

Kessler gathered the soggy towels, stood up, threw them under the sink. He squinted at the floor again, searching for splinters. Finding none, he adjusted his glasses and sat at the table again. "He went crazy," he said, "and broke into the lab with a gun. Killed the guard at the gate, and the guard in the hall killed him. Blew the top of his head right off."

"My God," said Angela, sitting down. "Was he trying to kill you, or what?"

"Me, Martin, who knows? He was just in a fury."

"Sick, you mean? He had rabies?"

"I don't think so. His son had recently died of it, and his wife had a breakdown. A serious breakdown, and Marsh just went off the deep end. His son . . . he was only eight." He took off his glasses and rubbed his eyes and said, "The poor, poor man." His lips were quavering; his voice had no strength.

Angela touched his shoulder and said, "Get some sleep."

"Sleep? How can I sleep?" he said. "I can't even get drunk." He put his glasses on again. "I should never

269

have gotten involved in this. Three stupid cases in Pennsylvania, how many years ago, and this is what I spend my life on. Spend all my time and money on, and what do I end up doing? Spreading the goddamn stuff."

"It's not your fault that it spread, it's the fault of those kids."

"They wouldn't have had it to spread, if it wasn't for me."

"No, they'd have had something else to spread, in Maryland or Utah or somewhere else."

"Maybe so, but . . . Christ." He held his head.

Angela chewed her lip. "Does it just spread through biting or infected blood?"

"What?"

"I mean, can it spread in other ways?"

He let go of his head and looked at her. "What other ways?"

"Well, maybe through sex?"

"Where did you ever get that idea?" His blood was loud in his ears.

"There are rumors," she said. "Of people who haven't been bitten who get the disease."

Shaking his head emphatically, he said. "It doesn't spread that way. Thank God."

"Let's go to bed," she said, standing up.

"I won't sleep," he said. "Not yet. I need more bourbon."

"All right," she said. "Just remember, it wasn't your fault. None of this was your fault."

"I wish I believed that."

"Don't punish yourself."

He said nothing.

"I'm going back up now."

"Okay."

She left the kitchen and went through the dining and living rooms. On the stairway, in darkness, she paused, her hand gripping the bannister tightly. Her heart was quick in her throat and her thighs were weak as she thought: You are such a terrible liar, Paul. You always were.

She took a quick breath, and tears welled to her eyes. For Jim Morgan was sick with much more than the flu. He had entered the hospital late last night, very sick. And if Jim had rabies . . .

The hallway darkness closed around her, making her clutch at her chest. "No," she said in a whisper, shaking her head. And she forced her legs to move again, to carry her up the stairway and into her bed.

When her husband entered the room an hour later, she was still wide-awake.

THIRTY-NINE

In Farrow's dream, Sharon Jensen was holding her hands out, and in them lay pieces of tissue and blood and bone. "See?" she said, and he frowned as the fragments leapt out of her fingers and coalesced, turned into a brain that pulsed and throbbed, and hardened into a skull. Then all was in ruins again in her hands, and she smiled again, so patiently, and again said, "See? It's quite simple." And once again the tatters of Walter Marsh jumped into the air and spun, so slowly, slowly, interlocking, this bit here and that bit there—

Farrow woke with the image white hot in his mind. He had only had three hours of sleep, but felt wide-awake, and he dressed and went out to the lab.

When Kessler pulled into the parking lot, he could scarcely believe his eyes.

Guards were stationed along the fence at ten-foot intervals, and two more stood in front of Building 6. As he left his car, a guard trained a rifle on him. "Jesus," he said with a shiver, and made his way down the walk.

At the gate he was told to show his ID.

"You're joking," he said.

"No sir," the guard said stiffly.

"Tell that soldier to lower his gun."

"When we see your ID, sir."

"For god's sake," Kessler said, and set down his briefcase. He took out his wallet. "Here."

The guard inspected it, nodding curtly. "Sorry to have to do this, sir, it'll take me a while to get to know everybody."

"Yes," Kessler said, and picked up his briefcase and walked across to the lab.

A guard opened the door for him. "Morning, sir."

"Morning," Kessler mumbled, thinking: Damn near afternoon. He had finally managed six hours of sleep, and now it was after eleven. He had never come in this late before in his life.

He went down the hallway and unlocked his office, set his briefcase beside his desk. He looked at the mail—nothing crucial, it seemed—then went to the closet and got out a clean lab coat.

As he entered Lab 1, Farrow turned on his stool and said, "I've got it."

Kessler suddenly loathed him. Good God, he thought, he acts as if nothing happened last night. He probably slept like a baby and got here first thing in the morning for business as usual. "Got what?" he said with a bitter tone in his voice.

"The answer to our problem with Series V."

"Oh really? That's wonderful, Martin."

"Get over here. Look at this."

He handed Kessler some sketches and notes done on yellow lined paper. Kessler studied them, frowning. Flicking his index fingers against the pages, he said, "What makes you think these liposomes are going to act this way?"

"I know they will. I feel it," Farrow said.

Kessler's eyebrows went up. "You actually feel things, Martin?"

Ignoring the comment, Farrow said, "Antigens will increase tenfold. At least tenfold."

Kessler looked at the pages again, and, after a space, said, "Well, maybe."

"I know they will," Farrow said. "Paul, we've got to get going on this."

In spite of himself, Kessler felt a sharp twinge of excitement. "You just might be right about this," he said. "We've been fooled before, of course."

"But sometimes we *have* been right, just not right enough."

"Yes," Kessler said, his excitement rising. "I think Kilgore's team could contribute a lot to this."

"Absolutely. And Hilton's."

"They might beat us out, you know."

"And you think that I care about that?" Farrow said.

Placing the notes on the table, Kessler said, "No, I don't think you do. It might be months, though, before we can tell if this works. It might—God forbid—be years."

"In the meantime, we go with the Protocol 4," Farrow said.

Kessler nodded. "Let's bring it before the committee. After last night I'm willing to try anything."

"I doubt if we'll have a repeat of last night," Farrow said. "You'd need a goddamn tank to get into this place. Which is good. Very good. Have you seen today's paper?"

"Why?"

"Take a look."

He reached to his left and picked up the *Boston*

Globe. Kessler took it and scanned the first page. MAN ATTACKS JILLSON LAB, KILLS GUARD, by Oliver Emmet, jumped up at his eyes. "My God," he said, "They'll probably descend on us in hordes after reading this."

"That's not the story that worries me," Farrow said. "It's the one on the right, up top."

Kessler looked at it. SEXUAL TRANSMISSION OF RABIES SUSPECTED—also by Oliver Emmet.

"No," Kessler said.

"It was bound to come out someday, we knew that."

Kessler straightened his glasses. "Well, where did he get this story?"

"From a patient sent down from Ellington, Cherry White. She got rabies without being bitten, apparently from her ex-boyfriend, who died last night."

"How did this guy, this Emmet, find out about her?"

"According to Hooks, he had a relationship with her."

"What?" Kessler said with alarm in his voice. "So he might be infected? And he's roaming around out there?"

"The word's gone out," Farrow said. "They'll get him."

"They damn well better," Kessler said. He laid the paper on the table and sat slowly down on a stool. "Angela asked me about this last night. I told her it wasn't possible. I don't think she believed me."

Farrow stayed silent. Kessler looked up at him. "Angela cheats on me, Martin."

"Don't jump to conclusions."

Kessler laughed sharply. "I've known it for years."

"Oh," Farrow said.

"Her latest fling was that guy from the bank, Jim Morgan. Do you happen to know . . . ?"

"They admitted him yesterday."

Closing his eyes, Kessler nodded and said, "Yes."

"I think we should give her the Protocol 4," Farrow said.

Kessler stared at his hands. "But maybe she hasn't caught it," he said.

"And you're willing to wait to find out?"

"No, of course not, you're right," Kessler said. "We have to give it to her, Martin, you're right. But how can I . . . bring this up?"

"Just tell her that this is the latest vaccine and give her the series. She won't resist. You don't have to say any more."

"All right."

"I'm going to call the committee together."

"Yes," Kessler said. He was staring down at the tabletop, at the test tubes and apparatus.

"Paul?"

Kessler looked up at him, dazed.

"This new one will work, we just have to get on it."

"Yes."

"I'll call the committee together."

Farrow's office was to the left, but he turned right instead and went to the end of the hall. He punched the buttons beside the door and went into the room.

The dogs started barking as soon as he entered. Without breaking his stride, he picked up the stick by the wall. He had checked Number 14 twice last night and things hadn't looked good, and as he approached now he saw the dog lying there, tubes in its nostrils and flesh, and he took a deep breath.

The monitor above the cage was flat. He looked at the dog for signs of movement, poked at its side with

276

the stick. Nothing happened. He poked again, harder, cursing, and said, "Come on, goddamn you, move!"

He stared at the dog and cursed again, then broke the stick over his knee. "Goddamn you!" he said, "You can't do this to me! You just can't do this to me!"

He dropped the pieces of stick on the floor and hurriedly left the room.

FORTY

Peace would not come to Amelia Rose. Even at home, in the still of the night, she heard the cries of the dying and sick in her dreams.

The crisis was nearing the two-month mark. Amelia had been involved from the very start, and now in the night her bones ached with fatigue, and at least once a day the mad rush would catch up to her, spreading a giddiness through her skull and making her sit down, breathe deeply, and close her eyes.

But the giddiness always passed, and she carried on. She'd been offered time off, a whole week off, but how could she take time off when the need was so great? If she and the rest of the staff worked full tilt, they would beat this thing. She would not allow herself to think otherwise.

Three nurses had already died, and the head nurse, Jane Mildrum, was now in intensive care. All had been bitten by patients who'd changed in the space of a minute from placid to violent. The dangerous ones were the new ones, those who had not been sedated. Once the drugs entered their blood, their fury was muted, if not their pain, but the new ones who came to ER were a constant hazard.

And ever since the story broke about sexual transmission, ER had been standing room only. One was tempted to draw the conclusion that every Blue Harbor citizen, permanent or transient, had been guilty of an indiscretion somewhere along the line, the demand for examination had become so great. Most cases were screened at the grammar school first, and were only sent on to ER if their symptoms were highly suspicious. In spite of this, the place was total bedlam.

Most of the self-referrals, it turned out, were suffering from a summer flu that was making the rounds with great rapidity, as stress and altered diet had led to weakened resistance. Amelia, who worked sixteen hours a day and existed on tea and granola bars, was amazed that she hadn't caught it. She didn't know how she kept going, really, and during the past week she'd made up her mind to retire once all this was over. She was forty-six, had put in her twenty-five years, and had savings enough to swing it. No husband, no children, just work all her life, and now it was time for travel and reading and leisurely restaurant meals, the theater, late mornings in bed. Once this was over—and if she was lucky.

As she left the quiet of intensive care—where breathing was done by machine—and entered the pediatric ward, the wails and cries and moans of the children rose up in a doleful wave. No matter how great her exposure to this, she would never get used to it, never. When she knew the children and their parents it was almost too much to bear; and, after a little while, she knew them all.

It was 8:25 P.M. A few parents were sitting in chairs in the hallway, their faces exhausted and drained, and Sandra Barnes, wearing a surgical mask, was among them.

Amelia went up to her. "Sandra."

279

Dark circles rimmed Sandra's eyes. Amelia, kneeling, took her hands.

"They're not getting better," Sandra said, her voice breaking.

"They seem to be holding their own."

Sandra let out a breath. "Has anyone beaten it yet?"

"Some look like they might."

"Be honest with me."

"I am being honest. Some seem to have stabilized. We have excellent supportive care now, the best, and we're quite encouraged."

Sandra let go of Amelia's hands and wiped at her eyes with gloved fingers. "If it weren't for you and Howard," she said, "I couldn't have made it this far."

"Of course you could have," Amelia said. "I guess Howard will be here soon?"

"Any moment now."

"And you'll go home and rest."

"I haven't been able to rest since the children fell ill."

"Are you taking anything?"

"Whatever I take makes me sick to my stomach."

A whine came out of the doorway beside them, and Sandra stood up and went into the room. Amelia went with her.

Lucy lay on her back with her head on the pillow, her hair soaked with sweat and her face drained and pale. Her wrists were bound to the bed's steel rails and her right arm was stiff with an IV board. "Mommy, I'm hot," she said.

"I know you are, sweetheart," Sandra said, and took the cloth from the pan on the bedstand, wrung it out, and wiped Lucy's pasty forehead with deliberate care.

"I want to be better."

"I know, sweetheart. You will be. Soon."

Lucy started to speak, then closed her eyes, and let out a quavering breath.

"You're so brave," Sandra said. "You are such a big girl. Just rest now, and Daddy will be here soon."

Lucy lay there, eyes closed. Amelia took the pan to the bathroom and ran fresh water; set the pan on the bedstand again.

Sandra went to the other bed in the room, where her son Matty lay, his eyes closed. High circles of red infused his cheeks and his chest didn't seem to be moving. In a sudden panic, she thrust her wrist under his nose—and felt his hot breath.

"Sandra?"

Turning, she saw Howard, there at the doorway. He entered and said through his mask, "Hello, Amelia."

Amelia answered his greeting and brushed at the front of her uniform. Howard's eyes, while worried, were not filled with exhaustion and fear like Sandra's, like everyone else's. Oh for a good six-hours sleep, Amelia thought, and said, "I have to be on my way. If you need anything, let me know."

"You're a saint," Sandra said.

Embarrassed, Amelia said, "I'll check them again shortly, Howard," and left the room.

In the hallway she met Martin Farrow, who said, "I saw Sharon Jensen just now and she seems to be stable."

"We're crossing our fingers, doctor."

"How many days has she been in the coma?"

"Three."

"But there's been no decline."

"No."

"Excellent. We may get some of them through this thing."

"I'm sure we will, Doctor."

He paused a second. "The Barnes children?"

"Not so good. They'll probably have to go into intensive soon."

He nodded. "Keep me posted."

"I will."

Farrow walked down the hallway past harried nurses, past orderlies pushing carts, past relatives, all masked and gloved, in chairs against the wall. Shouts, groans, and crying came out of the rooms and out of the beds that sat in the hall at intervals. He quickened his pace, trying to push aside his exhaustion. He'd been working since five o'clock this morning, and now he was off to the lab again, and he needed something.

The elevator doors seemed to shift as he stood before them, impatiently tapping his thigh with his latex-gloved hand. The dizziness passed, and he took the car up to the second level, got off, and went out through the front, avoiding ER. As he left the building, one of the guards at the entrance nodded. The other one, a giant of a man, a moon-faced adolescent, really, with beady small eyes and protruding ears, stared at him coldly. Accusingly, Farrow thought, and told himself: I *do* need something, and quickly crossed the parking lot to his car.

Bulkhead Morrison, rifle across his shoulder, watched Farrow drive off, then said to his partner, Kearney, "I'm takin' a leak," and turned and went through the door.

He stood in the corridor a second, letting his eyes adjust to the change in light. An orderly wheeled a guy into the lab.

It was time. Past time. As soon as he'd heard about Walter Marsh, he'd figured the order would come, but it never did. He could hardly believe it. How long were they going to let it go on like this? Eddie Mason was dead, Don Whipple was dead, and all those sick guys would soon be dead, too, and somebody had to stop

282

this thing. Had to stop it before it got them all, got *him,* like that guy Skinny Watts got Eddie. He had dreamed of that moment over and over, for weeks, waking up in a drenching sweat each time, his heart pounding, his eyes staring into the dark, where he saw himself shoot Skinny Watts and get sick. It was time to end those dreams. Right now.

He hurried past X-ray and laser lab, and stopped in front of the elevator. Pressed the button. Doctors and nurses walked by in a blur. The door came open and he got inside.

A stocky, no-nonsense nurse was in the car. "Where's your mask?" she said sternly, but Bulkhead ignored her. The car descended a floor and they both got out. "Stop at the nurses' station and pick up a mask," the stocky nurse said. Bulkhead nodded, his face sheened with sweat.

He found himself at a spot where three hallways converged. Where to start?

To his left a sign said Intensive Care. They were damn near dead anyway, right? so that wouldn't make sense. Down the hall, straight ahead, was a nurses' station; past that was a pair of doors. In front of the doors lay a man on a gurney, his mouth and nose behind a mask, an IV bag with yellow liquid hanging above his head. An orderly hurried past him and went through the doors.

Bulkhead followed the orderly with his eyes, then quickly turned to the hall on his right. Saw another pair of doors, and hurried through them.

Nurses and orderlies stared as he strode by, brisk and erect, his eyes on the window down at the corridor's end. Around him the cries and groans of the ill rose up; antiseptic assailed his nose. At the window he made an abrupt about-face, then entered the room on his right, and opened fire.

Loud terrified cries and then silence. Bulkhead crossed to the opposite room. The woman near the darkened window, limp and pale against the pillow, turned his way with dreamy slowness. Above her mask her eyes went wide, and Bulkhead dispatched her, then finished her roommate off.

The CAR 15 barked in the hallway, sending the nurses screaming. Bulkhead entered the next room. Faster, faster, he urged himself, and raked the beds with fire. The man near the window spasmed and jerked. The one near the toilet stiffened and screamed without sound.

Bulkhead ran to the hallway again. A light strong feeling suffused his chest; he was flying, his feet on air. He would get them all. He knew it now. He would get them all and the plague would be over and he would be safe and the world would be safe. He had waited and waited for orders that never came, and now the long wait was over.

Two more bursts from the CAR 15, and two more deaths. They were all as good as dead anyway, the rabies would kill them anyway, he was only speeding things up. Someday the whole world would thank him for this, they would give him the Medal of Honor.

He was out in the hallway again, and now an alarm was sounding. Hurry! he urged himself. A scream. He ended it.

The doors to the pediatric ward flew open; two nurses came through them screaming. Sandra and Howard Barnes, in chairs near the wall, both jumped to their feet. "What?" Sandra said, and the hallway was suddenly utter confusion, with visitors and hospital personnel shouting, running, and Howard gave Sandra a sudden shove, sending her into a room.

"Get down!" he yelled from out in the hall, and she heard a popping sound, again, again, getting louder, screams tore at her ears, and she dropped to the floor and crawled under the bed near the toilet. "Matty! Lucy!" she cried in a broken voice. This was not their room, she didn't know who the children were in this room, and the popping sound was vicious and loud now, the cries were deafening.

People lay on the hallway floor, some moaning and writhing, some dead. Bulkhead turned and looked into the room.

And saw in the bed before him a very young girl, maybe five or six, with blond hair, her eyes fastened in sleep. He licked his lips and swallowed hard and his throat made a clicking sound. Sweat poured heavily over his cheeks and his hands felt weak. *But you must* said a voice in his mind. One of the wounded down by his feet, an orderly, groaned.

He heard a sharp crack and his head snapped back and he grabbed at his burning neck and whirled, and there was Kearney.

"No!" Bulkhead yelled in a hoarse and horrified voice, but before he could aim his CAR 15, Kearney's bullets had torn out his throat.

When the firing stopped, Sandra ran to the hallway.

Howard was down on the floor, his entire shirt red with blood. His chest was making a thick sucking sound, and his lids were half-closed.

"No, no," Sandra said, weeping, running her hand through his hair. His mask was askew and she tore it off, then tore off her own mask, too. Taking his hands in hers, she said again, "No."

285

"Biological warfare," Howard said, his mouth hanging open, a line of red drool leaking onto his chin.

"What?" she said.

"Farrow . . . Kessler . . . Christian Charity."

She wept in utter confusion, shaking her head. "Howard . . ."

"Christian Charity," he said. "You have to . . . Sandra . . . No . . . I love you . . ."

His eyes rolled back and he slumped to the side. She squeezed his hands hard. "Howard. *Howard!*"

He didn't respond. Sandra jumped up and ran down the hallway, past wounded and dead. "Amelia!" she cried. "Someone, please! Amelia!"

She ran thrugh the doors at the end of the hall, and was greeted by total chaos.

Bodies lay on the floor, splayed, crooked, in puddles of blood, a young nurse was crying, two soldiers with rifles were running her way, an alarm rang and rang, a doctor was on the phone at the nurses' station, barking out orders. Another doctor was kneeling, his back to Sandra. She ran to him. "Doctor, please—"

Her words died in her throat. For the doctor was kneeling above Amelia Rose, and one side of her head was gone.

FORTY-ONE

Oliver Emmet, beardless, with spiky black hair, never wrote about Bulkhead Morrison. As soon as he'd filed the piece on the sexual transmission of rabies, he'd changed his appearance and rented a car and headed straight for Canada.

He knew that once that story broke, the feds would be on him in a flash. How well had he known Cherry White? they would ask. And was he himself sick?

He was indeed sick, quite sick, and was not going to die in Blue Harbor. He'd die on the road in a shootout first, he swore to God he would, though he owned no gun and didn't intend to buy one. No, he intended to get to Quebec just as fast as he could and check into a hospital there. Quebec was the closest city with top-notch medical care, and what with all the wolves in those northern woods, they probably knew one hell of a lot about rabies.

By the time he took off he was feverish, and his plan made perfect sense. He headed out Route 3 in the pale August dawn, his arms and legs aching, his genitals burning, his thoughts a confused melange of present and past. Random scenes from his childhood rushed at him—hitting a home run in Little League, dropping a blueberry pie that his mother had made, failing an English test in junior high—and merged with the present: Cherry White, the Great Day Cafe, sitting alone in the Starbuck Motel with his laptop computer, hammering out the day's story.

Then he'd enter long spaces of nothing, just nothing at all: no thoughts, no road, no anything, as he drove in a hot dim daze of pain and fear. And even the pain and fear would sometimes fade to a buzzing blank light in his brain, and then all at once he could hardly swallow. Out of his center a rage would build and consume his soul, and he'd stare with hot eyes at the ribbon of road and hate the entire world.

Each intersection was a trap, a shelter for cops, and he constantly glanced at the rearview mirror, expecting to see their blue lights. But the only lights he saw were the yellow ones deep in his brain, and his only pursuer was deep in his flesh, and one that he couldn't outrun.

By 6:00 A.M. he had reached the town of Skowhegan. He stopped for gas and the sun on the crest of the hills hurt his eyes. When he took off again, his brain said, The flu, that's all it is, there's a lot of it going around. In Quebec he would have a complete exam. He figured he'd be there in less than four hours.

But something happened that he hadn't anticipated: Twenty-five minutes later, at Solon, he encountered the Kennebec River.

Its brightness sent dazzling spikes at his eyes and the flow of it over the rocks made him gasp for breath.

He pulled over, heart racing, and looked at his map. If he stayed on Route 201, as he'd planned, the Kennebec would be right beside him for . . . what? Another hour? He traced the line with his fingers, thinking, No! and his throat closed off. He would turn here, escape it, he couldn't bear the sight or sound of it.

He went south onto Route 16, and the river was still

there, laughing, contracting his throat. He blocked it off with his visor and stared through the windshield, his jaws clamped shut, arms shaking and burning, a thick cold sweat pouring over his temples and cheeks.

Two miles down the road, in a desolate stretch of spruce and pine, he stopped and got out to urinate. He had used the bathroom at the filling station, and now, half an hour later, the pressure was urgent again. In the car his legs went rubbery, soft. The soles of his feet went numb, and he thought: I'm dying.

He looked at himself in the rearview mirror. The black of his dyed chopped hair made his skin look like chalk. He started the engine again and drove with fierce determination, staring straight ahead.

He left the river behind in North Anson and drove in a trance, sharp pains stabbing into his throat. He was lost in a dream of a hot summer's day in Boston, shopping downtown at Filene's for a cotton suit, and the next thing he knew he had made it to Kingfield.

Sugarloaf Mountain was close to here, a ski resort. He had come here before, years ago, with his ex-wife, Julie. That snow, so bright, tiny crystals of frozen . . . water.

Gasping for breath, he pulled up in front of a restaurant and checked his map. For a moment it made no sense whatsoever; then, forcing his finger across the paper, he saw a blue oval, which meant that a lake lay ahead.

No way to avoid it. And after that, another lake. And then, to avoid more water, he'd have to take small back roads in Canada, and God only knew how long it would take him— Don't think of that! he told himself, and started the car again.

The sound of the engine screamed in his ears, and he, too, was screaming, his hands stiff and dead on the wheel. He raced down Main Street, chest aching, crotch itching and burning, his legs hot and shaking and weak.

He was suddenly struck by a powerful thirst—an unbearable thirst! His mouth was parched and hot and thick and he needed a drink right now!

On the corner, in front of a general store, stood a blue and white Pepsi machine. He pulled into the lot, slammed the brakes and got out, the soles of his feet thick and numb.

As he reached for some change, the rage overtook him. He threw down a handful of coins at the dust and pounded the box with his fists till the plastic cracked. A screen door snapped and a man yelled, "Hey!" then backed off with wide-eyed fear as Emmet came charging, teeth bared. The man stumbled into his store, locked the door, and Emmet kicked it savagely, smashing the glass, screaming nonsense words in a squeaky high voice as saliva dripped over his chin.

Then he suddenly turned and ran off: past his car, down the street, kept running and running, his chest a bright ocean of fire.

Time drowned. Pictures popped in his brain like flashbulbs. He ran with the noise of jet planes in his ears, his own screams, ran, ran down the road, to the stream.

It stopped him dead. He was burning with thirst, but the sight of the water sent arrows of pain through his throat. He clutched at his neck as the spasms tore through him. A blinding pain ripped at his skull and he staggered forward, legs lifeless as stone, and the water was coming closer, closer, he managed to choke out a high pitched rasp—

Then slipped and fell and slid down the bank and went into the water headfirst.

It felt like sizzling fat on his tender skin. Grunts of pain left his paralyzed lips and he jerked in a spastic dance, arms flailing.

Above, on the bank, a crowd had gathered to watch this spectacular show. Emmet fell and went under, then shot up screaming. His whole being was fire and pain and rage, a dark bloody rage at the universe. Hot spasms attacked his stomach. Again he fell, and again he came up with a roar. On the bank someone shouted, "Don't help him! He's got the rabies!" but Emmet heard nothing at all. Even his own cries of pain had gone dead in his ears, and the sky had become a dark murderous purple, and angels with lances laughed into the slits of his sight. He went under the lava of water a third time and didn't come up.

That afternoon, a twenty-two-year-old reporter for the *Kingfield News* filed the story of Emmet's death, and it went worldwide.

FORTY-TWO

When Sandra Barnes's children died within ten hours of each other, her grief and pain obliterated thought. She had no memory of being driven home by Dr. Hoyt, and when he came back to give her more drugs, she at first didn't know who he was. He asked about her friends, but she had no friends—none in Blue Harbor, at any rate. They were dead, along with her husband and children. He came back again in the morning and gave her another injection and asked her about what to do with the bodies. His words didn't register right away. A long time passed before she said, "Cremation, of course. Like Howard." And what should be done with the ashes? "Scattered, like his. In the sea."

In the long delirious empty hours, her children kept coming back: their smiles, their voices, over and over, until she would cry out and bang at the walls with her fists. And Howard had helped those people—the killers—Howard had defended them. He'd understood the darkness of their work and had supported them, and now he was dead and his children were dead, cremated in Jillson's ovens. He had served his profession and Moloch, its god, all too well.

She received some calls from two Washington friends, Jan Hollis and Becky Kent, and had started out fairly well, but had lost it both times, ending up in hysterics, the receiver slick with her tears. She was stuck in Blue Harbor, she couldn't get out, there was nowhere to go to escape her pain except deeper into the drugs. But they made her sick, and after the third day of sickness, she told Dr. Hoyt, No more.

At the dining room table, dressed in her robe, her body trembling, she drank tea with sugar and milk, the only nourishment she'd taken since her children died, except for some apple juice Dr. Hoyt had forced upon her. She looked at the placid, silver cove, the flat gray sky, and drank the sweet tea, and a bitter rage filled her heart. Howard's sailboat was still at its mooring out there, and she pictured him in it, a smile on his face, the kids in their life vests beside him, and everything fine as they headed out into the bay. He always came back if the wind got too brisk, since he knew she would worry. And now she would never worry again about anything, for her life was completely superfluous.

She finished her tea, a dull ache at the base of her skull, and thought about Howard's last words. Christian Charity. Farrow and Kessler. She stood up and went to the bedroom.

She opened her top bureau drawer and took out the .22 pistol; looked at it there in her open palm for close to ten minutes, staring at it, feeling its comforting weight. She picked up the box of shells in the drawer, put the pistol and shells in her purse. She sat on the bed and gritted her teeth and punched at the mattress with tears in her eyes. Then she dressed.

When Farrow heard about Bulkhead Morrison's rampage, he did more coke and returned to the hospital. For three gut-wrenching hours, he helped with the wounded, and back in his cottage, the coke long gone, the thought of the dead Amelia Rose sinking tentacles into his brain, his fatigue overwhelmed him. He slept in his lounge chair and woke at dawn with an aching head and sore throat; brewed a pot of strong coffee and drank three cups and went to the lab, but right before noon the shaking began, and at two o'clock he went home.

His symptoms grew rapidly worse, as he'd known they would. He slept in a fever and woke in a sweat and heard voices, one of them vaguely familiar—Janice?—saying to get in his boat; and he'd actually gone through the door before something behind the voices said, Don't listen, go back.

In his lounge chair he slept again, and woke to a stillness, a sudden cool calm in which all became perfectly clear. He sat at his desk and wrote a letter, addressed it and drove to the post office, dropping the envelope into the drive-up box with a quivering hand. When he got back home, exhausted and hot, the voices started up again, and they lasted far into the night.

He woke late the next morning, a fierce stabbing pain in his throat and his mind a blur. He remembered the lifeless dog in the Jillson cage, the monitor, the tubes, and went in a haze from his bedroom into his studio, his study, the guest room that had never held a guest, collecting his paintings, taking them into the living room and setting them against the walls, the chairs, the tables, the TV set.

He returned to his studio for his paints, took them back to his lounge chair, and sitting down dizzily, sweating profusely, he picked up the tubes of oil, one by one, and squeezed them onto the table beside him, making a swirling mountain of color. He uncapped the mineral spirits and turpentine, brought the cans to his nose, took deep breaths.

The painting he'd worked on most this summer sat on top of the desk near the sliding glass doors, still unfinished. He hadn't been able to touch it since that day Paul had come here and told him a Jillson dog had bitten Teddy Marsh. It depicted the cove that now shimmered like molten lead under heavy gray skies. The day he'd stopped working on it had been spectacular, the last good day of his life.

When he stood up, he nearly lost consciousness; sparks spun through his eyes. He went to the desk where the unfinished painting sat and opened a drawer, removed a vial and a fresh syringe, then returned to his chair.

Hands shaking, he fixed the syringe. Miranda Shore, Amelia Rose, Sharon Jensen, Walt Marsh and his son, Gary Simmons and Tricia Stemmer . . . in the back of his mind, a parade of the dead and dying. He looked at the unfinished painting again and thought: If I had been really talented, this horror would never have happened. He shrugged. And what if Louis Pasteur had loved art more than science? Would the world be better off? One does what one has to in life; it's not always a matter of choice. I thought I could make a contribution.

He set the syringe down and picked up a book of matches. "Blue Harbor Inn," said its cover. "The finest in French and down home Maine cuisine."

The Blue Harbor Inn was a hospice now.

He tore a match out of the book with quivering fingers and struck it and stared at its flame. Beyond the flame, in the movie behind his eyes, he watched as a field flared up; saw a young boy stamp on the flames in excitement, saw the fire spread out of control, saw the boy run and run . . .

When Sandra Barnes finally got through to Jillson, a female voice informed her that Kessler was not available and that Farrow was not at the lab. Not at the lab, that was just what she wanted to hear. She went out to her car.

She knew where his cottage was, because Howard had pointed it out on one of their sails, and if luck was with her, that's where he'd be today.

Her white Saab turbo raced down the gravel road. The sky was a milky, depressing gray, and a fine mist coated the windsheild. She tore past spruce and fir and pine, past driveways snaking into the trees, past mailboxes: Hamilton, Wagner, Combs. All dead. As Farrow too would soon be dead. She thought of the gun in her purse: pictured pulling the trigger. It sent a hot thrill through her chest.

A few seconds later, blue lights came alive in her rearview mirror and, No, she thought, gritting her teeth, it can't be. Jesus Christ, they don't have anything better to do—?

She slowed and pulled over, shoving her handbag under her seat. Damn, her license was in there as well as the gun, she'd—

The police car sped past in a shower of gravel and dust, and before the dust cleared, two fire engines screamed down the road behind it.

Sandra pulled onto the road again, her heart thin and quick.

The cruiser blocked Farrow's driveway. Beyond it stood the fire engines, spewing high streams of water

296

onto the cottage, which crackled and danced with flames.

Sandra pulled to the side of the road and watched. Flames poured from the cottage's windows; huge sparks shot high into the sullen gray sky. She got out of the car. Even here at the head of the driveway she felt the heat. The cruiser's radio said something urgent and the trooper responded. The air howled with flames. A section of roof gave way with a silent crash.

Sandra went to the cruiser's window. "I'm his sister," she said. "Do you know if . . . ?"

"Not yet," said the trooper, his eyes cool blue.

"Oh," Sandra said, and went back to her car.

The rain began in a sudden rush. More fire engines came. The first two—out of water—sped away, and the new ones took their place. It took three more engines and two more hours of steady, heavy rain before the fire died.

At last the trooper came up to her window and said, "I'm afraid he was in there."

"I see," Sandra said. She looked at the cottage's smoldering black crooked sticks.

"Will you need a ride? Are you going to be all right?"

"I'll be all right," Sandra said.

When the trooper left, she started the Saab and headed for home again. She parked in her driveway, rain hammering down on the car's roof and hood, sliding over the glass. She banged her fists on the steering wheel, and said through clenched teeth as tears came to her eyes, "Goddamn you, Farrow, you son of a bitch! *I* should have been the one!"

FORTY-THREE

Dear Paul,

By the time you read this, I will be dead from cyanide injection. Painless and instantaneous, as you know. I had no choice. For the sad and depressing fact of the matter is, I contracted Flowers rabies from Protocol 4.

I started the series weeks ago, with high hopes. It was shortly after the dog became ill, that I, too, fell ill—after I took my last dose. I thought that perhaps the reaction would be a mild one. Then the dog expired, and my symptoms grew worse. It was clear I'd developed an active case of rabies.

In spite of this, I believe it is still worthwhile to administer Protocol 4 to those who sustain a lesion. The other dogs are doing well, and we know that the series has worked in mice. Let's face it: It's better than nothing. What can we lose?

In the meantime, press forward as fast as you can with the new vaccine. It is going to work. I know it is. And someday soon this terrible scourge will be stopped.

Now, Paul, I have something distressing to tell you, something you may have suspected for quite some time. (You are not as easy to fool as I once thought you were.) Our rabies research is funded by the Pentagon. It is biological warfare research, a project known as Christian Charity. General William Kromer is the man in charge. He will no doubt be in touch with you as soon as he learns I am dead.

You were right, Paul. We should never have worked on this project. Yet I couldn't totally discount Kromer's suspicion that Russia or somebody else had developed this virus, and was gearing up to unleash it on us. I wanted us to be ready if this was the case. I wanted to save our people, Paul. And be a hero, of course, another Pasteur. But fate would not have it that way.

Paul, the burden is now on your shoulders. Never doubt your capabilities, and you will succeed.

You are one of the best men I ever knew, and I wish you luck and health and long life. Say good-bye to Angela and the children for me, and forgive me.

Sincerely,

Martin

When Paul Kessler finished the letter, he took off his glasses and closed his eyes and rocked back and forth with his head in his clammy hands. "Martin, how could you do this to me?" he wept. "How could you, how could you? Leaving me alone like this. Disgracing me like this."

Biological warfare. A cold sweat coated his skin as he rocked. All this agony, all this death, a town ruined, the whole world threatened. That reporter who'd died outside of Blue Harbor, God only knew who he'd come into contact with.

And now it was up to him to stop it all. Oh sure, he had Kilgore and Hilton and all the rest, but basically, when you got right down to it, he was the one responsible.

Wiping his eyes, he put on his glasses again and read, *The burden is now on your shoulders. Never doubt* . . .

Never doubt. His breath caught in his throat and a wave of nausea struck him. "Oh, Martin, goddamn your soul."

Late yesterday afternoon the police had called him at work and had told him about the fire. Trapped? Burned to death? His mind had gone totally numb. He had driven right out there, shaking, his breath coming hard in irregular gasps, and had stared at the smouldering ruins for almost an hour. He hadn't been able to sleep until dawn, and had come to the lab today shaking and sick, to find this letter waiting.

He looked out the window: flat gray. The rain of the day before had turned into a peasoup fog, the perfect mirror of his mind. Biological warfare. He wished he had never been born.

The telephone rang. He let it ring five times. *General Kromer will no doubt be in touch* . . . With trembling fingers, he picked it up.

"Hello?"

"Sandra Barnes?" his receptionist said.

The name didn't register. Then: "Oh, yes," he said, "put her on."

The line clicked. "Hello?"

"Paul?"

300

"Yes?"

"This is Sandra Barnes. We worked together on the toxic waste campaign?"

"Of course." And your husband is dead, your children are dead—

"My husband—"

Is dead. And soon you will also be dead, because . . . No, he hadn't been infected, he died of a gunshot wound.

"—Howard worked on Christian Charity."

Kessler, catching his breath, said, "Christian Charity?"—as if he'd never heard of it.

"As you know, he was killed, and before he died, he gave me a message for you. A very important message."

"Yes?"

"I can't tell you over the phone, I have to meet with you. It's especially important now that Farrow is dead."

"Yes," Kessler said, his heart speeding up. "Where do you want to meet me?"

"I'll come to your office. I'll be there within the hour."

"I'll inform the guards that you're coming," Kessler said.

"I'm so terribly sorry about your family."

Sandra was sitting opposite him, on the other side of his desk. She nodded tersely. "Thank you."

"So many tragedies," Kessler said. In front of him, in gilt-edged frames, sat Angela, Jeff, and Mindy. His heart was sick for Sandra Barnes. "You said you have a message for me?"

"Yes." Sandra opened her purse. "It's right here. It's—" she pulled out her pistol and pointed it straight at his chest—"you're going to die."

301

Kessler's eyebrows shot up. "For God's sake!" he said.

"You thought you would get away with this?" Sandra said, her eyes fastened on his. "You thought you could murder a whole goddamn town and go free?"

"Sandra, listen—" He held up his hand.

"No, you listen, Paul. You're going to die. But not by my gun, that would be too easy. You're going to die the way my children died."

"Sandra—"

"Go get the virus, Paul."

"What?"

"Get it, Paul. You're going to infect yourself."

"Sandra, no!"

"Oh yes, Paul, yes, that's how you will die. You're going to inject yourself, nice and deep, where no antiseptic can reach, and soon you're going to feel what my children felt."

Kessler's forehead was soaking. His glasses had slid down his nose and he pushed them up. "But you don't understand," he said. "It wasn't my fault."

She jabbed the gun at him. "Go get the virus."

"It's in the lab."

"Let's go, then."

"We need to wear masks," he said.

She sniffed a laugh. "Fine. Let's wear masks."

He gave her one from a box in his desk. They put them on and she followed him out of the office. The hand that held the gun was in her purse.

They went down the hallway. Two middle-aged women in masks said hello. Business as usual at Jillson, Sandra thought, and if Kessler made a false move, she would shoot them all.

They entered the lab. White-coated people in masks and gloves—killers—sat at the tables.

302

Crossing to the refrigerators, Kessler pressed a combination lock and opened a stainless steel door. Vials of liquid lined the shelves. He picked one up, closed the door again.

Back in his office again, Sandra said, "A syringe?" She was pointing the gun at his head.

"Right here," Kessler said in a faltering voice, and opened a drawer in his desk. "Sandra, listen, you have to believe me, I didn't know—"

She tore her mask off. "Fix it," she said.

He swallowed hard, sweat making his forehead gleam. With pleading eyes he said, "I'm the only hope. Farrow's dead, I'm the only one who knows enough to stop this thing before it gets out of Blue Harbor. And I will stop it, Sandra, we're on the edge of a breakthrough."

"Fine," Sandra said. "Prepare the syringe."

"Don't you understand what I'm saying?"

"I understand that you killed my babies with biological warfare. It is time for you to receive the same Christian Charity, Paul."

"But I didn't know," Kessler insisted. "Your husband knew more than I did. I never heard of Christian Charity until today, I swear to God."

"Prepare the syringe."

Sweat poured over Kessler's cheeks. "Sandra, honest to God," he said, and he picked up the letter from Farrow. "Read this. Please."

She took the letter, glanced at it, then gave it back. "You read it," she said.

He did, the syringe in his other hand.

When he finished, she said, "William Kromer."

"You see?" he said. "I didn't know. If I had known, my God, I wouldn't—"

"Give me the vial," she said.

"What?"

She held out her purse. "Drop it in here. The needle, too."

He did.

"You have more needles?"

He nodded.

"I want them."

He reached in his drawer and took out a pair of syringes and dropped them into her purse. "Sandra, what are you doing?"

"I'm letting you live," she said. "But if you ever tell a soul I was here, the whole world will die."

"Sandra, please—"

"I'll inject it in birds, Paul. They'll go anywhere, everywhere."

"You wouldn't do that!"

"Don't test me."

"I won't tell a soul you were here. I swear."

"For the world's sake, I hope you don't."

When she left his office, he locked the door and hurried back to his phone; picked up the receiver and punched three numbers.

"Switchboard."

"This is Dr. Kessler. A woman just left my office who has to be stopped. She's crazy, she's got a gun. Alert the guards."

When he hung up, a cold wave washed through him. He looked at the photographs there on his desk and thought of how close he had come. She was crazy, crazy, but he couldn't blame her, he was half-crazy himself. If she'd killed him, though, the rabies research would have suffered a terrible blow.

He went to the door again; opened it cautiously.

Sandra was gone. They would get her, though, she

wouldn't escape, her gun was no match for the National Guard. She wasn't *that* crazy.

He sighed and went back to his desk and looked into his open drawer. No danger she'd spread the disease, at least. For the vial did not contain virus, but Protocol 3 vaccine.

He sat down in his chair and waited, a tremor deep in his limbs. They would get her, poor creature. The phone would ring any minute now, telling him that.

FORTY-FOUR

But Sandra reached the parking lot before the alert went out, and drove off into the fog to North Shore Road. By the time the police arrived at her house, she was driving down Roaring Spout Lane.

Crossing the mist-shrouded field at the end of the lane, she parked in a grove of pines. She and Howard and Lucy and Matty had picnicked here so many times, on so many glorious days. A trail in these pines led down to the cliffs and sea.

No one had yet escaped from Blue Harbor, but no one had tried the route that she planned to use. It was treacherous, perhaps out of the question, but it was the only way she could think of.

The barbed wire fence that the Guard had erected came to a stop at the cliffs, as the cliffs themselves were barrier enough to any escape attempt. But there was a hole in those cliffs, the Roaring Spout, and if you could get through that hole . . .

As far as she knew, no one had ever done it. Theoretically, though, it was possible. The channel through which the water rushed was maybe twenty feet long. If you tried at low tide, when the Spout was calm, and dived when the water was on its way out of the channel . . .

On the seat beside her was a waterproof nylon bag about eight inches square, an item that Howard had taken on sailing trips. It was navy blue, with two sturdy straps, and now contained a pair of nylon running shorts, a nylon T-shirt, a credit card, and five hundred dollars in cash. Next to these items she placed the pistol, the syringes and vial she'd taken from Kessler, and zipped it up again.

She got out of the car and took off her dress, revealing a black tank suit. The air was heavy and wet and cold and a shiver went down her spine. She strapped the nylon bag to her upper left thigh. It was heavy. Too heavy, she thought. She shivered again, then went into the woods, her running shoes crunching on dead black twigs.

At a distance she heard a foghorn: the lighthouse at Mussel Point. She hurried forward, spruce trees scratching her legs, and soon came to the path. A few minutes later she reached the cliffs.

Below her she heard the suck and swirl of the Spout, now hidden in dense gray fog. She started down the jagged granite outcrop, crouching, getting a handhold wherever she could. Down she went, and the sound of the water increased. And then she could see it, the gray turgid channel between the rocks, much wider than she had realized.

It looked impossible. Perhaps it was. Perhaps this was how she would die.

Well, then, this was how she would die.

She scrabbled down closer. The water was only a few feet away from her now, and even though the tide was out and the air was heavy and still, it surged with an awesome force.

Her heartbeat was suddenly racing. A tunnel of darkness, wet and cold. How long? Twenty feet? Twenty-five? Her life could hinge on the difference.

Above her the mat of gray fog pressed down, and the tops of the cliffs were gone. Kessler had surely reported her, the National Guard and police were combing the island, and this was the only way out of their net. She stared at the water, jaws tight.

In high school she'd been so good: in such great condition, and expertly trained. But she'd never have dared attempt this. And now she was twice her high school age and her only workouts had been daily swims in the cove—until two weeks ago, when her world had begun to crumble.

The water surged, and a sharp wave of fear hit her stomach. *You have to,* she told herself, *that's all there is to it,* and slipped off her running shoes.

On the other side of these cliffs lay Butterfly Island—a small hump of barren rock. It was only a hundred yards or so from the cliffs. If she could reach that rock and gather strength there, she ought to be able to make the swim to shore—another three hundred yards—without any problem.

If she could reach that rock. A very big if indeed.

She crouched on the granite shelf at the edge of the water and took a deep breath. An image of countless swimming pools came back, her body a coil of tension alert for the gun. The water rushed up to her feet, dashed spray on her shins, went out again, slack . . . and she dived.

She was used to the cold, she had swum in this water for years, and the blackness was just like swimming at night, but this wasn't night, this was walls of stone, a tunnel of stone. How long? How wide? Was it straight? Would she hit her head?

She pushed her arms hard to her sides and scissored her legs, propelling herself past thought, not feeling the bag on her thigh, a machine for motion, pushing, kicking . . .

And the water turned. It was coming up into the tunnel again and pushed against her with terrible strength. She opened her eyes upon utter darkness, just darkness and water, she had no breath, she would have to breathe water . . .

No! her bursting mind screamed, blind with panic, No! She struggled upwards, rose . . .

And came into air and breathed.

Here in the center of blackness: air. For the roof of the tunnel curved upwards here, there was air in here, for this moment at least, and Sandra gulped it, her lungs sharp and frantic. The water swelled up to her chin and she said to herself: *Go back.* You can make it back, give up, there must be another way. She hung there, her head tilted backwards, her cheek against stone, her breath eager and hard. No, no, she told herself, it can't be much farther now.

She breathed. The water rushed back to its source and she felt a lull; then it came at her hard again through the channel, black on black. She breathed, heart pounding, as it swirled and pulled; awaited its retreat. When it came, she dived again and pushed with every ounce of strength, shooting forward again into numb cold darkness, limbs aching, lungs burning.

Then light, gray light, then whiter, whiter, and out she burst into the fog, gasping, crying, her chest heaving brutally. Yes, she had done it, yes, and she sucked at the air with greedy hot lungs and wept, her feet dead from the cold as they pumped at the terrible sea.

But where was the island? Ahead of her all was gray.

She rested a moment, then started to swim with deliberate smooth strokes.

In the distance, the foghorn sounded. Behind her the cliffs dissolved. Just swim, she told herself.

She did: for a long time, too long. Her arms and legs turned thick and her thoughts turned thick and Where am I? they said. I am lost, they said. She wept again and cursed, jaw clenched.

The foghorn, mournful, far away, and then—the cracked cry of a bird.

The island, her sluggish mind said, and she pushed at the water harder, gritting her teeth.

She kicked and pulled and the island rose out of the fog. She scissored hard. A bird took off. The one that had cried out? The one that had saved her life?

She clutched at the jagged rock, sucking air, her lips retracted, weak sounds seeping out of her throat. She pulled herself up and rolled over, gasping, and saw her knee suddenly blossom with blood. She had banged herself on the rocks at some point, hadn't felt it, and tatters of flesh hung down. The sight made her sick and she looked away, but too late, too late, the sky in her head grew bright . . .

Sandra woke up in darkness, disoriented, her entire left leg in pain. She stirred, scraping her elbow, a thick bitter taste in her mouth; saw lights across the water, yellow squares.

The fog had thinned. The cliffs of Blue Harbor stood black against charcoal gray. She looked at the opposite shore again at the lights: cottage windows. Only two pairs of them, far apart, in the village of Cranberry Cove. There were very few people in Cranberry Cove. Most had left weeks ago, because of the rabies.

Her mangled knee sent sharp pain through her thigh.

She sat up, shivering, cold to her bones; took a deep breath and brushed back her hair. She had to get moving, to reach that shore.

Where they would be waiting for her?

She climbed down the rocks to the water's edge, and recoiled as her foot touched wet. Bracing herself, she lowered her body into the cold dark sea.

The water numbed her injured leg and she quickly found her rhythm; swam with determined, measured strokes towards a spot to the left of the cottages.

Fifteen minutes later she reached the shore and clung to the boards of a dock while she caught her breath. Except for the gentle lapping of waves on the pebbles and sand, it was silent. Holding onto the dock, she walked, hunched down, towards land.

When she reached the end of the dock she paused for a second. Hearing nothing but quiet surf and the foghorn, she looked up the beach both ways, then hurried into the woods behind the dark cottage that stood on the knoll to her right.

The earth here was covered with pine needles, soft on her naked feet. She walked through darkness; stepped on something sharp and winced in pain.

She went forward cautiously, pushing wet branches out of her way. Her injured leg was throbbing again, and every so often a low dead branch would graze it, sending a raw stab of pain through her knee and thigh.

Finally she reached the road, Route 6, her path to freedom. But she didn't dare walk on the road; they would catch her for sure. So she stayed in the woods, making her way with painful slowness through branches and rocks and roots, her hurt leg burning, her naked feet starting to sting.

The tank suit clung to her clammy skin and goose bumps covered her arms. She unstrapped the bag from her thigh, stripped, unzipped the bag and put on the

311

T-shirt and shorts. Not much more protection or warmth, but dry at least, and much less conspicuous. She'd look like just another jogger now, some crazy summer person.

But what to do with the bathing suit? If she left it here, a police dog would find it. Deciding to keep it for now, she wrung it out, and holding both it and the bag, started off again.

The tree branches tore at her forearms and thighs. On the road, a car went past. She stopped and watched it, wishing that she was inside it. A wave of giddiness struck her as she watched its taillights fade. For a second her balance failed, then she caught herself and pushed on.

The woods were formidable, black and dense. She would stop in the blackness, her breath coming hard, her knee blazing, her clammy skin scratched and torn, and feel hopeless. And then she'd remember Kromer, and make herself move again.

Shivering, numb, a pain in her ribs, she stumbled across a trail. It paralleled the road, and she laughed at her luck. She followed it down to a stream, where it rose again, and there was the road again, and a building—a store, with its windows dark. She knew the place, had passed it a thousand times on her way in and out of Blue Harbor, had bought gas there.

Behind it stood two garbage cans. She went to the one on the left and lifted its lid. It made a scraping sound and she held her breath. She listened. Nothing. She put her bathing suit in the can and put the lid on again.

A pair of headlights on the road. She crouched behind the garbage cans. The lights swished by.

She went to the side of the building and looked through the window. A clock with an illuminated face, a Miller's High Life clock, stood over the counter. Ten

312

twenty-two, it said. Already that late. The rack of chips in the clock's dull glow made her suddenly hungry. Smash the window, steal the food, and maybe there was a shirt in there, a pair of shoes. . . .

More lights. She hurried around the building, and the truck roared past.

When it disappeared, she crossed the road. This store wasn't far from Ellington, she didn't think. Ten minutes by car? She couldn't remember.

She walked along the edge of the road, the nylon bag in her hand. When headlights appeared in the distance she ducked off into the woods and crouched down. Not many cars this time of night, not these days.

A cluster of houses stood up ahead. In one of them, some lights were on. She cut back into the woods; fought her way through the branches and brush, cursing under her breath as the twigs lashed her damaged knee.

A quick rustle, a growl, and a dog was in front of her, barking its head off. Her heart skipped a beat and she froze. The dog, a bristling shadow, snarled, bouncing forward, its front legs stiff.

Her mind was racing. A dog on the loose. She had seen no dogs for at least a month, except for the German shepards used by the Guard. Through the nylon bag in her hand, she felt the gun.

The dog stopped, suddenly wary. Not rabid, she thought, and urged in her mind, Go away! Then from out by the road, near the house, came a gruff male voice: "Skipper! Get back here! You come in here!"

The dog started up again, louder. The voice by the house yelled, "Get back here, goddamn you! Now! Goddamn you, Skipper, there ain't nothin' out there, get up here!"

The dog's tension slackened; it turned with a frustrated growl and loped back to the house. "That's

313

all I need, you rasslin' a skunk," said the voice, faded now. A door slammed shut, and after a little while, the lights went out.

Sandra fought with the brush and trees again. Once she was well past the houses, she made her way out to the road.

FORTY-FIVE

Ellington was farther away than Sandra had estimated. Exhausted, she rested a number of times in the weeds by the side of the road, head aching, her knee on fire, her breathing the only sound. When she finally reached the town, it was fast asleep.

She walked along a back street past the dump and a lumberyard, past houses with blackened windows or dim lights burning upstairs. A cat, a black shadow, crossed her path and she held her breath. As the cat disappeared in the weeds, she reminded herself: I'm back in the normal world again. The cats and dogs are all right here. There is no rabies here.

Her wounded knee throbbed hard. A thousand scratches stung her skin. Her back and hips and ankles ached, and the soles of her feet were burning. The streetlamps, blue, with moths diving into their plastic shades, seemed hazy yet far too bright, and her thoughts kept floating up and away and blending into dreams.

She made it to Main Street, Route 1. A block away a red and green neon sign said, "Great Day Cafe—Open 24 Hours—Eat." She started toward it, expecting at any moment to see the blue lights of a cruiser flash on and a spotlight shine in her face. She went down the sidewalk from tree to tree, from shadow to light to shadow.

A dozen trucks and cars were lined up in the narrow parking lot, their noses aimed at the Great Day's cream-colored walls. An eighteen-wheeler with New York plates and Nationwide Hardware on its side was parked near a tall cedar hedge. Sandra hid in the cedars and waited.

Behind the diner's steamy windows she saw men drinking coffee, eating. Her hunger flared up again, powerful, painful. She clutched herself, shivering, feeling faint. The door swung open. Two men came out and went to a pickup truck.

She waited. More people came out and drove off. Another car arrived, and a young man slammed his door, flung his cigarette butt to the ground, and went into the diner.

So normal, so right, Sandra thought. While only a few miles away, people lived in a concentration camp. She closed her eyes and clutched herself harder, giddy.

The truck driver finally appeared. He came around the front of his rig and reached for the door of his cab, and Sandra said softly, "Excuse me."

The truck driver jerked and looked up. He was thin, about thirty years old, and was wearing a blue baseball cap with the red letter D. "Holy Christ," he said.

"I'm sorry if I startled you," Sandra said, stepping out of the shadows. "I wonder if I could trouble you to get me a cup of coffee."

The driver squinted and said, "Holy Christ, what happened?"

"My boyfriend threw me out of his car."

"Holy Christ."

"I'm okay," Sandra said, "I just need some coffee. And maybe a sandwich?" She opened her nylon bag and took out a ten, her smallest bill.

The truck driver took the money and said, "You don't look okay. That knee looks bad, and you must be freezin'. Here, sit in my cab," and he opened the door.

"Thanks."

"What kind of a sandwich?"

"Egg salad."

"You want your coffee regular?"

"That's fine."

He came back a few minutes later and got in beside her, gave her the change, then the food. Snapping the lid off the styrofoam cup, she drank. The coffee was hot and cloyingly sweet and tasted fantastic to her.

"Threw you out of the car, Holy Christ! The police station's right down the street, they'll get you fixed up."

"I'm okay," Sandra said, "it looks worse than it is, I just have to get out of here. Can you give me a ride?"

"Sure," the driver said, shrugging, and turned the ignition key. The engine caught with an oily metallic purr. Sandra drank again, then unwrapped the sandwich and started to eat. The truck backed out of the lot, started south on Route 1.

"I'm Danny," the driver said.

"I'm Ann," Sandra said.

"So where do you plan on goin'?"

"Portland, maybe."

"No problem, I'm headed for Buffalo."

Through the window she saw a flower shop, a hardware store.

"There's the police station," Danny said. "You sure you don't need them?"

"I'm sure."

Danny straightened the brim of his cap. "Okay." Heat was starting to filter into the cab, and felt wonderful.

"There's a flannel shirt in back of you," Danny said,

317

shifting gears. "On the shelf. I can't guarantee how clean it is, but it's somethin' to keep you warm."

Setting her coffee and food on the dash, Sandra reached for the shirt, slipped it on. "Thanks," she said.

"No problem," Danny said. "You can have it."

"Oh, no, I—"

"It's old, it's a rag. You can have it."

"Well thanks."

She ate again. The warmth in the cab was already making her sleepy.

"So where do you live?" Danny asked.

"In Ellington."

"I live outside of Buffalo. I make this run a lot. It's beautiful here—with the mountains and ocean and stuff."

"Yes, it is," Sandra said.

The shirt smelled of oil and sweat. She finished her coffee and sandwich and put her head back. Danny turned the radio on, and mournful country music filled the cab.

"Damn," Danny said, and Sandra woke up with a start—to see flashing blue lights up ahead.

"A goddamn roadblock," Danny said. "They're after the goddamn drunks again."

"Stop the truck," Sandra said.

Danny looked at her. "What?"

"Stop the truck, right here. I want to get out."

He put on his brakes and pulled over, frowning. "I thought you were goin' to Portland," he said.

"I changed my mind."

"You sure? It's two o'clock in the mornin', what are you gonna do in Thomaston?"

"My sister lives here," Sandra said, and she opened the door.

318

"Bye, Ann," Danny said. "Take care of that knee, now."

"Thanks, Danny. I will. And thanks for the shirt."

In the darkness behind the truck, beyond the red glow of its taillights, she crossed the road to a hill and a thick stand of brush. She ducked into the brush, her heart beating wildly now.

As Danny's truck pulled away to the roadblock, she scrambled up the hill towards a huge dark house. Her knee was on fire again and her feet ached and stung. She ran behind the house, across the yard, through other yards, and came into a wide wet field. The tall grass lashed her skin as she ran, and suddenly— railroad tracks.

She turned south on the roadbed, kept running. Her fear numbed the pain as her feet hit the ties. She came to a paved road and crossed it quicky, a cluster of houses on her right, on her left just open fields.

If they came down this road they would see her for sure, she thought, and urged herself to run faster. Her feet hit the ties, sending shocks through her knees and hips. Looking over her shoulder she saw no cars; kept running, running. Then, chest heaving hard and a bright sword of pain in her ribs, she flung herself onto the side of the roadbed, gasping.

She looked down the tracks at the road, now a couple of hundred yards distant. No cruiser. They hadn't seen her cross behind Danny's truck? He hadn't told them about her? She herself had been stopped at a roadblock once, and the cops had merely shined a light in her car and then let her proceed. They hadn't told her why she'd been stopped, hadn't asked her a thing.

She lay in the weeds by the side of the tracks, her heart calming down, and saw that the sky was clear now and filled with bright stars. After a while she forced herself up and started along the tracks again, this time just walking, and came to a metal bridge.

A river. Between the ties, no roadbed now, just air and the dark flowing water. She made her way carefully, fearful of falling, fearful that someone would see her, exposed like this. No moon, at least. When she reached the end of the bridge, she sighed with relief.

The tracks followed the river, curved past boatyards, then turned into town, and wove between houses. She walked steadily, trying to keep at bay the fear that at any moment blue lights would flash on and they'd have her.

A gully, a tunnel, and then to her right, a massive walled structure, the Maine state prison, the sky above it glowing orange pink. The tracks curved around to more houses, more empty fields. She was shivering, weak, she would have to stop soon and sleep. Go to sleep in these cold wet fields.

To her right, on a hill, stood a house and a sagging, tilted barn, and next to the barn was an ancient pickup truck. She climbed the hill, her thighs racked with pain, the pain in her ribs sharp again.

The house, as she'd hoped, was deserted. Its back porch was rotted, and here and there, on the top two floors, a window was missing.

Around the side was an old Chevrolet, early fifties vintage, its hood gone, its windshield shattered. A rock sat in the glass on its rotted front seat. She picked it up and went to the house and tapped it against a window pane. The glass cracked in two and a piece fell inside with a crash. She dropped the rock and reached through the hole and undid the catch and the sash went up crookedly, squealing.

She climbed through the opening, stood there in darkness. The room was filled with furniture: old tables and chairs and desks and lamps, some overturned, some piled on top of each other. Books littered the floor, along with beer cans and rags.

She went forward cautiously. Danny's old shirt was not much protection against the cold night, and she shivered.

In the next room she found a metal bed, rusted, and covered with bottles and cans. She picked up each bottle and can, placed it down on the floor, then swept the mattress hard with the palm of her hand. A musty smell filled the air and she sneezed, and shivered again, so cold.

The windows had curtains, gauzy and pale. She tugged at them and they softly tore and fell away from their rods. She went back to the bed and lay down on the mattress, covering up with the curtains.

The mattress smelled moldy and sour. Her body trembled with cold and she sneezed again; drew the rotted damp curtains around her; scrunched into a ball. Her knee was killing her. She sighed, remembering Danny, the warmth of his truck, that comforting coffee . . .

FORTY-SIX

A shaft of sunlight struck her eyes. Startled, she sat up quickly, throwing the moldy curtains aside. Her bladder was full. She found a toilet and used it. Someone had used it before in its waterless state; it was brown and rank.

The room she had slept in was flooded with merciless sun. Papers and empty cans and boxes littered the filthy floor. The wallpaper, gold with pink roses, was faded and streaked with rust-colored stains. She looked in the closet, hoping to find a pair of old shoes or something else she could use, but all she found was a pile of rags on the floor: men's underwear, torn and gray.

She searched the whole house, but found nothing of use. The bureau drawers were empty, as were the rest of the closets. Old *Farmer's Almanacs* and magazines and broken dishes, a few old seashells, a radio, cracked, with its speaker hanging out.

She looked out the windows. The house was surrounded by fields and trees, cut off from the rest of the town. The rooms were huge, with ornate baseboards and window trim and elaborate ceiling moldings. Years ago, this house had been someone's great pride, with its acres of rolling land and its view of the river. Built before the railroad came, no doubt, before the Civil War.

She went outside, through the window again. The sky was a perfect blue. To her right stood a tangle of red and white phlox, the remains of an ancient garden. The glass on the seat of the old Chevrolet sparkled wickedly in the sun. At the base of the hill, on the other side of the railroad tracks, the river gleamed.

As she walked through the field, her mind felt distant, detached from the beauty and warmth. Her knee had a huge purple scab on it now, and her legs and arms and feet were covered with scratches, some weeping, some healing.

She crossed the tracks and went through the bushes and mud to the riverbank; set her nylon bag on a rock, leaned down, scooped up handfuls of muddy water and splashed herself to wash away dirt and dried blood. She resisted her urge to drink, picked up her bag, and went back to the tracks again.

She walked in the high hot sun and the warmth felt good, but soon her thirst was terrible. The railroad ran through empty fields and stands of thick brush. Not a building in sight, not even on the river's far shore. Ahead, in the sunlight, the tracks flashed and wavered.

The drone of an airplane. Shielding her eyes with her hand, she saw it downriver, a small prop plane. Searching for her?

She hid in some brush by the side of the tracks, her dry tongue stuck to the roof of her mouth and her throbbing feet swollen and blue. When she lowered her head between her knees, sparks shot through her eyes. She took deep breaths as the plane passed over her head and kept going. When the sound of its engine faded out, she pushed herself to her feet again, felt giddy, and had to squat down. Her damaged knee sent

323

sharp jolts of pain to her groin.

She walked. The hot tracks curved into the distance. Just fields and the river, no houses, no roads.

Then, off to the right, behind some trees, a building, blue, with a shiny aluminum roof. She walked with fresh determination, ignoring her pain.

As the building came closer, she began to hear traffic; the heavy grinding of trucks at first, then the soft swish of cars. Then she saw it: Route 1 again.

She cursed. She'd hoped to find a back road, get a lift, and here was Route 1 again.

The building housed a business, Brad's Marine. To its right, past a line of poplar trees, two houses came into view and she headed toward them. One of the houses—its ridgepole bowed, its chimney falling—was ringed by a jumble of washing machines, old doors and windows, baby buggies, sinks, old bikes, tires, furniture, and God only knew what else. A sign above the open door said, Rhonda's Resale.

Sandra went down the wooden catwalk that led to the door. The way was lined with old TV antennas, cast iron stoves, copper tubing, aluminum chairs. She stood in the entry, letting her eyes adjust to the change in light. Behind a desk sat a huge fat woman of fifty or so with jet black hair, piecrust skin, and eyebrows like caterpillars. She was reading a book called, *How to Lose Twenty Pounds Fast.*

"Hi," Sandra said.

The woman nodded, crinkling her deepset eyes.

"Do you have any clothing?"

"Back room." It came out as a wheeze.

"Thanks," Sandra said, and squeezed past shelves of bric-a-brac, old books and magazines.

The windows were painted shut and the room was an oven, but it certainly did have clothes. Dripping with sweat, Sandra pushed through the racks, selecting a pale blue blouse and a pair of beige slacks in her size. In the corner a huge box held hundreds of shoes, and she found some sandals that fit her bruised feet. On a shelf near the ceiling, she found a straw hat.

Rhonda put all the stuff in a bag. It cost practically nothing. "Nice day," she croaked as she gave Sandra change.

"Just beautiful," Sandra said, feeling suddenly faint. "Is there any place around where I can get a soda?"

"Brad's Marine," Rhonda said. "Next door."

"Thanks."

"Come see us again," Rhonda said.

"I will," Sandra said.

A garage stood next to the neighboring house. Behind it, Sandra slipped the slacks and blouse on over her jogging clothes. The straps of the sandals hurt when she walked. She adjusted the hat, pulling the brim down, and went to Brad's Marine.

The Pepsi machine was beside the door. She fed it some change and grabbed the can that rumbled into the slot; popped it open and greedily drank. Closing her eyes and exhaling hard, she thought, Rhonda, you saved my life.

She got a lift right away, from a couple of kids in an old Pontiac. She sat in the back seat. A stuffed cat was grasping the window beside her with suction cup feet.

Both kids were about seventeen. The driver, a boy, had blond hair, hazel eyes, and slightly crooked front teeth. The girl beside him had dark hair and rosy cheeks. She turned toward Sandra, her arm on the back of the seat, and said, "Where you headed?"

"Portland."

"We're only going to Damariscotta," the boy said.

"Oh. Can you catch a bus there?"

325

"Sure."

"Can you drop me off at the station?"

Grinning, the boy said, "It's only a drugstore, but sure, I can drop you off. There's a bus stop in Thomaston too, if you want me to take you back. It's only a couple of miles."

"Oh, no, that's okay," Sandra said.

The girl smiled and said, "You sure don't look like a hitchhiker."

"No?" Sandra said. "Why not?"

"You just don't. You look like you're going shopping or something."

"Oh," Sandra said, and decided to leave it at that. "Do you live in Damariscotta?" she asked.

"No, Pemaquid," the boy said.

"I've never been there."

"It's great, you should go some time," the boy said. "You from Maine?"

"No."

"I didn't think so."

"Why not?"

"Don't sound it, don't look it."

"You mean you can tell a Maine person by how they look?"

"Pretty much. Where you from?"

"New York," Sandra lied.

"You mean New York City?" the girl said.

"Yes."

"We went there in April," the boy said. "Class trip. Saw the Statue of Liberty, Empire State Building, UN, all that kinda stuff. It was cool."

"But you wouldn't want to live there," Sandra said. They laughed.

They had just finished high school, they told her, and were headed for college in a couple of weeks. University of Maine. He was going to be an electrical engineer. She wasn't sure what she wanted to be, but liked psychology. As they talked of their plans, Sandra thought: This could have been Lucy and Matty. This could have been my kids, all grown up like this on a hot summer day like this, with the whole world lying before them.

The girl suddenly looked concerned and said, "Are you feeling okay?"

"Something got in my eye," Sandra said as she wiped at her tears. "It's gone now, I'm fine."

They let her off in the center of town, at the store with the Greyhound sign, and drove away into their futures.

She went into the store, her knee burning again; bought antiseptic, gauze and tape, a cheap digital watch, some toilet articles, some makeup, a comb, and sunglasses. After putting the sunglasses on, she bought a ticket to Boston.

In Boston she'd switch to a train for the rest of the trip. She'd thought of taking the bus to Portland, then catching a plane, but airport security scared her. They'd spot her for sure.

The bus wouldn't leave for another four hours. She went to the tiny restaurant next door and ordered the special, fried shrimp and potatoes. She'd had no food since that sandwich the night before in Danny's truck, and lingered a long time over the meal, having blueberry pie and three cups of coffee with plenty of sugar and cream. When she'd finished, she went to the ladies' room and washed her face and combed her hair and put some makeup on. It covered the scratches, and while she still felt like hell, she didn't look bad at all.

In the toilet stall she lowered her slacks and bandaged her wounded knee. The antiseptic burned as

327

she sprayed it on. She gritted her teeth, applied the gauze, pulled her slacks back up, and left.

At the store on the corner she bought a purse; transferred the stuff from the nylon bag, and discarded the bag in the trashcan that stood on the sidewalk.

In a tiny park on the waterfront, she sat on a wooden bench in the shade of a tree. Children played in the sun on swings and slides, and she thought of Lucy and Matty again. She thought of the vial that lay in her purse. If she actually used that vial, children might die. The plague would be out in the world, and innocent children would die. Children like these. Like hers.

It was dreadful to think of, and yet she would take that chance. For Kromer must die, and his death must be by rabies, no other way.

She watched the children, and tiredness claimed her in spite of the three cups of coffee. The laughter and shouts grew dimmer, dimmer, her head felt as heavy as lead. She dozed, jerked awake, and saw the children again at their play, and couldn't hold back the tears.

FORTY-SEVEN

Paul Kessler looked up from the desk in his study, blinking his owlish eyes.

"I'm frightened," Angela repeated, coming no closer, clutching the doorjamb. Her blond hair was hanging in disarray and her face was pale.

"Please, Angela, don't," Kessler said. "Don't panic, please, it's the flu."

"I feel so tired, and my throat . . ."

"It's flu, it has to be."

Tears welled to her eyes. "Paul, I . . . Jesus." She shook her head.

"Jim Morgan died last night," he said. As he said it, his heart felt sick.

She wept openly now. "Paul, please, you have to help. I'm sorry, I'm sorry, honest to God."

He looked at her there in the light of his lamp—her tears flowing freely, staining her cheeks—and remembered the girl she had been when they met, so long ago, at that dance at The Purple Drake. "If it isn't the flu, if . . ."

"Don't say you can't help."

"There's no cure, you know that. Once symptoms start . . ."

She stared at him, her tongue on her upper teeth. "Then I'm going to die," she said.

He shook his head. "Not necessarily . . ."

"Jim died."

"He did, but others—"

Her head on the doorjamb, she broke out crying again.

Kessler looked at his desk, at the papers he'd brought home to study, the lab reports. Tears misted his eyes. No, no, he thought, and the telephone rang.

It rang, it rang, he closed his eyes and held his head, then picked the receiver up. "Hello?"

He opened his eyes again, let out a breath. "So that's it," he said. He listened a minute. "All right, thanks," he said.

He hung up and stared at the lab reports. "They found one of Sandra's running shoes on the North Beach rocks," he said. "They assume she drowned."

His wife's chest heaved and she covered her eyes with her hand.

"Poor simpleminded Sandra Barnes," Kessler said, looking down at his hands. "Did she actually think I would give her the virus? Somewhere out in that lonely bay there's another running shoe, and Sandra Barnes, and a vial of Protocol 3."

His wife took her hand down. She looked at the floor for a couple of seconds, then stared at the lamp on his desk, and said: "She's lucky."

"Don't talk like that," he said. "Please, Angela, look . . ."

She was crying again. Kessler's face crumpled up. All right, all right, his wife was a cheat! She was also the mother of Jeff and Mindy, his children, who loved her. And in spite of her indiscretions, he loved her, too. He held his balding head in his hands and tried not to show

330

his tears.

He wished that Sandra Barnes had been lucky enough to escape and kill William Kromer. Swallowing hard, still unable to look at Angela, the only woman he'd ever loved or had ever made love to, he said, "We should go to the hospital now."

FORTY-EIGHT

In the dark anonymous intimacy of the bus, she had a long dream about Lucy and Matty. They were with her at the Smithsonian, staring up at a tyrannosaurus, and Lucy said, "It's extinct," and Matty retorted angrily, "It does not!" "Matty, no," Sandra said, "she doesn't mean it smells bad, extinct means it doesn't exist anymore. There are none of them left in the whole wide world." "In the whole wide *world?*" Matty said, his eyes wide. "But they have such big teeth!"

And suddenly Howard was with them, his lips drawn back, his teeth sharp fangs, he growled, he leapt—

She woke up with a start, her skin on fire, the nightmare dissolving, the horror of actuality taking its place. The lights of the harsh commercial strip on the outskirts of Boston, that garish jumble of motel and gas station signs, assailed her eyes, and the man beside her looked at her dully through half-closed lids then turned and went back to sleep. Her heart was dull, and the heat on her skin was not just from hundreds of scratches and cuts but from—what? She felt her forehead.

By the time they reached Boston, she was sweating hard. I can't have rabies, she said to herself, then thought: Who's to say that one speck of saliva from

Lucy or Matty didn't enter a break in my skin? I pulled my mask aside when Howard was wounded. There was blood all over the place that night. Who's to say that a speck of saliva or blood didn't find its way into my lungs?

As she left the bus her legs felt flimsy, and she sat in a plastic seat near the station's wall. The fluorescent lights were penetrating, harsh, and she got up quickly and walked out into the night. Two blocks away she went into a small hotel called the Somerville, signed a false name on the registration card, and paid in advance with cash.

In the tiny elevator, she thought she might faint. Sweat trickled along her temples and down her cheeks. She fumbled at the lock with the key, entered the room, lay down on the limp cigarette-smelling bed, and instantly fell asleep.

She woke to thin airshaft light and the sound of a garbage truck. It was five thirty-two, and her throat was sore.

I can't have rabies, she told herself, I'm just run down. It's something else, that flu—

She didn't convince herself.

She showered in the tiny stall; the slimy brown plastic curtain sucked at her tender legs. She patted herself with the scratchy towel, used the stick of deodorant she'd bought, brushed her teeth, changed her bandage, and put on her clothes again. The slacks and shirt still smelled of Rhonda's Resale Shop. She combed her hair, applied her makeup, put her sunglasses on, then her hat. She went shakily out to the street and hailed a cab.

*   *   *

333

On the Metroliner she, for God's sake, weaved in and out of hot dreams. She would wake, throat dry, tongue thick, and stare at dark factories, rows of old houses with wash on the line, sad swampy fields, stacks of rusted crushed automobiles. And if I have rabies? she thought. I just have to live long enough to accomplish one deed, and then I can die in peace.

The train arrived in Baltimore at one fifteen and she got off there, afraid they'd be waiting for her in Washington. It was hot, unbelievably so, and her head was now throbbing and thick. She bought Tylenol at the newsstand and swallowed three of them at the water fountain. On the street she felt dull and confused, but made herself walk.

Three blocks from the station she found a Dodge dealer who rented cars. She was forced to use her credit card, as he wouldn't take cash. The car was a black Dodge Shadow. The perfect name, she thought as she pulled away, tipping the sun visor down. What could be more appropriate? Well, maybe Avenger.

She'd hated to use her credit card, afraid it would lead to her capture. She drove down the Baltimore-Washington parkway, expecting the lights of a cruiser at any time.

But no, she made it to Washington, made it downtown, and drove into a parking garage. She parked in a slot on the third tier and rested a minute. Her heart was quick, her throat was sore, she was drenched with a clammy sweat. She wondered how long it would be till the pain began: the agony in the chest and throat that had made her children writhe and scream till she thought she would lose her mind. And after that the sudden weakness, the flaccidity, paralysis, when she would be incapable— She forced herself out of the car and went to the elevator.

Down on the street she was weak and exhausted, and

oh how she longed to get back in the car and go home: to Alexandria, her empty air-conditioned house and her very own bed. But that house would be full of the ghosts of her family now; she'd see the children's rooms again, their toys . . . and the cops would be waiting there.

She could hardly believe she was walking these Washington streets. The last time she'd been here, just weeks ago, her major concern had been the advance of the crow's-feet around her eyes. She'd had a husband, two wonderful children, a job; had been normal, contented, at home here, at home in the world. Now she was a stranger here—and everywhere.

When she reached the Rockwood Hotel it was after four. Too late to do anymore today, she told herself, and yet, by tomorrow, the spasms might start.

Don't think about that, she told herself. You will do what you have to do.

She paid cash for her room, signing a different name from the one she had used in Boston. She had stayed at the Rockwood years ago, before she had moved to the area. The place had declined since then, but still wasn't bad; it was clean and its bed was firm. She turned the air conditioner on, then took off her sandals, and looked through the telephone book. A Daniel Kromer in Alexandria, but, as she'd expected, no William. She looked for another number, found it, and dialed.

"Pentagon."

"Yes, when are your tours?"

"Every hour on the hour, starting at 10:00 A.M. Take the metro entrance. We're closed for today."

"Thank you," she said, and hung up.

She showered and rested awhile, then went to the deli she'd seen on the corner. In spite of the tropical weather, she ordered some chicken soup.

In her room she lay down on the bed. If they didn't

trace the car and track her down, she'd succeed. If her strength held out. No ifs, she told herself. It *will* hold out.

The soup hadn't helped. Her throat was worse. She got up and took more Tylenol, lay down again and slept.

FORTY-NINE

When Sandra woke up, bright sun rimmed the heavy blue drapes, and she couldn't believe her watch. It was almost noon.

The room was cool, but her skin was hot and her sheets were soaked with sweat. She sat up quickly. The room spun around and she lay down again on her back and stared up at the ceiling. A shiver of nausea swept through her. She thought, I'm already too sick, it's already too late. But she forced herself to sit up again, holding onto the edge of the mattress tightly, and after a few more minutes the dizziness passed.

She showered and dressed in the blouse and slacks. Everything seemed to take too long, and her limbs were so heavy, so slow. In the lobby she paid for an extra day, as she'd missed check-out time. The clerk, a frail old man with blue veins in his forehead, took ages to write a receipt, and she leaned on the marble countertop to conserve her strength.

The sunlight struck her like a blow, and her pupils contracted with pain. The sidewalk sparkled like diamonds, making her wince.

She stopped into the luncheonette on the corner and ordered a coffee to go. The place was packed—with normal people, far from Blue Harbor, normal oblivious people who lived with the missiles and chemicals daily, ignoring the peril, for what could they do? What could any one person do? Shrug it off and pay taxes and work in the factories making the bombs, go to work in the companies making the nerve gas, the germs that could wipe out the world. Good citizens eating their corned beef on rye. The sound of their voices set her head spinning. She paid for the coffee, went out again, and walked to the parking garage.

In the elevator, she leaned on the wall, the hand with the styrofoam cup shaking hard. She found the car, unlocked it quickly, sat behind the wheel. She again closed her eyes and breathed deeply, a sudden cold sweat on her brow. *I will succeed,* she told herself. *I will!* She opened her eyes, took the top off the cup, and drank.

The heat soothed her throat. She remembered Lucy and Matty drinking juice with parched red lips, then suddenly being unable to drink, screaming when she offered them the cup. When will that change take place in me? she wondered.

She finished her coffee and started the engine; turned the air conditioner on. Almost one thirty now. Hurry!

Passing the Smithsonian she wept, remembering Lucy say, "It's extinct," and remembering Matty's reply. She pressed her lips together and drove past the Jefferson Memorial and across the Potomac. Even with sunglasses on and a tinted windshield, the water's bright shine hurt her eyes.

In the Pentagon parking lot, she rested a moment; then, sweating profusely, she checked herself in the rearview mirror, straightened her hat, and got out of the car. After locking her purse in the glove compartment, she crossed the street.

The metro entrance stood under a metal canopy. She took the escalator down, went past the subway turnstiles, took another escalator up again, and found herself in the waiting area, along with scores of others. Visitors and Other Passes, said a gate, and a cluster of black girl scouts came through it, led by a uniformed guide, a young white man with closely cropped hair. The scouts gave him their badges and poked each other and went through the doors to the subway.

The line at the visitors' entrance stretched back to the gate. Good, Sandra thought. The bigger the crowd, the better. People went to the window, presented their driver's licenses, then sat on the wooden benches or went to the gift shop or just simply wandered around. Fast-moving people, most in uniform, showed badges and went through the gate. Beyond the gate was a pastry shop and a Woodward and Lothrop department store.

Sandra sat on a bench and waited. She'd done this before, and knew how it worked. You registered at the window, showing identification, and later they called out your name and gave you a visitor's badge. She had no identification, real or false, but it didn't matter: she'd get a badge without it.

She waited, dizzy from the swirl of people, the constant rush through the gate. Then another young uniformed man appeared, holding a basket. "All those for the three o'clock tour," he said loudly, straining to make himself heard. "The three o'clock tour. When I call your name, take a badge from the basket and pin it in a visible place. Wear your badge at all times and stay with the group." He looked at a paper and said, "Adams, Donald."

A middle-aged black man stepped forward and picked up a badge, and another name was called. When

339

the uniformed man got to "Friedman, Richard," no one responded. "Friedman? No?" said the guide. "Green, David."

There were always a couple of no-shows, people who signed up but changed their minds, and a few minutes later the guide called, "Jalbert, Helen," and got no response. He called out the name once again, and Sandra went up to the basket and took a badge. Thanks, Helen, she said to herself as she pinned it on.

Once all the names had been read, the guide led the group through the gate, past the Woodward and Lothrop's, and up to an Air Force display case. Ten minutes later, as they went down a flight of stairs, Sandra, lagging behind, waited until the guide rounded a corner, then took off her visitor's badge, turned back and ducked into a ladies' room.

She stayed there a moment, shaking with fever, then went to the hallway again, to the sign she had passed before: South Parking Lot. She went down the corridor, opened the door.

The mirror-bright rooftops of thousands of cars stretched before her, confusing her eyes. As she'd figured, the parking slots close to the door were designated: Bradshaw, Harris, DelVeccio, Marks . . . A hundred yards distant, a soldier got into a car and drove off. She watched his exit route closely, squinting behind her dark glasses.

She walked through the cars in the brutal sun and found no space labeled Kromer. The names gave way to numbers, and the thought struck her then that he had no car; he was chauffeured here. Christ, she thought, and a weakness hit her. She squatted between two cars and leaned forward, thrusting her head between her knees, and things went black for a second. After several deep breaths, the darkness passed.

Bracing herself on the tarmac she stood again, her heart beating hard in her throat, her damaged knee burning.

A few minutes later, right next to another door, she found it: a dark green Mercedes, brand new. How wonderful what murder can buy, she thought. She memorized the license plate; walked on till she found the gate that led out of the lot. When she saw the steel awning and metro stop, she realized that her car was in the lot across the street and went to it, drenched with perspiration, a high tinny whine in her ears. She got in and rolled the windows down and slumped back, her thoughts hot and thin. She checked her watch. It was twenty of four.

She rested awhile, then started the car, drove out to the street, and parked. The street was a no-parking zone. Cars passed her rapidly, the sound of them hurting her ears. Her skin was a hot stinging slime of sweat and her chest felt hollow and weak.

The gate to the lot across the way went up and a car came out. As the minutes passed, the exodus became more brisk. Sandra rolled up her windows and started the car, put the air conditioning on. She watched the gate, a dull throbbing pain in the back of her skull, her vision dim. Car after car came out, and at last, there he was.

His tinted glass revealed only a silhouette. She had to let six cars go by before she could follow. She weaved the Dodge Shadow from lane to lane, and was soon only two cars behind.

He went down the Shirley Highway to Alexandria, where he got off at King Street and drove for a couple of blocks, then went left.

And this was her neighborhood; her beautiful empty house was just four blocks from here. Kromer, one car

341

ahead of her, stopped for a light. When she put on the brakes, her head suddenly spun and she gripped the wheel tightly, gasping.

A few minutes later the green Mercedes turned into a shrub-lined driveway. Sandra, half a block away, pulled over and watched as a gray-haired man in a uniform left the car and walked to the house, a brick colonial with a portico. He waited a moment; the door came open; he disappeared inside.

Sandra drove down the street and parked two houses away from the brick colonial. She sat there, her flesh on fire, her pulse thin and quick, sweat coating her forehead and cheeks. I should have just shot him, she thought, just pulled up beside him and shot him, I missed my chance.

Taking a deep breath, she opened her handbag and took out her pistol and placed it on the passenger seat, then took out the vial of liquid and a syringe. She tore the plastic off the syringe, stuck its needle through the vial's top, and, shaking, extracted the liquid. She emptied the handbag, sticking the stuff in the glove compartment, then put the gun and syringe in the bag again.

Holding the bag, she got out of the car. The street seemed to jump, and she leaned on the hood to steady herself. Sweat poured down her face.

She would go to the door and ring the bell and shoot him as soon as he answered. If someone else answered, she'd run inside and find him.

She wouldn't shoot to kill, though, just to wound. His manner of death would be the same as hers, the same as her children's, the same as that of those innocent people who lived in Blue Harbor, Maine.

As she went up the empty sidewalk, nausea struck. She ducked behind the shrubbery lining the driveway and fell to her knees; breathed deeply and swallowed hard, her sore throat making her wince. She crouched there, clutching her bag—and heard voices behind the house.

She crept along the row of shrubs. She was fully exposed to the house next door, where a Buick and Cadillac sat, so she had to act fast.

The shrubs led behind the garage. She followed them, and through their dense leaves she could see a wide lawn, and there, on that lawn, stood Kromer.

His jacket and tie were gone, his sleeves were rolled up, and he smoked a cigar and talked while a younger man tended a grille. Sandra crouched in the bushes and set her bag down on the spongy black earth. She reached in and took out her gun.

For a second her thoughts faded out. As consciousness slowly returned, she found herself down on her knees again. She was shaking violently, drenched with cold sweat.

Now! a voice in her head commanded. *Now!*

She lifted the gun with both hands, her teeth chattering hard.

And the door to the back of the house flew open and two little children, smiling, their arms in the air, came out and ran up to the men. They were both little girls, and they yelled with bright faces, "Grampa! Grampa!" and Kromer knelt and hugged them both and something suddenly broke in Sandra's heart. With a sharp strangled cry she pitched forward, the gun flying out of her hand, her eyes rolling back into blue, into white, into nothing, no, nothing at all.

FIFTY

There was something between her legs and they had her tied down. She opened her burning eyes and saw white. She blinked. Saw the white was a stippled ceiling, saw the buried aluminum track, the curtain, the bag, and the plastic tube. Not tied down? Just an IV strapped onto her arm? The window, so bright—

"Hello, Sandra."

She turned to the source of the sound and her neck felt raw. Her lids were like sandpaper when she blinked.

Kromer sat near the door in a khaki shirt, black tie, black shoes. "Quite a rest you had. Almost twenty-two hours. We were starting to get concerned."

Her mouth was stuck. Her tongue tasted like rust. Tired, God, so tired.

Kromer's dead eye turned out as he said, "I've talked to Kessler. He was very surprised to hear you'd escaped. And quite sorry to hear you were ill."

Sandra managed to move her tongue. She wet her lips.

"The vial contained a vaccine, not a virus, Sandra."

She stared at his silver crewcut, that forest of

344

needles, her breath so terribly hot.

"An amazing attempt," Kromer said. "You'd have made a good soldier. Now that you're conscious, we'll have to restrain you, we really can't trust you. A pistol. Amazing."

Tears came to her eyes and she blinked them away. Thinking of Lucy, Matty, Howard, she saw him stand.

"I admire your courage," he said. "You'll get excellent care, of course." He stood there a moment, staring, then left the room.

A sudden rage blossomed in Sandra's chest. She reached down and pulled out the catheter, threw off the sheet. As she pushed herself up, the room spun. She gripped the bedrail, shaking, chilled with cold sweat, and moved to the foot of the bed. Stood on rubbery legs. Went to the head of the bed, reached up, unhooked the IV bag from the metal stand and cradled it to her chest, then crossed the floor.

Kromer was halfway down the hall, on his way outside, and she gritted her teeth and gathered her strength and ran towards his back on silent numb naked feet.

An orderly rounded the corner, pushing a cart. His blue eyes went wide and he softly said, "What?" A candy striper, stunned, stopped dead in her tracks.

Sandra ran. She tore at the IV tube in her arm, yanking the needle out of her vein and thrusting it into her mouth. A nurse in a doorway said, "Hey!" and Kromer turned.

Too late, for Sandra was on him. His milky eye jerked and he cried out, "No!" as she plunged the IV needle into his neck.

He tore at it franctically, ripping it out. Blood flowed from the hole it had made. His expression a mixture of terror and rage, he flung the tube down and it

345

swung back and forth from the bag Sandra clutched to her chest.

She smiled, her eyes half-closed, and let the bag go. "You'll get excellent care," she said, and heard whistles and bells in her head, so loud, and pitched forward and fell to the floor.

FIFTY-ONE

After they cleaned the wound in ER, Kromer got on the phone to Blue Harbor.

"I already told you," Kessler said, "we've just begun animal trials."

"I'll have a plane in Ellington within two hours," Kromer said. "Arrange to have it there."

"If there's even a *chance* you're infected," Kessler said, "you should be on that plane. I'll have the Guard meet you and escort you here."

Kromer laughed. "Have the vaccine waiting at Ellington," he said, and hung up.

Five hours later, he became the first human being to ever receive Series VI. His doctor, Peter Keltus, gave him shots in the wound and the deltoid muscle and said, "We're going to admit you."

"Like hell you are," Kromer said, and walked out of the office.

He went upstairs to see Sandra Barnes, but she was unconscious in intensive care.

His sore throat began three days later, a day before he was due for his second injection, and when he arrived at Walter Reed he was running a fever. "It's no goddamn good," he said to Keltus. "This new stuff is no goddamn good."

"You have to be kept under observation," Keltus said. "There's a chance you might just have the flu."

"Right," Kromer said, and refused the injection, and left.

Instead of going directly home, he went to his son's house. His daughter-in-law was there with the girls. Pale and sweating, he hugged them and gave them a gift of a silver dollar apiece. He told his daughter-in-law he was fine, he just had a little cold.

At home he went into his study, shaking and weak, and sat at his rolltop desk.

He knew only too well what was coming. He'd been to Blue Harbor weeks ago, had met with Farrow and observed the sick. That wasn't the way he wanted to die. It wasn't a soldier's way.

The rabies would disappear one of these days, for that was the nature of plagues. The virus would mutate and weaken. But who knew how long that would take and how many more lives would be lost? He thought of his granddaughters, saw their faces, their happy smiles as he hugged them and gave them the coins.

He opened his drawer and took out the .44 Magnum. The pistol felt heavy and cold in his shaking hand. It was loaded, of course; it was always loaded.

Barbara, his wife, had gone shopping and wouldn't be home until late. By then, the blood should have dried. And be safe to touch?

He lifted the pistol and frowned at the barrel, stared at the bore as he turned the gun slowly around. Yes, Sandra, he thought, you'd have made a good soldier, then thought: Please, Barbara, forgive me, I know how you hate a mess.

FIFTY-TWO

Beyond the trees, a bright band of gold skimmed the bay, and Wendell Renshaw squinted. In the distance a lobster boat made a turn, slowed down, hauled a trap. Wendell watched the lobsterman, tiny from here, pitch something out of the trap, rebait, and toss the trap over again.

So normal, he thought. So wonderful.

He looked back at the grave in front of him: George Jenkins, one of his oldest friends, who had died in the plague's last days. And off to his right was Dora Hobbs and the rest of the Hobbs family. Dora had worked for the *Blue Harbor Herald* years ago, at the reception desk. A good woman, unfailingly pleasant, thoroughly efficient, who never forgot a person's birthday, always made a cake.

So many good people buried here. Six hundred and thirty-eight, to be exact. A small tragedy, really, in the wider scheme of things, but monumental for a small Maine town. He looked at the rows and rows of crosses in what had once been Harper's fields, where, three years ago, the National Guard had camped in that horrible time. So many good people, a lot of them soldiers he hadn't known, young men, boys, really, who had done their best and had lost, as all these others had lost.

He walked down the rows of graves. Edward Mason; Algernon Morrison; Jill Pool, an out-of-stater, twenty years old; Amelia Rose. He paused before this last one a minute, then went on his way again.

He came to this place every week. How many years would he have to come here before he could start to forget?

At the next pair of gravestones he paused again: "Kessler—Angela, loving wife," and "Kessler—Paul."

He looked at the line of trees again, at the water, and saw that he wasn't alone. Fifty yards or so away, a woman was kneeling on the grass, her folded hands pressed to her mouth. Wendell watched as she unclasped her hands and stood up. She turned slowly and looked his way.

He looked down at the crosses, frowning. Every so often he met someone here. It was always the same; simply awful.

The woman was coming toward him. He concentrated on Paul Kessler's grave, hoping that she would ignore him.

"Wendell?"

The sound of his name was shocking. He looked at the woman, who stood twenty feet from him now.

"Yes?"

She came up to him, held out her hand.

"Sandra Barnes?"

She took his hand, nodding.

"Sandra," he said.

"It's good to see you, Wendell."

Her eyes were red; she'd been crying. She squeezed his hand, then let it go, and looked at Kessler's grave. "A heart attack, wasn't it?"

"Yes," Renshaw said. "He worked in a frenzy, night

350

and day. He wasn't able to save his wife, but he saved one hell of a lot of others, maybe the rest of the world. They say he was using drugs to keep himself going. His heart couldn't take it, just gave out one night in the lab."

Sandra stared at the gravestone. "Yes," she said.

"And he gave Farrow all of the credit. Told everyone Farrow had solved the puzzle."

Sandra frowned at the gravestone.

"You never had rabies, did you, Sandra?"

"No, just the flu."

"And Kromer was never infected."

"He had the flu, same as me. I gave it to him."

"Yes, I read all about it," Renshaw said. "And about the trial, how you were acquitted, the class action suit. You never know what to believe in the papers, though."

She looked at him sadly. "Your paper's dead."

"A young fellow's trying to start it up," he said. "I stop in and give him a hand every once and a while. I probably drive the kid nuts, but I can't seem to help it, ink runs in my veins. And I want him to be a success so badly. Blue Harbor could use a paper again."

"I read that one person survived the disease," Sandra said.

"That's right," Renshaw said, "just one—Sharon Jensen, the state pathologist, the one who discovered the rabies in Walt Marsh's dog. She was terribly sick, in a coma for months. Amazing how well she's done. She lives in New Mexico now. I understand she's back to work part time."

"That's wonderful," Sandra said. She paused, then said, "I'm here to put the cottage up for sale."

Renshaw nodded.

"It will probably take quite a while to sell it."

"I guess," Renshaw said. "Blue Harbor's a fishing village again. It's a lot like it was years ago, when I was a boy."

On the road behind them, a hundred yards off, a car appeared. "That's David," Sandra said. "My husband."

Renshaw reached for her hand again. He held it firmly in both his hands, and said, "Oh, Sandra, that's marvelous."

"We were married last year, and I'm already pregnant."

"I'm so terribly happy for you."

She squeezed his hand, then waved at David, who waved from inside the car. Looking at Renshaw's eyes, she said, "If I ever come back to Blue Harbor again, I'll stop in and see you."

"Don't wait too long," Renshaw said. "I'm seventy-six, you know."

"You'll live to a hundred and twenty," Sandra said.

"God bless you," Renshaw said.

"God bless you, Wendell."

She walked down the path to the car and got in. As it drove slowly off, she waved.

When the car was gone, Wendell Renshaw looked out at the ocean again, at the sparkling bright water, the flawless sky, a sky that a few years before had been filled with sails. He looked at the rows and rows of crosses, the graves that held the bones of those sailors, good people, dear friends. Under his breath he softly said: "God bless you and be with you, Sandra Barnes."

In the distance a single lobsterman hauled traps on a perfect Maine day.